STARSIDE

ALSO BY ALEX ASTER

THE LIGHTLARK SAGA
Lightlark
Nightbane
Skyshade
Grim and Oro: Dueling Crowns Edition
Crowntide

Summer in the City

STARSIDE

ALEX ASTER

BLOOMSBURY ARCHER

BLOOMSBURY ARCHER
Bloomsbury Publishing Plc
50 Bedford Square, London, WC1B 3DP, UK
Bloomsbury Publishing Ireland Limited,
29 Earlsfort Terrace, Dublin 2, D02 AY28, Ireland

BLOOMSBURY, BLOOMSBURY ARCHER and the Archer logo
are trademarks of Bloomsbury Publishing Plc

First published in 2026 in the US by William Morrow, an imprint of HarperCollins
First published in Great Britain in 2026

Copyright © Alex Aster, 2026
Jacket endpaper illustration © Justin Estcourt

Alex Aster has asserted her right under the Copyright, Designs and Patents Act,
1988, to be identified as Author of this work

This is a work of fiction. Names and characters are the product of the
author's imagination and any resemblance to actual persons,
living or dead, is entirely coincidental

All rights reserved. No part of this publication may be: i) reproduced or transmitted in any form, electronic or mechanical, including photocopying, recording or by means of any information storage or retrieval system without prior permission in writing from the publishers; or ii) used or reproduced in any way for the training, development or operation of artificial intelligence (AI) technologies, including generative AI technologies. The rights holders expressly reserve this publication from the text and data mining exception as per Article 4(3) of the Digital Single Market Directive (EU) 2019/790

A catalogue record for this book is available from the British Library

ISBN: HB: 978-1-5266-9433-1; TPB: 978-1-0372-0241-4; EBOOK: 978-1-0372-0237-7;
EPDF: 978-1-0372-0238-4; WATERSTONES EDITION: 978-1-0372-0247-6

2 4 6 8 10 9 7 5 3 1

Interior text design by Diahann Sturge-Campbell
Phoenix bird © eleyas emon/Shutterstock.com
Printed and bound in Great Britain by Clays Ltd, Elcograf S.p.A

To find out more about our authors and books visit www.bloomsbury.com
and sign up for our newsletters
For product safety related questions contact productsafety@bloomsbury.com

*For all those phoenixes out there—
keep rising from the ashes.*

1

This will kill me.

My sweaty palm curves around my dagger as I weave through the crowd of spectators. My blade is hidden up my sleeve, the sparkling metal cold against my pulse. One wrong move, and I'll stab myself, but it's better than having my weapon noticed this far from the front.

I lift to my toes to gauge my distance—and there it is.

The platform. A massive stone the size of a stage, black rock speckled with silver like a fallen slab of night. It's beautiful, one of the last remaining shreds of magic on this side of a land halved.

Soon, it will be covered in blood.

Hundreds have traveled from every corner of Stormside, armed with the best metals and years of elite training, to fight for a place on that platform. Thousands have risked their lives traveling down barren roads, just to watch.

The Questral only happens every fifty years.

Fifty of us mortals will be allowed past the gates, into the land of the immortals, to undergo a deadly journey.

Only a handful ever return. Most are killed by legendary beasts or the ruthless immortals themselves.

But the prize at the end of the quest is worth the risk. A goblet full of something that can turn miles of ash to fertile plains, summon storms after years of drought, cure any disease, grant power or wealth or even immortality.

Magic.

There are just fifty coveted spots. Hundreds will fight to the death for them during the king's mysterious Culling.

But to even qualify for the Culling, you must first reach the platform.

A ring of king's guards surrounds the stone, their well-worn silver armor glinting beneath the blazing sun. I squint, trying to find the one guard I need to stay the hell away from, but he's noticeably missing. *Strange.*

Relief slides down my spine. My chances are pretty much fucked as it is, but at least I won't be going up against *him*.

The king's eyes and ears, known only as the Watchman, stands just left of the stone, a gleaming silver hawk perched on his arm—one of the king's coveted rarities. Silver is the color of the gods. As the most powerful figure on this side, the king believes he's owed everything in that hue. Harboring creatures of the shade is a crime punishable by death.

Even so, I've seen the rare silver animal caged and sold in the illegal desert markets. They have to be caught young, when they can't put up a fight. Because the older ones . . .

They themselves are weapons.

The hawk's feathers shine like melted moonlight. Its long talons look like curved daggers. A chill sweeps down my arms, below the thick sleeves. I've seen guts spilled across streets, because of those talons. I've watched that hawk decapitate a thief, then fly off, head clutched in its claws like a damned trophy.

As if sensing my notice, the bird's head turns sharply, dark eyes boring into mine, and I fall back onto my heels, heart in my throat.

Ten minutes. Once the hawk gives its first scream, I'll have just ten minutes to make it onto that platform. Its cries will mark down each minute, until time is up. Any moment now, it's going to open its beak, and all hell is going to break loose.

I'm still too far away.

I quicken my pace while trying not to attract attention, part of my strategy. It's not just the king's guard to worry about. Some spectators will take it upon themselves to cull potential volunteers before they even get close to the front, in a twisted way to ensure only the best make it on.

Today, murder is sanctioned. *Celebrated.*

So, unlike the circle of armed hopefuls at the front, already staring down the king's guards, ready to fight, I'm trying to get as close as possible without being noticed. I shoulder through the crowd, head low. No one stops me, assuming I'm just a fellow onlooker. They must see the lack of muscle. Lack of sword. Lack of height. Pale skin without the healthy flush of nourishment. Hardly enough to go against heirs and warriors who have trained their entire lives for this day. Volunteering for the quest, in their eyes, would be a death sentence.

They're fucking right.

Someone slams into my back, sending me stumbling forward. *Shit.* I barely manage to keep my dagger flat against my skin as I topple forward, right into the woman in front of me.

She throws a scathing look over her shoulder that only deepens when I angle past her, apologizing under my breath. Judging by the thick, tightly woven material of the coat she now clutches in her hand, she's a traveler from far north.

Almost every village has sent volunteers or witnesses to our town of Nightfell, named after the black rock at the center of it. I slip past unfamiliar fabrics. All are faded, ripped, and covered in a layer of dirt, the tattered remains of something that once might have been beautiful, but is now only ruins. Just like everything else on this side.

A roaring has me wrenching my head back up. Next to the platform, a tower of flame shoots skyward, crackling in shades of shredded sunset.

I don't have to wonder what it's for—I know. The bodies that don't make it onto the stone will be thrown into the fire, left to burn.

I swallow. It's almost time.

"Looking to feed the flames?"

The gravelly voice comes from a slim, tall man with slicked-back hair, leaning all his weight upon a sword I'd bet my own dagger he can't hold up properly. Metal is heavy. Most men who visit the forge want the biggest weapon they can afford, but few can get it off the ground when it counts.

At his statement, several heads turn toward us.

Fuck.

Though my tongue itches to ask the man if *he's* looking to sharpen my blade, preferably between his ribs, I push my metal higher up my wrist and offer my most sheepish of smiles.

"Of course not. Just trying to get a better view." My voice says *That's ridiculous. Me? Try to qualify for the Questral? That would kill me.* It echoes what Stellan told me this morning when he saw the dagger in my hand.

"I didn't fish you from the ashes to watch you die in the gods-damned village square," Stellan said, yet there he is in the crowd, watching me from afar with narrowed eyes, his white brows furrowed in frustration. He shakes his head, letting me know, until my very last breath, that he did not sanction this.

"You've trained me for this," I told him in the forge, the place I grew up, the splitting of steel as natural as his endless whistling. He found me in the gutters of this world when I was just a child, an orphan with nothing to her name. Not even a name, really.

At that, his eyes lit with a fury so fierce it nearly diminished the forge behind him. Then that anger melted into something I had never seen in his expression before. Terror. "This isn't what I wanted."

Still, he didn't ask for the dagger back, even though it's the greatest weapon he's ever made, crafted from a piece of a world so cruel and deadly, he's refused to speak of it. Even to me.

Which is a shame, because the knowledge of how Stellan made it to be one of the Fifty would have really helped right about now.

No, he won't watch me die. Not yet. I'm going to make it to the platform. First, though, I need to get past this man who is digging a hole into the ground with his sword. He's still studying me far too closely.

I shrink into myself, as if unnerved by his notice. As if afraid of the sword he can't even hold up. I take a shaking step back, shoe sinking into the mud.

The man smirks, taking his time to look me over, his gaze snagging on my clothing. He must be wondering why I'm wearing long sleeves and fabric up to my chin in scorching heat. He must be noticing the clear lack of scabbard and baldric. He frowns when he reaches my worn boots, the fabric shrunken and split. The people to his left and right turn back around, already uninterested.

But he keeps looking, taking in my brown hair that I carefully braided and pinned at the back of my head, to keep the long strands out of my face—and to keep others from using it against me. It might be the most obvious sign that I'm here for something other than entertainment, but his stare just wanders, until it finally meets mine.

All at once, his interest grows. My eyes—they're dark blue. A rare shade. Now, I wish they were a different color entirely.

I don't drop my gaze. He tilts his head. Finally, he leans toward me, his metal leaning with him. "Don't let me stop you."

I smile my thanks and pass him by.

That's when his hand slides down my body. Squeezes. I freeze.

Bile crawls up my throat, but I swallow it and the urge to cut his hand clean off. I can't be noticed. Not yet, so many rows away.

I do what I've done for years. I bury the rage and keep moving.

That's when a scream cuts through the crowd like a scythe.

The silver hawk. Its sharp beak is opened wide, emitting a piercing wail.

It's time.

A flash of color snags my attention as a man hurls himself from a rooftop, attempting to get onto the stone by jumping. It looks like he might make it.

He almost does.

Then, just before his feet land, a guard's sword goes through his gut. He slips in his own blood right off the stone.

His body is quickly thrown into the fire. The flames roar, then crackle.

Fire or stone. Death or life.

This is the Questral.

In a wave of weapons, the first ring of volunteers rushes forward, only to be met with a wall of king's guards, all wielding the highest metal. *Silver*.

Metal is our last remaining magic—ore from the ground, infused with power. Some varieties hold more of it, making a weapon stronger. And silver is the strongest of all mortal metals.

They're dead. I see their swords from rows away, and I know for certain they stand no chance.

Still, they lift their blades. They bellow as they lunge forward, ready to duel.

And one after the other, copper, tin, and aluminum swords shatter against higher metal.

Their wielders are run through. They fall. *They all fall*. Their bodies are kicked to the side, then thrown into the flames, before they've even taken their final breaths.

Fuck.

The next surge of volunteers is already rushing forward. More metal fractures and breaks.

Panic rises within me like a bitter tide. My eyes widen at the blood, already spilling rivers across the stone and dirt around it. But my thumb traces the etchings down the hilt that I carved myself, the curve of a flame that mirrors the one currently melting a pile of flesh and bone. A reminder of why I'm here.

For you. I'm doing this for you.

The hawk screeches a second time. One minute, already gone.

No more standing still. I use the chaos as a cover and duck, slipping through rows, eyes fixed on the glimmering stone. Five rows away. Four—another screech. Three.

Clashing metal sounds to my left. The crowd erupts in mayhem as nothing short of a legion forces itself through its center, curved shields creating an orb-like barrier. They march as one body, inching forward, shoving anyone in their way to the ground.

Only when they reach the platform do the shields part, and out walks a man wearing glimmering armor that mimics the sun itself.

It's crafted from pure, unfiltered gold. Selling just a piece of it would feed our village for a year. It's nearly impenetrable, crafted with the utmost care.

I know. It was made in Stellan's forge.

The crowd murmurs to one another, but the displeasure doesn't rise above a whisper because Cadoc is the heir of House Bolter, one of the five remaining Great Houses on Stormside. Thousands rely on the house for food, since the Bolters own most of the remaining fertile land on this side.

It isn't an accident. Every Questral, House Bolter has sent its eldest through the gates, and they have returned with enough magic for another half century of prosperity. For themselves, at least. They've hoarded relics and knowledge that make it easier for their descendants to survive the next quest. Over generations, the house has ballooned in power.

Unlimited access to gold from their House's mines doesn't hurt either.

I don't have a legion. Thanks to Stellan, I don't need one. He taught me to be strong. Independent. Resilient even through tragedy.

You rise. You rise from the ashes like a phoenix, he told me when I was just a child who wouldn't stop crying.

Phoenixes aren't real, I told him.

"Not here," he said. *Not here.*

It was the most he ever revealed about the place beyond the gates. The one we're all now risking our lives to visit.

Starside. The land of magic and immortals. A place that is said to glimmer like diamonds and cut like teeth.

A paradise that is lusted after and feared in equal measure. Immortals don't die from disease, they don't bleed, they don't need food and water to survive. Their eyes glitter like gemstones. They are the descendants of the gods. The gods themselves live on that side, imbuing their land with endless resources.

We kill each other for scraps of that magic.

I'm so close. The crowd is still partially scattered, and I use that to my advantage. The stone glimmers brightly, winking beneath the sunlight. I take another step forward—

And nearly take an arrow in the eye. At the last second, I turn, and crimson spatters as the arrow goes through the skull of the man behind me. He slumps to the dirt, body crunching the glass of discarded goblets, drinks left by those who have waited days in the same spots to catch a glimpse of the action.

A sword is gripped in his lifeless hand. It's a lesser metal. Still, a half-starved man from the crowd lunges to take it. Another fights him.

My path has been noticed. I duck—then am slammed to the side as someone pushes past, making a run for the platform. A woman with tan skin and dark hair, cut close to her scalp.

The arrow was meant for her. That's made clear when another one whistles through the boiling afternoon air, right at her chest. She dips to avoid it, rolls, and pulls her own bow and arrow from her back so quickly, her movements blur.

She doesn't even stop, or slow. She just aims without looking, fires, and keeps going, before leaping onto the platform.

The archer falls from the top of a nearby building, his body hitting the road with a sickening thud.

A fourth cry.

Just seven minutes left.

I bolt, then almost trip over a body, curled low. The ridges of a spine are clearly visible through thin fabric. A head whips to the side, and—it's just a child. Clutching a jagged piece of glass as a weapon.

My gaze lifts to the platform. There's an opening, a gap between king's guards already dueling other opponents. I should run. I should take my chance. But instead, I find myself crouching.

"Don't do this," I tell the child. He looks at me with wide amber eyes. And I know I'm a damned hypocrite as I say, "You won't make it."

But his mind is set, just as mine is. "My family is starving. I'm—I'm their only chance."

I swallow past the knot in my throat. "Do they know you're here?"

He shakes his head.

I look down at my dagger. "Listen, I—"

Before I can finish, the boy turns and lunges. He makes a run for it. He's small. No one even seems to notice. He might actually reach it.

A moment before he does, someone steps into his path. A king's guard. His mouth turns into a cruel smile, looking down at the boy with relish.

Fifth screech.

I should stay back. Wait for the right moment. It's the only way I'll make it.

But when the guard's silver sword comes crashing down, I throw myself in front of the boy without thinking. The dagger I've tried so hard to hide slips from my sleeve, and I turn it midair, until the cold hilt hits my palm. I lift it right in front of my face at the last moment. Close my eyes tightly. The guard's sword slams against my dagger with bone-rattling force a second later.

And there's a glorious crash as that silver shatters.

The crowd has gone silent. Slowly, I open my eyes. The guard is staring down at me, mouth agape, as if still not comprehending what just happened. Not understanding how a dagger went up against his silver sword . . . and won. When he finally notices the metal of my blade, his face pales.

His hilt hits the ground and he staggers back, a coward without his sword. The boy has slipped away, and made it onto the stone. Before I can join him, the crowd stirs back to life, and half a dozen people hurl at me in a wave.

No going back now.

Sixth screech.

A copper blade reaches me first, and I turn, lifting my dagger, my metal just skimming its edge—but it's enough. The weapon breaks apart in a spray of splinters, just as a nickel sword aims for my neck.

Cracks spiderweb across its blade already, the mark of either bad welding or too many fights. Either way, it takes just a brush of my metal to turn it into shards at my feet and some of the people charging forward stop in their tracks. Rethinking going against my metal. Good. Just when I think I'm in the clear, a rallying cry sounds right behind me.

The man from before, with the wandering hands, is struggling to lift his sword up as he lunges at me, sharp edge trained right at my spine.

I don't think. I remember how those hands slipped down my body, and—

I cut them clean off. The Starside steel goes right through skin and bone. The blade glimmers even more than usual, as if savoring the blood. His heavy sword falls to the ground, fingers still curled around it. The man screams. A few people gasp.

Seventh cry.

When I raise my blade toward the crowd again, no one moves. Even the king's guards look hesitant to face me, now that they've seen my metal best theirs. They each only get one sword. Without it, they're dead.

My chest rises and falls wildly as I take a step back, inching myself toward the platform. Maybe I'll actually make it. I finally turn to jump.

And a man who looks like he was sired by the towering Dagger Mountains themselves blocks my path.

Shit.

Pagnus Ender, from House Ender, known for their magnificent size, rumored to have gods in their blood lines, takes a step toward me, and the very ground seems to tremble. I catch my horrified expression in his gleaming bronze armor, the top of my head not even reaching his stomach, his blade nearly the size of my body.

His house has eight heirs, and half are expected to make the quest this time. I see them now, positioned at the other corners of the platform, each sporting their house's metal. Already culling the potential recruits, alongside the guards, which aren't even *trying* to cut them down, likely from orders from the king, who has partnerships with all the Great Houses.

Of course, he's the one person standing between me and the platform. Of fucking *course*.

I take a deep breath. Steady myself. Take the stance I've fallen into as easily as sleep for years. Prepare for a blow that might be my last.

But Pagnus Ender just looks down at me and smirks. He steps to the side.

Something worse than fear sinks through my chest.

He doesn't even think me worthy of his killing blow. He doesn't think I have a chance at surviving the Culling.

Pride and anger battle behind my ribs, but I shove them down and opt for gratitude. I will do anything to make it onto that platform, through the Culling, and through those gates.

I step past him. I'm almost onto the glimmering stone.

That's when Pagnus seems to change his mind. Maybe he's decided he wants to claim my dagger. In a flash, I'm blinded by sun reflected off bronze, his sword arcing right toward my head.

He might be bigger, but I'm quicker, especially without armor. I roll out of the way, and then my blade is through his shin, my superior metal going right through his, reaching bone, and he roars. The rest of the Enders turn our way, allowing a crop of other competitors to make it through unharmed, including a girl with a whisp of red hair. Cheers erupt across the crowd.

Pagnus turns, eyes wide and gleaming with fury, his blade coming back around. I haven't injured him enough. Too late. I drag my dagger from his leg and throw myself through the air. Time stands still as I soar, waiting to feel his metal through my skin. The sun seems to wink at me, blocking my vision. My muscles clench as I brace myself.

My spine hits the hot stone. It burns through my shirt, but I barely register the heat; my every sense narrowed to the blade still hurtling toward my face. It isn't Starside steel, bronze is the lesser of even the mortal high metals, but with Pagnus's strength, it might as well be. There's no time to move. All I can do is stare at the sword that's about to cut right through my skull.

I'm on the stone. *I'm on the stone.* Any pride melts into panic as the bronze doesn't slow in the slightest. We're supposed to be safe here, under the king's protection.

Pagnus is in full view of the Watchman. He'll be disqualified. Or maybe he won't.

Maybe the same rules don't apply to him. Maybe he knows it. The fear of that bleeds through my chest as I brace myself for the death that already seems promised.

His blade stops just an inch from my face.

He snarls like a beast and says, "I'll see you in the Culling."

Then he steps up next to me on the platform.

Eighth scream.

Three minutes. I made it with *three minutes to spare*.

My ears ring. My heart batters my ribs. All I want to do is take a fucking *breath*, but I crawl away as fast as I can, knees nearly buckling as I finally get to my feet. I bolt to the center, next to the girl with red hair that nearly camouflages the copious amount of blood spurting from her skull.

She turns to me and smiles. I must look horrified, because she just shrugs. "I'm fine. *Lovely* eyes, by the way. Reminds me of home." She extends her hand. "Kira, from Brambleside."

It's a town at the westernmost tip of Stormside, along the sea. As far as I know, there isn't any magic left there. At least we still have the dregs of what once was, in the east. The farther west you go, the less you find.

The Culling hasn't even started. To be among the Fifty, I might have to kill her.

Still, I find myself taking her hand. Shaking it. Saying in a voice eroded by relief and exhaustion, "I'm Aris. From Silverside."

Her smile falters. Her green eyes widen. Shit. This exact reaction is why I haven't told anyone where I'm from for years. Not that many have cared enough to ask.

I'm the blacksmith's apprentice. Unworthy of notice. I don't really know why I share the truth of my origins with her now.

"I didn't know anyone survived from there," she finally says.

If I forgot for a moment why I'm here today, this reminder slams into my very marrow. A blinding rage flares in my chest, a fire that burns brighter than the one crackling just feet away. "Most didn't."

Ninth screech.

Just two minutes left. Volunteers are starting to get desperate. Sloppy. Launching right toward the king's guards, only to be slain and thrown into the fire.

Tenth scream.

Just one minute left.

Bellows, cries, and shouts of celebration reach a fever pitch. The guards grow in their brutality, reveling in the bloodshed, not stopping, even when the person is clearly incapacitated. Only two more make it through, and both are injured.

I can almost feel the seconds counting down, tension rising like the smothering heat of the flames. Last chance. Someone makes a jump for it, but they're pulled back by the hair, and slaughtered. No one else tries. And now there isn't any time left. Sun beating against the crown of my head, I turn and watch the silver hawk open its mouth one final time.

But the cry dies in its throat.

And, as if their screams have been ripped away by a brutal wind, the crowd suddenly goes silent.

"*No*," Kira whispers beside me.

No is right.

No. Fucking. Way.

The very people who tried to kill me now scuttle back in fear. They don't just lower their weapons. The crowd fully *parts* down the center, making a path straight to the platform.

And a towering knight steps forward. A black hood and silver mask hide his face.

Not that it matters. We all know who he is, and what he's done.

His silver armor is unmarred, because no one has ever gotten close to killing him. The only skin visible is his hands, white as bone. Thin, inky markings bleed across his knuckles and curl down each of his fingers.

He looks like a demon.

An enormous sword is tucked behind his shoulder. As he walks, his steps assured and almost casual, the slightest strip of silver is visible between the hilt and scabbard.

Sparkling, otherworldly silver, like melted-down stars. Starside steel. An entire *sword* of it. It makes my own blade look like a toy. His is the only one currently claimed this side of the gates. Ancient, powerful swords choose their wielder. This one chose a man who parts an entire bloodthirsty crowd with just his reputation.

Harlan Raker, head of the king's guard. The most famed knight on Stormside.

A man infamous for lacking mercy. I should know. I begged him for it, and he remained as cold as he is now as he studies the challengers. As he studies me. I can't see his face, but I can practically *feel* his notice. His disdain. By the set of his wide shoulders, he seems unimpressed. Bored.

Just feet away from the platform, Raker suddenly stops. Even the flames seem to still. He looks around, muscles taut for the first time, and I can almost imagine his eyes glimmering beneath that hood, just like my blade did, as if daring someone to come forward. As if *hungry* for bloodshed.

I almost wish for it, just to see that magnificent sword unsheathed.

But no one moves a muscle. All the guards bow their heads, staggering back. He steps onto the platform, unchallenged.

The hawk finally completes its final cry.

Murmurs spread through the crowd like wildfire. Why would the head of the king's guard risk the quest across Starside? Lesser members of the guard have before, but never their leaders. They already have what so many challengers want—a home, food, riches, glory. The king gives them all they could ever need. Still . . . I suppose there are things even the most powerful person on this side can't give.

The Questral is a journey across Starside, to the Land of the Gods, to claim a goblet of magic.

Everyone has their reason for going. Drops of magic can be used for medicine, or sold for riches, or—if an entire cup is swallowed—turn a human into an immortal. If they survive the Turn, that is. More often than not, humans don't, so most challengers don't risk it.

No, if a Questral challenger actually returns victorious, they come back heroes, and relish every drop, spreading their magic over decades. Entire villages have been pulled out of poverty by a cup of magic—their residents live in splendor while the rest of us starve and steal to get by.

Most of the Fifty never return at all.

Stellan did—but with an empty chalice. All he had to show for his journey was the sparkling metal that made the dagger I now hold tightly in my palm. People hated him, and questioned him, and so he became a pariah. He moved, but his reputation followed. The only reason he has any work at all is because his skills are undeniable. Still, he lives with little, when he could have returned with the wealth of the king.

I've always wondered why. I've asked him, of course, more times than I can count.

He's never answered.

Kira jumps as the hawk unfurls its wings in a flash of silver. According to the Watchman, there are two hundred and twenty-six of us on the stone.

The ones who didn't make it are strewn throughout the crowd, dead or dying. Their blood has turned the dirt into mud. Lesser members of the king's guard start to throw the bodies into the flames beside us.

The man I cut down is one of them.

Bile crawls up my throat again as the fire rages. Memories flash, choking me. I want to look away—I want to run. I want to sink to my knees and retch. But I can't be seen as weak. Not now, when the competition has hardly begun. I force myself to stand and watch as skin and bone and the flames themselves become nothing but heaps of ash.

The Watchman drags a bucket through the cinder.

One by one, he steps in front of each of the survivors—now, Questral challengers. I stand straight, gaze locked with Stellan's, sweat spilling down my back, cursing all the fabric I'm forced to wear, until the Watchman finally reaches me.

"Will you participate in the Culling?" he says for the fifty-seventh time.

Stellan is still in view off to the side. This is my last chance to back out. My last chance to step off the platform and return to the forge. There's work waiting for me. There's dinner to be made.

His eyes are pleading. *Don't do this,* they seem to say. *Say no.*

I break our gaze and say, "Yes."

The major dips his hand into the bucket. His hot, sweaty thumb makes an arc across my brow, a crown of ash.

"In the name of the gods," he says.

"In the name of the gods," I answer.

He moves on.

And I look up at the sky. Right at those *gods*. I wonder if they can sense the fury in my bones meeting the heat of hope—boiling metal hardening into steel. A sword of vengeance being forged within me.

This is truly in your name, I think. *This is* for you.

Because I'm not going to Starside to get magic, or to kneel before our beloved gods.

I'm going to kill them.

2

I was ten years old when a goddess burned down my village like it was nothing more than kindling. Every night since, I've seen her eyes in my sleep, glowing silver with power. I've seen her metal-colored hair, and gem-encrusted skin, glittering in the light of the flames. I've seen the curl of her cape as she turned on her heel and left us all to burn.

I'm going to kill her, and the rest of the gods who have forgotten this side of the gates. Even if it kills me too.

Which means I have to survive the Culling. I have to become one of the Fifty. *For them*, I will survive anything. Even the haunted look in Stellan's eyes as he watches me jump off the platform.

I can't deal with his disappointment. Not yet. So, I use all the excitement and celebration as a cover to slip away.

The roads are crawling with the king's guard. Their presence isn't unusual, given how close we are to their training grounds. Still, seeing them never fails to fill me with rage.

Four years ago, in the worst of the drought, I turned a corner with a bucket of water I had carried for three hours from one of the remaining working wells, only to see a guard leaned against the wall, high on hemdrake. He took one look at my dry, dirt-crusted face and straining white knuckles and said, "Here. Let me help you with that."

"No, I—"

I tried to turn, but he lunged forward, ripped the bucket from my hands, and poured the water out, little by little, right in front of my face, onto the broken cobblestones. He smiled the entire time, my horrified expression reflected in his marred silver armor.

He threw the bucket to the ground and passed me by.

I learned to take better roads. This one is usually clear.

The group I encounter now steps in front of me, and my bones clench. Fury alights in my stomach.

When they see the ash arc on my brow, though, they back away. They must have been instructed not to mess with the king's Questral challengers.

"Good luck," one says, his voice full of whispered mirth. I hear something else, a murmur about how many challengers Raker will kill within the first hour, but I scurry away before I can hear anything more.

Choking on hot air, throat rough with thirst, I weave through the lines of caravans and carts that have been hauled from distant villages. I don't stop until I reach the familiar patch of light brown soil at the base of the hill I visit almost daily, and then I begin to climb the weathered stone stairs.

Panic still bleeds through my chest like my body doesn't know it's not in danger anymore. My heart stutters. I stumble, before catching myself, blinded by flashes of the bloodshed—*metal shattering, bodies going limp, blood turning the soil crimson, skin melting from bone in the flames.* I grit my teeth, forcing the images into the dark corners of my mind as I focus on not twisting my ankle. I didn't survive all of this to be taken down by some half-crumbled steps.

As a distraction, I start undoing my pins, slipping them into my pockets. My hair gets in the way in the forge, so I always part it down the middle, then make two braids against my scalp at either side that merge into a big one at the back of my head. It usually hangs loose down my spine, but today I curved it into the gap between braids, like threading a needle, around and around until I could pin it all against my scalp. Now, I unravel it, releasing some tension as my braid hangs down again.

When I finally reach the ruins at the top of the hill, the full weight of what I've just done crashes into me. My knees buckle, and I collapse onto what's left of the white marble floor, heaving, hands trembling. Only when I can breathe normally again do I fully press myself against the floor, then turn onto my back to squint up at the storm-gray sky, what's left of the ceiling in pieces around me. My pulse drowns out all my senses, beating loudly, as if declaring, *I'm alive.*

I did it. I can't believe I did it.

I made it past the first step. I'm . . . going to the Culling.

I sit up. A breeze hisses through the columns of the ruins, prickling the ash arc on my brow.

This place is too broken to know what it once was, but a temple makes the most sense. Other than the Great Houses, the only structures built from materials this valuable are to honor the gods.

I found it years ago, while scavenging. At first, I wanted to try my best to finish the process of turning it to dust, because *fuck them*. But when the stone proved too hard to even make a dent, I tried to loot it. Everything of value was taken long ago . . . but there was one flash of color behind a massive rock. The border of what looked like a painting.

The idea of art, in a world of ruins . . . it seemed ludicrous. But it reminded me of finding wildflowers with my sister, years ago—a rare bloom in a wasteland. A spot of hope in a dark place.

So I came back every day for weeks, moving the stone blocking the color just inches at a time, until finally it was out of the way, revealing a landscape.

I instantly recognized the jagged horizon, formed by a mountain range like a serrated blade. I'd seen it multiple times.

Here.

I craned my neck past the wall and saw the same outline. This . . . was an ancient painting of this same view. But it might as well have been of another place entirely.

Because whereas this illustration was full of greens and blues, of forests and rivers and flower-brushed valleys—

Now I look out at endless dirt and ash.

"Why does the other side have all the magic?" I asked my mom when I was eight years old, while she combed through my hair, our nightly routine.

"We have our own magic," she said, as she gently worked through a knot.

"We do?" I asked, eyes wide as I looked at her through the mirror.

She nodded. "We have the magic of warm socks, and nights playing cards by the hearth, and laughter, and love."

I scowled at her. "That's not magic." I would have much rather had a dragon or magical sword from the stories she told before bedtime. The same ones her mother had told her.

"It's the only magic that matters," she said.

I didn't believe her then. I do now, when it's far too late.

With a grunt, I get to my feet, boots sliding in the rubble. I walk farther into the ruins, then crawl between two crumbled walls, reaching my hand deep, until my fingers brush against fabric.

I carefully withdraw my dust-covered pack.

It took years to save enough extra money from scavenging to get this simple bag and everything in it—a canteen for water, a bar of soap, some wrappings as bandages, a needle and thread, scraps of fabric, and a single gold coin that I traded everything of value for. It's all I could manage, and my best guess of what I might need during the journey.

Guesses are all I have. Preparation for anyone but Great House heirs is almost futile. When the gates went up, all our books about the other side were magically stripped of their ink. All the poems went blank. All the paintings were drained of color, leaving only blank canvases.

Only stories, orally told, remained, and I don't doubt the truth was twisted over time. All that's left is myths and legends. Even our knowledge of the gods is limited.

But the heirs whose ancestors have gone on the Questral . . . they have the most recent information.

If I can somehow convince Stellan to tell me what he knows, then I'll have it too.

I stare out at Nightfell, counting caravans, studying the crowds. Even if Stellan doesn't tell me what he faced, soon enough . . . I'll know.

I will survive the Culling.

I will cross those gates.

I have to.

And then, I will see for myself all that was meant to be hidden. I will see Starside, the world that birthed a thousand legends.

"I did it," I repeat, this time aloud, eyes on the direction of where my home once stood. I feel that relentless pull toward it, the pain and loss a gaping wound in my soul, as if part of me is still there, kneeling in those ashes. "I did it for you."

I take one last look at the mural, at the world that once was, and start the long trek down.

The streets are full now, packed with travelers already drunk on cheap ale. I take the long way around, through the ancient graveyard, along a row of abandoned houses, roofs caved in, paneling discolored, windows long broken. Each neighbor packed up and left in the middle of the drought, in search of more food and water.

I still remember finding their caravans on the road, years later, their carts looted. Their skeletons. The children . . .

I slip through the back, hoping Stellan is in the forge and won't hear me—only to find him waiting right at the back door, like he knew I would be too much of a coward to go through the front.

Stellan's eyes find my pack immediately. Then they find mine. I see the hurt there as he realizes this is something I've been planning for a while.

I lift my chin. "Save your breath. I'm not changing my mind." I try to walk past him, but he steps to the side, blocking me.

Then I proceed to stand there and listen to every possible reason not to go with the Watchman tomorrow morning. Every way I could die. He maps it all out for me, as if my death is inevitable, careful not to tell me anything that could actually be useful. He has a list of dozens of ways I'm woefully unprepared, and shoots down every counter I make.

But hours of arguing are nothing when compared with ten years of hatred. It's like lesser metal clashing against Starside steel and shattering into a thousand pointed pieces.

Finally, I throw up my hands. "Look. I'm going. You can't stop me. There's no use spending our last moments together fighting about it."

Last moments. I meant last hours, before the Watchman is at our door, loading me onto a cart that will take me east to the king's castle, but I watch Stellan's eyes flare with concern again and regret my choice of words.

We've never been good with them. We've gone days without saying anything to each other at all. Our language has always been that of smelting and shaping metal. He'd barely said anything during those first few weeks when he brought me here and all I could do was cry. I thought he didn't care. I thought he was a giant oaf, all beard, thick eyebrows, and grunts. I thought he would forget me in the closet of a room he had piled blankets in. I thought he might throw me back onto the streets.

One day he knocked on my door and came in to find me still crying. *This is the end of warm blankets and soup left at my door*, I thought. Tears were hot on my cheeks. *This is good. If he leaves me to die, maybe I will. Maybe that would be better than all this pain.*

But he didn't kick me out of his house. All he did was slowly kneel before me, so our eyes were close to level. All he did was hand me a figurine of a little girl holding a blade, in a fighting stance. It was painstakingly made of metal, so detailed, so expertly crafted that it could only be one person.

Through sniffling, I said, "But—but I don't have a sword."

He shook his head. Pointed his massive finger at the tiny figurine. "This here's a dagger. Not a sword. And you will, if you get up and stop your crying."

That was when he pulled a blade from his pocket. Something in me thought perhaps I should fear this towering man, with his hard eyes and weathered skin and long beard. He had a *weapon*. He could kill me. But I was so stunned by the sparkling metal, I stopped crying for the first time in weeks.

He quickly sheathed it.

"It's yours, when you're ready for it. You can even design the hilt if you want. But only if you get up. It's your choice."

He stood. Then he offered me his hand. I knew what it meant, even then. Either burn or rise from the ashes once and for all.

I took it.

And from then on, he spent his days teaching me to make swords and his nights teaching me to use them.

In the last decade, I never once saw his brow furrow. I never saw him display any type of emotion.

But now his face is all twisting lines. It's easy to see the time that has passed.

I take a step forward, pushing off the wall. My tone softens. "If—if you want to help me live . . . then tell me something. *Anything* that will keep me alive."

Stories about Starside are full of creatures and magic that are nearly too far-fetched to believe. But he knows the truth. He was one of the few survivors of the last Questral. He can tell me how he did it.

Stellan's face hardens again. I ready myself, believing he might finally tell me something about the other side, after all these years.

"You want to live?" he says.

I nod. Of course. I need to survive until the very end to get to the gods. "I do."

He leans in closer, as if about to tell me one of the world's great secrets. I don't dare breathe, in anticipation. It's so quiet, I can hear the simmering of the forge, and I remember all the work still left to do for the night. His mouth is almost to my ear.

"Don't go, then," he says, and then he passes by me on the way to the forge. I stay frozen in front of the hearth, hoping he might return, might actually tell me something useful, until I hear the familiar sound of pounding metal. It's only when I feel around in my pockets that I realize he's taken his dagger with him without my noticing.

Shit.

I don't know what else I was expecting. He's never said a word about Starside. Why would he help me now, when he's still hoping I'll stay?

In my foolish mind, I envisioned us sitting in front of these weak flames. Him—telling me everything I need to know. Me—planning my survival.

Now I take a lesser blade from its hidden place on a high shelf, cursing Stellan and his ever-present concern for my well-being, and duck out into the night.

It's suffocatingly hot, as always. A very convenient place for someone who must wear so many layers to live. Sweat already slips down the center of my chest, but I dutifully check the fabric at my throat, the way I have most of my life, just in case the collar has slipped.

Cursed markings.

As I approach the village square and see women wearing just bits of material, I wonder what that must be like. Feeling the wind against my bare skin. Having people look at me. Not hiding.

A curl of laughter spills out from inside a bar that is normally empty, considering few here have scraps of metal to spare. Through the open window, a teetering man spots the arc across my brow and tries to shove a chipped goblet into my hand.

I decline and cross to the other side of the road, making my way through a sea of strangers. I brush against fabrics worlds softer than the scratchy ones made by the local weaver, a woman with long, dirty nails who buys clothes I steal off corpses. Some weeks, she's the reason we have enough to eat. She's also the reason I have clothes that cover me, when usually so much fabric would be seen either as wasteful or dangerous in heat like this.

I turn another corner—then stumble back as a group of travelers pours out of the local inn. An inn I was sure was abandoned, given the fact that I have not, in the past decade, seen a single person inside of it. Now, its second floor is visibly sagging because of the crowd.

Stellan warned me of the throngs months ago. I thought he was exaggerating. Who would travel for days, or weeks, to see people die fighting to get onto a stone? It's not like they actually get to see the events of the mysterious Culling . . .

Thousands of people, apparently.

Merchant carts have been wheeled in from miles away. Their lines make mazes through the normally empty streets. I weave through them, eyeing foaming mugs, whipped sugar, and spice-encrusted pastries. Some travelers will stay for as long as their coins last, just to await news of anyone making it back through the gates.

My empty stomach grumbles. I introduce it to my empty pockets.

I might not have scraps of metal to spare, but there are some mushrooms still left from my foraging.

My stomach twists—and not just from hunger this time. Stellan and I should be making soup instead of fighting.

Regret sinks through me. He sounded so upset. So *disappointed*. I should go back home, but I don't. I turn again, toward the stone I barely made it onto. The crowds begin to thin, most people headed toward the carts. I see a wisp of smoke.

"There she is. The hands thief."

I jump, then whirl in the direction of the alley I just passed, blade clutched tightly. It's copper, barely worth anything at all. One of the first daggers Stellan let me make.

A man is leaning against the brick, swirling a drink in a rusted goblet. He has brown skin, dark hair, and is so tall I have to lift my chin to look at his face. I recognize him from the platform. He tilts his head at me. "Aren't you sweating rivers in all that clothing?"

Yes. Literal rivers, it feels like.

I ignore his question and raise my brow. "Tell me you aren't really going to drink that." It's one of the chipped goblets from the bar.

He cracks a smile. "Not even a drop. I'd like to make it to the gates. It would be a shame to have survived the platform only to be bested by bad ale."

"*Poisoned* ale, more likely," Kira says as she comes walking up to us from the other side of the street. Her red hair is now clean and combed, blood washed out of it. She's frowning at her own cup. "This even *looks* disgusting."

Poison wouldn't surprise me. Some of the Great Houses would do whatever it takes to ensure their heirs make it to the Fifty. We're all under the king's protection for now, but poison is difficult to prove.

Kira dumps the liquid into a half-dead bush next to her. It will likely be full-dead by morning.

A shame. There's such little green on this side to begin with.

"So," Kira says, turning to the man. She stays at the mouth of the alley, in a pool of moonlight. "You are?"

"Zane," he says. "From the Bladelands. Helmspeak, specifically."

Kira stumbles forward, her suspicion instantly melting into excitement. "Really?" The Bladelands are a stretch of mountainous territory to the west. Stellan says people lucky enough to be born there die there. The top of the mountains remain lush. Every year, hundreds migrate to Helmspeak during the spring, when the conditions are less harsh. Few survive the climb.

Kira's eyes are wide with a thousand questions. I just have one—if people die trying to reach his mountain's peak, why leave?

Why risk almost certain death?

"Tell me. Are the Helmhawks real?" Kira is in the shadows now, halfway down the alley. I remain at its mouth, hand still gripped around my blade. I should move on. The frustration curling around my bones has already softened. I should go back and help Stellan finish the last of his orders. It's the least I can do.

These are strangers. No—now they're challengers. We're all fighting for fifty placements. They're *rivals*.

But I don't move an inch. I'm curious to hear Zane's answer, I realize. I haven't been west at all.

"They were," he finally says.

The town weaver likes to talk while she makes my clothing. Listening gets me a discount. She claims she was once the personal tailor to a Great House heir, who wanted fabrics from all corners of Stormside. So she traveled to almost every one, collecting fabrics for her boss as she went. And for herself . . . she collected buttons. She has a drawer of them, locked with a key. Each button has a story. Over the years, she's told me almost all of them. I go to the drawer sometimes and pick one out. *Tell me this one again,* I'll say. That's how I know about Helmspeak and the hawks that once lived there.

Helmhawks are said to be larger than people and congregate on the highest peak they can find, which on this side is Helmspeak. Rumor is that hundreds of years ago they allowed themselves to be ridden.

"They're gone?" Kira says, so loudly a few passersby turn toward the alley.

Zane nods. "About a century ago, they left. Only a few giant feathers remain. The only proof they were ever there to begin with."

It's the story of this entire side. After the war, and the gates, all magic on this side faded. Nature withered. We rely on the magic that is brought back. These few years right before the next Questral are the hardest.

Maybe I should feel guilty for not having any intention of returning. Maybe I should be fueled by something more honorable than revenge.

The gods are the reason for our suffering, though. When they die, the gates will fall. Magic will not be hoarded on one side any longer.

Kira grips my elbow, and I nearly stab her through the chest on instinct. I'm glad I hesitate, though, because all she does is laugh and say, "Look at those fools. They're going to be retching off their carts tomorrow."

She's staring at the group of ash-crowned challengers sitting on the dark platform, in front of a newly started fire. They're drinking wine they must have brought themselves, because nothing that nice is sold anywhere close to here, even at the carts. Discarded bottles have gathered at their feet, over the blood-stained ground. The glass itself is worth something. I bury the urge to collect it. To make it into something I can sell.

Some challengers sit with women in their laps. Some are already passed out in the mud. Some aren't challengers at all.

Half the king's guard is here, standing and celebrating as if they each managed to gain a spot on the platform when it counted. My fists lock when I see them. My skin prickles with long-held fury.

Their leader sits in front of them, his massive sword dug into the dirt beside him. It's standing on its own.

It's the most valuable weapon on this side of the gates. I instinctually contemplate how much it would go for in the desert markets . . .

Useless, really. For even if it wasn't protected by knights, and Harlan Raker himself, I couldn't claim it.

I would have to be more powerful than Raker. An ancient sword isn't chosen; it's claimed by both sides. *Earned.*

As if sensing my notice of his weapon, Harlan Raker's head snaps up.

For a moment, the air seems to still. A chill licks down my spine. *Fear.* A creature encountering its species' greatest predator. A ruthless killer. His hood casts his entire face in shadow, even the mask doesn't glimmer. He would slay me where I stand if it wasn't against the rules. If it was worth his time at all.

My mind says to look away. To step back into the shadows of the alley.

But I remember that day in the rain. The day I begged him for mercy. I begged him to let me go.

He didn't.

I don't drop my gaze, even if I can't see his eyes. Mine narrow as if they could convey even a fraction of my hatred for him.

The bastard doesn't even look fazed. He doesn't look *anything*. Of course he doesn't. I can't see his face, but his unbothered posture shows enough. Someone taps him on the shoulder, and finally he turns, as if I've already been forgotten. As if he doesn't remember me in the first place.

"Chances are he kills one of us," Zane says, almost casually, motioning toward Raker. He's by my side now.

Kira gives him an incredulous look.

Zane only lifts a shoulder. "It's true. No use in pretending it isn't."

He's right. Harlan Raker once slayed an entire uprising himself. A hundred people against him, and he is said to have emerged without even a drop of blood on his armor. His movements were so precise, his blade so sharp, that it looked like he hadn't been to battle at all, according to the few merchants who passed through town, leaving behind gossip.

But he's not the only one with Starside steel going into the Culling. I'll convince Stellan to let me bring his dagger. He's angry . . . but he always promised that one day it would be mine.

Stellan likes lists. He makes one every morning of all our tasks and orders. On my way home, I make one of all the reasons he should help me.

Revelers stumble through the streets. The ash arc earns me a few bowing heads, and compliments, and—mostly—bets on how long I'll last in the Culling. Not long at all, apparently. No one tries to steal my dagger, though, which is a marked improvement from my typical walk home.

I don't hear Stellan in his forge, even though he locks himself in there all night whenever we get in an argument. Maybe he's decided to forgive me, I think, hope flaring in my chest. Maybe he's going to offer me the dagger. Maybe I won't need the list, which would be good, because it wasn't all that convincing to begin with.

I don't want to part on bad terms. I don't want him to sit here in this house alone, hating me.

"Stellan?" I say, floorboards creaking as I inch through the house. The hearth has gone dark. I use the poker to brush a layer of cinder away, uncovering the few glowing embers. I add some kindling and blow softly, gritting my teeth like I always do whenever I'm near fire. The logs flame.

I turn around, thinking he must have already gone to bed, and gasp.

Stellan is lying in the center of the room in a pool of blood.

Roaring fills the world. I'm on my knees beside him, feeling around for where he's hurt, my fingers finding gaping skin like screaming mouths. My hands slip in the blood. There's so *much* of it. I need help, I—

His hand comes over mine. It's cold.

"I—"

"Let me speak, child," he says. His words are labored, as if he's fought to stay conscious. How long has he been on this cold floor, in the dark? How long has he waited for me to come home?

Regret pierces me deeper than any blade could. I shouldn't have left. I should have joined him in the forge. This never would have happened—

His arm shakes with effort as he reaches to tap my pocket, and the copper blade inside of it. It's weak, nothing like his.

His. I look at his scabbard, only to find it empty.

No.

This is my fault. One of the challengers must have seen me use the dagger, seen how easily the glimmering steel cut through bone, and shattered steel. They knew it would be invaluable during the Culling. They came here to get it.

He hands me my own blade. I know what he means.

He wants me to kill him. He wants me to claim his dagger. If I don't, the person who did this will.

But I can't.

I shake my head. A sob rips from my chest, echoing through the room.

He takes my hand. It's trembling. "Listen to me. *Listen.* Find Vander Evren." His voice is so faint, I barely understand him.

"What?"

He doesn't answer. All he does is curl my fingers around my dagger. All he does is drag both of our hands toward his heart. His eyes are pleading.

"Kill me," he says, choking on the words.

I remember the figurine, still sitting on my bedside. I remember the day he let me accompany him to a Great House to hand-deliver a sword. I remember the village just outside the estate, and how he opened the tattered bag of metal scraps he kept in his front pocket and used one of his only copper ones to buy me a sugar-encrusted piece of fried bread. How I looked up at him and smiled wide after the first bite. How I stuffed half of it into his mouth, and he pretended not to like it, but I knew he did. How he taught himself to sew to make me long-sleeved shirts that covered my marks up to my throat—that kept me *alive*—when I was too young to make them myself, and before the weaver set up her shop. How, whenever I failed at something, he would tell me to rise from the ashes and call me a *phoenix*.

"I can't," I say, tears blurring my vision.

"Fool," he says, and then he dies.

I stay with his body until dawn turns the floorboards scarlet. Until the sun sparkles in his lifeless eyes.

Until there is a single knock on the door, and a high-pitched screech.

Carts creak outside. There's the murmuring of voices.

My tears have all been used up. They're dried against my heated cheeks. The dark pit in my stomach, the one where all my worst memories and emotions live, is churning. I push it down. I push it all down, because if I don't, I will never get up again. I will lie beside Stellan and finally let the rage and agony extinguish me.

The only thing that keeps me from doing just that is the fact that Stellan would have hated it.

My voice is pure conviction. "I will find who did this, and I will kill them. I will use everything you taught me, everything you made me, and I will kill them all." I press my lips to his cold forehead.

Then I take my things, get in a cart, and watch as my village becomes nothing more than a smudge of ash.

3

I've never been this far east before. Stellan used to travel to the castle often, to bring weapons to the king. He never let me go, even though I pleaded. Now I'm going to find out why.

Stellan. Thinking of him rotting on our floorboards makes my stomach turn. There was no time for a burial, but I should have dug him a plot. I should have listened when he told me to stay home that morning.

It's my fault he's dead.

It's my fault all of them are dead.

I push the pain and regret down, bury it all below my ribs and in the darkest pockets of my mind. I let it fuel the forge within me, hatred turning, boiling.

For him. I'm doing this for him now too.

Kira and Zane are in my cart, along with a few others. We sit side by side, with just enough room to stretch out our legs if we take turns. The road is ground dirt and jagged rocks for miles. The cart's wheels are uneven. Our bodies jostle and lurch forward, churning waves of nausea through me every few feet. Enough challengers in front of us retch that I'm grateful for my collar, pulling the fabric up over my nose, even though the sun burns so hot in the afternoon, I quickly sweat through my clothing.

Stormside's name is like a taunt—a reminder of what it once was. We pray for storms. We haven't had one in years. No rain at all. Only the beating sun, which often does more harm than good.

It's said that the first drop of magic brought back from the Questral always leads to rain. People leave buckets outside, waiting for it. I can almost feel the cold water upon my skin, if I close my eyes.

A flash of a memory has me opening them again.

Looking around, it's clear most of these challengers don't know how to survive long stretches outside in the heat. Some have already gone limp. Others are complaining loudly, asking when we'll stop for shade. I wonder if they spend most of their time inside, without having to venture out and scavenge, like most of us.

This is my advantage. I might not have the same metals as them, but I know what it's like to have to fight for survival. I've always found a way to live, even in the harshest conditions.

Kira watches as I tuck my braid back around and pin it up to keep it from sticking to the sweat on my neck, and also, in case I lean too far over the cart and it gets stuck in a wheel and breaks my neck. A few minutes later, she begins shedding some of her layers, until she's in only her underthings. Cadoc Bolter turns in the cart ahead of us and yells past the horse and guard leading our own wagon, "There's already enough vomit on the road. No need to make the rest of us sick."

Asshole.

She makes a vulgar gesture at him, but I'm close enough to see her pale cheeks go scarlet. She hugs her legs against her chest and looks away.

Cadoc's gaze shifts to me. "And you. Covered up to your chin. I wouldn't mind if you undressed."

I want to throw the sword in the scabbard along my spine through his skull. But I can't. Not until we're told the Culling has officially begun. Little is known about the challenges, since those that survive go onto the quest. Few ever make it back. All I know is they can't be long. The Questral always starts on the twenty-fifth day of the fifth month. Which is in just two days.

It would be a death sentence to face Cadoc now anyway. The sword I grabbed from Stellan's forge is titanium. A strong metal, but not a high one, and nothing compared to Cadoc's gold, two steps below Starside steel.

Cadoc opens his mouth again, but Zane says, "It's said that men who maim with words can't do the same with their swords. Is that true? I didn't get a chance to see your skill set yesterday . . . All those shields were in the way."

Silence.

Cadoc's eyes narrow, though his smile remains. He's trying and failing to look unaffected. "And you are?"

"Zane."

"Zane what?"

"Sterling."

This time, Cadoc's smile does drop. Kira slowly turns toward Zane. My eyes go to his weapon—an ax, sheathed. I realize now that I haven't seen the metal.

"House Sterling?" Cadoc says, his tone even but his posture changed completely.

Zane barely nods.

Cadoc straightens. "You'd be better off in our cart, then. My house has provisions handled for the entire journey." He motions to the distance, and there, on the horizon, is a convoy of men on horses. Of course.

They likely have food. *Water*, which might as well be Starside steel on this barren road. My pouch was drained hours ago.

Cadoc turns to one of the men in his cart and says, "Switch."

"What? We're *cousins*, Cadoc. My father—"

"No need," Zane says, his deep voice casual but his eyes narrowed. "I don't think there's room for me in that cart, with you and your ego in it."

Kira's mouth falls open.

Cadoc only gives a cold smile. "Suit yourself," he says, before turning back around. A few minutes later, his cart is too far ahead of us to hear him anymore.

That's when Kira whirls to face Zane. "You never said you were House Sterling."

Zane taps his fingers against the side of the cart. "I did say I was from Helmspeak."

"Yes, but you didn't say you own the *entire fucking mountain*," Kira counters.

And everything inside it. Including centuries' worth of mined silver. The Sterlings provide metal to the king's guard, and to blacksmiths like Stellan. Their own swords are why their house has retained control of the mountain all this time, without having to go on the quest. Which makes Zane's involvement even more mysterious.

Why does House Sterling suddenly need magic?

"You should have taken his offer," Kira says bitterly.

Her words are even truer later in the afternoon, when we watch Cadoc and his friends guzzle pouch after pouch of water, and eat meat dish after meat dish, throwing bones toward us when they're done.

Bastards.

My tongue is rough with thirst. My throat aches. My eyes sting from all the dirt kicked up by the endless string of carts.

Hunger hollows my insides, the hole growing by the hour. We keep going, only stopping briefly to relieve ourselves, and then we're back on the road.

I didn't sleep last night, or eat dinner, and now, I'm starting to feel it. My eyes flutter closed, before our cart's wheel hits a big rock, and I nearly fly out. I grip the side just in time, scraping my skin raw. I pick the splinters out of my fingers and decide I'm not going to fall asleep again.

Easier said.

My fingers begin to numb. My head leans forward, and I jerk myself awake. My stomach feels like it's gnawing itself. My lips and nostrils are dry. It hurts to breathe.

Just when I think the heat and hunger might kill me, Kira curls her hand around my arm.

"Look," she says.

It takes a few blinks to see the shape of a village up ahead. And . . . people. People standing outside, lining the road. Their hands are outstretched. *Begging?* No. Their palms aren't empty. They're holding things I can't see until we get closer.

Baskets, filled with food. Weapons, even, made of lesser metals.

"Offerings," Kira whispers.

I don't question it, though maybe I should. But I'm too fucking desperate. My hands are greedy. They take everything that's offered. Bread, which I swallow down without chewing well, nearly choking myself. Water, which drips down my chin, seeping into my collar. I pour some over my face, wiping the grime away, before accepting another pouch.

"Why give when they have so little?" Kira asks, while chewing something that looks like dried meat. A packaged cake barely misses her head as it's thrown right into the cart.

Zane unwraps it, sniffs, then takes a bite out of its corner. He makes a pleased sound. "They're hoping we survive, and that we don't forget their village when we come back with magic."

He's right. Some throw letters into our carts, messages for the gods, wishes, prayers. A woman whose bones I can see through her clothes manages to keep pace with our cart. When she sees me watching her, she rushes forward and presses a note into my palm. Her dirt-covered nails dig into my skin. "*Please*," she begs. "Take it."

I want to tell her it's useless. She's better off burning the letter. The gods have forgotten us.

But her hand is so bony, her eyes so glassy, her voice so frail, that I take it. I tuck it into my pocket. Her knees buckle. She thanks me from the ground as our cart passes her by, the wheels kicking up a cloud of dirt.

"They're so . . . hopeful," Kira says, swallowing a bite of bread as she watches the people fade away.

A man in our cart huffs out a laugh. He's been silent all this time, sitting as far from us as possible. His armor is covered in long scratches, and made of iron, a lesser metal below titanium. Still, any type of armor is valuable. "What they are is pathetic," he says. He isn't eating anything offered. In fact, he takes a handful of letters that are tied to rolls of bread and throws them right off the cart.

Kira's green eyes narrow. "Spoken like someone who has never had to beg for anything."

The man only smiles. His teeth are too crowded together. He looks amused. "Will you beg?" he asks, seeming genuinely curious.

Her pale brows knit together. "What?"

"When I have the tip of my sword at your throat, will you beg for your life?" He's serious.

"Will you beg for yours?" Kira finally counters.

The man's smile is slow and serpentine. "No . . . I don't think I'll have to," he says. Then he turns his attention back to the road.

The sun is relentless. By the time day turns to night, my cheeks are pink, the top of my nose burned. Kira's freckled skin is tanner and deep red at the shoulders. For once, I'm grateful for all my fabrics.

All I want to do is sleep, but just as I consider it again, a yell cuts through the darkness. Then, our cart jerks to the side as one of the wheels runs something over.

A body.

Another one.

Another.

I swallow, a chill rippling through my blood. The Culling hasn't started, but under the cover of night, it's hard to know if someone fell . . . or was pushed.

I keep my eyes open, and my sword gripped tightly. Kira and Zane seem nice enough, but we all want one of those fifty spots. I can't trust anyone.

Time crawls forward, until finally, night bleeds into day.

A screech peels through the morning. I look up and see a flash of silver. The hawk. A moment later, the Watchman comes riding along the carts with his horse. We know what that means. Another break. "Everyone up," he yells.

The carts park at the edge of a forest, and I stare up at the trees in awe. It's not the woods of the painting in the ruins. There's hardly any green at all. It's mostly dirt, and twisted branches, and tiny, prickling leaves. But I haven't seen anything like it in years.

A few people dart farther inside the trees to take advantage of the relative privacy. I stretch my cramped legs, fingers trailing along the bark, looking around in wonder.

There's a stream trickling nearby. A few challengers run toward it with their pouches. I stay in place and roll my neck.

Stellan's trips to the king never took more than three days total, which means we're close. The king will likely feed us before the Culling starts. No use in taking a chance on water that could very well make me sick.

Kira takes a step toward the spring, and my arm juts out. I don't even know why I do it. Her death would only help me. Friends are liabilities.

Still, I say, "I wouldn't."

"But I'm out." She lifts her pouch.

Zane steps next to me. He stretches his neck with a satisfying crack. "I once knew someone who drank from a bad spring and shit himself to death."

Slowly, she tucks her pouch back into her bag. "Okay, then. How much longer, do you think?"

"Half a day. Maybe less," I say.

Kira's shoulders slump forward in relief. "Good. I can't take another moment sitting in that cart. I have about a dozen splinters in my ass."

That almost makes me smile as we walk toward the Watchman, silver hawk now perched on his arm.

Instead, I freeze.

The carts are gone. Murmuring starts to spread through the challengers like wildfire.

Only when all of us have emerged from the forest does he speak. "There are two hundred and sixteen of you here." The number sends a chill through my blood. *Ten* challengers were killed on the road. "And there are only a hundred and fifty horses." I turn and squint. There they are, at the top of a distant hill just beyond the forest, saddled and standing in a line.

"The Culling starts now," the Watchman says.

And all hell breaks loose.

4

*R*un.

If I can run and get onto a horse, I'll have a third of a chance at making it into Starside. I could actually do this.

I'm not the only one with that idea.

I watch dozens of others run past me. And then I watch them fall.

Because half of our group has another plan. They're going to fight for each horse. Archers are already in the trees, shooting runners down one by one. I stop. Turn. Duck behind a tree at the last moment. Hear the splitting of wood as an arrow pierces its trunk.

Every single person who ran is now on the ground. Dead or dying.

I can't give my back to them.

I'm going to have to fight.

Zane sighs, a few feet to my left. I watch as he unsheathes his ax and rests it against his shoulder. My eyes widen. The silver is thick and reinforced with gemstones. I've never seen that before, the way the diamonds and rubies seem to melt right into the metal.

He sees me watching and shrugs. "It's been in my family since before the war."

A relic. Something the Great Houses offer. I look down at my own sword. Stellan was one of the best, but a blacksmith can only do so much with lesser metal.

"Hope to see you at the castle," Zane says, nodding his head. And then he charges forward.

Swords clash. Metal shatters.

Next to me, using the same tree as cover, Kira is shaking. "My sister," she whispers.

"What?"

An arrow just misses my side. I pull us both behind a larger trunk. It won't block us for long, not while the rest of the group is advancing.

"She's sick. That's why I'm here. She . . . she'll die without the magic."

And she might as well have reached into my soul and squeezed it.

My eyes close tightly as I remember my own sister. Her cries. Holding her body in its last moments as—

My cheek rips against a root as Kira drags me to the ground.

"What—" I look up and go still.

The entire top of the tree is gone.

The Enders. They're holding a glittering chain between them. It's—it's coated in a thin layer of Starside steel. They're using it to halve anyone in their path. Including the trees. Fuck. Bodies lay in pieces behind us. Trees fall in every direction, making the ground tremble. There isn't a safe place to hide. I watch a girl lunge forward, eyes widening, just before she's crushed by an oak. Blood spurts out her ears.

Kira throws up next to me.

"Come on," I say, dragging her up. I would have been halved if she hadn't pulled me down. I was too lost in my mind.

Distractions. My emotions and memories are distractions. They'll get me killed.

I have to bury it down. *All of it.*

The arrows have stopped. Most of the archers were cut down from their trees, thanks to the Enders. This is the best chance we're going to get. We start to run. Ahead, the forest has been flattened. The ground is a minefield of snapped trunks, sharp edges sticking up like broken blades. I sprint, careful not to impale myself on any of them, and—*I'm moving too slowly.* I can hear the stampede of challengers, not far behind. *Faster.* I push myself to run as fast as I ever have before, and Kira's ragged breaths make me think she's about to pass out, but she manages to keep pace. Branches split below our boots, already hollow and weak.

An arrow whistles past my head, and burrows into the ground in front of me.

Fuck. At least one archer is back up.

I leap over a downed tree, then nearly trip over another. I duck arrow after arrow, ignoring the sounds of those dying around me, burying the instinct to help.

There's a thud as a woman running a few yards to my left goes down, her body drudging up dirt. Ahead, a man is hit in the neck, and I barely avoid trampling his body.

The archer is close. And so are the next wave of challengers. Their steps thunder and crack against the broken forest floor. Some simply bolt past, others lash out, striking those around them, trying to increase their chances.

I don't turn, I just keep going, the hairs on the back of my neck rising, anticipating being struck at any moment. Their yells are getting louder.

"They're coming," Kira says. And then she goes down.

Go, my mind says. *Get a horse. Leave her behind.*

But I think of her sister. I couldn't save mine . . . Maybe Kira can save hers.

I stop. Whirl around. And my sword meets iron.

The man from the cart. His crowded teeth glint as he smiles. Kira's screaming, a hand pressed against the back of her head, blood pouring between her fingers. That's when I see he's holding a thick strand of her hair. *He fucking ripped it from her skull.*

"Protecting someone who will surely die? That seems foolish."

Our swords meet again, and this time his fractures. The line is like a vein running down his blade. A few more strikes, and it will shatter completely.

"So does fighting someone with greater metal," I say, slamming my blade against his. He stumbles back. Frowns, as if not expecting I might be able to hold my own against him. His eyes narrow in fury, and then he's lunging at me again.

But I'm ready.

A decade of Stellan's training steadies me against the panic, and I fall into my stance. I block his next sharp blow.

He spins then lashes out in a brutal mess of strikes, like he thinks his speed will catch me off guard.

It might, if Stellan hadn't been far faster than him. If I hadn't done this exact practice every morning. The titanium sword is nearly weightless in my grip as I block his every advance and force him back.

The arrows have stopped, at least. The archer must assume we're going to kill each other, and doesn't want to waste their limited stock.

I could kill him. I know I could. But it would take time we don't have. Not as we're passed by swarms of challengers running toward the line of horses.

That should be me. I should turn and run.

He tries to disembowel me. My blade meets his.

Another fracture.

"Waldron," he says. Sweat spills down his brow. He's not looking at me. He's looking at my titanium sword. "You . . . you will belong to Waldron."

Great swords have been known to betray their wielder if they encounter someone more powerful, even in the middle of a duel, but this isn't that kind of sword.

And Waldron isn't proficient enough to get in even a single strike.

Our blades meet again.

This time, the fracture runs completely down his sword, nearly splitting it in two.

Without a weapon, he has no chance in the Questral. He seems to know that, because before I can strike again, he steps back. "I'll have your blade," he says. "Another day, I'll have it. I'll carve my name right into its hilt. I'll carve it right into your corpse." *Carved names.* My breath catches. A memory chokes me. By the time I shove it down, all I see is his smile, promising a heinous death, before he runs past us.

Kira is still on the ground. She's staring at me, wide-eyed, her blood staining the dirt. "You—you saved me," she says, a hand gripping the back of her head.

"You saved me first."

"Yes, but . . . I didn't—"

"Get up," I say.

She does.

And we run. We run before we're cut down by the dozens still behind us. We run until the forest ends, and then we have to climb.

Kira is slow, bleeding profusely, but I drag her up with me, my legs burning. Thunderous hooves drown out the clashing of weapons, and we leap out of the way just before horses with House Bolter crests on their armor nearly trample us. They're carrying Cadoc, who is tucked between two warriors, covered by their shields.

Pathetic.

Many more have passed now, not bothering to stop and kill us, caring more about getting a seat on a horse. I wonder if there are any left. I wonder if I should have just left Kira to die.

But I pull us both up the hill until we see them. A line of horses. All of them taken.

No—not all.

Two, side by side, in the back, without riders. We run. Steps rumble behind us.

"Go!" I scream, and Kira is breathing wildly as she throws herself onto the first horse. I fling myself onto mine, a great brown one with a white marking on its forehead. Someone tries to pull me off by my foot, but I kick, and they go down.

And then I'm seated.

We made it.

Kira is still bleeding, but she's beaming.

A few others stumble out of the forest. Even more don't make it out of the trees at all. We hear the cries of the dying, begging for help. Begging for someone to come back. The young boy from the platform . . . I don't see him. I wonder if he's one of those voices. *Bury it down*, I remind myself. *Your empathy is a liability.* I look around at those who have claimed a seat and find Zane. Cadoc, of course. All four Enders. Waldron, the sick bastard. The archer, with dark hair. A few others I recognize. One person is markedly missing.

That's when I spot Harlan Raker, still at the edge of the forest, leaning against one of the only remaining trees.

He's just . . . watching.

Even with that massive sword at his back, it doesn't take long for him to make it up the hill. It's useless, though. There aren't any horses left. Challengers have already turned toward the castle. They've already begun the journey to the king.

Just when I think Raker has been left behind, he reaches back and launches his sword through the air in a glimmering blur. It flies as fast as an arrow, with just as much precision.

And pierces right through Waldron's chest. He slumps forward.

Raker outstretches his hand—

And the sword cuts back through Waldron, before returning to Raker's fist.

My mouth goes dry.

Magic. The sword . . . it has magic. And Raker knows how to use it. My blood is roaring. I've never seen a weapon do that before.

Waldron's lifeless body slides off the horse.

Raker takes his place.

Silence.

Somewhere nearby, I hear Zane say, "Welcome to the Culling."

5

The king has invited his surviving challengers to a feast.

We're forced to leave our weapons at the door with his guards. Killing isn't allowed inside, because, according to the Watchman, "The king thinks there are too many gods-damned wraiths already haunting the castle." He looks around at us. "The dead don't stay quiet here. Kill someone within these walls, and the king will have you hanged on the closest cliffs."

The castle itself has magic. All the Great Houses do.

I can feel it in the air like a whisper upon my skin as I walk over the threshold.

Someone shoves me to the side with their shoulder, and I would have cracked my head against the obsidian floor if it wasn't for Kira keeping me upright.

I look up to see Cadoc wink at me before he strides down the corridor.

Killing might not be allowed, but there are other ways to hurt a person. I'll be sleeping with furniture against the door of my room, if I sleep at all.

When I make it through the grand foyer, my lips part. The outside of this castle is pure fortress—three rings of thick stone walls, high enough to keep all the hungry subjects out.

But the inside is gilded to utter excess.

Silver, everywhere. The king's collection isn't hidden behind a vault, it's proudly displayed, hung upon every wall.

There are monstrous silver wings that once might have belonged to a great beast. Silver feathers that look dipped in starlight. Enchanted chalices, sitting upon stands, next to ancient books with blank pages.

I look around in awe and horror, at all the king has kept for himself, until I reach the base of a grand double staircase.

The Watchman is standing on the bottom step, hawk nowhere to be seen. "Pair up," he orders. "Find a room and make yourselves presentable for dinner."

Then he strides away, likely to go give the king a full report on everything that's happened.

Kira grabs my arm. "Come on," she says, wincing, like her head still hurts. "Let's get a good room."

I don't think there is a bad room in this castle, but I follow her lead up the stairs, marveling at each step. These are nothing like the ones leading up to the ruins. Every stair is whole, and made of thick marble that's shined so perfectly, I can almost see my reflection in them. At the top, we turn left, taking the opposite hallway as Cadoc and his group.

"He isn't so intimidating without his militia," Kira says. His personal guards were turned away at the castle's entrance. "Or his fancy gold sword."

I grunt in agreement, but I don't take my eyes off him until he turns the corner.

The Culling has begun. Everyone will be looking for a way to rise above the others. Treachery will be celebrated. Plans will be forming.

Kira makes a choking sound. I whirl toward her, hand going for a sword that isn't there—

Only to find her standing in awe in front of an opened door. She isn't even being dramatic, I decide, when I slowly step next to her.

And nearly fall to my knees.

A *bed*. A real mattress, with thick blankets and pillows on top. Luxuries that would be ridiculous in Nightfell.

A rush of guilt poisons my excitement. Stellan might not have given me a true bed, or pillows, but he gave me a home when mine burned to the ground. He gave me everything when it would have been so much easier to just let me curl up and die.

Look where that got him.

Kira kicks off her muddy boots and hurries in. "There's a private tub!" she yells. "I'm using it."

I hear a door slam and then the sound of water running just beyond it.

Steps echo. The hall fills with voices as the rest of the challengers find their rooms. I finally walk inside, shut the door, then slide all the way down it, not wanting to sully the bed with my dirty clothing. From the floor, I run my fingers down the pale lilac wallpaper made of—*is that silk?*

Shit. It is.

The *wall* is wearing the most luxurious fabric I've ever felt in my life. And the rest of the room is just as opulent. I look around, taking in the gold trim of the ceiling, the four-poster bed, the massive hearth, the thick, richly woven curtains, and door-sized silver frame, surrounding a simple painting of a knight.

What a waste of good metal.

I'm not in that broken and blood-soaked forest anymore. But my body doesn't seem to know the difference between a castle and a battle. It isn't fooled by this finery.

My heart is still racing, anticipating the next danger. My pulse beats against the stone wall. I breathe in slowly, the way my mother taught me a long time ago, whenever I would get so overwhelmed, the world seemed to narrow into a keyhole. Her warm hand steady against my back, she would count for me. Eight seconds to draw a breath. Eight seconds to hold. Eight seconds to breathe out.

Breathe . . . just . . . breathe.

I do, and eventually, my heartbeat slows. My mind settles. My eyes close, as I drift into a half-sleep, waiting for my turn to clean up.

Kira doesn't surface for twenty minutes, leaving little time for my own bath. But when she emerges beaming, I can't bring myself to be annoyed. The soft, floral scent of soap fills the room. My breath catches.

I haven't smelled flowers in years. Nightfell had only the occasional blossom. Once, a wildflower sprouted just outside the ancient graves, about a mile from our home. I visited it every morning, watching it bloom—then watching it die, far too quickly. *You are a phoenix,* I told it as the petals withered away, repeating Stellan's own words to me. *You grew in poisoned ground. You'll grow again. You will* rise.

It never did.

Kira twirls in a plush towel, another luxury. The patch of missing hair has been covered with a strip of wrappings she must have found inside the bathroom. "I've never seen a tub in a house before. We bathe in ponds, mostly, since the sea's too briny. Or the common tubs." She makes a face. "They make you share sometimes."

I shudder at that image, suddenly grateful for the bath that Stellan installed in a closet for me.

"Go," she snaps. "You'll make us late."

I sigh as I walk inside the bathroom. Then pause.

This isn't just a closet. It's nearly the same size as the room. There's . . . polished stone on the walls, and the floor. The faucets are plated in gold. The mirrors are lined in bronze.

Kira drained the tub, at least, and turned the taps on to replace the water. I let it run, and my eyes widen at the curl of steam. The water is *warm*.

I lock the bathroom door and try the handle twice. Only then do I begin to strip off my clothing, until it's a muddied pile on the marble.

A clean, large mirror shows the skin I've hidden for most of my life.

Thin silver rootlike markings spread down my throat, shoulders, arms, chest, and sides.

Silver is a forbidden color for mortals. It's the color of the gods. My markings make me strange. Dangerous.

Sky-touched, according to my parents.

If the king knew of my marks, I would be imprisoned by his guards. Or added to his collections. Or carved open and studied. I'm not sure which of those fates is worse. Stellan taught me to wield a blade, in fear that one day I would be found out.

And now here I am, right in his castle . . .

I swallow. I've hidden my skin for so long that my nakedness almost feels wrong. My own body feels illicit.

I shoot another glance at the door, making sure the lock is turned, then lean over the counter, studying myself more closely, checking for newer markings and injuries. This mirror is so damned *clean*. I see myself more clearly than I have in years.

I wince as I get a good look at my face. I look exactly like someone who has lived out of a cart for the past day and a half. The cut is a crust of blood. Dirt is smeared across my cheeks, obscuring the dusting of freckles. My eyes are red, but the dark blue still shines brightly. Strands stick up wildly through the braids in my hair. I'll have to wash it more than once to get the grime out.

Still . . . I've gotten to the castle relatively unscathed.

For now.

The tub is full. I dip in each leg, tensing at the scalding heat—then sighing as I sink down. My hands are tired from tightly gripping my sword, the muscle along my forearm screaming as I grip the edges of the bath. My thighs are aching after hours on the back of a horse.

Now, my sore muscles seem to melt. For the first time in a while, my body goes almost boneless. I wish I had more time to enjoy it, but I don't. The feast is waiting.

I begin to scrub myself with one of the bars of soap. One time isn't enough. I scrub again, and then again. I undo my hair, then wash it several times before attempting to comb the strands with my fingers.

A knock sounds against the door, and I jerk in panic, then remember it's locked.

"It's almost time to leave," Kira calls from the other side.

With a whisper of regret, I step out of the tub and into a soft towel. Another knock on the door has me tightening it around myself.

"There are clothes in the wardrobe. Open up."

I tense.

Kira knocks again.

I don't move a single inch.

But I can't just hide in here. I need clothes. I can't be suspicious. I wrap another towel around my shoulders, shrouding myself. I open the door just a sliver.

Kira isn't even looking as she tosses the clothing toward me. I close the door again and stare at two options.

A simple dress with a low neckline. I wish. I throw it to the side without a second glance.

Pants and a long-sleeved shirt. Perfect.

My throat will still be visible, so I tear the sleeves off my old shirt, then put it on beneath the new one, to keep its high collar. I turn and look at myself in the mirror. The color is nearly exact. It's not an ideal solution, but when I have more time, I'll do a better job of fixing the new shirt with the supplies in my bag.

Quickly, I begin to braid my hair in its usual style, adding the pins, then open the door to find Kira, hand lifted as if she was about to knock again. Her hair is tied up now too. She must have realized the liability it posed, after what happened with Waldron.

Her stomach grumbles. Mine echoes the sound.

She sighs. "Finally." She takes my hand and all but drags me from the room. "Let's meet the king."

Long tables fill a room larger than the entire Nightfell square.

Swords are hung along the walls like decoration. *Silver* swords, enough to arm a battalion.

It's a testament to the current peace between sides that they aren't being used right now. It's all thanks to the gates. Thanks to the agreement that the immortals would allow fifty of us to pass through them every fifty years to try to get some magic of our own.

I'm not the only one staring at the swords. The man next to me looks up at them with unadulterated longing. His cheekbones are visible. He doesn't fit his new clothes; the fabric is rolled at his hips.

During the Culling and the Questral, our weapons will be the difference between life and death. Only a handful in this room have swords that compare to the ones shimmering just above, just out of reach, as if they're mocking us.

We remain standing, crowded against the back wall. No one wants to be the first person to sit.

The thin man begins to fidget as attendants bring in silver trays of food. Through gaps in the group, I see piles of potatoes. Meats. Fish, even, which is perplexing, given how far we are from the coast.

On my other side, Kira swallows. "I don't know which one I want more. That sword or that turkey leg."

Her stomach growls.

"Definitely the turkey leg," she says, just as the doors across the room swing open. There's a moment of stillness, of anticipation.

Then in walks the king.

"He's shorter than I thought he would be," Kira whispers, and I dig my elbow into her arm.

She's right, though. He is far shorter than he looks in the propaganda his guards occasionally leave throughout the villages, which I collect and use for kindling.

His skin is smooth, youthful, even, but with a waxy sheen. His smile doesn't reach his eyes. He wears a crown of pure silver, with points sharp enough to draw blood.

He could be considered handsome, I suppose, but not by me. I wonder for a moment how this man has been able to keep us all under his thumb for so long.

The king of Stormside is legendary for his ability to survive countless obstacles. Stellan used to call him a roach. He's said to be more than two hundred years old—impossible for anyone on this side . . . without magic.

He claims his youthfulness and unnatural lifespan is gods-given. He uses it as proof that he should rule.

Seeing him now, it all makes sense.

His people are dying, yet here he is hoarding magic.

My hands curl into fists. The gods might be to blame for keeping magic on one side, but the king has clearly kept much of what comes through for himself.

For the first time, I wonder if more challengers returned than we knew about . . . that never made it past the king.

Is that what happened to Stellan's cup? Did the king . . . take it?

A single drop of magic from Starside can make a field fertile for a century. It can revitalize a village. It can heal the sick.

It can also extend a life.

At once, the challengers in front of me start to bow, and I would rather die, but Kira pulls me down beside her. "What are you doing?" she snaps at me, and I don't know. I shouldn't care about the king. He's just a step toward my fate. I'll never see him again.

Still, kneeling before him feels wrong. Especially now that I wonder if the Questral is truly meant to serve our people . . .

Or *him*.

"Please, rise," he says, his voice easygoing. We do. "Sit."

We do that too, each of us shuffling toward a chair. Kira drags me toward the two right in front of the plate of turkey legs.

Once we're all seated, the king's eyes roam over us, and they are not casual at all. No, now they are calculating.

The king is no fool. I can see it in the way his eyes immediately linger on who I've already marked as my greatest competition.

Cadoc, if only because he seems to have endless resources and his friends under his thumb. He might not have guards anymore, but he has a handful of challengers willing to kill for him. Two of them are archers. I wonder what he's promised them.

The Enders, who look like a mountain range, sit side by side at the same table. They have weapons forged from shreds of Starside steel. I never thought that such a small quantity could be dangerous, but I was wrong. Whoever made that chain was ingenious in how they got so much out of so little. Their swords are all bronze, the lowest of the high metals, but strong, all the same.

Valen. The archer I watched kill dozens in the forest with her bow and iron-tipped arrows. Her tan skin is covered in glimmering chain mail. It's iron too, a lesser metal, but any type of armor is costly. Her dark hair is cut short. She turns sharply to look at me, and I glance away.

Then, of course, there is Harlan Raker, who sits at the end of the last table, as far from the king as physically possible.

The king nods at the head of his guard. Raker gives the slightest tilt of his head in return.

He does not lower his hood or mask, even inside. Even at a feast. Even in front of the *king*. I wonder if he'll be ordered to.

But the king doesn't say a word. Is he afraid? Has he ever seen beneath Raker's famous mask or his battle helmet?

For the first time, I realize Raker must be making the quest on the king's orders. Of course. It's the only way the king would allow someone so valuable to take the risk.

Why? To get the king more magic?

Is the king finally after immortality?

If so . . . chances are good he'll get the opportunity to make the Turn. If any of us is making it back with a full cup of magic, it's Harlan Raker.

The king continues speaking. "You have already survived several obstacles to be here. The platform. The journey. You have been culled from two hundred and twenty-six to just one hundred and fifty." His gaze sweeps over us once again. "Tonight, you will know peace for perhaps the last time. Killing is forbidden. You may wander these halls as you please. You may eat your fill. You may sleep soundly. And sleep you should." His eyes glisten with amusement. "Because tomorrow, the Culling begins in earnest."

Next to me, Kira swallows.

The king looks around at us, brown eyes lingering on each challenger. "You each have a reason for leaving your lives behind and going on this deadly quest." He lifts his chin. "But the Questral is not just about individuals . . . The magic you bring back helps us *all*."

Him especially, it seems.

"Some of you have survived by pure luck. But luck won't get you through Starside. Neither will alliances. Every day on that side will test you, and you alone must be strong enough to fight, if you are to take one of the coveted fifty spots. Bravery is admirable. But skill is better.

"You can only survive a quest across ancient, unforgiving lands by being resourceful and ruthless. The Culling is simple. At sunrise, you will leave this castle and race to the gates. The first fifty through them will embark on the quest."

I blink. That's it?

I just have to beat most of the other challengers there. It seems almost simple.

As if sensing relief from most of us, the king frowns. "The way to the gates is laden with challenges." Of course it is.

He stands dramatically. The food in front of us is going cold. He doesn't seem to care. Kira's stomach growls again.

"Now . . . a choice." He looks at the walls. "These swords were sired by my own legendary blade, Maverick." He pulls the sword from its scabbard, and a gasp spreads through the group. It's thick—made of several sheets of pure silver. Perhaps even several swords blended together. He sheaths it just as quickly. "I will offer you a chance to claim one of my swords . . ."

Kira perks up next to me. Her own sword is of far lesser metal—nickel, the most common across Stormside.

". . . in exchange for an oath. You will swear on your sword that should you survive and return with magic, you will give half to me."

There. The confirmation I was waiting for. He *is* taking some of the magic.

Half wouldn't be so bad, if the king planned to disperse the magic across his lands, but the current state of Stormside is proof he hasn't. No, he's keeping it.

So this is how he has kept himself alive all this time.

The thin man stands. "I'll do it," he says, practically wobbling with exhaustion.

The king looks at him as if he's dirt. Still, he reaches up—and one of the swords flies into his awaiting palm. Just like Raker was able to call his own blade.

Gasps fill the room.

Sword-magic. Can all swords be called, with skill, or only ones made from high metals? Could Stellan do it?

"Come here, boy," the king says, and the man slowly shuffles forward. His hands tremble as he reaches toward the blade. The king shakes his head. "This blade would never have accepted you, to be sure, but I am bestowing it upon you. Do not disappoint me."

The man is practically in tears as he says, "I won't. Thank you, King." He bows before him and then happily returns to his seat.

"Anyone else?"

Almost *everybody* else. It isn't a surprise that nearly the entire group takes the king up on his offer. Over and over, I watch him call the metal down. Kira tries to tug me forward, but I stay seated, even though my own blade is several steps down from silver.

I don't trust the king. If these swords were made from shreds of his own . . . could he control them? No, I have no business making any oaths. Not when I don't plan on returning anyway.

And I certainly have no business making any oaths on my sword to a king I would rather see dead at the end of it.

The only others who also remain seated are Zane, and the handful of additional challengers who have high-quality metal.

And Raker, who has a better sword than even the king.

When the last sword has been called down, the king walks over to the head of one of the tables. *My* table.

His eyes sweep across the challengers before landing on me. They narrow. His mouth is turned up in an amused smile, but his tone is cold as steel as he says, "You, girl. What kind of blade do you have that is better than my own?"

A hush settles around me. Kira tenses. For as grimy as the king is, he is the most powerful person on this side. He could order me dead, or kill me where I sit, and no one would think twice about it.

"It's titanium, sir," I say, keeping my voice measured. Docile, even.

He scoffs. "That would surely shatter against one of my blades. Why not take me up on my offer?"

I will my smile to be pleasant. "For my blade to shatter, someone has to block it."

Silence.

His eyes narrow. "Silver is silver."

"Metal is metal when it goes through skin and bone," I say, smile tight.

Another second of silence. Two. Fuck. I should have just taken one of his damned blades. My heartbeat rattles my chest.

The king tilts his head.

I swallow, sure he's going to call one of the remaining swords down from the wall and stab me through the throat for daring to speak back to him.

But he only turns toward another table, and I finally exhale, leaning forward. Kira sighs sharply next to me, as if she was also holding her breath.

The king finally remembers to tell us to eat, and plates screech against the tabletop as they're dragged toward each challenger. The room goes quiet save for the king's voice as he sits next to challengers he has clearly deemed to be his early favorites. Soon, guards come in to take each claimed sword and put them with the others.

I reach for everything I can, eyes on my own plate, grateful for having been forgotten.

"Can you die from eating too much?" Kira is currently lying in the center of the bed, her limbs stretched out wide. "I feel like I'm about to burst." She strains her neck to look at me with what looks like, from where I sit against the door, great effort. "I wouldn't know. There's never been enough food in Brambleside to be full."

I nod. I know what that's like.

Kira frowns. "Aren't you going to get in bed? I can move."

She doesn't make a single attempt to shift to one side.

I shake my head. "No. I'm going to stay here, in case someone tries to get in."

Kira blinks at me. "You can't sleep on the floor."

"I do it all the time."

Not on purpose. I often wake up on the ground after having fallen off the piles of blankets that make up my bed, after nightmares so vivid, they have me clawing at my skin and screaming.

They're always the same.

Lately, I've been finding mushrooms for the village apothecary in exchange for a tea that makes my nights dreamless.

I don't have the tea now. I forgot to bring the few leaves I had left.

I left it behind in that house, along with everything else of value to me.

It's fine. I won't reach deep sleep tonight anyway, knowing the Culling starts tomorrow and that Cadoc could kick down our door at any moment. I tell Kira as much.

"Right. I probably won't sleep that much either, with the nerves and all."

She's snoring approximately five minutes later.

I almost smile. I envy her deep sleep.

I really should try the same. But I think about what the king said. We're allowed to explore. Is there something here that can help me? Am I putting myself at a disadvantage by staying put?

I weigh both sides. I sit in the dark, Kira's snoring counting down the minutes. I shut my eyes, willing rest to wash over me.

It doesn't. I'm too riled up.

So, I slip out of the room. I'll stay close. At the first sign of danger, I'll come back.

The halls are dark and quiet. I turn several corners without hearing anyone at all. One floor down, there's a rush of commotion. *Challengers.* I take the opposite direction.

Every door I try is locked. I trail my fingers down the silver hung on the walls, but they're mostly ceremonial objects. Goblets, tapestries, star-stitched capes. Either too heavy or unnecessary to be of any use during the quest.

I'm just about to turn back to my room when I hear whispers—

From voices I recognize. The *king's*.

Then another, deep and slightly rasped, torn from one of my worst memories.

Harlan Raker.

Even his name in my thoughts sends a chill through my blood. I should run. But instead, I inch closer, careful that my boots don't make a sound.

"And you have everything you need?" The king.

"Yes."

"You know your orders?"

"I won't return without it," Raker says, deep and low. I frown. Without what? The cup of magic?

"Good," the king says. "It will be the start of a new age. I feel it coming . . ."

I lean closer, to hear more, but then the steps retreat. They're leaving. I lean around the corner, to see if I can follow, but they're gone.

I should get back to my room. It's getting late.

I take the same halls back, studying each object again, in case I missed something. But it's all the same finery that I could sell in the markets for buckets of metal—and won't do me any good on the quest. So much for getting anything useful. My steps hurry, panic sinking through my chest. What if Cadoc and his friends are wandering these halls? I turn around the corner—

And smack right into a wall of armor.

Slowly, I look up—*and up*—only to see a hood. I swallow.

Fuck.

6

He's enormous. Even bigger up close. Even unarmed, his presence nearly makes my knees buckle. With sword in hand . . . no wonder rebel armies surrender as soon as they see him coming. No wonder some have chosen to fall onto their own swords rather than face him. No wonder people whisper about him like he's a demon.

His head tilts, and I catch a sliver of that silver mask. "Interesting," he says, his voice rumbling along my bones. "You aren't pissing yourself yet."

It takes everything in me not to run. He would catch me in a second. But a worse fate would be a death at his hands before I even started this quest. So I summon every shred of courage I have, reinforce it with my hatred, and lift my chin. "Is that how people normally greet you?"

He seems shocked that I'm speaking to him, or that my voice isn't shaking. *I'm* fucking shocked my voice isn't shaking. I don't wait for a response.

"Sorry to disappoint," I say.

At that, I hear him growl beneath his mask. When it's clear just his presence won't make me stand down, he takes a step toward me. "*Everything* about you is a disappointment," he says, with so much venom, I bristle.

"You don't even know me," I say.

"I know a street rat when I see one. I know a thief."

Rage flames through me, blazing past my better judgment. I lean forward. "And I know a king's *lapdog* when I see one."

The moment the words leave my lips, I know I've made a big fucking mistake. He doesn't need a sword to kill me. He could crush my throat in one of his hands. He could snap my neck with half a thought. I swallow, waiting for him to end this conversation by ending *me*.

But instead, he ducks low, in an attempt to meet me anywhere close to my height, and says, "You're lucky the king doesn't permit killing in his castle . . . but the next time I see you, I won't hesitate."

Shit. I don't know whether to feel relief that I actually get to survive this encounter, or dread that I've made the worst enemy imaginable.

Still, I manage to keep my head high. "Neither will I."

He huffs in cruel mirth as he walks past me. When he's out of the corridor, I finally slump against the wall, heart pounding against the stone.

Fuck. Fuck, fuck, fuck.

I never should have left my room. I race back, then shut the door, slide down it, and keep it closed with my spine.

Kira is still sleeping. Her breaths are long and heavy.

Sure that she can't see me, I begin to trace the markings at my neck, the way I do when I'm anxious.

That voice. *His* voice. Hearing it again . . . suddenly, I'm thrust back two years ago to a rare day of rain.

Gray eyes, buried in a battle helmet, staring me down. His glimmering blade against my throat, and—

No. I won't think of him, and what happened afterward.

I close my eyes tightly, pushing him from my thoughts, focusing only on following the path of silver up and down my throat. It lulls me into a calmness that leads to a few hours of sleep.

Until a flash of silver has me sitting up, gasping.

The room is still dark. Kira is still snoring. Another memory, from far before I ever encountered Harlan Raker. The day on the hill. The day my sister and I disobeyed my parents and went far past the village.

The day I got my markings.

I jolt when a knock rattles the door behind me, my veins aflame with panic. But it's only the Watchman. "Outside in ten," he yells, before moving on.

How is it already time? My eyes still burn with exhaustion.

My legs are sore from being folded beneath me. I wince as I struggle to get up, then slowly make my way to Kira.

I poke her shoulder. She just snores louder.

I tap at her arm, and she just turns to the side.

My sister was like this. A heavy sleeper. It would take ten minutes sometimes just to wake her up.

We don't have that time.

"Kira," I say loudly, and she startles awake. Her eyes widen with fear before seeing me. That fear dims.

It shouldn't.

Today, we're enemies. I won't save her the way I did before. Not if she stands between me and being one of the first fifty through those gates.

"Is it time?" she asks, voice heavy with sleep.

"It is."

She nods and gets up, swinging her legs over the side of the bed. She looks at me, using seconds we don't have to spare, her green eyes filled with regret. "I really hope I don't have to kill you," she finally says.

And by the sudden hardness of her tone . . . I know.

I know she would kill anyone and anything to save her sister . . . the same way I would have. The same way I *will* in vengeance for her death.

"Me too," I reply, meaning it as well.

Then we pack up our things and leave the room.

THE KING'S GUARDS return our weapons one by one.

When they reach Raker, they each bow their heads, then motion toward the front of the castle. I hear whispers, and—

No one was able to move it. I can almost imagine his great sword still dug into the dirt, untouched.

Raker opens his hand, and there's a sky-splitting crackling as the sword arcs over the castle in a flash of silver—before landing in his grip.

It leaves the rest of the challengers speechless.

Until, of course, Kira leans down to whisper, "I heard he's terribly scarred under that mask. That's why he doesn't show his face."

I've heard the exact opposite.

I've also heard that he's a creature. A venomous beast. Rumors abound when it comes to Harlan Raker.

She quirks her lips. "Is it bad that I don't really care?"

Zane huffs on my other side. "The only thing that's ever gotten close to Harlan Raker is his sword. I wouldn't put it past him to kill a woman for even *suggesting* she wanted to be with him."

I don't know why anyone would suggest that.

"He's a monster," I say, voice cold with long-held rage. At that, Raker's grip tightens on his sword, as if he's heard me.

I would think it a good thing if I didn't need to survive this journey.

The next time I see you, I won't hesitate . . .

A guard stops in front of me and hands me my titanium blade. Kira is given her new silver one. Zane is reunited with his ax. He frowns as he looks at it from all angles, as if surveying it for damage.

I stare out at the gardens in front of us, at all the land separating me from the gates.

Green. So much green, in a brighter shade than I've ever seen it. Trickling water sputters from a fountain surrounded by statues depicting all the gods. The water is just . . . for decoration. The king is using it for *beauty* when I've watched countless neighbors die from dehydration.

I swallow my anger. All that matters now is making it to Starside. I need to focus on strategy.

Besides the few shrubs and sculptures, there's hardly anything to use as cover. It's just flat grass until a sharp slope that hides everything beyond it. If the archers start trying to take us down like they did in the forest, I'll have little defense against their arrows. I just have to run as fast as I can, and hope by the time they set their marks, I'm down that hill.

I slip my sword into my back scabbard.

This is a race. The first fifty to the gates get to go on the Questral. Holding my blade will just slow me down.

Once everyone has their weapons back, the Watchman appears.

He motions above us, and I look up to see the king on one of the highest balconies. From his viewpoint, he can likely see all the way to the gates. He's going to watch us kill each other. He's going to see which of us make it.

"With your blessing, King," the Watchman says, bowing.

"Given," the king replies, waving his hand.

The Watchman looks down the entire line of us. Nods. Then—

"May the best fifty win."

7

Magnus Ender turns and slices the challenger next to him clean in half.

A man with a graying beard, without armor. He had no chance. His torso hits the grass.

I run.

The wealthiest have armor. I don't. I'm *faster*. I use that advantage by running until Kira isn't by my side anymore.

I hope I don't have to kill you.

An arrow slices through the air just inches from my ear. I watch it get buried in the grass in front of me. *Fuck*. That was fast.

There's nowhere to hide.

A bow twangs as it's released, and I duck low, barely escaping an arrow that would have been buried in my skull.

The ground starts to slope—but the arrows don't stop. The archer must have crested too. Down below, there are walls, though. Some sort of towering structure. Somewhere to use for cover. Just a little farther—

An arrow hits my spine, knocking the breath out of me. I fall from the force, tumbling down the hill, the cut on my cheek ripping open against an errant root, hot blood streaming, before I finally go still, face down.

I gasp for air, dirt filling my lungs. I wait for the wave of pain. Wait to feel the crushing sadness that I'm going to die in the king's fucking *garden*. That, after everything, after *Stellan dying*, I didn't even make it to the gates.

But there's nothing. It doesn't make any sense.

I felt it.

I reach back, expecting blood, only to find the arrow buried in the blade on my spine. I remember Valen's arrows now. Iron-tipped. A lesser metal.

My titanium sword stopped it.

I close my eyes, grateful for Stellan and the swords he gave me, made from scraps of metal collected over time, far nicer than I would ever be able to afford.

He saved me.

Relief and desperation have me up and running faster than I ever have in my life. I reach around and wrench the arrow from my blade, then break it in half before discarding it, so it can't be used against me a second time. Kira is ahead of me now, her red hair already slipping out of its braids. I wonder if she saw me go down.

And if Valen is readying her bow again.

The structure isn't far. I can reach it. My lungs burn. My legs are already sore. Still, I keep pushing. As I get closer, I realize that it isn't a structure at all. It's nature. Part of the garden.

Ten arched entrances stand tall, framed in twisting vines. Ten paths. I race into the last one, grateful to see it empty. No one follows. They've all picked different roads.

I collapse over my knees, my breaths wild, my heart beating too quickly.

I'm alive. For now.

My gaze slides up. Walls five times my height box me in. I take a step toward one. A hedge? No. It isn't made of shrubs or trees.

I brush my finger against the wall with the slightest touch—then tense. A thin line of blood spills down my hand.

Thorns. The walls are completely made of thorns.

They might as well be walls of daggers for how sharp they are. Distant yells echo around me. *Can't stop now.* I start to run, careful not to brush against the barbs.

When I reach the end of the path, I expect something new. Gates, if I'm lucky.

Instead, it's another trail, with more openings. A dozen of them. I swallow, realizing that this isn't just a pathway.

This is a labyrinth.

A maze of thorns.

Panic spikes through me. I don't just have to find my way out—I have to do it quickly, before the rest.

I think of the king sitting up on his balcony, with a clear view of the maze, and us, and the exit.

The bastard.

Screaming pierces the air, and I run in the opposite direction, picking a corridor. I bolt, arms tucked in.

This one is shorter. I turn a corner only to see another challenger, a blond woman with long cuts down her side, as if she's been scraped against the maze walls. We both look at each other and run in opposite directions.

Another scream—then silence.

I'm in the middle of a path so long, I can't even see the other end. The maze doesn't have a pattern. Or if it does, I haven't figured it out yet.

Hissing pulls me out of my thoughts. I unsheathe my blade and turn.

A snake weaves through the wall of thorns, protected by silver skin like armor.

Silver. Did it get trapped on this side of the gates? Did the king steal it from its home, to add to his vast collection?

The serpent stops. Its head turns, and we look at each other for a moment. I don't make a single movement, but it lingers, as if it could possibly sense the silver beneath my clothes.

Then the world turns as I'm shoved to the side. My head hits the compact ground. My ears ring. A challenger runs by, not bothering to kill me on his way. His calf is shredded, a chunk of skin hanging off his leg, revealing muscle and bone.

What? From the ground, I turn to look behind me.

And I see the end of the path . . . is gone. The thorns along the walls . . . they're lengthening, quickly, becoming meter-long barbs, both sides meeting in sharp clashes. It's happening in a ripple. The thorns around me begin to tremble, like a mouth readying to close.

Run.

I do, and the faster I move, the faster the hedges close in behind me, as if they're carnivorous, like the thorns are teeth and the maze is starving.

A light. There's a light at the very end.

I just need to make it.

As if sensing my hope, my own desperation to make it through, the walls shake, thorns shooting out until they're daggers, then long as swords, all rushing toward me. I can hear the rustling on both sides, the hissing of snakes within, the screams of those being eaten by the labyrinth.

I've survived so much already. This maze will not kill me. A grunt scrapes against the back of my throat as I push my legs harder, painfully, as I ignore the thorns just inches away.

But they're so close. I turn sideways, buying myself seconds, their sharp points scraping against the scabbard on my back with a high-pitch screech, and then I launch myself through the closing gap, hoping I don't hit another wall.

My body lands hard on the compact ground, the air stolen from my lungs. I gasp, turning around—only to find a wall of thorns.

The path I was on is gone.

I turn again and see more entrances. More pathways.

And something else. A towering figure, stalking toward a short woman with dark hair, tied back. Her name is Helra.

She's my age, barely twenty. Instead of a sword, she has throwing knives, a pack of gold ones she's trained with for years. I overheard her telling another challenger about them during dinner. They were her grandmother's. She survived the last Questral. Helra's completely oblivious to the giant right behind her. My lips part, but it's too late to warn her.

I watch in horror as Pagnus picks her up—and throws her against one of the walls, the thorns already lengthened into barbs.

Her body gets stuck in them. She dies instantly. My hand muffles a scream.

Pagnus picks her pockets. I watch him slide those gold throwing knives out of her pants and into his own before moving on. Anger churns as I remember Stellan's missing dagger. Was Pagnus the one who stole it?

Someone here did. Someone here killed Stellan.

All of a sudden, Pagnus turns in my direction, and I throw myself through another entrance, hoping he didn't see me.

I wait one second. Two. I'm not breathing.

Heavy steps sound just feet away.

I swallow. Reach back for my sword.

Just when my fingers curl around the hilt, a yell echoes from the other direction. *Cadoc*. I don't move a muscle. Neither does Pagnus.

See you in the Culling. That was his promise. He's walked with noticeable strain since I stabbed my dagger through his shin.

He takes another step forward. I inch my sword out of its scabbard.

Then Pagnus turns around. I hear him getting further away, until his footsteps all but disappear. I don't release my breath until a few moments after that.

I look around the corner. He's gone. The corridor is empty.

Cadoc's and Pagnus's houses are now working together. *Great*.

Still . . . if they haven't found their way out of the maze yet, maybe most of the challengers haven't either.

Or maybe they have. Maybe some have already reached the gates. Maybe I've already lost—

Think, Aris.

I try. I walk along the path, considering each entrance, head pounding. So many roads. I barely survived the last one I picked.

The king said the Culling was a test of resourcefulness and ruthlessness. I look around, but I don't see a solution. All the paths look exactly the same.

I turn in circles, until panic finally roots me in place.

Move.

But I don't know where to go.

Indecision will get you killed. I can almost hear Stellan's voice in my head. At night, we would walk down to the ancient graveyard and duel beneath the stars. *Instinct is your heart telling you the truth. Listen.*

He said it whenever I hesitated. Whenever my mind got in the way.

There isn't time. Heavy armored steps are approaching. I hear labored breaths just walls away. Far in front, there's a loud cheer. Someone must have made it out.

If your eyes fail you, then close them and listen, Stellan once told me.

I do now.

I listen, beyond the screaming. Beyond the footsteps. Beyond the rustling of the ever-changing maze.

I listen, until I hear it. Metal against metal.

A familiar sound in a forge. That's how I know, without a single doubt, that a large weapon just hit something.

And that thing shattered.

It happened immediately. No multiple strikes needed. A far superior sword just bested lesser metal.

I keep listening.

More metal splits apart.

Again.

Again.

Only one blade could break four swords so quickly.

Harlan Raker is near.

Instead of terror, hope rises to the surface. If anyone is making it out of this maze, it's him.

I take off before I can think better of it. I race right toward the sound, *listening*. And soon enough, I see his hood going around a bend.

I follow, careful to stay far enough away, running then stopping, making sure I catch him before each corner he turns.

A fool jumps from behind one, in a desperate attempt at his weapon. Raker doesn't even look the man's way as he cuts him down. More shattering.

An arrow flies right at his face. His blade stops it. A few steps later, the archer is gutted on the ground. I step over his entrails and keep going.

Raker doesn't even walk around with his blade in his hand. No, it stays in the scabbard behind him until he needs it, and then it goes right back in.

His movements are fast. Precise. No one stands a chance. He's carving a path for me, even if he doesn't know it.

I scurry after him, careful not to touch the walls, the thorns lengthening as I approach. One of the passageways is so long, I lose sight of him. *Fuck.* I sprint down it, then turn, hoping I haven't missed his next move—

Only to run right into a wall of metal.

I fall on my ass, head spinning.

He knew I was following him. Of course. There he was, waiting.

I look up. Only darkness, with a glimmer of silver beneath, meets my gaze. He's about to reach for his sword. He's about to bury it through my chest.

The next time I see you, I won't hesitate . . .

Instead of begging for my life, I glare at him with every ounce of buried fury. I can't see his eyes, but I hope he can see the pure hatred in mine.

I assume that will make it even more satisfying for him to cut me down.

But all he does is step over me, like I'm no more than garbage. Not worth killing. Not competition.

The bastard.

I should feel lucky he let me live, but I just hate him more.

Still—just because he thinks I'm useless doesn't mean he isn't of use to me.

He knows I'm following him. No use in hiding it now, especially when he clearly doesn't think I'm worthy of his blade. Now I follow close behind. I take each turn. I run past thorns that grow in waves, narrowly escaping their edges.

Until the maze ends.

Sunlight beats down from directly overhead, unblocked by the enormous walls—I was in there for *hours*. I squint against the sharp rays, taking in a stretch of grass leading into a forest.

A living one, with hundreds of leaves per tree. With . . . color.

I look around quickly, searching for Zane and Kira.

Only to lock eyes with Pagnus Ender.

Fuck.

His crooked mouth turns up in a smile just before he charges forward.

I run. I'm *fucking tired of running*, but I bolt. Already out of breath, already sore, I run for my life into the forest. It's not just any forest, I realize, when I almost trip over a stone.

It's a graveyard.

There are more challengers far ahead. But instead of racing toward the finish, they're just . . . standing there, heads lifted skyward. Kira is among them. I feel a rush of relief seeing her whole. *She made it.*

Why isn't she running?

Only when I'm closer do I see what they're staring at. Hundreds of swords are tangled in the trees.

Stellan said great swords are buried with their wielders. I imagine some of the blades were ready to bond again. They cut up through the ground . . . and got trapped in the branches.

I look over my shoulder, hoping Pagnus has been distracted, only to see him barge right through a branch, wood chips flying.

Shit. I turn around again, just as Valen confidently reaches up toward the weapons, arm flexed taut. A blade soars down right into her hand.

It's been claimed. They've been matched.

Magnificent. The silver sword she's claimed, with an emerald in its hilt, is nothing short of brilliant. Every challenger is now reaching toward the swords, furiously trying to claim one. One of the blades, etched in intricate designs, wriggles back and forth before wrenching itself free. It soars down into an awaiting hand.

Kira's. She grips it and beams. It's old metal . . . rusted and chipped, but it's silver. Better silver than the king's, even. It has a glimmering purple stone in its hilt and flower designs up its blade.

She turns when she sees Pagnus crashing through the trees. We lock eyes, and hers widen.

I nod at her. *Good luck,* I hope it conveys as I keep running.

More branches snap like twigs. They do nothing to slow Pagnus. I hope a sword will fall and go through his skull, but I'm not so lucky.

Especially not when I see who's waiting up ahead.

Cadoc and his friends. They're standing below another cluster of swords, throwing rocks at them. Reaching for them clearly didn't work.

He sees me, and Pagnus not far behind, and raises a hand.

Pagnus stops, like a trained dog.

I don't. I keep going, until something hits my temple. The world spins before I hit the ground.

A rock. One of his friends just hit me with a fucking *rock.*

Cadoc slowly walks toward me. I wonder why Pagnus is listening to him at all when he could tear Cadoc in half with his bare hands.

"Look at you," Cadoc says, smug as hell. "So close to the gates. You could join us, you know." He smirks. "I have needs that require attending to."

I get his meaning immediately and unsheathe my sword, standing.

That only seems to amuse him. "Is that a no?"

I spit at his feet. "It's a never."

His amusement falls away completely. "Very well." He waves a hand, and I watch as one of his friends, a thin man in his early twenties with pale skin, pulls an arrow out of his quiver.

I can't duel against an arrow.

I take off. There's a whistling as the arrow flies right over my head. I can feel its wind rustling my hair. *Close. Too close.*

I duck behind a tree and hear the bark break as another arrow pierces nearly all the way through.

There are just seconds between reloading, and I use them to run to the next tree. This time, the arrow nearly catches my arm. The next trunk is too far. I throw myself behind a massive tombstone instead, pressing my spine against the coarse rock. Its writing has been eroded by time.

Panting, one hand clutching dirt and the other my blade, I wonder if I can just stay here. If I can use this tombstone as a shield. If they'll forget about me . . .

I don't matter. I'm not important. Is Cadoc's ego truly that big, that he has to kill me for turning him down?

Apparently, yes.

"Hiding, are you?"

He's not far. I hear a tombstone shattering, like he's just swung at it with his new silver sword.

Then another. And another. He's getting closer.

Pieces of rock fly around me, coating me in dust.

He's right behind me.

I take off again, darting toward the next stretch of trees. A twig snaps just behind me, and I whirl around.

Only to find myself face-to-face with Cadoc.

I gasp as his sword settles against my throat. In a flash, he turns me against him. His arms band around my body.

I want to retch. I want to run.

I go very still. I'm not breathing.

"Now. Was it worth—"

I throw my head back as hard as possible and hear a crunch. Before his blade can slit my throat, I slip away, grateful for his clear lack of practice. Reflexes aren't learned easily. They're developed with training. Not by hiding behind guards.

If I thought a broken nose would delay him, I was wrong. I turn my head, and he's right behind me. Chasing. Teeth bared.

The look costs me.

I stumble over a rock, my knees hit the ground, and by the time I stand, I'm surrounded. Every direction I try is blocked by one of his relatives or one of the towering Enders. There's no way out.

And he's already raising his weapon.

I swallow. There's nothing to do but lift my own lesser metal. My hands shake around the hilt. Stellan made this. I should be proud of it. Stellan made *me* the warrior I am, who won duels against men double my size in the desert tournaments, winning a prize that fed us for a month.

I might be better than Cadoc at wielding a sword. But it doesn't matter. The king was right. *Silver is silver.*

"You should have taken the king up on his offer," Cadoc says through his teeth, coated in blood pouring from his nose. He wastes no time now. His sword arcs through the air. I lift my own to block it. His silver hits my titanium—

And it shatters.

The last piece of Stellan I have. Gone.

I'm knocked onto my back with the force, head just missing an ancient gravestone that has crumbled into ruins.

He takes a step toward me. A smile crawls across his face as he spits out blood. Sword lifted high, he pauses. He reaches his other hand into his pocket.

And pulls out a dagger. *Stellan's* dagger.

No.

His smile widens. "Thank you for showing this to me," he says, taking another step, twirling the Starside steel in his hand. His smooth, noble fingers touch the etchings I painstakingly made over years. The flames. *The flames that cost me everything.* The carvings I touched every morning when I woke up before Stellan to train, to remind myself of my fury. The reason I'm so eager to run full speed toward an almost-guaranteed death. I guess I've found it now. "I'm going to use it to carve my name into your corpse."

Carved names.

My fists curl with anger. He gets even closer.

No one is going to help me. I'm surrounded. I don't have a weapon. The hilt of my broken blade falls to the ground, useless.

But behind Cadoc's head, something glimmers. One of the ancient swords stuck in the trees. Of course.

I reach up desperately to see if any of those blades might claim me. I reach out with every shred of fury, and pain, and desperation.

Nothing happens.

Cadoc laughs, the sound pealing through the forest. "Did you really think that would work?" His friends laugh with him. "Did you really think you were worthy of any of those swords, when we weren't?"

Another step. He's so close. I extend my arm, over and over, the same way the other challengers did.

Please, I beg the world. *I know this will kill me, but not today. Not like this.* Nothing.

I think of my sister, her eyes widening as she realized no one was coming to save us. Nothing was going to stop the flames.

As she realized she was dying.

Anything. I would give anything to see her again. But, since that isn't possible, I will do anything to make sure the god who killed her will feel the same pain she did.

"*Come on*," I scream to the heavens, my voice trembling not with fear—but with fury. Cadoc is right above me now. He slides the dagger Stellan once promised me back into his pocket. The one he *died* for. Cadoc *killed* him. My anger is an inferno, heating me from the inside out.

But it's all for nothing. It's over.

Cadoc reaches his sword above his head. He roars as he leaps forward, his blade aimed right at my neck.

And I surprise myself by not looking away. Not flinching. If this is my death, I will look it right in the face.

No. I don't want to die. Not yet.

The piece of me that accepted my end now burns to ashes. Fuck that. Fuck *this*. I didn't come this far to be stopped by a man who has never wanted for anything, who killed Stellan, who will continue to bring back magic to enrich his greedy house.

From the cinders of that fear and doubt and acceptance, an ember of fight ignites. Not just rage—but resistance. A will to live strong enough to smother death.

I reach up, palm open, in one last attempt to claim a sword, as silver fills my vision. It's the last thing I do.

A blade does not fall from the trees. No.

It cuts up through the ground, from the grave below, right into my palm, just in time to block Cadoc's weapon.

And I watch his silver sword shatter into a thousand jagged pieces, in a storm of starlight.

8

Cadoc stumbles back, hilt still in his hand. His eyes narrow at the sword in my grip. I lose the opportunity to strike him down because of my own shock.

Sparkling, Starside steel. An entire sword of it.

It has an energy, a force I can taste. A current runs through the hilt, searing into my blood.

Then the blade shines glorious silver, bright as a star, blinding the world. Wind tears through the woods, roaring, energy rippling. In a flash, the light retreats into the weapon, leaving only me glancing down at my reflection in the glimmering metal.

The forest has gone still. The challengers have stopped.

Everyone is looking at me lying on the ground, holding a sword that rivals Raker's. He's there, on the other side of the woods, and has paused midstep. As if, for once, the famed warrior is stunned.

That's when I realize this blade might have just saved my life—

But it also just made me a target.

I scramble to my feet. Challengers break free from their shock and close in, just like the thorns of the maze. Closer. A dozen blades are pointed at me now.

I try to lift my sword like I have a million times with Stellan, but this weapon weighs as much as it's worth. I have to use both hands to even continue to hold it—it's fucking *heavy*. The sparkling blade glistens, as if excited for the fight. I swallow, decidedly less thrilled. Losing this sword just moments after claiming it would really fucking suck.

Then don't, I think. I groan as I try to lift it over my head. Weaponless, Cadoc turns on his heel and runs. One of his friends lunges, ready to strike—

A rustling.

Faint at first. Nearly masked by the wind.

Then it's a roaring. Yelling. *Running.*

Challengers, *screaming*. My body stills, trying to hear the words they're belting out, but I can't. I can see them, though, in the distance. There's a wall of them, running for their lives—

Only to be overcome and crushed by nothing short of a stampede. Creatures with horns like javelins are running toward us, heads dipped low, cutting down everything in their path.

"*Oryx*," I hear someone say.

"Run."

The crowd around me scatters. I take off after them, then stop myself. I remember the first trial of the Culling, in the forest. How some challengers ran and were killed by the archers who scaled the trees.

I won't be fast enough. I'll be crushed.

Just sheathing my new blade nearly makes me fall over, but in a rush of panic, I do, then race to the closest trunk and begin to scale it. Some around me have the same idea. Others flee.

The lower branches aren't stable. My sword adds too much weight. Wood snaps below my foot, and my back hits the ground, stealing my breath. I gasp for air, fighting to move, but I can't. *They're coming.* The ground rattles beneath my spine.

Fucking move!

I throw my body around another tree and force my way up, nails shredding, the bark scraping my hands raw. I turn. The first of the oryx are almost here. I'm still too low.

With a groan that scrapes the back of my throat, I reach for a higher branch and hope it doesn't snap this time. My fingers lock around it, and then I'm hanging.

A thud sounds a few yards away. A challenger has fallen from her tree. She's scrambling to get up.

Too late. The oryx are here. She's crushed beneath their hooves.

I'm still too low. I fight to pull myself up, but my new blade is pulling me down. My arms tremble as I lift, inch by inch, and reach for the next branch.

If it snaps, I'm done. It's a risk. As it stands, though, the creatures will tear my legs to ribbons.

I wrap my hand around the wood and pull—

My entire body lifts, just out of the way of the first pair of horns. I swing wildly, bending my knees, feet barely clearing the oryx's head.

I reach to the side, shifting my grip, muscles clenching and burning, until my legs can wrap around the trunk.

Then they're all right below me, and I hold on for dear life.

The stampede tears through the forest, and my very bones rattle. My teeth chatter. The tree sways from side to side, but I hold on, my fingernails slicing through the wood. Branches snap around me. Another challenger falls and is skewered on a pair of horns. Her body rides the charge like a wave, her eyes wide, blood spurting everywhere.

The swords trapped in the trees clash together. I look up—and barely swing out of the way of a fallen blade, cutting branches on its way down. My grip loosens.

One of my hands slips.

My stomach drops as I hang, feet kicking, just above the sea of horns. There's no gap in the stampede. If I fall, I'm dead. My palms go slick.

No. I will not let fear be my death. My eyes close. I think of climbing trees with my sister, in that rare stretch of forest. I think of running and playing games until we had to lie down because our hearts were beating too fast. I think of smiling up at the sun and being excited to do it all again tomorrow.

This will not kill me. I will survive this. I will hold on.

With all the strength I can summon, I pull myself back up, arms shaking, until I reach a steadier branch. I wrap my limbs around the trunk again and will the tree to hold. It shakes so wildly I nearly retch from the movement. My hands begin to bleed, and my fingers almost slip, but I hold on. With every tremor, I hold on. As trees fall around me, I hold on.

Until the forest stills. It's several moments before I open my eyes and slowly look down.

All that's left are bodies, mangled beyond recognition, and a few gleaming swords that were shaken from the branches. Some remain on the ground; others fly up and are trapped yet again. None rivals my new weapon. The remaining tombstones are now just piles of ruin.

One by one, challengers start jumping down. How many were ahead? How many have already gone through? I swing to a lower branch.

An arrow slices away a curl of bark an inch in front of my face.

Valen. I see her in another tree. The Culling is far from over.

I scramble down and run, jumping over what's left of the bodies. Another arrow whistles nearby, but I use the trees as cover. I run as fast as I can with this blade on my back. All that's on my mind are those gates.

The forest ends—

And there they are.

The gates that divide our lands are tall enough to scrape the clouds. They're crafted from pure, sparkling Starside steel, hewn into curling currents of wind and waves and flames, as if casted by the elements themselves. A wall of ancient, unyielding energy pulses from its glimmering metal. The sword on my back jerks against my spine, as if it can feel it too.

Only a deep trench and the long stone bridge across it sits between our side and theirs.

I'm so close.

The bridge isn't narrow, but it doesn't have sides. The drop must be hundreds of feet, maybe more. Mist clouds everything below. Challengers have already started down it—more than fifty. But the gates are still closed. There's still time.

I run. Muscles already aching, breath raw in my lungs, I take off toward the silver gates, panting. This is the last step of the Culling. I'm too close not to make it.

My new sword is heavy on my back, slowing me down but invigorating me all the same. This ancient weapon saw something in me worth claiming. Just as Stellan saw in me something worth saving.

I will make it through. I will be one of the Fifty.

Suddenly, the bridge lurches, and I go flying. I land roughly, rolling, body scraping against the rock, until I flatten myself, holding on however I can. I fight to remain in the center as the edges of the bridge crumble away. One of the challengers ahead falls right over the side. His scream is swallowed up by the drop.

The gates have started to open.

They are magnificent, shining, rattling the very foundation of this world as they reveal a slice of *green* on the other side. A shade of the color I've never seen before. One I didn't even know could exist.

I'm flung again as the gates settle. They're open.

They're open.

We all get to our feet and run.

There are more than fifty challengers in front of me. An arrow flies past my ear and takes one down. Then another.

Still, too many remain.

The first challenger is almost through. He punches his blade right up toward the sky, as if he's trying to stab it, unleashing a victorious bellow. And then—

No one ever mentioned this. Even the most far-fetched legends about the gates and the Questral never mentioned dozens of hill-sized *creatures* barreling through the gap.

Right toward us.

Fuck.

The first challenger turns around, and I'm close enough to see the whites of his eyes before one of the beasts swallows him whole.

FUCK!

We all turn and run in the opposite direction.

I make it all of three steps before I hit the ground. Someone's hand is wrapped around my ankle—a man holding on for dear life as he's dragged back by one of the creatures. He's taking me with him, my stomach grating against the stone. I kick against his hold, but it stays strong. Desperate. His nails claw at my skin. The beast opens its jaw, and he slides inside, screaming for help. Then, his pull goes limp.

All that's left is his arm, his fingers still locked around my ankle. With trembling hands, I tear it away, then get back on my feet, and make a run for it while the creature is distracted.

I stumble to the side—right in another beast's path.

Heart in my throat, I leap out of the way, landing just inches from the bridge's edge. My arms pinwheel, rock crumbling beneath my feet. I stagger back, the weight of my sword against my spine helping me barely keep myself on steady ground.

My mind races. My senses are filled with the smell of blood, the roaring of these creatures, and the stampede of challengers running for their lives. I can't turn and flee back into the forest. Not when I've made it this far.

Not when some are about to go through the gates.

I watch as a tall, hooded figure calmly walks toward them, without a care in the world. Harlan Raker's sword rings as he unsheathes it—and the beasts begin to fall. His blade moves in arcs of silver in front of him, so fast I barely see his movements as he clears a path right *through* the creatures.

Others follow him, just like I did in the maze.

A dozen of them.

I can feel my chances slipping away as Raker steps through the gates. Then the rest. There are only thirty-seven spots remaining.

Bridge slick with blood, I bolt forward.

In front of me, a challenger is sprinting in the opposite direction. He's crushed beneath a massive foot. Another is flung off the side of the bridge.

The next beast doesn't slow as it charges right toward me.

It bares its fangs. Opens its mouth like it's going to devour me whole. *Fuck.*

I can't outrun it. So, I need to think.

I might not be the strongest, or the fastest, or have any of the right tools, but I have my mind. And I've had to fight to survive every day for the last decade, without a family. I've always found a way out of every snare. Sheer desperation has made me resourceful.

A plan forms, and it might be the worst one I've ever had, or the best. I won't be sure, until it's too late. The beast rushes at me and, with a shaking breath, I stand my ground, both arms reaching back, sweaty fingers gripping the hilt of my new blade. I slowly pull it out, letting its weight bring it forward, until its tip is against the ground.

Time slows, and I wonder if it's because it's my last seconds. I wonder if it's a mercy from the gods. Then I remember that the gods are merciless. This is not my end.

This creature will not kill me.

The stone beneath my feet shakes as the beast gets closer. It moves in long, vaulting strides. Its face is twisted. It has dark scales, thick legs, and a body that could fit a dozen of us in its multiple stomachs. Its mouth is full of rows of teeth like a fully stocked forge. I can almost see my reflection in those gleaming fangs as it gets closer. Closer. Until I can feel the heat of its rancid breath against my face.

This better fucking work.

At the very last moment, I fall back, knees bent, legs in angles at my sides, body flattened—and lift my newfound sword all the way up with both arms and every sputtering ounce of strength I have left.

And the blade cuts right up the beast's stomach, splitting it open. Guts and hot blood rain down on me. I barely close my eyes in time. A primal roar thunders above.

Its body crashes behind my head. I hear it slide . . . before that howl fades away, as it slips right over the side. The drop is so far, I don't hear it land.

Alive.

I'm . . . still alive.

My crushing relief doesn't last more than a few seconds. I can't stay here, buried in a pile of guts. I can't retch at the smell. I need to move. I open my eyes and am met with a stretch of cloudless sky. It's almost peaceful. It's almost too easy to just *take a breath*. But I can't.

I will know what the sky looks like on the other side. I will see it for myself. I will see the gods, in all their glory, on their knees, begging for someone to save them the same way my family did.

I rise, just like Stellan taught me. Covered in guts, I get to my feet and lift my blade once more, fighting to keep the metal steady. Another beast is hurtling toward me. I brace myself, trying not to slip in all the blood—

But the next creature runs right past me. The one after that doesn't even seem to notice me, not like the one I took down, which seemed to be *hunting* me. I study its face closely as it passes me by.

That's when I realize the creatures don't have eyes.

They can't see. They are going off scent.

I smell like them.

Covered in their blood and guts, *I smell like them.*

Up ahead, I catch a flash of red hair. *Kira.* She's on her hands and knees, crawling to the other side of the bridge, arms shaking.

"Forty-two have passed!" someone yells. It's one of Cadoc's friends, calling to the others.

Before I can think better of it, I drag my hands through the blood and guts at my feet, then bolt toward Kira, shoes slipping, skin hot with the beast's blood, until I'm at her side.

There isn't time to explain. I smear the red on her head, on her arms, down her sides. She gasps, but once she sees my face, she stills.

Trust, I think. So, that's what that looks like.

The beast hurtling toward her changes its path.

"Go."

The creatures that ran down the length of the bridge are now turning back around. They're hungry for more. I drag us to the side, rolling, and a foot the size of my body barely misses us.

Another person isn't so lucky. A challenger just short of the gates gets crushed, bones snapping like twigs.

Blood. Mortal blood everywhere, and we slip in it, falling, sliding, taking each other down. I try to grip anything, *anything*, but the stone is slippery, and—

A hand.

No. A *handle*.

Zane's ax.

He's right ahead of us. "Forty-six have made it through," he says, just as Valen runs past us, making it through the gates. "Make that forty-seven."

Three spots left.

But we're here, just feet shy of the entrance. We race forward. Kira's through first. Zane's next. I leap—

And am dragged back by my braid, that's gone loose from its pins. My head rings as it bounces off the stone. One of Cadoc's friends. I'm too late. He's about to walk through. He's about to be the fiftieth.

All of this . . . for nothing.

I watch from the ground as Zane does the unthinkable. He strides back through the gates—and shoves the man off the side of the bridge.

I look up at him, stunned. Zane just reaches out a hand. "Everyone deserves a chance to die a brutal death," he says.

I take his hand.

And we both walk through the gates.

9

Walking into Starside is like stepping into a diamond. Everything glimmers. The sheen of magic is a paint, a lustrous stroke over us all. Even the sun feels different—the heat revitalizing, instead of draining. I tilt my face up to the sky to revel in its warmth, only to be met with a shock of the brightest blue I've ever known.

My lips part in wonder. The sky isn't gray on this side. It's the color of the morning glories my mother had in her book of dried flowers, collected over generations.

With a world-shuddering tremor, the gates begin to close behind us. There are challengers still on the bridge. Most are bleeding out. Screaming.

"Fifty days," Zane says, watching the intricate designs of the metal as they perfectly lock together.

"What?"

"That's when they'll open again. At sunrise. They'll close at sunset."

I knew the quest usually took around two months, but an exact timeline is the type of knowledge I had hoped Stellan might share with me.

Zane's from a Great House. I should ask him a hundred more questions about what he knows, but one spills from me before I can think of anything else. "Why did you save me?" He risked his own spot to secure mine.

He just shrugs a shoulder. "You're less likely to kill me than one of Cadoc's friends." His gaze dips to my ruined clothing. "And I saw what you did with the blood. It was smart. I want to work together."

I don't pretend that my new sword doesn't also have something to do with it. He knows I'm stronger with it . . . Or maybe he'll kill me, to try to claim it.

I consider his words. Now that we're not fighting for fifty spots, we aren't rivals.

Even so . . . we all want to make it to the Land of the Gods. He might betray me in a second, if it meant reaching the end of the journey.

My eyes drift to the rest of the Fifty. Teams are being formed. The only person who is striding into the unknown alone is Harlan Raker, the black cape of his hood curling in the wind.

I can't trust anyone. But to make it to the other side, and to survive possible encounters with these teams . . . I'll need one of my own.

I face Zane again. "Only if Kira can join too."

Zane frowns. He seems to be considering the same thing I already did, that Kira could slow us down.

But she's survived this far. And Kira is here for her sister. That motive alone, knowing she will do anything to succeed . . . it's valuable.

"Fine," he says.

"I'm going to pretend you didn't hesitate," Kira says, glaring. She looks him up and down. "What exactly do you offer, other than wielding that ax?"

Zane reaches into his bag. Uncurls a scroll. We all watch as ink spills across the blank parchment, shapes and letters forming before our eyes.

A map. Part of one, at least. It's just a single path, all the way from the gates to the Land of the Gods.

"Fuck. Okay, that works," Kira says. I nod in agreement. It's a huge advantage.

He quickly puts it back in his bag. The last thing we need is other competitors taking it. But before he did, I saw a mess of mountain ranges, rivers, and something called the Storm Woods.

Fifty days total. Anyone making it back to the gates will have to do the entire journey to the Land of the Gods in twenty-five. Seeing the landscape . . . I'm not even sure that's possible.

Kira has a clump of green in her hand. Grass, she ripped from the ground. She sighs deeply. "At least we get to die in a beautiful place."

Ever the optimist.

Yells sound to our left. Cadoc's group is huddled around someone covered in blood. One of the Enders. The eldest. She must have been wounded by the beasts on the bridge. She's screaming out in pain. I watch as Cadoc lifts his blade—and drives it through her heart. She goes still. Her siblings . . . they did nothing to stop him. They don't do anything now either but stand still, as if waiting for instruction.

Forty-nine Questral challengers remain.

"Let's go," I whisper, hoping Pagnus or Cadoc doesn't turn our way.

Zane nods. He leads us southeast, to where his map starts. The same path someone successfully made the journey on.

We walk the first few steps—and then we run.

HOURS LATER, THE blood on my face has dried into a painful crust. My energy begins to wane.

The sun dims, and so does the brilliance of everything around us.

Just when I've started to think this entire side's ground is made up of one color, the grass gives way to a shimmering pool of blue.

"Finally," Zane says, and he runs into the water, ax still on his back. Kira is right behind him. She dives forward, soaking the crown of her head, before angrily scrubbing her face.

I glance down at my clothes. If the material gets wet, will they see my skin?

Do secrets matter anymore, on this side?

I take a careful step forward and gasp at the coolness of the pool. My canteen was drained a while ago. I swallow, throat rough with thirst, knowing I can't drink this. It isn't running water. But do the same rules from the other side apply here? I'm not sure. Best not to test them so soon.

I walk until the water is up to my waist, feet firm against the bottom.

Water.

So much of it.

Clear water. Not the cloudy liquid from the well. Not the rare bucket of bitter rainwater.

"This can't be real," I whisper, letting it pool in my hands.

"It certainly feels real," Kira says, sighing as she dips her head back and then shakes her hair, droplets spraying all around us.

I slowly lower myself back, and relax. The cold is a welcome relief, weaving across my scalp.

What would it be like to sink into it? I close my mouth, plug my nose, and slowly, hesitantly, bend, until my knees reach the smooth bottom.

And the world goes dark and quiet.

Underwater is thoughtless, emotionless, problemless. *Nothing can reach me here*, I think, until my lungs constrict, and I have to surface again.

I break through the water, sputtering, blinking too many times, before my vision settles. My eyes meet another pair, across the pool.

A pair that glimmer like gemstones.

My hand immediately goes to the sword on my back, though my muscles are so spent, I doubt I could even take it out of its scabbard. There's a scraping as Zane's ax leaves its sheath.

The man only inches closer. And when he's at the edge of the pool, I see that his skin is too smooth. His limbs are lithe and just slightly too long. The way he moves is almost feline.

And his eyes . . . They are a sparkling violet, like an amethyst.

He doesn't have a weapon. He doesn't seem too concerned about Zane's ax. Does he not need one?

I wonder which of the legends are true.

Are immortals faster than us? Stronger than us? Could he, unarmed, kill us all?

His body is lanky, devoid of muscle. He isn't in a defensive stance. He's wearing a gray robe made of rough fabric. He takes another step forward, and I stand very still. He stops just short of the water.

Silence. None of us makes any move. We just stare at each other. I hear Kira swallow behind me.

"You're . . . immortal," I finally say, stating the obvious.

The immortal grins, showing white teeth. His eyes are gleaming with excitement. His voice is practically quivering with it. "And you . . . you are *not*."

I finally unsheathe my sword, arms drooping with its weight. I can't imagine ever being able to hold it without both hands.

Still, I ready myself to fight this creature, to learn through battling him the extent of immortals' mysterious abilities.

That only makes him grin wider.

"What do you want?" Zane demands.

The immortal motions behind him. "To extend an invitation. My dwelling is just beyond the forest."

I was so focused on the water, I barely looked at the trees. Now I see that they're ancient and twisted, roots knotted together.

"You're . . . offering us a place to stay?" Kira says, sounding the words out slowly, as if she still can't make sense of them.

The immortal nods. "You'll die out here," he says matter-of-factly.

"Why?" Zane demands.

"Night is a deadly time, even for us." What does that even mean?

Nothing in life is given freely, regardless of which side of the gates we're on. I know that for certain. "And in exchange?"

The immortal's purple eyes twinkle in the growing darkness. "Let me see your clothes. The contents of your pockets. Tell me about the other side."

I blink, having expected anything but everything that just left his mouth. Also—why would an immortal care about our *pockets*?

"I'm not letting you *see my clothes*," Kira practically spits at him.

The immortal shrugs. "Have it your way." He turns his back to us. "I'll search your bodies tomorrow. If there's anything left."

Then he makes his way back into the forest from which he came.

Zane looks over at us.

"He could be lying about night being deadly, just to get us to go with him," I offer.

"Yes, but what if he's not?" Kira retorts. "We aren't close to the first village on your route, are we?"

Zane shakes his head. "We won't reach it for days. I assumed we'd camp outside." Because we didn't know about the threat of night.

The person who made this map clearly didn't face the same challenge, given their path. It could be proof the immortal is lying . . . but the last Questral was half a century ago. Things could have changed. I turn. The sun is almost touching the horizon.

My stomach twists with hunger. Already.

I wonder if the strange immortal's offer comes with food. They don't eat, do they? Would he have anything for us?

Evening wind whips the strands of hair that have gone loose. Chills ripple down my arms.

We all look at one another.

Without another word, we rush out of the pool and into the forest.

We catch up to the immortal quickly, and he brightens. "Good. Yes, good. Alive is better. I have so many questions for you."

I frown. "Why?"

He glances at the sinking sun and hurries his pace, making me think the threat might actually be serious. "I'm a scholar, of course. Do they have those on the other side?"

I almost laugh. We don't study—we *survive*. But historians did exist, once. I know, because Stellan had a book that he kept in his room, with a dusty cover and yellowed pages. About a year after he found me, I snuck in and started to read it, hoping it would be entertaining.

It wasn't. I promptly slammed it closed and never opened it again. Maybe I should have.

The thought of Stellan makes my throat tight.

"No," I say simply.

"Then my work is even more important," he says, almost to himself. "I'm Pelas. Level Five."

"Level Five?" Kira asks.

"At the Tower of Knowledge."

He offers his hand to each of us, his expression a mixture of disgust and curiosity as he considers having to touch us.

Even after washing in the pool, red is soaked into our clothes. Our hair is dripping wet.

Kira shakes his hand first and recoils. When it's my turn, I realize why. His skin is *freezing* and too smooth, like touching stone.

"*Warm*," he says excitedly, taking a notebook and a quill from his robes. He looks at us as he writes while walking. "Warm everywhere?"

He reaches out as if to touch us more, and Zane snarls at him.

The immortal simply laughs before writing something else. "Territorial about warm skin. Fascinating."

"Are you all not territorial over your skin?" Kira demands.

He blinks. "For knowledge, I'm not territorial over anything," he says. "*We* are not. How old are you?"

"Twenty-two," Kira says warily.

The immortal chokes on an excited laugh. "How short. How insignificant! I've been training to be Level Five for *fifty years*. You will be dead before I reach Level Ten."

Kira is glaring at him.

"What happens at Level Ten?" Zane asks, and I don't miss how his hand is scratching the back of his neck every few seconds in a ruse to be closer to his weapon, should he need it. And we might.

Pelas is an immortal. As lanky as he looks, he could likely turn around and kill us at any moment.

"Level Ten gets access to the peak of knowledge," he says, eyes wide, as if entranced. "The forbidden floor. Enlightenment you couldn't imagine."

The light from his sparkling eyes dims as he turns to look at us. "Fewer questions from you. More from me."

By the time the trees part, he's already asked dozens of questions, and Zane looks close to burying his ax into his back.

I wonder what would happen. How hard is their skin? How are immortals killed? I want to ask my own questions, but I stay silent.

Then a great cone-shaped tower comes into view, the size of a mountain. It's the tallest building I've ever seen.

"This . . . is your castle?" Kira asks.

"Oh, no. This is the Tower of Knowledge."

"You live . . . in the Tower of Knowledge?" I ask.

He gives me a withering look. "Not in it. Next to it. All scholars do. At least the ones not on expeditions," the immortal says, scribbling something that looks like *not very intelligent* in his notebook.

He thinks we're idiots. Good.

A plan begins to form.

"Are we going into the Tower of Knowledge?" Kira asks, staring up at the structure in amazement.

Pelas spins to face her, and for the first time, he looks almost violent. "Of course not," he spits. "Only scholars are allowed inside."

Instead, he takes us to a building at the base of the tower. Before we reach the entrance, the door swings open, and a tall immortal walks through. He's wearing similar robes as Pelas, though his are almost silver.

"I thought that color wasn't allowed here," Zane says.

Pelas sucks in a sharp breath. He almost looks like he's going to hit Zane. "How *dare you question*—"

The tall man places a hand on his shoulder. His voice is deep and resonant, as if he's speaking inside a well. "Pelas. Remember. Sometimes we learn more from the questions asked than the answers given."

He turns to Zane. "You are correct. Silver is the color of the gods. Only those of us who are given permission from them are permitted to wear anything that approaches it."

The color isn't silver, really. More like a very light gray.

"You—you speak to the gods?" I ask, trying my best to sound casual.

The immortal looks at me as if I'm a foolish child. "Of course not. The texts are the closest we get. But the first scholar. He . . . he was a friend of the gods. Level Ten wear robes from his own collection."

Pelas looks at the other immortal's robes with something like longing.

"I'm Ellis." The tall immortal moves to the side and motions us forward. "We're always pleased to have guests pass through. Shall we prepare food? Drink?"

"You . . . eat?" Kira asks.

Behind her, Pelas shakes his head and angrily scribbles *IDIOTS* in his notebook.

"Not often," Ellis says. "For pleasure, mostly. How often do you eat, mortals?"

I frown. "You don't know?"

His smile is almost pitying. "Our study is typically reserved for . . . our own kind." A gentle way of saying that our short, mortal lives don't matter. Not to them. "And your knowledge was taken to your own land during the Great Divide."

The Great Divide. Is that what they call the period when the gates were erected? Our side might have books, but there are hardly any people who can *dedicate their lives* to reading them. Knowledge has been kept within certain families. And all information about Starside faded away—literally—a long time ago.

Ellis leads us down plain stone hallways with just a few cressets holding flames for light, and into a dining room, with a long oak table, and simply carved seats. A small group of immortals with darker robes scurry to meet him, their heads tilted in reverence. "Get our guests food," he commands.

They bow, then run back into another room with hardly a glance in our direction.

Ellis positions himself at the head of the table. Pelas sits five seats to his right. He roughly motions for us to sit at the other end.

We do, even though we're still dripping wet. Word of our presence must have spread, because a few more men in robes walk in and take their seats.

They all look expectantly at us. Then the questions begin in earnest.

"What does the other side look like nowadays?"

"Barren, mostly. There are hardly any fertile patches left," I offer. Desperate scribbling.

"What do you eat?"

We turn to one another. "It varies based on where we live," Kira says. "My side, to the west . . . we eat mainly fish. We're by the coast."

"I'm from the mountains," Zane says slowly, studying them, hand not far from his ax. "We eat pheasants. And roots that grow up high."

"Fascinating. And you? Where are you from?" Ellis is looking right at me.

I swallow past the knot in my throat. "I'm from a place that doesn't exist anymore. But—we used to eat mostly grain. And there was a single, giant fruit tree. It would feed our whole village, during infrequent blooms."

I grip the side of my chair as an image flashes through my mind of that fruit tree on fire.

"I . . . moved to another village as a child. There, I ate scraps. Pieces that were handed out at the town square." *Or that I stole.* "I foraged too. Mushrooms and such."

None of their expressions change.

"Do people die of hunger on that side?"

All the time, I want to say. Because all the magic is *here*. Because you all are in a fancy tower, studying books and looking down your noses at us while we are *dying*.

"Yes" is all I say.

"What does hunger feel like?" one of the other scholars asks, his voice devoid of any emotion.

"It feels like desperation," I say, a bite in my tone.

There were seasons when no one was buying anything from the forge. When Stellan would go without food for weeks so that I would get both rations of scraps.

Even that wasn't enough.

Hunger is a knife, twisting, *carving*.

These immortals . . . they've never been hungry. They are *disgusted* by us and our lives. They eat *for pleasure, mostly*.

My hands grip the chair harder, and Zane gives me a warning look.

Before I can say anything else, the doors burst open, and steaming bowls of broth are brought out. They are placed roughly in front of us, liquid sloshing onto the table.

Mysterious pieces float inside. Kira sniffs the bowl and nearly retches.

"Eat," Ellis says, before taking a spoonful of his own soup.

It could be poisoned. Though the other scholars continue asking questions. We aren't much use to them dead.

I take a sip and fight not to twist my face. The soup is bitter and acidic. The pieces are hard.

Still, it's food. And I don't doubt I will know hunger on many days during this journey to the gods.

The questions keep coming. About our climate, about our limitations, about our birth rates.

Finally, I fix a big smile on my face, and say, "We would love to know about you. Are you truly immortal? Can you not be killed?"

The table suddenly goes silent. Pelas is glaring at me.

Ellis humors me. "We can be killed, of course. We don't die of old age, however." He looks closely at me. "Our bodies are more durable than yours. We don't have disease here. Only high metals can wound us."

He doesn't even glance at our swords, as if not considering for a moment we could be carrying strong ones.

"Do you bleed?"

Pelas's look is nothing short of withering. "Of course we bleed," he says, and there's a legend that has proven to be false. He continues with a string of mumbled insults I only partially make out.

"If your people rarely die . . . are there many of you?" Kira asks.

"Far less than there are mortals, I assume. Recently . . . more have perished," Ellis says simply, and I don't miss how the other scholars seem to hunch forward with serious expressions. "Births are rare."

"Why recently?" Zane asks.

Silence.

I wonder if it has anything to do with the pure fear I saw on Pelas's face as he glanced at the moon and the incoming night.

Night is a dangerous time, even for immortals.

Ellis stands from the head of the table. "We've kept you long enough. It seems like you have survived . . . a great ordeal. Perhaps you would like to retire for the night. We can continue our questions in the morning." He nods at the other scholars, and they begin to stand one by one.

Pelas blinks too many times. He looks from his notes to us. "But I—I had more—"

"I'll stay with you," I offer. "While they rest. I can answer your questions."

Zane and Kira look at me as if I've lost my fucking mind. Maybe I have. I only smile tightly at them and hope they trust I know what I'm doing. Or, at least, I think I do.

"Very well," Ellis says. "Level Ones will escort you two to your rooms." The dark gray–robed men scuttle out again, leading Kira and Zane away.

I turn back toward Pelas. "What is it you want to know?"

Two hours later, Pelas has asked me an endless stream of questions. The latest was about how he compares to a mortal man.

"You're ... fine," I say, careful with my words. "Most mortals have more muscle, if they aren't starving. But ... your face is ... not revolting?"

SUFFERS FROM VISION PROBLEMS, he writes.

I fight to mask a laugh, and his eyes dart up to my face. His demeanor completely changes. "Were you reading my notes?" he demands.

Fuck.

I blink quickly, then divert my gaze to the floor. I hunch my shoulders and will red to stain my cheeks. "Oh, no—I ... I can't. I was just marveling at how quickly you make the shapes."

He reaches a finger out to touch my cheek. His touch is clinical as he studies the rush of color in pure fascination. I wonder if immortals' durable skin means a blush looks different on them.

He tilts his head. "Mortals do not read?"

I smile weakly. "We have no use for such things."

His aggression melts away, replaced by something worse: conceit. "Of course not." He shakes his head. "Of course you have no use for such things, simple creature."

I smother the urge to bury my sword in his skull. "Where do the words live?" I ask innocently.

He blinks. "The books, you mean?"

I nod quickly, eyes as wide as I can make them.

He sighs. "You simple, simple creature," he says, stroking my cheek, and I have to stop myself from recoiling. "Stand. I will show you."

And I wonder who the simple creature is.

It's the middle of the night, and the corridors are quiet. Pelas looks around before lighting a candle. I watch as he takes a quill with a sparkling metal point out of his pocket. *Starside steel*. Though here, I'm guessing it's called something else. The quill has a jagged edge. It almost looks like a key.

Pelas slips it through a crack in the wall and turns it. A door punches out of the stone, then we're in the tower.

He frowns at my dirty clothes. "You're not worthy of being in here, mortal. Be grateful I have charitable instincts."

Charitable. I know men like him. Men who are treated as if they are lesser, then take the first opportunity to do it to others.

I nod deeply, almost bowing. "You have my gratitude."

I'm not a threat to him. He thinks I'm too stupid to lie. He's too eager to feel important.

My boots click over a mosaic that makes up the entire bottom of the tower. Its pieces form a ring, with a much smaller silver circle at its center, filled like an orb. I stop right atop it, frowning, studying the two thin lines of silver erupting from the middle to the outer ring, shooting from opposite directions.

Before I can ask what it is, Pelas turns, motioning around him. "This. *This* is half a century of work," he says. "Being able to walk in here whenever I wish." His pride is a drug. He looks up and points at the levels overhead, floors and floors of shelves all visible from the center of the hollow cone-shaped tower. "Half the library. I can access *half of it*. You wouldn't understand. You have no idea how rare this is."

I do. And it's getting hard to mask my excitement. I force my voice to be casual as I say, "Do . . . do any of these books include accounts from those who have completed the Questral?"

I swallow, waiting, *hoping* he answers.

Pelas only frowns. "I haven't encountered one yet. But it wouldn't be from a *mortal*. It would be an immortal's account, of course."

I blink. "Immortals used to make the quest?"

He scowls. "Of course. Before it became a death sentence." He laughs, then stops himself.

"What do you mean?" I ask.

He sighs. "Immortals used to journey to the gods to ask for favors. Or to win a cup of magic. Some even *drank* it." His lip curls in a sneer. "Most turned into beasts, of course. Cursed by their greed. The gods have only deepened their cruelty, as is their right. Only the truly desperate would ever try to visit them now."

He looks over at me with unfiltered disdain and perhaps a bit of amusement. I want to ask more, but his eyes begin to narrow.

"Come. You've sullied this place long enough." He drags me back through the door. His grip is punishing, his nails digging into my shoulder. He's so close, he spits the words, raising his voice as he says, "You are not going to tell anyone you were in here."

I nod slowly.

Only then does he release me. I'm led back to the dining room and Pelas relishes commanding a Level 1 to show me to my quarters. I follow, head bent.

When the hallway is quiet again, I sneak back toward the tower. And slip the quill I stole from Pelas between my fingers.

The scholars don't visit at night. The structure is windowless, save for a large skylight that takes up the entire pointed ceiling. Daylight is clearly preferable for reading. I have nothing but the light of a candle I took from the hall.

The shelves are positioned in rings, with the stairs going around and around. Each level up is smaller than the last, leading to the peak—Level 10. Just a small circle of books.

I don't waste a moment. I run up the spiral stairs to Level 1 and begin with the first book. As I go to pull it off the shelf, it pulls back.

Shit. The books are *chained* to their shelves, making it impossible to steal them—and hard to open at all. I can only view them if I'm hunched over at an awkward angle. Each chain is locked.

I try Pelas's quill, and it works. The book is freed.

There's nothing inside but half-empty pages. Something about plants, with detailed drawings of leaves.

I move on.

I open book after book, flipping through each quickly, looking for *anything* that might help me complete the quest.

I reach toward another text, but I stop just short of it. There's an energy . . . a thrumming inside.

Something is contained in that book. I'm not sure what it is, but I move past it. A few others have that same strange feeling. I finally pick one up and read its cover. It has to do with magic.

Useless to me right now. I just need any information that can help me get to the gods—and kill them.

Level 1 doesn't have anything relevant. I go to Level 2. The books here are about history. War. Great Houses rising and falling.

Level 3. Creatures. Endless books about beasts and beings, most of which I've never heard of. It could be useful, but I don't have time. I need to find something that can specifically help me on this quest.

The darkness begins to fade.

I look up. The first rays of light are gleaming through the peak.

Shit.

Pelas said he had never encountered an account from someone who had completed the Questral. It must be because it's on a higher level.

I skip Level 4 and Level 5 and go straight to Level 6.

Here, most of the books are thrumming with that strange energy. It makes it easy to pass those. Only a few don't have it, and I hurriedly turn their pages.

Orange rays spill down from the ceiling, slowly illuminating the mosaic below. As soon as the sun hits that silver circle at the center of the ring . . . it glows, producing its own column of light that shoots right up through the center of the tower.

Beautiful. But it means my time is almost up. Scholars should be walking inside any moment now. I look around, frantically, knowing I don't have time to go through each book. This level has *hundreds*.

That's when I see it, across the way. A book that looks more worn than the others, as if it wasn't written in a place like this.

I walk around the ring of shelves until I'm standing right in front of it. It's absent that thrumming energy. I pull it from its shelf, and the chain pulls it back.

A Quest of Life and Death.

I sink to my knees, not bothering with the lock this time, knowing Pelas's key won't work. I flip through it as light completely fills the tower, sun pouring in through the skylight like wine entering a goblet.

Some of the pages have been torn out. Some of the ink has smudged, as if the pages got wet.

My quest starts at the Beast Tree. Some of my group hits the ground. Others are luckier. They say you won't survive without a creature. Most don't survive the tree at all.

I will report back.

My quest did not end there, I am happy to say. I survived the tree. Many did not. My beast is stubborn, but strong. With him, I feel confident that—

Voices sound below me. My hands tense around the worn cover, the book's chain rattling.

Pelas. He's with a group, which is why, I assume, he hasn't noticed his quill is missing. His voice is full of excitement. It echoes up the tower.

"They're sleeping now," he says.

A voice I don't recognize says, "Good. And the poison you're making will keep them alive?"

"Yes, yes. I'd rather study their insides while their blood is still flowing. We'll keep them alive for as long as possible while we conduct our tests."

I go still.

He's going to slice us open and study us . . . while we're still *alive*.

Of fucking course he is.

I flip through the pages faster. I had hoped I could read the entire text and commit it to memory, but there's no time now. My fingers pause at one of the last pages.

The author . . . he drew a *map*.

Unlike Zane's, it's complete, and strikingly detailed, showing all the way from where we are now to the other edge of Starside, where the gods live. Every town. Every mountain range. Everything he encountered.

This is invaluable.

Pelas is only Level 5, but still, desperately, I try the lock, just in case. The quill gets stuck then drops against the wood.

The voices go quiet.

Then—"Who's here?"

I remain very still.

"Scholar?"

I take a slow breath. Another.

The stairs groan as they begin climbing.

They're going to find me. The tower is hollow. There's nowhere to hide. I don't even try. They spot me immediately, from several levels down.

"Mortal!" one yells.

Pelas starts running, his gray robes furling around him.

No use being quiet. I pull the chain, clumsily unsheathe my sword—drop it—then begin slamming my blade down against the metal with all my might. The chain is sparkling Starside steel. But so is my sword.

I start banging and banging at it, watching the metal slowly chip away. *Too slowly.* Fuck, this sword is heavy. I'm already panting. My arms burn.

The scholars are on Level 3. Then they're on Level 4.

They're yelling for help. I bang my blade over and over and over, but then they're on my level.

There's no time. I rip the map out of the book, stick it in my pocket, and run.

Pelas is right behind me. The rest of the scholars block the stairs. I feel the magic all around, humming, thrashing.

Pelas might not be muscular, but he's fast. He's on my heels in a moment. I turn around and raise my blade high.

His eyes widen in fear.

Not for his own life, apparently. "Put that away, you *simpleton*," he cries out. "You'll harm the *books*. Some of them are fragile. Some are filled with things you won't want to unleash."

I should kill him for what he planned to do to us.

Instead, I slice my blade along the spines of books closest to us, the ones boiling with magic.

And the world explodes.

I get thrown back and nearly fall over the railing as black, sparkling smoke erupts, each text bursting apart in quick succession. My ears ring. A metal taste coats my tongue. My knees nearly buckle as I stand, then I'm off again, using both arms to slice my sword across another row of texts.

Some books break off their chains, some howl like beasts, others burst into flames. I hear screaming somewhere.

Then Pelas's voice: "Stop! Stop!" I do no such thing.

The tower is filled with different colors of smoke, and I use its cover to run down the stairs, past coughing scholars who have spent their lives holed up in this place.

Chaos meets me in the hallway, but the yelling immortals press themselves to the walls when they see my weapon. I turn a corner, and someone grips my wrist—I lift my blade.

Kira and Zane.

"What did you do?" Kira asks, eyes wide.

I wince. "Far too much."

We race down the steps toward the front door. There, in front of the towering oak stands Ellis, wielding a thin sparkling sword of metal slightly different from my own. It has an intricately carved hilt and a pearl in its pommel.

I lift my blade, ready to fight. Kira and Zane raise their weapons too.

The immortal glances at my metal and pales. "Where did you get that?"

My chest is burning, lungs filled with the mysterious smoke from the tower and constricting from all the running. "I think we've had enough questions, don't you agree?"

I wait for him to advance. I plant my feet, readying myself, blinking quickly so as not to miss any sharp movement.

But he only lowers his sword. "I underestimated you, human," he says. Then he steps away from the door.

It doesn't make sense. There's no time to question it. The sounds of yells and running surge behind us. The scholars might have scurried away at the first sign of a weapon, but all together, who knows what they're capable of?

Zane inches toward the door, eyes fixed on the immortal, and opens it. "It's clear," he yells back at us.

He steps through. So does Kira.

The immortal pays them no mind. No. He's staring at me—at my *hand*. I lower my gaze, and my chest goes cold. While I was flipping the pages, I folded my sleeve up and never lowered it.

Just the smallest bit of silver is showing, but those immortal eyes miss nothing.

Slowly, his gaze meets mine again. I keep my grip on my weapon, waiting for him to strike me, or yell out his discovery—

But he doesn't say a word. And as I back away and flee into the morning, I realize his silence wasn't the most surprising part.

It was that he didn't look surprised at all.

10

"There's a place where creatures can be claimed, like swords." We finally slow down a mile from the Tower of Knowledge, just beyond a grove. I show them the map, pointing at the Beast Tree, a mountainous oak sticking up from a forest, with a ring of wings circling its crown.

Zane unfurls his own. We compare them. His avoids the north of Starside entirely until the very end, when the path curves up northeast, to the entrance of the Land of the Gods.

He chews his lip as he considers both options. "A winged creature definitely would make things easier . . . and give us time to make it back to the gates."

Easier is putting it lightly. The new map shows a smattering of ominous illustrations. Dueling Rings. Great Houses. Something called the City on Fire. Endless forests and lakes and mountain ranges sharpened into treacherous points.

We could fly over it all . . .

I know which path I want to choose, but I'm not alone anymore. We look at each other awkwardly, silence spilling over.

Kira sighs deeply. "Well, then. Let's get this out of the way." She throws a hand up. "We don't trust each other. And for good reason. Just yesterday, we were rivals." She looks at me. "But I saved you, in the forest. And you saved me . . . on quite a few different occasions." She points at Zane. "And he saved you, on the bridge."

"No one's saved me," Zane says.

Kira pauses. Frowns.

"The scholars were going to poison us, and cut us open to study," I offer.

"See! She saved you too." She brings her hands together. "Now. Since we're all in this wonderful *circle of saving* . . . I propose we make a pact."

Zane raises a brow. "A pact?"

She nods, red hair spilling out of its loose braids. "We're not enemies anymore. We're a team with one goal: making it to the end. In service of that, we should agree on a few rules between us."

No one says a word, and she continues.

"First, we vote on each big decision." *Like choosing a path we know works or going north to try to claim a creature.* "Second, we vow to protect each other, if doing so won't lead to our own deaths." Fair enough. "And . . . finally." She swallows. "If one of us is slowing the rest down . . . we cut them loose. Nothing personal. The quest must come first."

It's a brutal truth none of us want to admit . . . but she's right. It isn't betrayal, if it's agreed upon from the start.

Kira lifts her silver sword so its tip is pointed between us both. "Well. Do we have a pact?"

I've never made a pact or an oath with metal before. I'm not even really sure how it works.

And I don't have friends. All the ones I did have, as a child, are dead. I don't know what it's like to trust anyone other than my family, or Stellan. Every day on Stormside is a fight for survival—and this journey is only going to be worse.

But Kira's right. We've all saved each other. Maybe if we keep doing that, we could actually make it to the end of this.

And . . . a weak thought flits through my head. *I don't want to be alone.* Not anymore. Not if I don't have to be.

With both hands, I lift my weapon.

Zane just looks at us both, a crease between his brows. He shakes his head, sighs, then unsheathes his ax in a glorious arc, the multicolored gemstones glittering beneath the morning sun. Our metals all touch.

A current sweeps through my blade, into my bones, and I wonder if we actually did make some sort of promise beyond words.

I plan to honor the pact. Looking at them both . . . I hope they feel the same.

"Our first vote then," Zane says, still sounding wary. "Path of relative safety . . . or the Beast Tree?"

"Beast Tree," Kira says immediately. She looks up, staring at a crop of bright blue birds that soar overhead. "I've always wanted to know what it's like to fly."

I've never had that desire. But I also don't see how it's possible to survive this deadly landscape on foot. "Beast Tree."

Zane nods. "Not that it matters, but we're all in agreement." He outstretches a hand toward the parchment in my grip. "May I?"

My first instinct is to hold the map tighter, just like I hold everything—in fear that it will be ripped away from me, like everything I've ever cared about.

But we're a team now. I slowly hand it over.

Zane gives me a reassuring smile, as if sensing my hesitance, and then pours over the illustrations. "It'll take at least a few days to get there," Zane says, using the miles we've already crossed as a reference.

Kira bites the inside of her mouth. "Where are we going to sleep? Was that creep telling the truth about night?"

All of us look at the sun, steadily moving, counting down our hours of safety outdoors.

"I don't know, but I don't want to find out." Zane points at the map. "Here. This road. If we can find it, it should lead right to this village." *Westwere.* "There could be an inn. Food, maybe."

Kira snorts. "And what? We'll rely on the charity of the *immortals who tried to just use us for anatomy lessons?*"

"No," I say, reaching into my pack and bringing out my coveted gold coin. The amalgamation of everything I've ever sold, all melded into this one small piece of metal. "We'll use this."

A slow smile spreads across Kira's face. "And here I was, thinking you were just a pretty, blood-spattered face." She looks over at Zane. "How about you, *Sterling?* Is that pack full of coins?"

Zane's eyes find the ground as he leads the way toward the path. "No" is all he says.

"Why not?" Kira demands, clearly not getting—or caring—that Zane doesn't want to talk about it.

His jaw tenses. "All the silver is kept under lock and key. I left in the middle of the night."

Kira's eyes widen. "Without telling anyone?"

"Just one person," he says. Then he strides forward, outwalking this conversation.

Kira looks at me, shaking her head in disbelief. She lets out a low whistle. "Great House heir leaving for the quest, with just his weapon on his back, and a few provisions . . ." She purses her lips. "That's the type of thing people write songs about."

It's true. Minstrels pass through villages, singing legends, charging scraps of metal to hear them. They're the keepers of the stories that were drained from our texts.

They only came near Nightfell once, and I scavenged for weeks to save up enough to listen. I did, for hours, in pure fascination.

Until the stories turned to the heroism of the gods, and then I stood and left.

The road is easy enough to find . . . and empty. It's made of ancient sparkling cobblestone, grass growing between the mismatched squares, cutting right through the forest like a blade.

"I would think more people would use this road," Kira says, squinting into the distance. We hear nothing. No sound of an approaching wagon. No footsteps.

"Maybe we shouldn't be on it," I murmur, studying the stones for wear. I find almost none. All the cracks are covered by overgrowth. There are *flowers* sprouting right in the middle of the road, in between stones. I reach down and gently rub the soft petals through my fingers, chest tight.

They would have been run over if this road was used often. They wouldn't have grown in the first place. I stand. "I think we should—"

A hush falls, like the forest is whispering. Then we hear the familiar sound of clanking metal. I reach back for my sword just as an immortal in gleaming armor steps onto the path.

He's wearing a mask. It's made of a sheet of gold, completely covering his face, etched in intricate designs I can't make out.

With it . . . he almost looks faceless.

My hand stills on the hilt of my weapon.

Zane pulls out his ax.

Another figure steps from the trees. Another. All wearing masks and armor.

"Mortals," a woman says from behind a glimmering red mask, a slice of ruby. She turns to the second man. His mask is emerald green. "They didn't hear the screaming from the last ones, then."

Shit.

Kira makes to run into the forest, and the green-masked man produces a bow and arrow so quickly, he blurs.

The scholars were hardly a good example of their kind. Immortals are faster. *Stronger.*

Kira goes still.

"What do you want?" Zane spits, still wielding his ax.

The first man tilts his head. "Payment."

With sinking regret, I take the coin from my pack and hold it up. "Here. You can have it. We don't want any problems."

The woman just laughs. It's a beautiful, melodic sound. "Our god has no use for coins, stupid girl."

God. My body stills.

"Who is your god?" Kira demands, voice trembling.

"The god with many names," she says. "The god of journeys and in-betweens and thieving. She controls the roads. All must pay her price."

"And what is that?"

"A face," she says simply.

Silence.

"What do you mean, '*a face*'?" Kira asks.

The one with the green mask opens a bag at his hip. He lifts something up. Kira tenses.

A head, held by the hair. Eyes wide in fear. Blood dripping from the neck.

I recognize that face. It's a man from Eros, a southern town that was abandoned during the droughts. Their villagers now wander Stormside, in search of water. His group was so happy when he made it onto the platform. His cobalt cape had been a patchwork of history, generations of stories stitched into it.

That cape is now probably soaked in blood.

The woman tilts her head, considering us. Her voice is bored. "Just one. You can choose. Or we'll choose for you."

Zane turns to look at me. For a split second, I think he might be getting ready to chop my head off with his ax and toss it at the thieves in front of us, pact be damned, but instead he mouths something.

"*Your blade*," he says.

I blink. What does he want me to do? Unsheathe it? Offer it as payment?

His words barely make a sound. "Throw it. Like he did."

Like he did. He's talking about Raker, when he threw his sword at Waldron and somehow called it back to his hand.

He thinks just because I claimed this ancient sword I know how to use it? I can barely hold it upright. I haven't even had time to look at it properly, let alone learn how to do anything like that.

I can't, I mouth back. Still, I try. Nothing happens.

"Enough whispering, we can hear you," the woman snaps. "And I assure you, if you try to throw your blade, it's not going to work." She takes a feline step forward. "We are faster than you. Stronger than you. We hear everything. Smell everything. Even your fear . . ."

She looks back at the two masked men. "Mortals are so weak. So pathetic." In a flash, she's right in front of us, hand outstretched. "The blade. Let's see it."

I don't make a single move.

Her glittering eyes narrow. The archer cocks his arrow. He aims it right at my head. "Leave it right here, or you die. But not before I slice your face off, slowly, carefully, so that you feel every single turn of my dagger."

I swallow. Dread spills through my bones as I reach back toward my sword.

"Try something, and your friends die too," she warns. I'm not stupid enough to try anything now. Not when I just saw her cross a few yards in less time than it takes me to blink. I curl my hand around the hilt. Lift it with all my strength, teeth gritted with the effort. Bury the blade right between us, in the dirt of a missing stone.

I step back just as she steps forward.

Her eyes widen. "Look at this," she says, turning back toward her companions. "She must have stolen it from somewhere important . . . The diamond alone . . . What kind of favor do you think it might be worth?"

The green-masked thief steps forward. "A good one," he says. He still hasn't lowered his bow. "You know how much our god enjoys rarities."

The woman nods, eyes flashing with greed. She curls both hands around the hilt. Pulls.

Nothing happens.

She frowns. Pulls again. *Again.* She digs her steel-plated boots into the ground, bends her knees. A frustrated groan escapes her lips.

The sword doesn't move an inch.

There's the twang of a bow. I close my eyes, bracing myself for a flash of pain.

Nothing.

I open them to see the arrow sticking out of the woman's forehead, right through the mask. Her hands are still around my sword's hilt.

She drops to the ground, blood dripping in a line down the ruby. It's red, just like ours. Not the fabled silver blood of the gods.

Metal clashes. The gold-masked and green-masked thieves are dueling. They fight in wild streaks of color.

"*Run*," Zane says. I pull my sword from the dirt, and we shoot into the forest. It's not long before more steps join us. *Faster steps.*

A beam of silver metal arcs to my left, and I just barely stop it with my blade, both arms hardly holding it up. The green-masked thief. There's a sickening crack as his sword breaks in half against mine, but that doesn't stop him.

A moment later, his halved blade is at my neck. My pulse beats along the jagged metal.

Then a sword is through his chest. He falls, only to reveal the gold-masked thief standing behind him. The first one we encountered on the road.

"Where did you find it?" he demands as he lifts his sword between us.

My back is against a tree. There's nowhere to run. Even if there was, he would catch me.

"The—the other side," I say, trying to buy myself any time.

My blade is still in my hand. Just as I wonder if I have the strength to raise it again, the tip of his weapon is against my heart.

"*Where?*" he demands. "*Where exactly?*"

I open my mouth to answer—

And close it against a spray of blood.

The man . . . his head is gone. It's on the ground, right in front of my foot. I push the rest of his body away before it and his blade can fall onto me.

Zane is standing there, blood coating his ax, panting. Kira is just behind him, looking like she's going to retch again.

"You—you didn't run," I say, looking between them.

The corner of his mouth lifts. "We made a pact. Remember?"

I remember. Kira rushes forward, pulling a scarf from her bag and using it to wipe the blood from my face. "There's a lot. Hold still." I do. I do, even as my heart races, energy coursing through my veins.

Without Zane and his ax . . . I would be dead.

My sword makes me a target—even here. I can't forget that.

Once the blood is wiped away, we collect the two immortals' heads. We go back to the road, and Zane cuts the woman's off too. We each hold one, by the hair, and continue down the path, through the rising dusk.

When the trees rustle again further down, Zane merely holds up one of the masked heads and says, "Consider the price paid."

IT'S NEARLY DUSK when we reach the village of Westwere. A wall sits around it, with a moat, and a narrow bridge that's already being pulled up.

We race forward, heads still in hand, and jump. The bridge stops.

A foot above us, a window in the wall slides open. "Get off," an immortal man barks. "It's almost sunset."

So the danger of night is real.

"We need a place to stay. *Please.*" I take the coin out of my pocket and hold it over my head, hoping it's actually worth something here.

He eyes it, and us, warily. Then he notices the heads.

For a moment, I wonder if keeping them with us was a mistake. We don't know how immortals work. Maybe they all serve the same god.

The window slams closed. Panic floods my chest.

Just when I think we're about to be locked out, it opens again, this time, as a full door. And I see the man wasn't standing on a platform. He's seven feet tall, at least.

"In, quickly," he says. "You're playing with fate, being outside this close to sundown." He shakes his head before pulling the thick chains again, raising the bridge completely in just a few tugs.

Immortals are powerful. So why are they so afraid of night?

What could be so bad that even *this* immortal fears it?

He runs his large hand down his face, before sighing with his entire body. "That time of the century then, is it?" he says, seemingly to himself. He frowns down at us. "Come with me."

We all look over at each other, surprised. I really thought he would leave us outside the gates. Our encounters with all immortals so far haven't exactly been pleasant.

The village is modest. All the structures seem to slope, one way or another. He leads us down a mostly empty street. We pass by countless doors and hear lock after lock turning.

He stops in front of a quaint house with four stories that is noticeably tilting to the side, held upright by an equally precarious-looking tower.

He knocks three times. A moment passes. Another.

Then a tall, beautiful immortal with violet eyes and blond hair tied into a single braid that starts at the top of her scalp opens the door. She looks up at the man and smiles.

Then she sees us.

Her face pales. She shakes her head. "No. I told you after the last time, *no*—"

He's leaning casually against the threshold. "They killed three Masks."

She blinks. Her eyes slide down to the heads we still hold.

The blond immortal opens the door wider. "Come in." Her face scrunches. "Leave those outside."

We step into a bustling room. It's a tavern, filled to the brim with immortal knights, still in their full armor. They're massive, towering figures, like statues. Fear sinks through me.

The room goes quiet.

"They're guests," the blond immortal says, her voice firm, and the chatter gradually starts up again.

Still, I feel eyes on us. Some curious. Others disgusted.

"I'm Xara. Welcome to my inn."

"Thank you," I say warily, watching as she bolts three different locks at the door.

"Weapons at the front," she commands, motioning toward a patch of swords at the entrance, all dug into the floorboards.

Zane doesn't look happy about it, but we each dig our weapons through the wood. It feels wrong walking away from my sword . . . but we need a place to sleep. This is her inn. She makes the rules. I only hope it'll be there in the morning.

Xara puts her hands together. "Hungry? Thirsty? Tired?"

"All three," Kira says.

Xara's mouth turns up knowingly. "You mortals are *always* all three." She leads us through the crowd toward the bar. Even massive immortal warriors stumble aside to let Xara pass.

She motions for a few of them to make some room, and we are presented with three seats at the counter. "It's been a century or so. You'll have to remind me. Do mortals drink ale?"

Kira barks out a laugh. "Most drink far too much of it."

Now behind the bar, Xara eyes some of the warriors in the tavern. "Immortals have that problem too." She presents each of us with a tall, foaming glass.

The color of the ale is different than it is on Stormside. It's less yellow and more sparkling gold.

I take a tentative sip and sigh, in spite of myself. It's cold, and bubbly, and refreshing. I look up, only to see Xara smiling at me.

"It never gets old," she says.

"What doesn't?"

"Watching mortals try something for the first time." She lifts a shoulder. "We've been alive for centuries. Nothing is ever new anymore." She looks at us. "But for you . . . everything is new. Your lives are so short. There's not enough time to try everything." She says it almost reverently. She puts her hands on the bar. They're small but callused in the same places mine are. "I'll be back with some food."

A few moments later, we're presented with three bowls of soup that taste decidedly better than the ones the scholars gave us. It has vegetables not too different from the ones I've seen sold in the nicer markets, and meat that has been seasoned. I'm too damned hungry to question the fact that Xara doesn't ask for payment. We finish our bowls, and Xara brings us a second helping. Then a third. Zane and I keep looking around for any approaching danger, but Kira chats happily, telling Xara our names and all about Brambleside. The immortal listens intently, interrupting only to ask questions.

When we finish eating, we must look exhausted, because she hands us each a key and leads us up to our rooms. Mine is right off of the narrow stairs. In the hall, I finally try to hand her my coin, and she curls my hand back into a fist.

"The Masks have tormented our area for too long. The faces they've collected . . . are not just from travelers." Her eyes glisten. Do immortals cry?

I should shut my mouth, take this favor, and go into my room. But nothing is ever given freely. I duck to peer down the stairs, expecting to see my sword gone. It's not. It's standing upright, just where I left it.

My eyes sweep over the slender hall, searching for some sign of danger. My pulse races, awaiting the trap. The betrayal. But there's no one there.

Xara just stares at me, brow raised.

Finally, I just spit it out. "Why are you being so kind to us?"

She frowns. "Why wouldn't I be?"

I motion to myself. "We're mortals. You're . . . not."

"Ah." She smiles knowingly. "Not all immortals are Masks waiting in the trees, Aris. Just as not all mortals are looking to loot my inn, the way some tried two Questrals ago." Her eyes flash with a whisper of irritation. It's gone in a moment. She looks me over. "I don't know you. I don't trust you. But I trust metal. A sword like yours is drawn not just to the strength of one's abilities . . . but to the strength of one's soul." She tilts her head. "Now, that strength might be good . . . or evil." She shrugs. "But this world has enough rot in it. I choose to see the good first, and the bad only when I have to." She nods toward the door behind me. "Enjoy your stay. I'm downstairs, if you need anything."

Before I can say a single word, she turns to leave. By the time I blink, she's already down the stairs.

Her words cycling through my mind, I finally step into my room.

It's small but warm, with a bed brimming with thick blankets. My eyes nearly water with gratitude, seeing them. A fire is already burning in the corner. And I discover, with soul-melting relief, that there's a bath.

I take my time scrubbing my skin, then each item of clothing. The king is a bastard, but I'm grateful for the new clothing, especially the extra undergarments I grabbed before leaving. I hang it all up to dry near the hearth.

Then I slip below the sheets, and groan. My body sinks into the mattress. I've never been so tired in my life. My exhaustion hits me all at once, my muscles going slack.

Through half-shut eyes, I stare at the crackling fire. Memories flash of other flames, all-consuming, *killing, destroying* flames.

"I'm here," I whisper to the goddess who set those fires. "I'm on your side now. There are no gates between us." I watch the flames flicker. "And when I reach you, you will wish you killed me too."

I WAKE UP on the floor, tangled in my sheets. They're stuck to my skin by a film of sweat. I take a panicked breath, nearly choking on the fabric, before kicking them away, gasping.

The nightmares. They haven't stopped.

At least, it means I actually slept deeply last night.

There's a knock upon the door, and I jump.

Xara. "There's food waiting downstairs," she says through the wood, before the floorboards creak as she moves on.

I take a quick bath, braid my hair into its two that converge in one, pin it up, then slip my dried clothes back on. They're warm thanks to the hearth, and I wriggle my toes in my boots, relishing the feeling.

Pack over my shoulder, I step out of my room, not expecting someone to be right there, filling the hall with their wide shoulders, passing by at that exact same moment.

I smack right into them, then stagger back, falling—

Right down the stairs.

Or at least, I would have, had a hand not fisted the front of my shirt, keeping me on the ledge. A massive hand, with thin, dark tattoos curling down every long, pale finger.

Shit.

I look up. And up. Into the darkness of a hood.

"Are you actively trying to find your death?" a voice spits out.

I swallow, grateful for the shirt I'm wearing below the one crumbled in his hand, that's currently keeping my markings hidden. "It certainly seems like it."

And he hasn't saved me yet. I'm still leaned back at an angle. If he were to let me go, I would fall and break my neck on these stairs. Xara might be an immortal, but if I screamed right now, I doubt she could reach me in time. That fact alone should probably make me more agreeable. Pleasant, even. He probably wants me to beg him to pull me back up. But I've already begged him for mercy before, and I'm not doing it again. I just lift my chin in defiance.

His head tilts.

Then he loosens his grip, sending me lurching back just an inch, and I gasp. My heart sputters.

My eyes narrow. *Bastard.*

On instinct, I reach behind me, blinded by the need to at least injure him before he drops me, because apparently, yes, I am *actively trying to find my death*. But my fingers brush my empty scabbard. There's nothing there.

Fuck. It's in the floorboards.

I hear a huff of cruel mirth—and maybe shock—above me.

Heat prickles my cheeks, but I don't drop my gaze, refusing to show an ounce of fear or shame in front of this monster. This monster that currently has my life clutched in his *fist*. His grip tightens again, long fingers slipping down my chest.

Just when I think he'll finally let go, he slowly pulls me up, inch by inch, right toward his hidden face to say, "Careful. You just might find it."

Then, he shoves me back onto the landing, and passes me by without a second look, taking the stairs in a flash. The front door opens and slams closed.

Asshole.

Asshole . . . who saved me.

Why?

I shake off the question. He likely didn't want to get his boots dirty with my blood, which would have no doubt formed a puddle at the bottom of those treacherous stairs, had I fallen.

And he's right. *I do need to be more fucking careful,* I think, as I finally start down the steps that were nearly just my end.

As promised, there are plates of cooked eggs and meats waiting below, spread out across two tables. Sun shines through the dust-glazed windows. Most of the warriors are gone, but some are still milling around the door.

I stop midway down the stairs, watching as they each take turns trying to lift my sword. They're twice my size. Their arms are thicker than my head. I watch them groan and strain, and I tense—then nearly laugh, which seems absurd, since I almost just died.

I clear my throat, and their eyes shift to me.

Yeah, bad idea. I go still, remembering the best way for them to claim my sword is to *kill me*.

But right at that moment, Xara walks through the tavern and says, "It's a bit early in the day to wound your egos, isn't it, boys?"

Those *boys* look like they could rip the limbs off a person with little effort. But amazingly, they begin to disperse, after mumbled apologies and goodbyes to Xara.

I slowly turn to face her, and I know that she can feel me looking, but she doesn't meet my gaze.

I step down the rest of the rickety stairs, toward the spread of food.

Three glasses sit full of violet liquid. I sniff one, then take a tentative sip. It's sweet, with a slightly bitter aftertaste.

"Berries," Xara says. She frowns at my pale face, as if she can see the lack of nutrients in my body. "Drink it. You need it." I do. I finish it all, then, once it's replaced, I empty a second glass.

I finally motion toward the door. "Did you know you were housing a monster?" I ask.

She blinks at me. "The mortal in the hood?"

I nod.

She lifts a shoulder. "He was nice enough. Came just after you did. Was surprised to see him in one piece. Cleaned up after himself, which is a rarity, unfortunately."

I scowl. Just when I'm about to tell her about how awful he really is, the stairs creak. Zane. His eyes immediately go to his ax, still buried in the floorboards. His shoulders melt with relief.

Then, he says good morning and starts unceremoniously eating *everything*.

Kira surfaces not long after, still wrapped in one of the blankets from her room. She turns to Xara, who's behind the bar, wiping glasses with a rag. "This is the softest fabric to ever exist."

Xara smiles. "A friend knitted them for me, from Arladan goat fur."

Sensing our confusion, she says, "It's a place in the north. Cold, white, vicious. The goats grow the softest coats."

It isn't on the map. And, as much as I want to know all about it, the quest must come first. I reach into my pocket and slowly bring out the crushed parchment. I gingerly smooth it out on the table. "We're here, right?" I point to the illustration of the village.

Xara stops her movements. Her eyes widen as she walks around the counter.

"Where did you get that?"

No use in lying to a woman who has housed and fed us for free. "The Tower of Knowledge."

Xara carefully takes the paper. "The God of Travels had most maps destroyed . . . This much land covered . . ." It's the second time hearing about this god. Why ruin maps? Xara gently traces across the markings. "Yes. You're in Westwere."

"We're trying to get here," I say, pointing to the Beast Tree. Her mouth tightens as she nods.

"What is it?"

"What do you know about the Beast Tree?"

"That creatures can be claimed, like swords."

Xara studies me for a moment. She works her jaw. "It's tradition for the heirs of Great Houses of Starside to visit the tree when they come of age. Their blood is filled with old magic, you see. Their connection to this land is deep-rooted. It's a great ceremony . . . but it hasn't happened in decades. The heir goes to the top of the tree . . . and jumps."

"The fall is hundreds of feet. The only hope of survival is if one of the creatures catches you. But there are no guarantees. There are very few creatures willing to bond . . . and few who have survived the hunters."

"Hunters?" Kira asks.

Xara nods solemnly. "Swords infused with dragon scales or pegasus feathers or griffin talons hold great power. Creatures have been hunted into near extinction. Many have gone into hiding. There are fewer than ever at the tree . . . so fewer people have decided to take the risk." Her fingers curl around the edge of the table. "What I'm trying to tell you is the practice has mostly died out, because most of the people who try it hit the ground. Nothing saves them. And they . . . *they* are immortals."

Her eyes meet mine, and her implication is clear. The chances of one of these mysterious creatures choosing us, *saving us* . . . are low. It's not a cruelty. It's truth.

I look down at the map. The land we have covered from the gates is almost nothing. And in those short miles, we have nearly died several times. We need creatures. They could be the difference between making it to the Land of the Gods . . . and not.

"I'm still willing to take the risk," Zane says.

"Same," Kira agrees.

I look up at Xara. "How do we get there?"

She sighs. "Stay off the main road. Even if you wanted to travel with rotted heads, the Masks will be seeking revenge. They'll hunt you down."

"So, we go through the forest?" Zane asks.

"Gods, no," Xara says, shuddering. "Avoid forests at all costs. Ancient creatures lurk within most. Others are perfectly harmless. It's hard to know the difference before it's too late." She points at the river. "Here. It flows north."

Xara must sense my apprehension, because she says, "I have a boat. You can use it."

"You would . . . give us your boat?"

She shrugs a shoulder. "I'm letting you borrow it. When you're done, it will return to me."

Before I can ask how, glasses begin to clink at the back of the bar, the sound like music. A dozen people must be working to make that much noise. I peer around her. "Do you . . . do you have employees?"

Xara smiles, and motions for us to follow. When she pushes the door to the kitchen open, the clanking intensifies. I expect to find a roomful of immortals efficiently scrubbing dishes.

But it's empty.

Glasses fly through the room. I duck, barely avoiding a mug to the head. Water splashes. Towels lift as if held by invisible hands.

I stumble back, and Xara chuckles.

"Is—is this magic?" Kira asks, clinging to the doorframe as if afraid to take any step closer.

Xara nods. "The inn was gifted to me. Enchantment is built into its very foundation. It runs itself, just like the Great Houses."

I remember her hands—the calluses. The respect of the warriors. She turns her head, long braid shifting over her shoulder, and that's when I notice markings down the back of her neck, sparkling silver lines melted right into her skin. My chest tightens. They almost look like *mine*, but no . . . they're thicker and shaped—

Like a sword.

"You're a knight," I say.

Xara tracks my gaze, and fully lifts her braid, revealing a fully illustrated hilt up her neck. The rest of the sword must run down her spine. The ink glimmers, just like metal. It's as if her weapon has been melted down and imprinted onto her skin.

She reaches back—and with a brush of her fingers, the hilt of the sword peels off, becoming solid in her hand.

My mouth drops open. *Is that an option?* Carrying this great sword in my scabbard is making my muscles ache. I'd much rather it be reduced to a tattoo.

She releases her hold, and the sword falls back into its glimmering lines.

"I was a knight. Not anymore." With that, she leads us out of the kitchen. Xara must sense the questions we're barely too polite to ask, because she adds, "I led a battalion to victory, and this was my gift." She motions to our surroundings.

"And the boat?"

Her smile speaks of a long story she'll probably never tell us. "Another gift," she says simply, her eyes glazed over with a memory. The edges of her mouth twitch.

Then she's facing us again. "If we time it right, you'll be on the water through the night and arrive the next day." She nods to herself. "Yes . . . yes, that's the best plan."

With a casual order from Xara, the kitchen gets started on packing a sack of food and filling three fresh canteens. The door opens, spitting out the filled basket when it's ready.

We fetch our weapons from the floorboards, and then we're outside again, bathing in sunlight. It's instinct to look for shade. On Stormside, I track the arc of the sun like an enemy, scavenging in certain places depending on its position in the sky. Here, fully hydrated and fed, its rays filtered through the sheen of magic, I tilt my head back and sigh, taking it all in.

It's the third day of the quest. With a creature, we have plenty of time to make it to the other side of the map.

I hope.

"Is that another imprinted weapon?" Zane asks. He's looking at Xara's fingers. There, along the side of one of her pointers, is the glimmering tattoo of a small blade. Xara runs her thumb down it quickly, like striking a match, and it flips onto her palm.

She twirls it expertly between her fingers, as if she's done it a thousand times before. "It marks me as part of an order. The Dagger Sisters, we call ourselves," she says, eyes lost in a memory. The metal sinks into her skin again.

"How do you do that?" I ask. *Can I* are the words I don't say.

She smiles at the hope in my tone. "It's a long, painful process, unfortunately. You have to be well bonded with your blade to even attempt it. It's a commitment, of sorts."

Kira examines her own weapon as we make it to the edge of the village, Xara's presence parting the crowds of curious immortals.

"Beautiful craftsmanship," Xara says, glancing at it. "May I?"

Kira hands the sword to her, and Xara smooths her fingers down the hilt. Flowers are carved delicately up its blade. There's a glittering purple stone in its grip, the same color as her eyes.

"This was made by faelings," she says, turning it over. "A long time ago."

"Faelings?" Kira asks, carefully taking the sword back.

"Forest fairies," she clarifies. "It's rare to see them nowadays, but they're some of the only safe beings in the forests. Some try to seek them out, but the woods kill travelers more often than not."

"Which forest do they live in?" I ask as we pass through the village wall. A different warrior is on watch. He nods at Xara. She nods back.

We walk down the short bridge, then take a turn before the main road, onto a light green plain.

"All of them, I suppose. Their home is enchanted. It's constantly moving, so as not to be discovered. The only people who happen upon them do so by chance, or by invitation." She looks at Kira. "It's a valuable blade, with a history, though the metal might not be of glimmering steel."

Kira frowns, and Xara shakes her head. Her words grow fierce. "That doesn't mean it isn't a great sword. Metal matters. But heart matters more. Swords grow stronger based on their wielder. They draw upon our strength . . . just as we draw upon theirs." She nods at Kira's blade. "Keep it close."

Kira grips it tightly, staring at its etchings in wonder.

"And her sword?" Zane asks, nodding toward the one on my back.

Xara doesn't even look at it. Her eyes remain on the horizon. "Hers is dangerous," she says. "Keep it sheathed. The more people who see it, the more people who will want it." She grimaces, gaze drifting toward my spine. "Immortals will do anything for better metal. Swords like that . . ."

She looks straight ahead again, as if forcing herself not to look at it. As if something within it is dragging her attention . . .

I think about the warriors in the tavern. Each taking turns. Each pulling, over and over, as if in a trance. I think about the Masks doing the same.

A babbling river breaks me out of my thoughts. It sits below us, water whispering over worn stones in a sheet of rippling silk. The only streams I've seen on Stormside are mostly dried up. This one looks close to spilling onto land.

We stop along the slanted trees lining the river. A boat is tied to one of them. It's small and made of expertly sculpted wood, with intricate designs running along its side.

Xara's expression turns grave. "No matter what, find shelter before sundown. A village, if you can. You'll be fine tonight, but for the rest of them . . ."

"Why?" I ask. "Why is night so dangerous here?"

Xara looks around, as if someone might be listening, just beyond the trees. She leans toward us and whispers, "The God of Death's demons emerge from underground at night, killing everything in their paths."

The *God of Death*. At the sound of his name, the shadows at our feet seem to lengthen. The birds stop chirping.

Still, Xara pushes on. "Even our best knights have been torn to shreds by teeth like swords." She closes her eyes. Swallows. "It wasn't always like this."

"What happened?"

She lifts a shoulder. "Only the gods know. All *I* know is, one night, everything changed. Hundreds were lost. We woke up . . . and blood was smeared everywhere. We found . . . only pieces." She cuts herself off. "The night kills even immortals. Do you understand?"

We nod.

"Good." She leans down and whispers something to the boat. Directions, maybe. She drops the pack of food and canteens inside, then motions for us to board.

Zane does without issue. Then Kira. Then me. The wood shifts beneath my feet, sending me falling onto my ass. I sit up quickly, heart in my throat.

"My boat never flips," Xara assures me. "It is no ordinary boat. You'll be safe on the water." She opens her mouth as if to say something else—then stops herself.

But there's something I need to know.

"I thought immortals were better off than us," I say, quickly. "And you are, of course . . . but the gods don't serve you either. They've damned you too."

It's not really a question. But Xara nods.

"The gods only serve themselves," she says. "Whatever legends you've heard about them, they're worse. Do yourself a favor and never cross one."

Then she unties the rope.

11

For a while, we just sit in the boat in silence.
    Kira breaks it. She turns to me, offers me her sword, and says, "If I hold my hair up, will you chop it off?"

I gape at her. "You . . . don't want it anymore?"

She sighs. "No, I do. My hair's my favorite part of myself, really." She spits out a lock that blows into her face from the breeze, her few braids now almost completely loose. "But it's getting fucking annoying."

Right. I don't know how to do this, how to be friendly, how to *be* a friend . . . I'm out of practice.

But I remember how Kira wiped the blood from my face with her scarf, without question. "Here," I say, hesitantly. "Before you choose to cut it, let me help you." I lift my hands, motioning for her to turn around.

Kira brightens. "Really?"

Before I can nod, she's settling in front of me, legs folded in front of her, sword across her lap.

Gently, I begin to undo the braids, before starting over. She tenses with even the slightest pull, so I take my time. We have plenty out here, in the middle of this river.

Zane just stares at us, reaching into the basket, taking out a flower-speckled muffin from Xara's inn, and taking a bite.

"So," Kira says, nodding toward him. "Why are you here?"

Zane just takes another bite of the muffin. Chews. Swallows. "For the magic, obviously."

She tilts her head, my fingers slipping through her hair, making me lose my place. I start again. "You're from a Great House. You live in paradise compared to the rest of us. Can't have been easy to leave everyone behind, hike down that mountain, and get east to the platform." She juts her chin forward. "So why? Why risk your life for this? And don't just say the magic."

Even though Kira's tone is slightly accusatory . . . I've been wondering the same thing. I finish one side of the braid, before moving on to the other.

Zane just leans against the side of the boat, then stretches his long legs out in front of him, feet nearly reaching us. Finally, he says, "On a clear day, at the top of our mountain, I could see the glimmer of the gates. But never anything past them. There was . . . a fog, wiping everything from view." He lifts a shoulder. "I just wanted to see what was on the other side."

Kira snorts. "You're risking dying brutally at the hands of creatures or immortals . . . for curiosity?"

He shrugs again. "The mountain is paradise, as you say, but it's cut off from the rest of the world. I've known the same small group of people my entire life. There's no advancement. No changes. Just everything we've done for centuries. Our resources will one day dry up. Everyone tries to deny it, but we've all seen the signs. The Helmhawks leaving. The mines producing less and less. I'm not the eldest. There are four brothers ahead of me in line. My life will never mean anything. Unless—"

Unless.

Zane's mountain could be transformed with magic. His motivation might not be the same as Kira's, or mine, but it doesn't make it any less true. He's trying to save his people. Even if their suffering isn't imminent, if it's anything like the rest of Stormside, it is inevitable.

He sighs, leaning back. "And I think everyone should go on a wild, transformative journey at least once in their lives."

He's probably right. "So now that you're here, what do you think of the world?" I say over Kira's shoulder as I finish the second braid, then begin weaving them together. "The world outside of your mountain?"

He shakes his head. "I'm thinking I probably should have stayed put."

I laugh first. Kira joins in. Then all three of us are shaking with laughter and perhaps a bit of regret.

"You know what? I'm not scared of dying. I'm scared of not having lived in the first place," Kira declares.

Something in me awakens at that—a foolish shred that mourns the life I might have lived, if I wasn't rushing into my almost certain death. So I decide that I'm going to drink up all the wonder of this place, while I can. As I work to finish Kira's hair, I look around, watching as the forest along the bank changes. It becomes lusher, full of trees I've only seen the skeletons of, in the bare woods of Stormside. Pines, covered in needles. Willows, hunched forever in mourning. Birches, with their curls of peeling bark. I wonder what kind of creatures lurk within these woods—and if they're watching us back.

The braid is done. I curl it up and slip it through the gap made by the two braids, just like I do for myself, again and again, until nothing else hangs down. Then I slip one pin from my own hair and use it to secure Kira's. I'm finished. She turns and beams at me, reaching up to touch my work. "I look like you now, don't I? Wonderful. How'd you get so good at this?"

"I had a sister. Once," I say, surprised by the words spilling out of me. Just like when I told her where I'm from, seconds after meeting.

I guess I just want someone to know. Because if I stop talking about where I'm from, and who I lived there with, then that's when they'll all be truly dead.

Her grin fades. She knows about what happened to my village. Everyone knows about the place that was burned down by the wrath of the gods. It was used as a warning. People whispered that we must have done something wrong to invite their fury.

"You're the only one that survived, aren't you?" she says.

"Yes."

She squeezes my hand. "If you survived that . . . you can survive anything," she says, nodding, like she's already decided my fate.

If she knew who I was hoping to go up against, I don't think she'd be so sure of that. But I nod back anyway.

"Here." Zane looks like he doesn't really know what to say, so he reaches into the basket and shoves meat pies and muffins at us. "You should . . . you should both eat."

Kira smiles wryly at him. "You don't have sisters, do you?"

"Only brothers."

She laughs loudly. "Now, look at you. Stuck with both of us." She takes a bite out of the meat pie, then says, mouth full, "Holy gods, I want a magical kitchen."

I crack a smile. "I'm sure a few drops of claimed magic would do it."

It's not why she's on this journey. We both know it. But for a few moments, it's nice to pretend that the greatest thing we need is food prepared at our every whim.

Kira hums. She leans back in the boat, lying beside Zane's legs. "Now that I'm thinking, I could also use a magical goblet that refills with wine whenever I want. *Good* wine." She looks over at Zane. "Like the type you drink up in your fancy mountain." He rolls his eyes, and she nudges against him. "What ridiculous dreams will you use drops of magic on, Sterling?"

Zane shifts. His expression is serious. But his voice is light as he says, "A magically refilling bath would be nice."

Kira groans in agreement. "A bath at all would be heavenly! One that would stay warm the whole time. Can you imagine?"

Zane grunts.

"How about you?" Kira asks, propping her head up to look over at me. "What ridiculous dream are you harboring inside, Aris?"

Several. None of which are possible. I chew my lip. "Magic in the forge would be nice," I say. "Something to mute the hammering. Make metals easier to carry . . . or keep the floors magically clean." I open my mouth, then close it, realizing that even if I somehow survive confronting the gods, I'll never be working in that forge again—at least not with Stellan.

"Maybe after this, you won't have to work in a forge at all," Kira says, her words light.

I swallow past the lump in my throat and take a bite of the muffin to keep from having to say anything else. The sugar is sour on my tongue, as I try to imagine a future beyond this journey, back on Stormside . . . but I can't. There's nothing left for me there.

There's nothing left for me anywhere.

Something hits me square on the head, and I startle, the muffin slipping from my fingers. I look up, only for another drop of water to land between my eyebrows.

Rain.

I haven't felt it in far too long, and this water . . . it's *clear.* It's cold, and clean.

I part my lips in wonder—then the rain falls in earnest, a faucet turned all the way on. *Shit.* I pick up the muffin and shove the rest of it in my mouth to keep it from crumbling. Zane rushes to cover the pack.

Kira just sits up, staring up at the sky, filling her hands and drinking from them, even though she has a full canteen of water by her hip. Her sword is still in her lap, rain dripping tears down its silver.

Wind blows my hair back, and this isn't just rain. It's turning into a storm. "We—"

The boat lurches to the side, and Zane nearly falls over. I grip the edge of the boat to keep still.

"Fuck. Hold on," Zane says. He's facing the front.

The blood drains from my face at the sight of surging whitecaps just ahead.

Before we even reach them, the boat hits a rock, shredding its bottom, and my head jerks down painfully, teeth clashing together. Then the prow rises, taking us all up—before we land roughly back against the water.

Xara said the boat never flips. I hope she's fucking right, as we jolt to the side, everything sliding. I barely keep my hold on its edge, fingers cramping and slipping against the wood. It hits another rock, turning sharply in the other direction, and for a moment, I'm weightless. Time seems to stand still as I watch all of us and our belongings lift—then fall again.

We don't have a single moment to prepare before the next current hits, sending us all flying. The basket opens midair, spilling food. The canteens soar.

But I'm not looking at them. I'm looking at my pack, which slips off my shoulder—

Right into the river.

No. Everything I worked so hard to save up for. My soap. My canteen. My bandages. My fabric. All of it but the coin in my pocket . . . *gone.*

Just when I think it can't get any worse, we hit another rock, and Xara's basket is lost.

Fuck. This. Current.

Howling wind batters my face, forcing tears from my eyes. I duck low against it, but it's like a wall, pushing me back. My body slips, but my grip holds.

Everything here is heightened. Even the storms. If I'm going to survive, I can't forget that, for even a moment.

We hit the biggest rock so far.

Kira goes flying, and I don't think. I risk my hold by grabbing her by the back of her shirt, keeping her in the boat. But not all of her.

Her sword slips out of her hands, into the water.

"No!" Her scream pierces even this tempest. Desperately, she stretches her arm to her side, palm open, the same way she did when she claimed the sword. The same way Raker called his own.

Nothing happens.

"Stop!" Kira shrieks.

The boat obeys. We all go flying as it suddenly halts. I land in the middle with a thud, bones screaming. It immediately jerks to the side, fighting the current.

"What are you doing?" Zane yells from the front.

Kira doesn't answer. She makes to throw herself off the side, before I pull her back. "We don't know what's in there," I bellow over the onslaught. "And the weather . . . you'll *drown*."

She looks back at me, tears streaming down her face, mixing with the rain. Her voice trembles. "I've—I've never been chosen by anyone. Or anything. This—this blade *chose me*. I can't leave it behind."

"What about your sister?" I say, my voice breaking on the last word.

She shakes her head. "I'll never get her the magic she needs without a weapon like this." She slips from my hold—and before I can say anything else, she's jumping over the side.

I gasp, gripping the wood, peering into the sloshing water, watching as her figure disappears.

It doesn't surface again.

A minute passes. I throw a look over my shoulder at Zane, who is clutching the sides of the boat, being tossed about wildly by the surging streams, waves crashing into the prow, and sputtering foam all around him. The boat is filling with water. We have to keep going.

She's gone. Trying to save her would be a death wish. Even if I could. Even if I could—

Metal clangs at my feet, glimmering through the deluge. *Her sword.* I rush to the side and see her hand reaching out. I take it—

But a rush of current pulls her away, past the boat. She disappears beneath the waves again.

"Follow her!" I scream, and the boat is released from its hold. I'm knocked onto my back. The wall of rain blurs my vision. I lose sight of Kira in the whitecaps.

Then I see her hand again.

I reach over the side, grazing her fingers, before she's pulled under. *No.* I strain, curling toward the water—and the boat lurches again. I fall forward.

Zane pulls me back, arm around my middle.

"Look. There she is."

Up ahead, she's clinging to a massive rock. The boat bounces back and forth before reaching it.

Zane pulls her into the boat. She gasps, retching water, her legs folded beneath her.

I crawl to her as the wood groans and rocks, fighting to stay upright. "Are you okay?"

Kira nods weakly. She grabs the hilt of her recovered sword, knuckles pale. She's freezing. There's no time to speak, no time to do anything at all but hold on as the boat races forward.

The river churns into a series of whirlpools. The rain turns into relentless throwing daggers, aimed right at us. The wind becomes a rampart. All conspire to flip the boat. Only its magic saves us. We cling to the sides. My hands grow cold and sore, but I don't let go.

Once dusk falls, the weather only worsens.

My eyes close against the storm; I curl my body to preserve as much heat as possible. I think about hot meals and warm socks and soft bedding. The *magic* my mother once told me about. All things that I might never have again, but I imagine them, until the river finally smooths. Until the rain thins.

I finally look over at Kira. Without the constant rain and water splashing into the boat, I now see it.

Red, puddling beneath her.

"Why didn't you tell us?" I demand, rushing forward, searching for where she's bleeding.

Her legs. One of them was shredded by a rock.

I take a strip of ripped fabric from her pants, and wrap it around and around, as tightly as it will go. She looks up at me with heavy-lidded eyes.

They close.

"No," I say, clutching her hands. They're freezing. "Stay awake."

It's almost dawn. We'll be at our destination soon. I'll be able to wrap the wounds better. We could find her help. But she needs to stay awake.

Her eyes close again. I pinch her fingers.

"Tell me—tell me something," I plead. I said the same words to my sister as she was dying.

Kira goes quiet. I pinch harder.

"Tell me about your sister," I say.

At that, she smiles. "She's—" Her voice fades away.

"She's what?"

"She's a terrible liar," she says weakly. "Everyone always beats her at cards."

I nod. "What else?"

Quiet. A rock jostles the boat.

My voice rises. "*What else?*"

She takes a shaking breath. "She . . . she hates lying, but she lies for me. She lies when she says she's had enough to eat. She lies to the neighbors about the firewood missing from their backyards." She swallows. "She—she lied in front of a guard and kept me from the jails when I was accused of stealing food."

Her eyes glisten as they open again and hold mine. I don't drop her gaze, gripping her fingers tighter, and she squeezes back.

"She's only twelve, but she's *so smart*. I used to steal her books from the ruins of an ancient house. It had been almost completely looted, but no one cared about the books, of course. Every time I would go out thieving, I would bring one back. She would be waiting with the most delicious food. Somehow, she made potatoes taste good without salt. I can't explain it." Her sigh shakes her whole body. "I would give anything for her potato soup. She puts—she puts some sort of pepper in it."

"You'll have that soup," I say, putting both of her hands between mine, trying to give her some warmth. "What happened to her?"

Kira frowns. "Our mother—she was addicted to hemdrake. She didn't stop using it when she was with child . . . and my sister was born weak. Frail. My mother abandoned her at the outskirts of town, next to a forest, hoping the wolves would get her. I snuck out and brought her back. I began stealing milk and fed her every day. She gripped my finger—like this." She wraps her hand around my pointer finger. "And those eyes . . . they looked at me like I was the only person in the world. And I was . . . for her. I still am."

She shakes her head. "The drug killed my mother soon after, and there we were, alone. She was always feeble. She couldn't leave the house, but she was smart and capable and began weaving for money. Between that and the thieving, we carved out a life. But then . . . she started having the same signs my mother did. Shortened breath. Uncontrollable shaking. I saved everything I made from stealing to bring a medic to our home, but he said she's beyond help. Her lungs are too small. She'll suffocate to death one day soon. The only hope—"

"Is magic," I finish.

She nods. "I knew the Questral was approaching. I promised a merchant a portion of my winnings if they took her in. They did. I didn't tell her until the last day, and you—you should have heard how she screamed at me. How she told me she could live with her own death but not mine . . ."

She looks up at me. Her eyes are glassy and dejected.

"You are not going to die," I say, gripping her hand tighter. "Her name. Say it."

Tears stream down her face. "Anise. Her name is Anise. I named her—named her after the flowers my mother abandoned her on." She laughs. "There are so few flowers on our side. But there they were . . . a patch of them . . . as if they were holding her."

I nod, throat tight. "Anise will get medicine. Anise will get better. *You* will survive this."

I have no business saying these words, or caring if she *does* survive this. But I do. *I do.*

Her gaze locks onto mine. Something in her changes. Firms. The fire in me spreads to her, like inviting a person to share the heat of a hearth, and I see the resolve set in her face. "I will survive this," she whispers.

"*You will survive this*," I echo.

She holds on to my hand with the strength of a person who hasn't already lost a good portion of her blood. She doesn't let go, until our boat knocks against the riverbank—and stops.

"We're here," Zane says softly.

The sun is creeping over the horizon. Kira is still clutching my hand. We lift her out of the boat, and Zane curses as he sees the extent of her injuries. Her leg—it's ruined. Her knee buckles, and we catch her. We all take one step together. She screams with pain.

"Stop," she says, shaking her head, her hair still pinned back. "You both—you *know*," she chokes out. "You know I'll never make it. You know I'm going to put you both at risk and—and it'll be for nothing."

"I'm not leaving you here," I say, voice firm. I couldn't save my sister, but I will save hers. "We will reach the end—together."

Zane looks over at me. He says nothing, but I can read it in his face.

I look down at her leg. Even if we can heal the cuts, she won't be able to walk alone, let alone run.

"Aris," she says, voice low and serious.

"No." I remember my sister telling me to leave her. Telling me to save myself. My eyes burn with the memory. I close them. "You will survive this. *You will.*"

"*Aris*," she repeats, and it might as well be my sister speaking. "We made a pact. Remember?"

The quest must come first.

I open my eyes. She grips my hand. "Put me in the boat. It will sail back to Xara. She'll help me get back to the gates—I know she will."

"But your sister—"

"You're going to make another pact," she says, her voice firm. Her green eyes are blazing, searing into mine. "You're going to promise me . . . if you make it back . . . you will get magic to my sister."

It isn't a fair request. I've only known her a handful of days. I don't even plan on going back. But if somehow I do . . .

"I promise," I say, meaning it.

Zane and I walk her to the boat, which sits there as if waiting for a command to be let loose again. We lay her inside. She looks up at me, on her back . . . and I can't help but feel like I'm looking into a grave.

She grabs my hand again. "I believe you," she says, tears slipping down her face. In her other hand, she holds on to the hilt of her sword. The purple gem sparkles.

The boat departs from the riverside, fighting upstream. Our fingers slip past each other. And it reminds me of the night I lost my sister.

12

"Let's go," I say roughly to Zane, after washing my bloody hands in the river. I walk past him.

Bury it down. I try, with every step I fight to forget, because crying would only slow my journey. My emotions are only distractions.

The quest must come first.

We spot the tree from miles away. It's sticking up from the center of the forest, its trunk thicker and taller than a tower.

But that's not the part that makes my breath catch. No, it's the ring of flying creatures, soaring above its crown so quickly, their scales turn into smears of light.

Any of them could help us finish this quest.

First, though, we have to reach them.

"How are we supposed to climb that?" I ask Zane, taking in the height of the tree. "I've never—I don't have much experience climbing." The highest I've ever been is up to the ruins on the hill.

He glances over at me. "Lucky for you, I know a thing or two about it."

The Beast Tree's roots begin at the edge of the forest. We follow them like a map. They're enormous, winding in and out of the ground like a massive stitch all the way to the town-sized shadow beneath the oak.

I swallow as I stare up at the hundreds of feet above, not knowing how the hell I'm going to climb this.

Every hard thing is conquered in steps. That's what Stellan would say. I just have to be brave enough to take the first one.

With a steadying breath, I do—before Zane roughly drags me out of the way, grip tight enough to bruise. "*What—*"

A body lands right where I was standing.

The limbs are twisted. The bones are snapped like twigs. Blood pours out of a shattered jaw. He's one of the challengers. One of Cadoc's friends.

"They're here," I breathe. They're trying to get creatures. They're failing.

Fear sinks into my chest, but it's quickly smothered by fury.

He killed Stellan. He stole his blade.

I look up. *He's somewhere up there.*

I make the decision right then. When I get the chance, I'm going to kill him.

"Look," Zane says, and that's when I see all the bodies, spread out in a ring that reflects the band of winged creatures above. Challengers. A half dozen of them. Clearly, we weren't the only ones with this idea. Did immortals tell them about the tree? Was it written on pages they brought over? I look away from the broken bones and blood, Xara's warning flashing through my mind.

She didn't think this was a smart plan. But we made it too far to turn around now.

I climb the pile of roots, then press my hand against the bark. It's as rough as the stone pillars of the ruins, ancient—yet still alive. I look up, squinting through buttery beams of sunlight, taking in the short, twisted branches above. They get thicker and longer higher up, until they're as sturdy as bridges.

"Ready?" Zane says next to me.

"Not at all." *Here goes nothing.* I jump, trying to reach the lowest branch. My fingers don't even brush the bark.

Well, fuck. I look around for something to step on.

Zane takes a few steps back. Then he runs, jumps, and buries his ax into the branch. It stays put, even as he groans, using his weapon for purchase as he pulls himself up, inch by inch.

When he's over the side, he turns and offers his hand.

No going back now.

I run and jump just like he did, reaching out—

And his fingers lock around mine.

I gasp with pain as my entire body hangs below me, just like it did during the Culling. Zane groans again, then pulls me up, little by little, until I collapse next to him.

"We can't do that the whole time," I tell him through ragged breaths. There are limits to what a body can take, especially after everything we've done since the platform.

He looks up. "It's a good thing we won't have to."

I follow his gaze, and relief rushes through me. Stairs are carved into the bark, wrapping around and around the trunk in massive spirals.

That relief quickly curdles behind my ribs. Entire steps are missing. The way they're slanted makes it almost impossible to climb down. I swallow. There are only two ways off the Beast Tree—on the back of a creature . . . or falling to your death.

Zane motions me forward.

I take the first step.

There's no railing, of course. If I lose my balance, I fall. I don't look over the edge. I just focus on every stair and the weight of my blade clanging against my back with every movement.

It claimed me. It saw something in me worth saving. Hopefully, during my plunge, a creature will see the same.

I take another step—and a scream sounds to my side, sending me stumbling forward in shock.

My knees hit the stairs, pain spiraling up my legs. I turn toward the noise, just in time to see a blur of color. It's followed by a thud.

Another challenger who didn't get picked.

Pulse racing, I straighten and keep climbing. The screams happen every few hours. I don't look again. I keep my gaze on the next stair, and my hand against the trunk, leaning part of my weight against it.

Sweat spills a river down my back as the heat intensifies, then fades away. At least the rain didn't reach these steps. I would have slipped off hours ago. My worn boots manage to hold on. My stomach grumbles, but I ignore it. My throat is dry, but I'm used to that.

I just keep climbing.

The melodic screeches above, from winged creatures, get louder, and that's how I know we're getting close. I make it a few more steps, before finally taking a break, bracing my palm against the bark, breathing heavily.

Fuck. If I didn't already hate stairs from my near-death encounter yesterday . . . I despise them even more now. My calves burn. My lungs feel like they're shriveling up. I glance to my side and see we've reached the thick, higher branches. *Finally.*

I risk a look over my shoulder. Zane's leaning against his knees, shaking his head. His gaze flicks up to mine. "Stairs suck, don't they?"

"They really fucking do," I say, and he cracks a smile.

I almost smile back.

But that's when I see movement in the foliage in the closest branch. A rustle, then . . .

Eyes. Blinking back at me.

"Zane—"

"I see them."

Slowly, a creature creeps forward, out of the shadows of the leaves . . . and my shoulders melt. *Oh.* It's just a small, rounded fuzzy animal with big, sad eyes. It looks at us curiously.

Cute. I turn back around, break over. I take another step.

And the circle of fur launches itself at me, mouth open, revealing razor-sharp teeth.

Shit. I move at the last moment, and it hits the trunk. It slides down, before unveiling claws that find purchase, carving lines into the thick wood. It turns to look at me in a flash, growling.

"Really?" I yell. "The climbing wasn't hard enough?"

I bolt up the steps, Zane at my heels. Another one launches itself, just missing my face. Its jaw snaps, and I stumble to the side before finding my footing again.

There's a missing step ahead. I jump over it, teetering, barely dodging another set of flying teeth. I turn to warn Zane.

But he's looking at the creatures. He misses the step, loses his balance—

And falls over the edge.

NO.

I lunge forward.

And catch his hand. He nearly pulls me over the side with him, but I manage to dig my sword into the stairs, rooting us.

"Don't let go," Zane says, dark eyes wide.

"I wasn't planning on it," I say through my teeth. My shoulder screams. My arm is at risk of getting pulled out of its socket.

Then one of the creatures leaps from the branches, and bites Zane's shoulder, teeth going right through muscle.

His yell of agony echoes through the tree. His fingers slip—

I grip them harder. I lean back, kick the creature off him and clench my jaw as I pull and *pull*. He's too heavy. Especially with his weapon.

"You—you have to let it go," I say, straining, one hand on my blade, keeping us on the tree, the other clutching his.

He knows what I mean. He shakes his head. "I—I can't."

"I don't—I don't want to have to let you go," I say, my voice a ragged whisper.

I will let you go are the words I won't say. But he knows. *He knows.*

We made a pact.

Zane's eyes harden. I hope he isn't going to try to use his ax to stay on, when doing so could crumble the entire step below my feet. He reaches behind him . . . and drops it. It falls, then crashes. But not far. We both hear it bury itself in one of the branches below.

It's not lost. Not completely. Though climbing down would be its own death sentence.

I pull him up without the added weight, then collapse against the steps, gasping. The creatures shriek. They're still rising from the branches, right at us.

Zane turns. "My ax—"

"Come on," I say, urging him forward.

He follows. Mercifully, he follows. We run up each step, panting, until finally the creatures give up their chase. We don't stop. Not until the branches thin—and the sun is searing my scalp as we surface.

The top. We made it. The crown of the tree is as steady as the ground, thick leaves and branches solid below our boots. I take a tentative few steps.

A shriek peels through the air, loud as thunder. I look up and my jaw goes slack.

The ring of creatures is a mesmerizing band of color as the animals bleed together, following a single path. *Dragons.* Most of the creatures are dragons, of all different shades. Some are iridescent, their scales gleaming beneath the sun. Others are spiked. Some have wings that look like shards of stained glass. Their sizes range from large as a hill to small as a cart.

Some of the creatures aren't dragons at all. Some are massive beaked birds.

"Helmhawks," Zane whispers, sinking to his knees. "This—this is where they went." His eyes glisten. "A century years ago . . . during the Questral. That's when they left. I should have known . . ."

I put my hand on his shoulder. *We did it. We made it here.*

But we're not alone.

A group of challengers waits by the edge of the treetop, at the fringe of its greenery. I instinctively reach for my sword—but Cadoc and his friends are not among them.

Did they get creatures? Did they fall? I didn't look at the rest of the bodies while we climbed.

Slowly, we approach the edge, keeping a healthy distance from the others.

"Make the leap," one of the challengers says. She's tall, with dark skin, wearing a baldric filled with daggers of various high metals. She's speaking to a tan man with brown hair, who has a silver sword strapped to his spine. "I believe in you."

Their foreheads press together, and they stare into each other's eyes, speaking in a wordless language that I imagine was learned over a thousand scattered moments. Finally, he nods. Straightens.

Without a single look back, he jumps off the side of the treetop.

I race to the edge to watch what happens. The other challengers barely spare me a glance. The man falls, falls—

Shit.

My heart is in my throat as the woman at my side sinks to her knees. Her lips part in a strangled cry. Her hands grip the thick leaves below us.

But then a winged creature swoops down from the ring high above, fast as lightning—and catches him. The woman jumps to her feet. Tears of joy slide down her face.

The man emerges on the back of a spiked dragon. He beams at the woman, and their group erupts in cheers. His smile is triumphant. He unsheathes his sword and lifts it to the sky in celebration.

Then he jerks forward as an arrow pierces through his chest. He looks down, slowly, as if in shock. The yells go quiet.

His body slumps forward. He slips right off the creature.

This time, the dragon doesn't save him. The woman's cry shreds my senses.

He hits the ground, and one of Cadoc's friends surfaces from the lower branches. He leaps onto the back of the dragon—and flies away.

My blood goes cold.

Cadoc and his friends couldn't get creatures by leaping. Now they're *taking* them by killing those who have bonded. Just like stealing swords.

I look over at Zane, the woman's weeping swallowing the world. Even if we don't fall to our deaths ... Cadoc's archers will kill us.

He looks down in the direction of where the arrow came from. Just a few branches below. Then he looks back at me. "Go. I'll deal with the archer."

I frown. "Wait—"

He doesn't. He strides back toward the stairs, and I race after him. I catch his wrist. "Zane. You can't go alone. They'll kill you."

His face is as serious as I've ever seen it. "I'm getting my ax."

He makes to move, but I pull one more time. "The reason you gave us for making the quest," I say, the words spilling out of me. "That wasn't the only reason, was it?"

It shouldn't be important. For some reason, it is.

A flicker of surprise passes across his tanned face. His dark brows lift. He looks at me for a second, before saying, "No. It wasn't." Then, he slips from my grip. A moment later, he's disappearing beneath the leaves again.

I wait. I wait for him to come back. Wait for some sort of sign that he was able to reach the archer. No one else jumps, so I can't be sure. They're all just mourning.

Zane doesn't have a weapon, at least not until he recovers his ax. Did Cadoc and his friends get to him first?

The sun isn't overhead anymore. It's rapidly sinking. I wonder if we would be safe up here from those night demons. If maybe we can wait out Cadoc's friends.

I just keep sitting.

Until the spot beneath me begins to tremble. I stand and take a few steps back, away from the moving branches.

Just before nothing short of a giant bursts through the treetop. His eyes glimmer when he sees me. When he sees my sword.

Pagnus Ender.

Fuck.

By the time I'm on my feet, he's already traveled multiple yards. He has a new sword, and it's taller than I am. It rings through the open air as he unsheathes it.

Fuck!

He swings it down, and I roll to the side, barely missing being sliced in half. The branches below crack at the contact. My breath spills out of me.

No time to think, just move. I unsheathe my own sword with both hands, then launch forward. Pagnus bellows as I stab his leg, my metal piercing two layers of armor, right through bone.

He falls to his knees.

I turn around just as Cadoc and his friends emerge. My eyes desperately search for both archers, and I only find one. The other isn't with them.

Did Zane kill him? Did he kill Zane?

Arms straining, I force my blade from Pagnus's bone. I take a step back. Another. The archer points his arrow at me. I dive past Pagnus, still on his knees, using him as cover. He roars as the arrow buries itself through his armor.

I spring up before he can cut me down. Arrows slice past both my ears. They barely miss me. I run until I reach the edge. And then there's nowhere else to go.

"You have to know you have no chance," Cadoc says, stepping forward. He rips the bow and arrow away from his friend.

He wants my sword. *He* must be the one to kill me.

Just like he killed Stellan.

Another step. "I'll give you one more opportunity. Sink to your knees and beg me for mercy, and I might just give it to you. If you hand me your sword . . . I might just *keep* you."

I spit in his direction.

He sighs. "Very well." In a flash, he raises the bow. Docks the arrow. Pulls back. There's a twang as the arrow is released, headed right toward my heart.

It's the last thing I see as I turn and jump.

13

No creature is coming to save me.
 When the man leapt, the dragon instantly parted from its pack. I hear nothing as I fall, nothing but the howling wind.

It stings my eyes, burns my nostrils, whips against my cheeks, as if in punishment for my being so very stupid.

I got lucky with the sword. No creature wants to claim me. Why would they? My intentions are not pure. They are not honorable.

My heart is a pile of ash in my chest, made of pure vengeance and regret. I mean to destroy this land. I mean to claw my way into the sky, pull the gods down from their clouds, and paint the world with their blood.

So close, I think. I got so close.

But close isn't ever enough.

Roaring fills my ears as the ground rushes up to meet me. It's stone on this side of the tree. Pure stone with sparkling veins. It would almost be beautiful if it wasn't about to be my grave.

I close my eyes and hear the rock shatter just before darkness swallows everything.

DEATH FEELS LIKE flying.

I'm carried by a wind, and it's almost peaceful. Almost beautiful. Until the pain hits me like a battering ram.

"I'm not supposed to hurt anymore," I croak, surprised by my own voice. My eyes open, and I realize I am—somehow—very much alive. The stars blink back at me, diamonds threaded through a dark quilt. The moon is just a fingernail crescent.

I'm in the sky.

I'm flying.

I try to move my hand. It takes a few moments for the sensation to reach my fingers again, and then—

Scales. Beneath me. I turn, only to see a shredded silver wing.

A dragon. I'm on a dragon.

It saved me.

It takes several tries to get up, and then I'm promptly blown back down by a gust of wind. My spine hits the scales, tearing the breath from my lungs. Choking, I turn carefully, clutching ridges, until I'm on my stomach.

I sort through my memories, trying to make sense of this. None of the dragons above claimed me, I know that for certain. I remember the ground fracturing . . .

It couldn't have been me who did that. I would be in pieces. The dragon must have been below. It must have risen, just like the sword, to meet me.

Not that I want to complain about someone saving my life . . . but why?

As if feeling that I'm awake, the dragon begins to fly lower, and my sweaty hands fight for purchase again. *Shit.* I grit my teeth as it soars down, right toward a field. The dragon lands smoothly, but my body slams against its back, then slides. I barely manage to stay on.

The moon is still out. It's dark.

My chest clenches with panic, just before I spot the sun, just beginning to crest the horizon. The dragon flew all through the night. For hours. For *me*.

It sighs loudly beneath me, as if the journey cost it something. I finally stand, wincing at the pain in my bones, grateful I somehow didn't break any. Then, I slide down its leg and promptly fall on my ass.

The dragon is staring at me.

It has large silver eyes, and scales like a mosaic of moonlight. A crown of spikes adorns its head, continuing down its neck, between a set of glimmering spiral horns.

"You—you saved me," I say from the ground, like an idiot.

It just breathes heavily through its nostrils, like it was an awful imposition.

I stand slowly, studying the dragon up close, aware that it could kill me a thousand ways before I even reached for the sword I can barely carry. But it wouldn't have saved me and flown all this way if it planned to kill me . . . right?

Its head is larger than my body, and its body is larger than a house, but it's not the largest dragon. There were bigger ones in the sky above the Beast Tree. Still, despite its relatively small size, it has an energy around it, just like my sword.

Its color is the most special part of all.

"You're silver, like me," I say, pulling down my collar. Showing it what I've never shown anyone but Stellan and my family before.

The dragon dips its head to my level. I should stumble back—but I take a step closer. I extend my hand, aware the creature could eat it, or incinerate it, in a moment.

Instead—it bows into my touch.

All at once, a spark jolts through my arm, down to my feet. A connection, just like the one I formed with my sword. A light erupts from its forehead in the shape of a star, which fades into a glimmering scar.

I don't know what it means. All I know is that this creature is the reason I'm not splattered across rock right now.

"Thank you for not letting me die," I say. The dragon huffs through its nostrils. It flares out its wings.

The beautiful silk-like silver webbing is shredded.

I gently touch one of them, and the dragon makes a warning sound.

"What happened to you?" I ask. The dragon just looks at me. The star on its forehead glimmers again and somehow . . . somehow, I know it's a girl.

"Do you have a name?"

I don't know what I'm expecting. Nothing, really. Which is exactly what I get. That doesn't stop me from talking, though. Apparently, this is how lonely I am.

"I'm Aris. From Silverside. It's on Stormside, past the gates. I'm here on a quest to reach the gods."

She just blinks at me.

Then, she shifts onto her side, as if she's resting.

Right. Of course she's tired. As she sleeps, I take out the crumpled map from my pocket. Only when it's unfurled do I remember Zane.

Zane. Was he able to find his weapon? Did he reach the Helmhawks?

He doesn't have the map now.

I close my eyes as another thought clenches my heart and mind.

Kira. Floating away in a boat. She'll also be okay. I say it confidently to myself, as if I can will it to be true.

Circumstances change in moments. This map is one of my greatest assets. My dragon is asleep, and it's not like I'm going anywhere without her. Carefully, I sit, lean against one of her legs, and decide to memorize the map, just in case I lose it.

The way to the gods is treacherous. There are several mountain ranges. Forests with various names and shading. Wide fields. Bogs. Countless villages. Stretches of land that seem uninhabited. And there it is again, the City on Fire. I frown. Could it possibly be on fire? Or has it been burned away, just like my own home?

I draw the entire thing in the dirt with my sword, arm straining with each stroke. I memorize every name. Every peak and valley. Then, I erase it. I make it again from memory. Check my work. Try again. Again, until it grows tedious.

Then, I finally allow myself to study my glorious blade.

Every moment since I claimed it has been full of danger. Or I've been too tired to do anything but sleep. Now . . . I have a few seconds to simply admire it.

The hilt is storm-silver, with intricate etchings that are so small, so precise, I need to squint to see the details. Its pommel is sharpened into a point. Its cross-guard juts out like two wings. A diamond is buried between them. The entire piece almost looks like the front of a crown.

"Masterful," I whisper. I make weapons. I pride myself on my focus, and the meticulous way I carve metal. It's the only task that can truly quiet my mind and sorrow.

Still, even if I had years—even if I had *lifetimes*—I could never make anything like this.

The blade itself is sparkling, otherworldly Starside steel. It glimmers as if a million diamonds and stars were melted down to make it.

"Why me?" I ask it, and I must be out of my mind, asking questions of beings and things that will never answer.

The blade—it glints. And I really must be losing it, because it almost feels like a response.

"Maybe you should have chosen someone who could actually get you off the ground," I say, through my teeth, as I stand and use both arms to lift it. Every single inch up feels like its own battle. Without panic running through my blood, it feels impossible to even get it to my waist.

I need to learn. This sword will help me reach the end of this . . . but only if I can use it.

The dragon watches as I fall into my stance, the one Stellan taught me. I lift my sword again, using my core and legs to ground me. It helps, a little. But this sword is heavier than anything I'm used to.

I clench my jaw. Pretend that there is an enemy. I slice up through the air, and the weight sends me forward, until I end up skewering the ground.

The noise the dragon makes sounds almost like a laugh.

I glare up at her. "I'm trying," I say.

Then I tug and tug at the ground, *trying* to get my sword out of the dirt. I'm sure I look like an utter fool. I pull so hard that I end up stumbling backward and falling on my ass.

This time, the dragon does laugh, a huff that feels like steam upon my skin.

I take a deep breath. Settle myself.

And try again.

The dragon watches as I cut invisible enemies to ribbons, both arms fighting to hold the metal. As I stumble more times than I don't. As I fall more times than I can count. As I get up. Again. Again.

I'm practicing advancing, feigning blocking hits, when, in a flash, silver is hitting my own. I gasp, stumbling—only to see that the dragon has launched her tail at me.

For a moment, fear grips my heart. I think this dragon has grown tired of my inferiority and is about to skewer me with her spikes.

But no—with an impatient growl, I see that the dragon . . . she's helping me train.

Her tail battles with my sword, lightly striking. It's thicker than my entire body, but it clashes just like a weapon. It moves as fast as one.

And having an opponent, having someone to practice against . . . it helps. It helps me find my energy. Find my strength.

My arms tremble. I can't get the sword up high enough, but the dragon doesn't give me a break. She doesn't go easy on me. She strikes again and again, and I'm forced to haul the metal up as high as I can to escape the wrath of her tail.

I steel myself and fight. I'm strong. I can master this sword, just like I've mastered plenty of impossible things. Step by step. Hour by hour.

We duel until finally my sword slips from my hands. The dragon's tail stops just short of me. She looks me over and huffs with something like approval.

I sink to the ground with exhaustion.

With a sigh, the dragon curls herself around me.

"What do you eat?" I ask the dragon hours later, when it feels like I can move again.

At that question she gets up, and I'm knocked onto her back in a flash. Before I can recover my stolen breath, she's in the air.

"You can't just—" I cough, sputtering. "You *can't just*—"

She looks at me over her shoulder, as if to say, *I'm a dragon. I can do whatever the fuck I want.*

That smug look shuts me up. I grip her scales and see where she might take me.

The air is cold up here. It feels like flying through an icy river, without fear of drowning. I peer over the side and forget to breathe.

This far up, the land looks like the weaver's quilts—cut into patches. Forests I've been told to fear are just streaks of green. Mountains that would have taken days to scale are just daggers, dug into the ground.

Stellan taught me never to trust anyone. But all I can do up here is trust. If this dragon shifts to the side, I'm dead. If she decides her food is *me*, there's nothing I can do about it. That doesn't scare me. No. Because she saved me. I trust her, and it means I don't just have to count on myself anymore. Someone is leading the way. Someone's got me.

We fly for less than an hour before she begins her descent. This time, I hold on better, and only slightly bruise my ass when she lands.

We're in the center of a small field, at the base of a mountain, in front of a sparkling gray rockface.

I look around, confused. It's . . . empty. There aren't any creatures roaming about. I can't hear anything. I slide off my dragon and onto my feet, then pause. Listen.

Nothing.

"What—"

The dragon turns in a flash of silver. With a thunderous whip of her spiked tail, the stone begins to fall away, revealing cluster after cluster of glimmering red gems. Rubies? My mouth goes dry. I inch forward, blinking quickly as if this could be some sort of illusion. *Priceless.* These gems must be worth enough to feed a quarter of Stormside.

My dragon lowers her neck—

And devours the stones, teeth crunching them into powder.

I watch, dumbfounded, as the wall slowly goes gray again, picked clean. Only then does my dragon sit back, tired, having had her fill.

"You eat . . . gemstones?" I ask, incredulous. "You're going to be an expensive creature, aren't you?" She huffs as if she's saying, *Look at me. Were you expecting anything less?* I frown. "Your diet. Is that why you were underground? Do all dragons eat precious stones?"

She doesn't answer, of course.

I sigh. "Strange creature," I say. By the way she nuzzles up against my side, she takes it as a compliment.

Unlike the dragon, I don't eat rubies. It doesn't take long for my own stomach to grumble. After a few minutes, my dragon seems to tire of the sound. She sighs, then lowers her neck. *Come,* the motion says. Then we're off again.

I understand now why the writer of the journal said a creature was so crucial to this journey. My dragon knows these lands better than a map ever could. With her, I likely don't need a map at all. Before long, she's landing in the center of a forest.

Red is everywhere, just like the rubies. But instead of gemstones . . . these are berries. I slip off my dragon and grab handfuls greedily, smelling them for a moment, then shoving them into my mouth, eating just as quickly as my dragon did. I close my eyes and groan. *Sweeter than honey. Sweeter than anything I've ever tasted.*

I eat until my stomach twists in pain, and then I gather the rest to keep for later. "Thank you," I say, offering some to the dragon.

Her huff says, *I don't eat anything as pedestrian as fruit.*

Very well, then. More for me.

The sun is almost setting.

My dragon takes off into the sky, and I grip her scales. We glide like that through the pinks and oranges, flying through the sunset. Tears prick my eyes. I'm not alone. Not anymore. She is going to take care of me.

We are going to take care of each other.

My chest is flush against her back. I can hear her heartbeat somewhere deep inside. It's in sync with mine.

"Thank you," I say, because I'm not sure I did before. "For giving me a second chance."

Her chest rumbles beneath me, a response.

"I never thought I would do anything like this," I tell her, my words being swallowed by the wind. I huff a cruel laugh as I think of all the impossible things I've done in the last few days. "I was never brave, not really. I would run into my parents' room almost every night, as a child. Every creak of the wood of the house scared me. But then . . . my sister came, and I realized I needed to be brave for her. So, I was. I *tried*, and—"

Sometimes trying isn't enough.

I go quiet, wondering if the dragon heard me at all, but then her chest rumbles again. She hears me. She's *listening*.

So, I keep going. "What I'm trying to say is I never thought I would leap from a mountainous tree. Or wield a sword. Or race toward certain death." I smile, a little. "I never thought I would fly through a sunset."

I reach down to brush her scales—

And jolt back as she shudders.

She screams, and the sound doesn't just pierce the sky. It lances through *me*. I look down to see if I've been struck, but no. Just her.

There's an arrow through her side. It's long, sparkling metal. Starside steel. Strong enough to go through her scales.

A roar rattles the skies.

Then a monstrous dragon like a barbed shadow blocks out the rest of the sinking sun. He's twice as large as mine. He parts his jaws in another bone-rattling shriek, then dips, revealing his rider, holding a bow.

Cadoc.

Fury flames through my bones. He killed Stellan. Now, he's wounded my dragon.

How was he able to claim such a creature? Did he kill its original rider? If dragons are anything like swords, the connection must be accepted both ways.

Which means this beast is just as wicked as Cadoc.

Everything in me wants to kill him. But I can feel my dragon's panic as if it's my own. We won't survive this fight. I grip her scales. "Go," I say, and she rushes down, fast as lightning, but it's useless.

The creature is beside us in a moment. Wind howls in my ears as I turn to see Cadoc, grinning.

"First, I'll take your sword. Then I'll take your dragon," he yells through the wind. "I'm going to feed it to mine." His dragon turns his head. Through the beast's dark scales, red rises. Orange. Like a sunset spreading through his stomach. *Fire.*

I gasp just before a column of flames shoots right at me.

My dragon lifts her wing at the last moment, blocking the flames like a magnificent shield.

I can feel her pulse quickening—the move has cost her. Some of the fire goes through the thick shreds of her wings, setting them ablaze.

"Down!" I scream. "Go down! We can't win up here."

He's larger, and faster. Perhaps lower, in the cover of the trees, we have a chance at escaping him.

At first, I think my dragon either doesn't hear me or isn't going to listen. Then, just as Cadoc's beast opens his maw again, fire rising, she nose-dives like a shooting star, right into the forest.

Fire paints the sky like a second bleeding sun. We crash through the trees, branches snapping, dirt ballooning all around us, and land with a bone-splintering thud.

Then the woods go quiet.

Everything hurts. It doesn't matter. My dragon is injured. The fire through its wings is out, but I can smell the burned flesh.

The arrow is buried close to where I sit, and I lean around, snap its end—and slowly slide it out. She tenses. The scale the arrow hit is now missing.

I'm going to kill Cadoc. *I'm going to fucking kill him.* But not today.

I slip off her back and face her. Her eyes are looking in all directions. She's focused, listening with her superior hearing.

She goes still, and I know what that means. They're close. They're coming.

"He wants me," I say.

She looks at me almost in warning, as if she could possibly anticipate what I'm about to say.

"You're injured. That dragon—he'll tear you to pieces. He'll burn you to ashes."

She huffs steam out of her nostrils. But that's the extent of her power. She doesn't have fire. She doesn't stand a chance.

A shriek tears through the skies, just above us.

They're here.

There's no time. I lean forward, my forehead against hers, and she lets me. I think about all the people lost because of me. I won't lose anyone else.

"Go now. He'll see you're without a rider. He'll chase me instead of you. I'll be fine. *Go*."

She doesn't move an inch.

The forest trembles as the monstrous dragon lands nearby. "*Go*," I say, my voice breaking on the word. "I will find you. I promise. But for now—for *both of us*—go."

She looks at me with an intensity I don't think I'll ever forget. Silver eyes. The star on her forehead gleams.

Then she's gone. She shoots up into the sky. I hear yelling. I tense, watching.

But no one chases her.

They're going to chase me.

I run.

There's more movement. More creatures approaching. I see them in the sky, through the treetops, a mess of wings.

Cadoc and his friends have all claimed creatures. They're all hellbent on getting my weapon.

The forest floor trembles as they land, one by one.

"You can't hide forever," a voice calls, close by. "Night is approaching. And you're going to be trapped on the ground."

Fuck.

In my attempt to save my dragon, I forgot the simplest rule of this side: Be anywhere but outside at night.

I shoot a glance at the horizon. The orb of the sun is completely gone—only its smear remains. And even that is weakening.

I run faster.

Suddenly, a pillar of flame charges through the forest, roaring like a beast, burning everything in its path.

The fools are going to try to trap me. They're going to try to burn their way to me.

If I can just survive until nightfall, they'll have to take off into the sky, right? But then I'll still be here, in this burning forest. Without a plan.

Another roar. Flames getting closer, lighting up everything. I run through the burning trees, racing, panting as I look behind me.

And nearly crash into the side of a rocky cliff. I look up—and there's an opening. A cave? All I see is a place to hide. A vantage point. Can the night demons climb? Will I be safe here?

Behind me, the trees rustle as if something is tearing through them. Getting closer.

It seems my choice has been made for me.

Dirt lodges beneath my nails as I scale up the rock face, fear melting down my spine as I hope the trees don't part and they don't see me here, vulnerable, on the side of this cliff.

The sword is heavy on my back, weighing me down, but soon enough I'm reaching into air—the opening.

I haul myself inside and scramble to my feet. I turn to look out into the forest below, and swing my scabbard to the front, my hand curled around the hilt, ready to unsheathe my weapon.

I swallow.

They've made a maze of the woods. Long lines of crackling fire burn everything in their path. Smoke curls into the crimson-brushed sky. My heart hammers, remembering. Everything is burning. Just like it did that night. *That night.*

Leaves fall in balls of flame. Branches crash down and ignite the forest floor.

Everything alive and beautiful is gone. *Gone.*

A brutal command echoes through the forest. *"Find her."* Cadoc.

I take a step back, moving farther into the cave, and tense. Somehow, I feel it, prickling the back of my neck—an awareness.

I'm not alone.

With trembling hands, I slowly unsheathe my sword, inch by inch, and hold it in front of my face. In its reflection is a towering shadow right behind me. A monster in human form.

Harlan Raker.

14

His armor gleams silver. His own sword is not drawn, though I know it could be in just seconds.

An instinctual fear grips my bones, everything in me telling me to *run*. Run where? I'm surrounded by enemies.

I wonder which is worse. A burning forest full of challengers and dragons hunting me down . . . or Harlan Raker?

Definitely Harlan Raker.

Still, I don't move an inch. I just stare at his reflection in my blade, metal trembling.

"Leave" is all he says, in a deep, gravelly voice forged from the strongest steel.

He says it like it's an *order*.

But I'm dead down there. And I guess I really am *actively trying to find my death*, or whatever he said in the inn, because I summon every shred of courage I have left and whirl around to face him, blade still drawn. "I'm not going anywhere."

There is a moment of silence. I can hear my own breathing. This is the stupidest thing I've ever done, but I stand firm, spine straight, even though my heart is beating so wildly, I can feel the strain in my chest.

He takes a step forward. There's another type of gravity around him, a force that thickens the air and quiets the incoming night. I lift my chin, refusing to show an ounce of fear, but still, I swallow. This close . . . I'm reminded of how much bigger he is. How much stronger.

Harlan Raker. *The destroyer. The battle ender. The ancient sword wielder.*

He is known by many names, and all of them mean death.

I can't see his face, but I can feel his gaze on me, sharp as a sword's edge. "Either you leave of your own will. Or mine."

I can imagine grown men tremble under his notice. They piss themselves, apparently. But I've made it this far. A warrior I despise with every ounce of my being is not going to be the one to make me fail at my purpose.

"Then I guess you're going to have to finally kill me," I say, my voice as vicious as his. My stomach tightens, as if predicting the metal that will slice through it.

But he doesn't move.

We stay like that, staring each other down for a moment. Two. Twenty. Sweat slides along my spine. Still, I refuse to look away first. I refuse to lower this sword that has numbed my arms with its weight.

Just when I think he's going to cut me down, he sighs and turns instead. There's a slight rustling as he gets his things. Then he's back. He makes to move past me, toward the mouth of the cave.

I blink, shock rendering me useless.

It isn't the fact that he didn't actually kill me. It isn't that he clearly let me win. That's surprising, sure. But what's even more surprising is that he would rather *leave this spot than be in my presence.*

I should be relieved. I should watch him go.

Instead, I'm reminded that I'm alone, in the middle of a strange land, without a creature. Surrounded by fire and enemies hunting me down. Standing in nearly extinguished sunlight, unsure if I'm about to be torn apart by mysterious night demons.

He's my enemy. I've hated him for years. I remember that day in the rain. The day he could have taken mercy but didn't. The scars on my lower back are proof of that. The fact that he caught me on the stairs doesn't change any of it.

But enemies often make the strongest allies.

"Work with me," I say, before my pride can silence me.

Those words were gathered from the very pit of my desperation, but he doesn't stop. It's as if I haven't spoken at all. My fury melts into prickling shame. I used to think hatred was the worst thing someone could feel for another. Now I know it's apathy.

He's almost at the cliff's edge. He's almost gone. I don't know why I do it.

But before he can leave, I raise my sword to strike him.

He turns in an instant. His weapon is unsheathed in half a second, his metal hitting mine, and—

Music. It's like music, the ringing.

Two glorious swords meeting. Neither yielding.

A bolt races down my arm, spearing through my stomach, down my legs, and into the ground. The very world seems to tremble.

I wonder if he feels it too. I wouldn't know. The hood blocks everything.

But not his voice.

"Have you lost your fucking mind?" he snarls, the words like rocks grinding together.

Yes. Almost certainly so, for being bold enough to try to strike Harlan Raker, the warrior without marks on his armor.

"Work with me" is all I say, panting from the simple movement.

Our blades are still touching.

His voice is even deeper and more chilling than I remember. He takes a step forward, and our blades scrape together, emitting a high pitch that echoes around us. "Why would I ever work with someone as pathetic as you?"

Fury and shame burn my face, but I swallow them down. I'll do anything to make it to the gods—even if it means working with this bastard.

I glare at him, trying not to let the strain reach my expression. Both of my hands are gripped on my hilt—he's only holding his with one. "We have the same sword. Clearly, I'm not as pathetic as you think."

I can almost *feel* his revulsion. He spits out his words. "Our swords are not the same."

"I don't see any cracks," I say in a sharp whisper. Silence. Our swords are still together. A shred of moonlight gleams between them.

Both are unmarred. As if they are equally matched.

He quickly sheaths his, as if he can't bear to face that fact, his sparkling metal disappearing like all the stars guttering out at once. I lower mine, trying hard not to drop it, but don't sheath it.

He turns to leave again, but the words are out of me before I can stop them. "I have a map."

That makes him pause. He turns, very slowly. I carefully reach into my pocket and pull it out, my sword still between us. I shake it open. "It's all here. Everything."

I imagine he's looking at it. I can almost tell from the direction of his head.

Then he turns slightly, toward me. I keep my posture straight, my skin prickling beneath his study.

"I could kill you and take it." He says the words without feeling, as though it would take little effort, time, or space in his conscious. If he even has one.

I was expecting that. So I curl the map into a ball—

And throw it past him, right off the cliff. We both watch as it falls into the fire and burns into embers. "You fool, you—"

"I memorized it." If he wants that knowledge, he can't kill me. Not until we reach the end of the quest, at least. I stand there watching him, the darkness of his hood like a second mask.

He tilts his head at me. There is something predatory in the way he does it, like a beast staring down prey. He looks like a demon. A nightmare. His cruelty is not just a rumor. I've experienced it firsthand.

And he doesn't even remember.

"You will regret this," he says, before taking a step forward. It's not a threat as much as it is a promise. But it isn't a no. His hands are halfway curled into fists. "If you slow me down, I will kill you. If I find another way across the land without you, I will kill you. If you try to touch my sword, I will kill you. Understood?"

I know I should feel fear, but instead, all I feel is crushing relief. He'll help me reach the end of this. I know it.

"Same to you," I say, because *he*, I think, will be the one to regret ever underestimating me.

He doesn't even look at me as he walks past, deeper into the cave. I remain fixed in place, refusing to follow.

I don't plan on getting anywhere near him for the rest of the night, but then I hear it. The faint gurgling of a water source far behind me. In the direction he went.

I swallow, my throat rough with thirst. Now that he's gone, now that I'm not running, the full force of my hunger and exhaustion hits me at once. My knees nearly buckle. *Don't show your weakness*, I think *You've gone this long without water. You can last a few more minutes.*

I try. I stand, battling with my pride, but I lose. I turn and rush toward the sound, not even looking for the demon knight, eyes and mind and senses solely focused on a stream of water so blue, it's almost glowing.

Fuck it. I'm so thirsty, I fall to my knees and drink from my hands. I gulp it down greedily, the water streaming down my neck, soaking my shirt until my throat is finally smooth again.

That's when I finally notice him. He's turned toward me, leaning against the side of the cave. He's still wearing his hood. Of course. Does he ever take it off? How about the mask? Is there even a face beneath it? If the rumors are true, there isn't. He's a beast. A true devil. I might not be able to see his expression, but disdain is clear in the way he looks down at me. He thinks he's better than me. He's probably right.

What he doesn't understand is that I will do *anything* to reach the end. I will do everything he said he would do to me and more.

I can't see his eyes—which I know he has, because I've seen them, beneath a silver helmet—but mine aren't obstructed. I glare at him, and I hope that he can feel my hatred. It hasn't dimmed in years. If anything, it's grown.

I will use him the same way he's using me, and then I will kill him for what he did. And he'll deserve it.

My mind shifts to a flash of him in the rain. The hatred in his eyes, his metal against my neck, and—

My hands tense against the cold stone floor before I slowly start to wash my face. Then, when I feel relatively clean, I sit back against the smooth cave wall.

No way I'm sleeping tonight. Not when I'm half convinced Raker is going to gut me in my sleep and take my sword, map be damned.

He could do that even if I was awake, I think, but I'm not risking it. I grip my blade against my chest and stare out at the opening of the cave.

Darkness has nearly swallowed the sky. The moon is out. Shrieks echo as creatures take off into the fading light, the forest still roaring with flames. They've stopped hunting me. For now.

My head falls back against the stone, my body going boneless, relief rushing in, my fight leaving me. I'm tired, so tired. And I'm not even a fifth of the way there.

My body might be worn out, but my mind races. Before, all I could think about was survival. Now all my thoughts catch up.

My dragon. My flameless dragon.

I hope she's okay. I hope she doesn't do anything stupid like look for me. Not when trouble always tends to find me.

Some part of me grieves, even though we didn't know each other for long. She is beautiful and powerful—but I could tell some shred of her needed a shred of me. And that maybe . . . maybe, if we'd had a little more time, we could have found our fire together.

Kira. She must be on the other side now. I wonder how her leg is doing. Xara helped her. I know she did. *I hope she did.*

Zane. I wonder if he claimed a Helmhawk. I can almost imagine him on the back of one, blue feathers turning silvery beneath the moonlight.

I can also imagine him mangled in the tree branches, an arrow through his forehead.

My eyes tighten against the image. No. Zane is strong. So is Kira. So is my dragon. And so am I. This will kill me, but not yet.

Not yet.

I continue to stare at the sky, lost in my mind, until the stars break through the darkness, sparkling like my sword. They shine brighter here on this side. There are so many, a galaxy, like infinite versions of the freckles across my cheeks in summer. My sister had more. She had them all over. I used to count them, one by one, to help her fall asleep. I used to sleep beside her, because she feared the dark. She used to sleep with an arm banded around me, because she was convinced one day someone would try to take me away in the middle of the night, and she told me she wouldn't let them.

I laughed. "What is your arm going to do if a demon is intent on taking me?"

I'll wake up, she said with pure conviction. *I'll save you.*

I believed her. I believed she would save me from anything.

If only I could have saved her.

My eyes close against the memories. A tear slides down my face. It's incredible I have any left. But they are endless, just like this agony. Just like this guilt.

Because I'm not just doing this for them. I'm doing it for me too. Maybe—maybe if I kill the goddess that ended them, maybe that will absolve me just the slightest bit. Because I'm the reason they're dead.

I'm the reason they're all dead.

I used to crave sleep, because in my dreams, they were still alive. But over time, the memories dimmed. As much as I fought to keep them clear, they were like sand in my palms, falling through my fingers. I tried everything to strengthen my memory. I memorized pointless things, read books then recited them backward, trying to train my memory like a muscle. It worked, partially. But still, with every year that goes by, I remember less.

Now I have more nightmares than dreams. For even though the memories of the good times have faded, those of that night never have. They are still as real as when they happened. I relive that night all the time. It always has the same ending.

And I *wish*. I wish I had anything of value to give to the gods, to try to go back and change it all. But even the gods can't do that. So I'll kill them instead.

My mind cycles through the memories. There are ten of them, the ones I treasure the most. The ones I refuse to forget.

Number one is the first time I held my sister. I was only three years old, but I remember the way she looked at me and smiled. When her tiny fingers curled around one of mine, I thought, *You. I would do anything for you.*

She never stopped looking at me like that—like I was someone to be trusted. Someone to be admired. Someone worthy of anything at all.

Even in the end, she didn't doubt me. She didn't *blame me*.

She—

A whisper. It barely breaks through the crackling of the forest fire. It's so gentle, it could be the wind.

But I would know that voice anywhere.

"Aris."

I don't dare breathe. My imagination. It's a memory. It's my head, messing with me, it's—

"Aris, it's me."

I stand. Raker is hunched over, asleep against the wall. His sword is dug into the ground in front of him like a guard.

I know it's impossible. I know it's not real. Still, I turn toward the sound. I walk all the way to the mouth of the cave, and then a sob spills from my lips.

Because right there on the forest floor is my sister.

She looks just like she did that last night. Same white sleeping gown. Same ribbons in her hair.

My sister.

She smiles when she sees me. *Smiles.*

"You look so different," she says, her face lighting up. "So beautiful, Aris."

She's here. I know it's impossible, but *she's here*. And she's never said those exact words before, so this can't be a memory. It's real. It must be.

My arms are trembling. I choke on a sob. "You look the same," I say, eyes burning. Behind her, the forest is on fire. She shimmers like moonlight.

A specter. She must be a specter, like the ones in the king's palace.

This is Starside, the land of magic. Somehow, *she's here*. She's been here this whole time, waiting for me.

"I miss you so much," she says, and the words are claws, curling through me, piercing and hooking. "I've seen everything. You've been so brave."

I shake my head, my vision smudged with tears. They bleed into the fabric at my neck.

"It should have been me," I tell her, sinking to my knees. The words have cycled through my mind for years. I've wanted to tell her this, needed to tell her this. "I'm sorry. Please—please forgive me."

My sister only smiles. "No, it shouldn't have. You were meant for this. You know that, right?"

I don't know anything. I don't know anything but this blinding, all-consuming, swallowing rage I've felt since that night.

She frowns, as if she hears something I can't. "I have to go," she says.

I get up. Go? Go where? "*No*," I say. Not again. "Please, please stay—"

"I can't," she says. She turns as if to walk through the flaming forest. To walk through the fire again, like that's where she lives. Like that's where she's been this whole time, trapped in the flames that took her away from me.

I move without thinking. I crawl out of the cave and climb, then leap to the ground, my muscles seizing as I land. But I don't care. I barely feel it. I turn and run toward her.

I couldn't save her that night. But I won't let her burn again. I won't let them take her from me.

She's right there, her glimmering nightgown twirling behind her as she walks. Her hair is falling out of its braid. I tied it. It was one of the last things I ever did for her.

I reach out, my fingers uncurling, as if I could rip her from death's grip. My fingers brush against her sleeve. She turns.

But it's not my sister. It's a creature, with blood-crusted fangs and claws like daggers.

I scream.

My sword is in my hand in an instant. I cut the beast down without hesitation, the weight of the metal helping strengthen my downward blow. The creature falls onto the forest floor.

When it lands, it's my sister again.

I fall to my knees with a sob that rattles my bones. Rattles the world. My fingers dig into the ground, my veins igniting with every thornlike feeling I've buried, every jagged piece of pain and anguish that will never go away. It's all too much, overtaking me, pulling me under, a sea of agony.

A hand grips my shoulder.

Tears streaming down my face, I look up into darkness. Into a hood like a rippling shadow. The voice is harsh. It's brutal, like a truth shoved down my throat. "Get up. This isn't real."

I bare my teeth at him—

And the forest . . . Even aflame, the forest stills, as if it's taking a breath. Raker looks up. A second of silence.

Before he can say a word, the darkness splits open. High-pitched screams sound from everywhere. Tremors throw me to the side, like a hundred creatures are rising up at once.

"Idiot," Raker barks above me.

We run.

The ground is uneven. It's undulating, like a wave of beasts are crawling just beneath the surface.

Demons. Finally, the first breaks through. Then, the next. Then, them *all.*

Dirt sputters as dark, night-spun creatures emerge all around us, sprouting like wicked plants. They're made of dried, rotted skin, fitted tightly over mangled bones. They're the devils my mother would tell stories about, the God of Death's underlings.

Killing one awoke more. *So many more.*

Raker reaches the rock face first and climbs. I'm right behind him, tiny stones falling onto my face from his boots, dirt clouding my vision. I can't see the creatures, but I hear them when they reach the cliffside, their claws scraping against it, just below me, the sound piercing my skull.

The cave—we need to get to the cave. I blink through the darkness and dirt and watch as Raker moves toward it—but beasts are already blocking the entrance. One parts its mouth in a mind-piercing shriek, revealing rows and rows of fangs.

Fuck.

Raker shifts immediately, as if he's going to climb the whole rock face. My arms tremble as I take in the distance to the top. My fingers are already slick with sweat. I'm not sure I'll make it all the way.

Something grabs my ankle.

I don't turn around as I kick, dislodging its hold, and then I'm climbing for my life, following the glint of Raker's sword like a guiding star, my own heavy on my back. Tears blur my vision as I remember my sister, or whatever demon it was that crawled into her skin. She wasn't real, but this pain is. The memories are.

This time, instead of letting the grief choke me, I let it ignite me. *For her.* I will fight until every bone breaks and I can't stand anymore, and even then I will crawl to the edge of this world for her.

Those memories from before, I cling to them as I grip each ledge, as I ignore the shrieks below me, as nails scrape my ankles. My mind narrows to arrow-like focus, and I climb until we reach the top, and then I'm pulling myself up, and panting as I run as fast as I ever have before.

Far ahead, something sparkles silver—the moon, reflected off water. That's where Raker is headed.

Water.

I remember the small moat around the village. The fact that Xara said we would be safe on the boat. The stream in the cave. Of course. The beasts must not be able to pass water. Raker must know that.

Hope flares in my chest. We just have to reach the lake.

My legs burn as I push them, as dirt sputters behind me, as I use my arms to take me farther. Raker isn't in front of me anymore. Did he take a turn? Did he go off in a different direction?

I finally look over my shoulder, only to see teeth, glistening like metal. I gasp and run—

Until my feet leave the ground. For a moment, I'm weightless, as if gravity has taken pity on me and released its hold. I'm free. Floating.

Then I'm falling.

I hit the water, and it swallows me whole.

I gasp, my lungs filling as I sink. My arms reach for the surface—

but it's gone. With my sword on my back, I'm going down quickly. The lake is black as ink. My blade pulses against my spine, as if in panic.

The moonlight fades, giving way to an almost comforting darkness.

Dying is peaceful. It's so quiet. So cold. It *is* like flying. I seize, my lungs burning with water, my throat contracting.

If I die, I'll be with her. But will I be able to face her, and my parents, and Stellan, without anything to show for it? Will I be able to explain that I failed them all yet again?

Their deaths cannot be meaningless. They will be the spark of the flame that ends the gods once and for all, and then, *maybe*, all this suffering will have had a purpose.

I can't die. Not yet.

I reach—*reach*. For in me is a flame desperate to live. Wanting to see just how far this rage might take me.

But I'm too far down. I kick my legs, but it's useless. I'm fighting so hard, but I have no idea how to make it mean something.

My fingers are numb. They separate as my reaching hand begins to sink. My chest lurches. My heartbeat stutters.

The fire in me begins to die, every ember burning out, one by one. The world goes still and silent.

Far above, the water parts as something heavy breaks through it. Death has come to claim me.

He wears a hood.

It slips off his head as he swims, revealing a mask of glinting metal. That's when I see them. Steel-gray eyes alit with fury, just like they were that day in the rain. I fight to keep hold of reality, so I can see more of him.

But I can't. I blink and see only impending darkness. Only fingertips, inches apart, reaching—*reaching*—but not touching. Too late.

The water rushes in to fill my lungs as the darkness wins.

15

"Of course you can't fucking swim," a voice says above me as I seize, then promptly empty the limited contents of my stomach. "Of course you take a fucking *gulp* of water in shock. Like an idiot."

That gulp of water burns my throat as I retch it up.

When I'm done, I look at him through my dripping eyelashes, wondering what I'm going to do with two massive swords when I murder him.

He doesn't move an inch. All he says is, "Of course, mere hours into working together, you almost get us both killed. Over an illusion." He shakes his head and curses.

My eyes prickle, remembering that *illusion*. My throat is raw from the retching. "*You* . . . you are a bastard. Do you know that?"

He tilts his head. His hood moves with it. Now, though, it's firmly in place. I remember the sliver mask, though. I remember gray eyes. "What an interesting way to thank me for saving your pathetic life."

"Thank you?" I laugh, then cough some more. My ribs ache. My skin is ice-cold. "We both know you would let me drown in an instant if you didn't need the map."

He doesn't deny it.

The water was freezing. I shiver in spite of myself, my teeth chattering. He doesn't give a damn. Of course he doesn't.

He doesn't seem cold at all. He's prepared. He must have layers on beneath that armor.

I lean forward, nails sinking into the ground for purchase as another wave of nausea rocks through me. At the sound of gentle lapping, I look to my right. We're on a tiny island, right in the middle of the lake.

And we are surrounded. Every inch of shoreline is covered by rancid, flesh-rotted demons. Waiting. Watching. I grab my sword.

Raker's voice is grating. "Don't waste what little energy you possess. They cannot cross. They'll be gone when the sun rises." I look over at him, sitting, his sword dug into the dirt in front of him.

He isn't worried in the slightest that I might take it. I probably can't, I think, after having seen so many people try to take my own.

Could he move mine? He's Harlan Raker. Maybe he's capable of moving any sword.

I don't plan on finding out.

I have every intention of staying awake. My heart is beating wildly, the panic still pounding through my blood. But I'm worn out from the retching. My energy fades quickly.

I fall asleep curled around my sword in its scabbard, to the memory of furious gray eyes.

SUNLIGHT RAINS DOWN, its heat like a blanket. I groan, luxuriating in its warmth, before it's ripped away completely.

My eyes slowly blink open, only to find a hooded figure blocking the sunlight like an incessant shadow. I'm still curved around my scabbard, my legs and arms wrapped around it.

His voice is emotionless. "You weren't moving. I thought you might have died."

I glare up at him. "Sorry to disappoint."

He walks away, murmuring something that sounds like a curse against me. I'm sure he's regretting saving me. I'm sure he thinks even the map isn't worth it.

As long as he keeps working with me, I don't give a shit. And even though I would be dead without his interference, I can't summon even a shred of gratitude. Because I know the truth about him. I know he doesn't have feelings, or mercy, or *anything* resembling a heart beneath that spotless armor.

The demons. I jolt, turning toward the shore where they watched us sleep all night.

They're gone. Just like Raker said they would be.

His deep voice cuts through the morning. "The next part of the map. Draw it." He points at the dirt.

There he is again, *ordering* me to do something. My pride rises, but I snuff it out. He's already proven useful.

I begin drawing with a stick. I'm not stupid enough to draw the entire length for him. I'll just show the closest part to us.

There are several mountain ranges. A few roads. Forests. I draw all of them in proximity to where we are, grateful for all those nights spent strengthening my memory.

Finally—"The Prism Pass. *Land of rainbows* was written beneath it." I wait for a reaction that never arrives.

These mountains seem separated, full of steep drop-offs and deep valleys. And . . . waterfalls. I draw from memory and perk up. "This is perfect—because . . . because of the water." I draw at least a dozen of them that were marked.

I put the stick down and marvel at my work.

Raker studies my drawing for a moment.

Then he wordlessly turns around. His sword glistens as he pulls it out of the dirt and slides it back against his spine. He grabs his pack.

I blink. "That's it? You aren't going to tell me where we're going? You aren't going to consult me at all?"

"Your voice is *irritating*," he says, reaching his hand into the darkness of his hood. Is he . . . pinching his nose over the mask? I think about all those rumors about him being a monster beneath there. Maybe he is. All I saw were eyes. The rest could be anything. "Speak to me as little as possible."

"You do not order me," I say, getting to my feet, because fucking *enough*.

"That's where you're wrong." He takes a step forward. "You asked to work with me. Those are my conditions. Listen. And don't speak."

My hands clench into fists. I did ask him to work with me. I practically begged him to. And even though he's proven himself to be more of a bastard than I anticipated, I'm alive. I'm closer to the gods. That's all that matters.

"Fine," I say through my teeth.

He turns away, toward the water. That's when I realize we'll have to cross it.

"I can't—"

"*Fucking swim*, I know," he barks. He sighs, the movement raking through his entire mountainous form. He really is absurdly huge. A foot and a half taller than me, and ridiculously muscled . . . but not so big that his size would slow him down. The exact form I would expect from the most feared warrior on Stormside.

He lingers, looking over at me, hesitating.

For a moment, I think he might offer his hand. He might take me in his arms, the way he must have last night to drag me from the depths of the lake and onto this isle. But that's stupid of me, because in the end, he seems to think better of it as he shakes his head and growls, "Figure it out."

He steps into the lake and is gone in a moment. He swims effortlessly, even in his armor. I open my mouth. Close it.

Will he leave me? Will he decide the map isn't worth this?

I won't wait to find out. I look around, searching for anything to help me get across. That's when I see a few trees. Some bark is hanging off. Bark is buoyant. I know that from the time it rained when I was five, and my father used a rare slice of it to make two small boats we raced in a puddle.

My hands grip its edges, sharp pieces digging into my skin, and I pull. It's thick and tough. My teeth slide together, my shoes digging into the dirt as I tug, and tug, muscles straining. Slowly, it begins to come apart. I wince, my fingers slipping in my own blood as sharp wood pieces dig into them, but I don't stop, the sound of the water diminishing as he gets farther and farther away. He could leave me. Especially now that I've given him the surrounding area of the map.

I take my sword, force it up with a groan, and hastily slice off the rest of the bark, then sprint toward the water, hands bleeding. Everything in me screams to stay on land, my lungs burning as if remembering how they filled with water, but I can't hesitate. Not anymore.

I fling myself into the lake, the thick bark beneath me. And it floats. I kick wildly, eyes on the shore. The water is freezing, just like it was last night.

Last night. I remember the burn of my chest, the constricting. My body both fighting to stay alive and resigning itself to death.

He might be the most miserable person I've ever met, but Raker is right. My weaknesses will seal my fate during this journey. I have no choice but to overcome them. That's the only way I'll make it to the end of this.

Starting with getting to the other side of this lake.

If I slip off the bark, I'm dead. Raker won't save me a second time. I don't even hear him swimming anymore. No, the only thing cutting through the morning is my ragged breathing, my kicking legs, and the water sputtering around me.

If he left . . . I'll be alone again. No dragon. No Kira and Zane.

I didn't expect to have allies on my quest, and only now do I see how stupid that was. Did I really think I could make it across Starside alone? Yes. I did. I thought this rage in my chest and the years of training with Stellan would be enough to carry me through.

Now I understand why Stellan was so against me going. Now I understand why he was so afraid.

Find Vander Evren, he'd said. Who is that? And how am I supposed to find an immortal in the middle of nowhere, surrounded by challengers and immortals alike who would kill me for this sword on my back?

I kick harder, and the bark dips low, sending water spilling into my mouth. I spit it out, hoping Raker didn't leave. Being with him is better than being alone.

It's only halfway across that I see him, leaning against the cliffside, watching me struggle. His posture says *unimpressed*.

I grit my teeth and kick, eyes locked on him, refusing to let him see me fail, letting my stubbornness overpower my muscle cramps, until I wash roughly up on the shoreline. The rocks cut my fingers again, but pride fills me.

I made it. I figured it out.

Raker doesn't seem too pleased about that fact as he turns around, like he wishes he could have watched me die.

We don't speak. All I do is follow as Raker walks at a pace that means I have to half jog. His legs are far longer than mine. I race to keep up, already exhausted from crossing the water.

My sword is heavy on my back, but he carries his as if it's almost weightless. The same with his armor. That is, I suppose, his training.

The king's guard has unmatched training outposts and resources. They know how to build muscle and keep it. Stellan taught me everything he could, but my own instruction was nothing compared to Raker's. My nails dig into my palms, remembering the one time I tried to get access to that training and where that got me.

My hatred of him has had years to simmer. How many nights have I fallen asleep, dreaming of gutting him with his own blade? Of being strong enough to hurt him at all?

I glare at his back, imagining a dozen swords buried in it.

That's how I pass the time. Imagining the various ways I could kill him. I picture a thousand sparkling knives going through that armor. An ax chopping away that hood. A lance going into his chest.

My sword hums on my back, almost with approval. It makes me smile.

I'm definitely not smiling hours later when my legs feel like they've been reduced to clay, and my feet feel like they've decided to merge with my boots. Maybe working with Raker wasn't the best idea.

He doesn't take breaks. He never slows. His posture never slips. I might be impressed if I wasn't in so much fucking pain.

I nearly whimper with relief when the sun dips toward the horizon and Raker begins to deviate from the path, toward the faint sound of rushing water. *Finally.*

As we get closer, that whispering water turns into a roaring. Then the forest clears, revealing a riverbank with white, foaming crests, streams of water hastily moving in various directions. There's a small strip of land at the center of it.

I clench my jaw, remembering how quickly a similar river swept Kira away, and how rocks just like these, sticking out of the water like fangs, shredded her leg.

Surely, Raker doesn't mean to camp here.

Without a single glance at me, he steps into the rushing current and walks straight *through* it, his armored form cutting across the thrashing water like a blade. He steps onto the bit of land as if it was no trouble at all. He puts his stuff down. His back is to me.

Figure it out.

Figuring it out means me making camp at the edge of the river, hoping my proximity to the water will keep me safe.

A moment later, I hear a sharp click, followed by a roaring. I turn to see Raker has made a fire. In less than a minute.

It was a skill I taught myself, before coming to the Centennial. But even in the best conditions—not next to a sputtering *river*—it took me several tries and over ten minutes. I watch him slip something back into his pack.

A flint rock. I scowl. Of course, a king's guard would have one. They're rare and expensive.

It's not even that cold out. But as Raker stalks to the edge of the piece of land and peers into the water, I see the fire isn't for warmth. He slides the sword from his spine. Lowers it in front of him.

With a speed that makes me jolt, he stabs it into the river.

I almost laugh that he would actually think that would work. That he would think he would be *fast enough to*—

That laugh dies in my throat as he turns around, and I see the large, pink-scaled fish impaled on his blade.

Well, fuck.

He expertly descales it. Cuts it. Then begins to cook it on the fire. Of course, he doesn't offer any to me. Not that I would take it. I've never had fish before. Best not to test my gut when I'm not even that hungry.

My traitorous stomach grumbles at the smell anyway. I turn away from him and his roasting food, toward my bed for the night.

It doesn't matter that it's dirt and a few patches of grass. The moment I'm off my feet, my entire body melts into the ground. Not even the river, roaring in my ears, nor the stars glimmering brightly overhead, nor the danger lurking nearby can dull the pull to sleep. I tell myself I should stay awake, I should test this theory about the water, but it's not long before my eyes close, and everything fades away.

I'm not even an hour into sleep when I'm jolted out of it by a slow scraping, like a claw grating across tree bark. My eyes open immediately. And the sound . . . it stops. As if it was never there at all.

It could have been a dream; it could have been nothing. I lay very still, listening beyond the river. Beyond Raker's steady breathing.

Nothing. Nothing but quiet for several minutes, and my eyes slowly close again. Sleep rushes in like a hungry tide, washing over me, pulling me under.

That's when I hear it again. And this time, there is no doubt.

I sit up, hand clenched around the hilt of my blade. Heart racing, I squint into the darkness of the forest.

Nothing. I *see* nothing.

But I feel . . . I feel the hush of the woods. The breath it holds. On shaking, tired legs, I stand. My arms ache with exhaustion as I haul my sword in front of me, the metal pierced into the ground. I wait. And wait.

Until a single foot steps out of the trees. It's made of flayed, putrid flesh. Its smell hits me at once, and I nearly gag.

Rot. The demon smells of pure and utter death. It takes another slow step toward me, and a shard of moonlight illuminates its face.

Twisted, mangled features, skin dried into a peel. Similar to the others, but this one isn't encased in shadow. No, I see every inch of its graying skin and waxen bone.

Its eyes are two pits of darkness, looking at me. Its mouth is scarred tissue, as if it has been sewn closed and ripped open a hundred times before. Was this demon once alive? Is that what the God of Death does? Create armies from his corpses?

Its mouth parts, breaking skin, oozing onyx blood, and emits an ear-splitting scream. Its teeth go back rows and rows.

It doesn't waste any more time. It lunges forward, claws outstretched toward my neck.

I stumble back. Right into the river.

My spine hits a rock, and light explodes behind my eyelids. There's no time for pain. I'm immediately swept into the current's relentless hold, my body turning, toppling, scraping against the daggerlike stones, sharpened into points by the rough water. I reach out blindly and manage to grab on to a rock, splitting my palm in the process.

With a desperate jolt, I grip it, nails breaking, and lift myself out of the shallow water, fighting the current, fighting for air. I turn the moment I can and see the flesh-stitched creature, peering into the water. Right over me. Waiting.

Head pounding, spine a lightning bolt of pain, I reach for another rock. Another. Slowly, I pull myself through the current, sword still clutched in my other palm, toward that narrow strip of land, until I can throw myself onto it, coughing up water. Whimpering as my tattered hand scrapes against the dirt.

The creature waits for several minutes at the edge of the river, staring me down, before slowly slinking back into the woods.

Trembling with cold, my pants rasped and loud, hot blood dripping all over me, I turn toward Raker. His back is still to me. His glorious sword is still dug into the ground right where he left it.

He had to have heard my struggle. The beast's scream. He must be awake.

He didn't move a single inch.

Of course he didn't. He wants my map—but he must have decided the extra effort of saving me again simply isn't worth it.

The sound of ripping fabric cuts through the night as I tear the extra length at the bottom of my shirt, and wrap it around my hand, wincing at the pain. Watching it soon turn crimson.

To heal, to prepare for another relentless day of walking, I need to sleep. Body shaking with cold, I lie on my side. Somehow, rest finds me.

The next morning, I'm awoken by the sound of Raker splashing through the current. He doesn't even turn. Doesn't even alert me to his leaving.

Heart in my throat, I rush to my feet and throw myself through the water in a hurry, boot slipping against a rock. Pain shoots through my limbs as my knees both hit the jagged bottom.

I grit my teeth and rise, then race onto the riverbank after him. He makes no move to check if I have followed.

Another day of silence. Another day of Harlan Raker completely ignoring me, as if I am below even a moment of his notice.

Good. I don't want to hear about all my shortcomings anyway. My own voice inside my head is enough.

It tells me I'm too slow. Raker won't adjust his speed for me. Either I match his pace . . . or I get left behind.

We don't have creatures. Not anymore, at least. Most—if not all—of this journey will be made on foot. Just like the swimming, this is a weakness that needs to be strengthened. *I* need to be strengthened, like pouring high metal into a lesser blade. Like reinforcing it.

I vary between walking quickly, jogging, then resting. Sometimes, I lose sight of him altogether and run at top speed, only to crest a hill and see his unmistakable form below, armor glimmering beneath the sun.

My bleeding hand quickly becomes irritating. I replace the bandage again, using more torn fabric, knowing it could get infected. And then what? I have no medicine. And no illusions that Raker won't leave me feverish and dying.

No, he won't leave me. He'll likely kill me and take my sword.

That's fucking comforting.

Distractions prove to be their own medicines. I study the curve of the landscape, how this world is like an endless painting, each mile more sparkling than the last. Right now, the grass is dark green. Large rocks rise from the ground in sharp angles. Some form clusters of mountains. We walk by ruin after ruin. I feel the whisper of their histories as I pass them by, as if there are secrets hidden between those stones. As if they once formed a magnificent place.

Now they sit in forgotten piles.

The path tilts up and down, alongside craggy mountains, through wildflower-speckled glens. When the sun is shining brightly above, we reach a valley covered in violet.

Tears well up in my eyes. Lavender, foxglove, catmint—I count all the flowers I've previously only seen pressed into pages, in my mother's book.

She loved flowers. They were so few on Stormside. But she had one plant, from a seed she said came from Starside. A flower she claimed had been passed down through our family for generations. Only something magical could survive so many centuries.

My sister and I would sneak away and search the fields of dirt for any wildflowers to bring back. Most of the time, we came home empty-handed, but finding one was a treasure. We would rush home and—after scolding us for going too far away—our mother would take us to the coveted book, and we would flip through the pages until we found one it resembled. Then we would press it into the parchment. Sign the date.

All of it is now ashes.

Over the hours, the grass lengthens. Its color brightens, until it's light green, just as it was near the gates.

Our path tilts up, and my calves burn as we climb, Raker's body blocking the sun. Blocking everything. I keep my head down, focused on the grass in front of me, on the blades that sparkle even in shadow. I don't even realize we've reached a bluff, until Raker stops, and I almost run into him. I stumble to the side, to see what he's staring at, and my breath catches.

The Prism Path.

Endless, towering mountains ripple in steep waves, all covered in that light green grass, as if the god that created this place coveted the color. In between each sit long, thin waterfalls, like towering blades, sunlight skipping from one to the next in rainbow arcs. I've never seen so many colors. I didn't think the world could look like this.

"It's beautiful," I whisper.

Raker makes a sound of contempt next to me.

Soon, we're in the middle of it, walking through a valley. I feel so small down here, just a pebble compared with these mountains that stand tall like rows of knights, wielding their sparkling swords.

There's an energy to this place, a pull. Something different from everywhere else I've been. Even if I wanted to ask Raker if he feels it too—even if I thought he would respond to anything I say, and if I even wanted to speak to him in the first place—I wouldn't know how.

The feeling is wordless. It's pure emotion, bleeding through my chest. An ancient, long-lost sense, awakening.

We walk a mile through the valley, until Raker turns, shifting our path into the mountains. I know better than to ask where we're going. He stops in front of one of the many waterfalls. A cave sits just behind it. Raker unceremoniously throws his pack through the water and walks away, in a different direction. He's gone before I can even think about speaking.

"Bastard" is what I eventually say, far too late for him to hear it.

Slowly, I unpeel my makeshift bandage, wincing, but grateful that I don't see any signs of infection. Yet. I carefully wash off the blood and dirt in the cool water, before wrapping my hand again. The inside of the cave is dark, smooth stone.

I sink down onto it. The cold is a balm against my sore calves.

If only I still had my dragon, I wouldn't have to do this all on foot. I wouldn't have to work with Raker.

More than that . . . more than the help she offered . . .

I miss her.

My stomach twists with hunger.

I glance over at Raker's pack and have half a mind to search it for food, before deciding against it. He's made it very clear how he feels about me touching his things.

Figure it out.

To forage is to survive on Stormside. Barely anything grows. You have to be clever and patient enough to seek out the small fertile patches. It's late afternoon. I still have an hour or so until sunset.

I leave the cave, then follow the slope of the hill, down into a forest.

Mushrooms are rare on the other side. I once found a bundle beneath a rotted tree stump and felt the joy of discovering gold in a rock.

Here—here, they're *everywhere.*

Some are as large as my hand, others are thin and small, bunched together in a bouquet. Some have thick stalks and curved edges. There must be hundreds of them.

Relief rolls through my empty stomach . . . along with a flash of bitterness. This is all untouched. This place . . . It's abandoned. How many villages could this forest feed on Stormside?

I look up at the sky. If the gods were fair, they wouldn't allow this all to go to waste. They wouldn't allow one side to be brimming with food while the other goes hungry.

And maybe I'm no better than the immortals, because when I see all this food . . .

I take it. I grab it all, tucking everything I can fit into my pockets. Then, I keep wandering, until I reach a streak of color.

Berries. A rainbow of them. Purple, blue, pink, red. *Red.* The same type my dragon found for me. Just like I did then, I grab them by the handful. I put some in my mouth.

I bite down and groan.

They're sweeter than the previous berries, even. Anything on Stormside is a cheap comparison. Watered down. This is straight from the source. Perfect, a sugar that melts through my marrow. I groan as juice slides across my tongue. I pack as many berries as I can into my pockets.

Wildflowers bloom in a petal-swept trail, and I follow them into a grove, filled with blossoms.

I go rigid. Before now, I could count on my fingers how many flowers I'd seen in my life.

But here . . .

In a place like this, every page in our book would have been filled within hours. We would have needed an entire library of them.

I start picking some of them, weaving their stems into a bracelet, then a chain, then a crown, the way my sister and I used to weave together limp sticks we found outside. These are much more pliable. I rest the ring of daisies on my head, knowing it's stupid, knowing it's a waste of time, but remembering my promise to myself to soak up all the wonder I can on this quest.

"I wish you could see this . . ." I whisper, my voice getting lost in a gentle wind.

The trees are farther away from each other here, in two rows, but their tops lean together, making a canopy. Thick shards of sunlight filter through, in glimmering crosses. I run through them, leaving a path of petals in my wake, turn into another grove—then stop in my tracks.

A green dragon is sleeping on a bed of clover.

I tense. It could be vicious. Or . . . it could be friendly. Having a dragon would mean I wouldn't need Raker. It would reduce my travel time significantly. Maybe, it could help me find my silver one.

I step forward, and its eyes open immediately.

They're green. They sharpen, a ring of fire flashing through the irises—before they close again. That simple movement is a clear warning.

It doesn't want to be claimed. It will kill me if I try.

Hint taken.

The dragon continues sleeping. I step around it carefully, and the more I walk, the more the forest thickens. Sunlight strains through the treetops.

Something lands on my nose, and I startle. But it's only a grasshopper with a pink, blooming flower on its back. The flower . . . it's part of its body. I slowly reach up to touch its petals. The moment I do, it flies away.

Then, the insects melded with flowers are suddenly everywhere, taking off from the trees, and swirling around me like a living bouquet. I whisper the names of the ones I know. Bluebell. Bloodroot. Honeysuckle. Cowslip. Daisy. They wear their blossoms on their backs.

Some fly around my head, sweeping down, examining the flowers I wear in my hair, then leaving. I almost smile.

Then something zips by my ear, nicking it, and I gasp, reaching up. There's a tiny spot of blood on my finger.

I unsheathe my sword and whirl around. An arrow. *Cadoc.*

But no one's there.

Something else buzzes by, too fast and loud to be one of the floral insects. I turn quickly, reach out—and catch it. I'm expecting another type of bug.

When my fingers uncurl, a tiny being is sitting in my palm. It looks like a child with the wings of a dragonfly. It bites my thumb, and I startle, loosening my hold.

It zips away in a rush of sparkling light.

Suddenly, the light is everywhere.

Shit. My hair is pulled in all directions, out of its braids. I turn and see only my own brown locks, being smothered right against my eyes and mouth, suffocating me. I trip over a rock and fall into the grass.

I swear I hear *laughing.*

"Stop," I say, picking the creatures out of my hair and trying my best not to crush them as I throw them back into the breeze.

They don't. They pull *harder,* and I clench my teeth in pain. It's like they're trying to rip my hair from my skull.

"Enough," I growl. My nails dig into the ground until I clutch dirt, then I throw it into the air, into my own face.

Release.

There's soft coughing and what sounds like cursing as they're momentarily stunned, and I use that chance to fucking bolt. I push the loosened strands out of my face and rub the dirt from my eyes with my arm as I tear through the grove.

I sprint, panting, until . . . *silence*. There aren't whispers in the trees. There aren't any winged insects buzzing. There aren't even grasshoppers. I sigh and run my fingers through my hair to ensure I've lost them.

A branch snaps behind me.

My hand on the hilt of my sword, I whirl around—

An elk stands just two feet in front of my nose.

Its fur is green, just like the dragon. Its horns are a crown of white, flowers caught on every point.

Its eyes are large and sparkling. It blinks at me and takes a gentle step forward.

It isn't afraid. Even though my sword is halfway out of its scabbard. It doesn't even look at the weapon; it just looks at *me*.

Slowly, I lower my blade back down. Something within me is called forward. I extend my hand toward it, the same way I did to my dragon.

This creature isn't meant to be claimed, no . . . But still, it steps toward me, as if allowing me to touch it.

Its horns glisten in the fading sunlight. It leans into my touch—

And seizes. Its sparkling green eyes widen. *No.*

The creature collapses, a sword sticking out of its side. I fall to my knees, still reaching, eyes still locked with a gaze that is now unblinking. A horrified gasp spills from my lips.

I twist sharply. "What have you done?"

Raker ignores me as he walks to retrieve his sword. He cleans it on the grass, then reaches down and effortlessly lifts the creature onto his shoulders.

I remain in the dirt, next to a hot puddle of blood. "You didn't have to kill it! We have food!"

He doesn't even look at the mushrooms and berries in my shaking hands.

Finally, after a day of silence, he speaks. "Everything dies," he says. "Get over it."

Then he turns and walks back to the cave.

16

*M*onster. That's the only thing I can think of as I finally make my way to the waterfall. The sun is setting. My hands are still shaking.

The elk's eyes are in my head. It was *looking* at me. I distracted it. I got it *killed*.

Just like everything else in my life.

We're on a journey of survival. I know that. This shouldn't matter. But for some reason . . . for some reason it does. For some reason, that elk just feels like someone else I let down.

By the time I approach the cave, Raker has already skinned the creature. I look away, fighting the urge to vomit. He's made a fire. He roasts the meat and unceremoniously ignores me as I step through the curtain of water and make my place as far from him as possible.

I count my mushrooms and berries, eat a portion of them until my fingers are bright with color, then carefully wrap what's left in giant leaves I collected.

My stomach isn't full—but I'm not hungry. Not that Raker ever offers any of his meat, even though it's enough for several people to share.

Its smell fills the cave, making my traitorous stomach rumble, and that just makes me hate myself even more.

I fall asleep to the sound of falling water, my cheek against my blade.

Buzzing in my ear wakes me up.

Then a sharp pull.

"*Ow*," I say, getting up and reaching toward the source—but a blur of light zips away before I can catch it.

It makes the mistake of getting near Raker's hood. It tries to pull it down—and Raker's hand smothers it in half a second.

I inhale sharply. He killed the small creature, just like the elk in the woods. But before I can even think about mourning the menace that has been trying to scalp me, Raker cocks his arm, and throws the tiny creature right through the waterfall, in a shimmering arc of light.

It's alive. Still, that couldn't have been pleasant.

"Damned pixies," I think I hear him say to himself, like he has forgotten entirely that I'm here.

He packs his stuff without even a glance at me. Then he leaves.

I sigh as I follow him out of the cave.

The sun has barely risen. We walk through the near darkness, and I watch this glittering world wake up.

The grass rustles like a song. Birds chirp in response. Wildflowers bloom in mismatched patterns. Some have the same stripes and spots as creatures. Raker looks completely out of place in the middle of it. A towering shadow in the center of this fertile place, black cape curling in the wind.

Against my spine, my sword hums. I reach back and brush its hilt, even though I know I'm being ridiculous.

Has it seen this place? Did it battle here? I wonder about its history.

"Maybe you'll return one day," I say under my breath. "Maybe your next wielder will have bigger dreams than me."

Green and arcs of reflected prisms fill my vision for hours. The grass is soft beneath my boots. My sword is heavy on my back, so I take it down and drag it behind me.

Raker turns to look at me for the first time in hours, and I can't see his face—but I can almost *feel* his derision.

I glare at him until he turns back around.

The mountains are endless. We climb them all, one after the other, until my legs go numb. Just when I think my body has reached its limits, those limits expand.

It's like my tears, I think. Just when I think I've cried enough for several lifetimes, they prove me wrong.

If you believe you're limitless, then you will be, Stellan used to tell me. When I told him I was tired, he would say, *You think you're tired.*

No. I am fucking *tired,* I would think back, scowling at the fact that he acted like tiredness was a choice. Like weakness was a choice.

Now I can't deny that his unwavering strength was always more mental than physical.

We enter another grove. A small pool sits in its center, clear and sparkling, water running in from the mountains. It's clean. Raker bends to fill a canteen from his pack. I should really try to get another one using the coin in my pocket.

For now, I sink to my knees and pool the water in my hands, washing my injured palm before rewrapping it. Then I drink.

When I'm done, and the water settles before me, I catch my reflection and wince. My face is still covered in the dirt I used to get rid of the pixies. Blood is crusted on my ear from where one bit me. My hair is a knotted mess, several pieces sticking up from the thick braids. My clothes aren't faring any better.

I straighten my spine, turn to Raker, and say with what I hope is the utmost authority, "I'd like to bathe."

He barely looks over at me. *Then bathe,* his silence says.

I swallow. Even if it wasn't for my markings, I wouldn't be rushing to strip in front of him.

Politeness isn't getting me anywhere. My chin rises. "You need to leave." I order him just as he's ordered me countless times before.

He stills. Very slowly, he turns to face me fully. His voice is pure malice. "Do you think I would waste even a moment of my attention ogling you? Do you think you matter at all?" And now I realize that his silence thus far has been a gift, as I am reminded of how cruel his words can be.

"Then it shouldn't be any trouble for you to leave," I say through my teeth.

He does very much the opposite. He drops his pack. From it he produces a thick bar of soap. Another useful item I don't have anymore.

Then he begins to undo his armor.

"I'm bathing," he says. "You can do whatever the fuck you want." He digs his sword into the ground. It stands tall and proud in front of me.

He undoes his boots. I swallow, wondering what's next. He has to lower his hood and mask to bathe, right?

Curiosity momentarily stuns me.

Then I get my fucking mind together and scurry into the woods. I am not going to sit here and stare at Harlan Raker bathing. That's ridiculous. And likely a death sentence, as he clearly doesn't like anyone seeing him without his layers, much like I do.

Asshole.

When I'm done imagining just what lurks beneath that hood—each iteration becoming increasingly demonic—I distract myself by foraging. There are some of the same mushrooms I found before. A few different ones. Some leaves that are edible, given their smell. Others that smell bitter, poisonous.

Another advantage of having a mother who loved plants—she taught my sister and me which ones we weren't allowed to touch. The ones that would burn our ankles . . . the ones with enough poison to kill a horse.

By the time Raker emerges, I have an armful of provisions, wrapped in leaves. Some roots and nuts, even.

He walks right past me with not so much as a grunt. His hood is slightly wet. It's the only indication that he was ever in the water at all.

My own skin is dry and dirty, but I swallow my bitterness and follow him up another hill. The sun is almost setting.

When we reach a waterfall, he throws his pack down and turns without another word. To hunt, I know. He didn't have enough time to cure the elk's meat. Much of it was left behind uneaten.

I close my mind against the memory of that elk's lifeless gaze and begin washing my mushrooms in the waterfall. I scrub the dirt off them and the leftover berries and spread them on a smooth rock to dry.

I watch as the sun is pierced by the mountains and melts into a golden smear. It vanishes quickly. Then I make my way into the cave. Raker follows a few minutes later. Empty-handed.

I try and fail to hide my mirth. "What's wrong? Couldn't find another gentle creature to kill?"

He steps past me without a single glance.

"Maybe if you'd let me bathe, you could have found your dinner," I say, chomping happily on one of my roots.

His sword carves into the stone floor with a sharp crack, the rock rippling.

I shrug. "Ignore me. Sorry, I forgot the rules. Shut up and listen. Don't bathe. Don't protest when friendly beings get murdered right in front of you."

At that, he whips around. "Just because it had fucking flowers in its horns doesn't make it *friendly*," he says, with just about all the disdain in the world.

I glare at him and get to my feet. "It was a gentle creature in a grove. It was looking at me with more awareness than *you*, you demonic brute."

His voice is venomous. "That *gentle creature* was a moment away from skewering you through."

My laugh echoes through the cave. "Oh, so that's it? You were protecting me?"

He makes a sound of contempt. "Your life is meaningless beyond you possessing something I need. I need you alive for now. Unfortunately."

I bow at the feet of my past self for setting the map aflame, for I have no doubt in my mind that Raker would have cut me down days ago if I still had it.

He won't kill me. Which gives me the courage to finally, truly get under his skin. He's ignored me for days. He has *left* me behind. He has insulted me at every turn.

Fuck. Him.

I take a slow step toward him. "I repulse you, don't I?" I say, tilting my head, searching within that hood for *anything* to glare at. Even a hint of those gray eyes. I see only darkness.

"You have no idea," he says.

I look him up and down, wondering why I bother him so much. I come up with a decent theory. "You think I'm unworthy of this blade."

He takes a step forward. "You are unworthy of *any blade*," he says, getting closer. He doesn't stop there. "You are weak. You are reckless. You can't even fucking *swim*."

My cheeks burn. His words sting like knives, skinning my weakest points. Still, I tilt my chin up. "Yet it's mine anyway," I say, right below him.

"Not for long," he says. Not even a threat but a promise.

He isn't wrong, but I hate that he's right. I hate that he knows this will kill me, because I'm in far over my head and blinded by this unrelenting pain.

He sees that. He sees my weaknesses. I don't want him to see *anything* about me.

I'm almost panting in anger. He's a shadow towering over me. I have to fully tilt my head just to pretend to look at whatever face lies beyond the mask and darkness. I've gotten a rise out of him. I want to twist the knife of my words, since I can't stab him with a real blade. Not yet.

"You must hate that this sword chose me . . . because it means we're not so different. It means, in some way, we're matched," I purr, hoping my words hit their mark. A smile curves my lips. I can sense the change, the rippling in energy, as his anger simmers.

He leans down like he wants me to hear every word. "Swords are only as good as their wielders. Yours is just as pathetic as you are." I flinch, that word sinking into my heart deeper than any dagger could, but he doesn't stop. He gets lower. "Nothing about *you* is any match to me."

Raker stares me down, as if daring me to say anything else. As if he's thinking that he has finally broken me. His words were meant to hurt. They did. But I am not a flame that can be extinguished. I won't let him look at me and only see weaknesses.

I look into that darkness, unflinching.

Enough of the mystery. Enough of *hiding*. Enough of him insulting me when I can't even see his *fucking face*. In a flash, I reach toward his mask to remove it.

His hand juts out just as quickly, wrapping painfully around my wrist. I gasp at the tightness of his grip, enough to nearly break bone.

"Don't," he snarls.

I bare my teeth at him. His hold doesn't weaken in the slightest. "They say you're a monster beneath that mask. That's why you wear it," I spit at him. "It would be good, I think. For your face to match your wicked heart."

His head moves as if he's looking me up and down.

I know what he sees. My collar, pulled right up to my chin. My shirt that covers me all the way down to my knuckles, even though it's hot. "I could say the same thing about you," he says. Of course he notices everything. I glare at him.

I can almost *feel* him glaring back.

This is a duel, one I want to win, but as the moments bleed together, as I stare so long at the place beneath his hood that I can almost see those gray eyes, and that silver mask, as our angry breathing fills the cave, as his grip tightens even more—

He drops my wrist as if he can't bear to touch me any longer, then walks off, leaving me burning with shame.

Bastard.

I hate him. His words shouldn't sting—but they do anyway.

The previously sweet berries are nearly tasteless on my tongue. I swallow them down, then some water, before packing my food up carefully.

I look over at where Raker went. I can see the outline of him on his side, sleeping. His sword is close to me, dug into the ground. I don't even attempt to move it.

His pack, though. His pack is right there by the entrance.

I watch his form as I step toward it. Slowly. *Screw you.*

With careful fingers, I slip my hand inside—and find what I'm looking for. The soap. I slip it into my palm, grab my sword, then jump through the water.

I am not pathetic, I think, as I venture into the darkness.

UNDER A MUTED crescent moon, I take my clothes off.

My markings glow faintly, like they sometimes do. They're thin. Not too different from the color of my skin. They would be almost unnoticeable if they weren't so very *silver*.

The water glows faintly through the darkness. A few bulbous white flowers float along its surface, alongside elaborate lily pads that look like expensive lace, tiny pieces cut out of them in patterns. Beautiful. Everything here is *beautiful*.

Sword and soap in hand, I wade into the stream, toward a pool of water that barely moves.

I can't use too much, or he'll notice, I think, as I begin to scrub myself. I get my legs, then stomach, then remember the dirt that crusted my cheeks and rub the soap all over my hair and face.

I pause.

This soap—it's the best smell I've ever encountered. Something in nature . . . something I can't place.

I breathe it in deeply and sigh. The demon smells good.

Bastard.

With regret, I throw the soap onto the rocks. I wash the bubbles off my skin and tilt my head back, running my fingers through the knotted strands of my hair.

At some point, I realize I'm waist-deep in water . . . and I'm not afraid. My pulse isn't racing. Before, I used to hesitate even being near bathhouses, not that there were many to speak of.

That fear has dimmed. And I hate that it's because of him. Because he forced me to *figure it out* instead of carrying me through it, and I did.

I sigh, letting the water melt away my pain and anxiety and anger. It swirls effortlessly, beautifully, massaging my skin. I blink up at the moon, thinking I could learn to love this. I could so easily live here, and be among nature, and learn to swim.

But this is not my life. I've spent far too much time in this stream already. I sigh. Straighten.

And pause.

A man in dark armor stands there staring at me. No. Not just a man. Darkness crawls up his throat, across his cheeks. I remember the obsidian blood, from the creature of the night.

He's a demon. That's why he hasn't reached me yet. That's why he's been waiting. Though his face doesn't look as decrepit as the others did. It almost looks normal, with the exception of his black irises, and those veins.

Slowly, he extends his hand toward me. "Come."

I just blink at him.

Maybe Raker is right. Maybe I am pathetic, and an idiot. Because for some reason I thought it was a good idea to have a bath at night, knowing very well what lurks in the darkness.

The stream was so close. I thought, between the waterfall and the pool, I would be safe. Cocooned between two water sources.

At my silence, the man takes a step forward. I flinch. The tip of his boot stops just short of the water.

He's only a few feet from me. I back away a few steps, but the bottom slants, and I'm forced to stand my ground.

Raker's horrible voice is in my head. *You can't even fucking swim.*

I should have learned. I should have demanded Stellan teach me. But there were no bodies of water nearby. The springs all dried up decades ago. We lived far from the sea.

"Come. You will join them."

"Join who?" I demand, water now up to my chin. My skin has erupted in chills. The previously refreshing water now feels ice-cold.

"The stolen brides," he says simply.

Stolen brides? I start to laugh. The man doesn't make a single movement. The idea that anyone would want me as their bride . . . the idea that someone would want a bride badly enough to *steal* them . . .

Wait. Is it the God of Death? Does this demon work with him?

Finally, the man's eyes narrow at me. "I will wait."

Fuck.

The water is freezing now. It'll be hours before daylight. I consider my options.

I could wait here and potentially find my death in these cold waters. I could scream and see if Harlan *"I Need You Alive, For Now"* Raker would save me. Or, I suppose, I could take this man's hand and see what life might be like as a stolen bride.

I sigh. "Then I guess I'm stuck here staring at your ugly face all night."

The man frowns.

I stare at him. He stares at me. He doesn't say anything. He doesn't drop his hand, as if believing I'll just give up and take his mysterious invitation.

Stolen brides.

On Stormside, people rarely get married. Survival oftentimes means betrayal. Families divided. Killed. Most don't live that long in those conditions. Love or care or even sex take lower priority than hunger and thirst.

You're on the wrong side, I think. Thousands on Stormside would take this man's hand willingly if guaranteed a lifetime of enough to eat.

My feet go numb. So do my fingers. I shiver, teeth rattling, and curse myself. Curse this man. Curse a god who can't get a bride unless he *steals one*. I curse this entire forest, and all its creatures, and even Raker's heavenly soap.

Just as the sun is about to surface, the man turns and disappears into the woods. Shivering, I wait for the red-tipped slice of sunrise to reach me.

A little cry sounds in the back of my throat as I rush through the stream, faint heat finding my limbs again.

My skin is pruney. My nails are blue. Tears sting my eyes at the sensation of the sun on my frozen skin.

The shivering makes it almost impossible to put my clothes on. I didn't get a chance to wash them.

I grab the soap and my sword and rush up to the cave.

Raker is sharpening his metal when I enter. He takes one glance at my dripping hair and trembling body and looks away.

"Idiot," he says beneath his breath.

I can't say I disagree with him. Behind his back, I slip the soap into his bag, grab my food, and leave the cave. I braid my hair, then lie outside beneath the sun, waiting as it warms me just the slightest bit.

When I can feel my toes again, I find the coin in my pocket and lay it on the grass.

"Come back," I say to the skies, willing my dragon to sense the gold. To want it as much as she wanted rubies. *"Please."*

Please, give me a path to the gods that doesn't involve this asshole.

My coin glimmers beneath the sunlight.

She doesn't come.

THREE DAYS PASS in the same way. Endless silence. Raker, doing his best to pretend I don't exist. Me, doing my best not to risk it all by smothering him in his sleep.

Sometimes, we'll make camp at one of the waterfall-doored caves earlier than sunset. It gives Raker more time to hunt, and he regularly returns with food. I stop looking. I stop complaining. He never offers anything to me.

It's fine. I don't need it. I collect a pile of sticks and, over the days, make a small basket, with skills the weaver taught me over the years. I forage so much that it's overflowing with fruits, mushrooms, and nuts. The Prism Pass is nothing if not fertile.

I'm wading through a moss-laden forest, brimming with buttercups and asters and violet-tipped tulips, pockets full of crimson berries, when I hear it.

A blade, smashing against something hard. I go still. My blood turns to ice.

Another challenger. Or an immortal?

No. The sword didn't hit metal. And that sword . . . I know it. Unless there is an immortal walking around with a blade as large as Raker's, it's his.

He's out hunting.

Raker has eaten plenty. There are more than enough berries and mushrooms here. Maybe . . . maybe if I could save one creature . . . My feet move before I can think about all the reasons getting in Raker's way is a bad idea.

As quietly as I can, I sneak through the woods, careful not to step on anything that will give me away, using skills learned through years of thieving just to get by. I duck low under branches and walk only on roots covered in spongy moss. The sounds of his sword get closer, and I slow. I curve around a tree dripping wisteria.

There he is.

Raker's armor is off. He's just in a shirt that he must wear underneath, thin fabric that molds to his form. His hood is still up.

It's the first time I've seen his body without his armor, and—

Fuck. He's not as repulsive as his personality.

I curse every single muscle—muscles so defined they are visible even through the fabric, ones I didn't even know existed, ones that do not have any right looking so good on someone so horrible—then drag my attention back to his blade.

He isn't hunting. He's training.

It makes sense. Of course, someone that skilled has only gotten those abilities from ceaseless practice.

I should be practicing. I've been too focused on keeping pace, and surviving, but I should be learning how to handle this massive sword.

Raker wields his like it's weightless. He growls as he turns. His blade flashes silver—before slicing through a tree. *An entire fucking tree.* It topples over, making the ground tremble.

Gods. The strength that would take ... the sharpness of the metal ...

Raker snarls again. He takes down another tree. Then another. His body is wound tight, muscles flexing.

It seems like he's getting aggression out. Good, I think. Good that he's using the trees as targets, and not my neck.

An innocent creature isn't at risk of becoming his dinner. I should leave. I should find more berries. I should erase the image of Raker's perfect body from my memory. Instead, I take a step closer, watching through the cover of branches and leaves, transfixed.

I can see now why he has so many names. Why his reputation is enough to leave grown men shaking and pissing themselves.

He is unparalleled.

Raker's movements are pure strength, matched with perfect precision. He turns to a tree, and cuts along its side in wild slashes, etching notch after notch up its bark, each line so close it's almost touching, with control I didn't think was possible.

His wide shoulders are tight. The frustrated growl that leaves his mouth makes me think there was a mistake—or maybe he's really that upset.

Definitely upset, I think, when he turns—and launches his sword directly into a tree. The trunk trembles with the force, before the blade flies back into his palm, just like it did during the Culling.

Leaves fall from the shaken tree in a flurry.

Then time slows to a crawl as he moves with a smoothness completely at odds with his towering form, with a speed that shouldn't be possible—

And slices every single falling leaf in half.

I don't breathe. I don't blink as I watch him lurch to a stop. The leaves are at his feet, in perfectly symmetrical pieces. He doesn't even look winded.

Fear inches through my blood as I realize I should be *absolutely terrified* of Harlan Raker. *Immortals* should be afraid of him. He is known as the best warrior who has ever lived, on Stormside. And I see every bit of that training, every bit of that mastery now.

I finally take a breath, watching him in knee-trembling awe.

Then that breath shoots out of my nostrils as I'm sent back against a tree, my spine hitting the bark. I gasp for air, unable to find it. My mind spins.

Raker's sword has skewered me here, through the fabric of my shirt. Slowly, I glance down, seeing the shining metal blade not even an *inch* from my waist. One hair in the wrong direction, and my guts would be all over this forest floor.

When I look up, he's right there, staring down at me. *Glaring*, if I had to guess.

I was quiet. I was far away. The fact that he could even have sensed me . . .

His voice is punishing. "You might think you are quiet, and clever, but you are loud, and clumsy, and a fool to think you could sneak up on me."

"Then teach me," I say, through ragged breaths. I want to learn how to wield this sword with even a whisper of the mastery he possesses. It's the only way I stand a chance at killing the gods once I reach them.

He wrests his blade from the trunk, sending me sliding down the wood as the fabric is released. I barely keep myself upright.

"You aren't worth even a moment of my time," he spits, before turning around. "Besides. You'll be dead soon."

He leaves me seething and panting against the tree, wondering if it's a threat, a promise, a prediction—or all three.

17

Just when I start thinking I have this land all figured out, the green ends.

It's replaced by ash. Mile after mile of ash.

It looks just like the Prism Pass but ruined. It looks like Stormside. The trees in the forest are rotted. The branches are bare.

But there are streams. I rush toward one, my throat throbbing with thirst, and pause just before my fingers skim the surface.

The water is red as blood.

Even on Stormside, the water isn't this shade. Most sitting water is murky and not safe to drink . . . but not crimson.

I look up at Raker. By the tilt of his head, I can tell he's studying the liquid. Without a sound, he turns away from it. Undrinkable, then.

We walk until the sun hangs low, and then we find a cave, with a red sheet of water in front of it. Raker stalks off to either hunt or train.

He won't teach me to wield my sword. Foolish, really, for me to even ask. But seeing how expertly he uses his has convinced me more than ever that I must learn.

Figure it out.

Under the fading sunlight, just beyond the cave, I lift my sword.

I haven't practiced since my dragon. I almost smile, remembering how she helped me. How her magnificent tail struck over and over.

If I thought days of walking with it would have made the weapon feel lighter, I was wrong. No, the steel feels even heavier now. My arms feel weaker.

Maybe berries and mushrooms aren't enough to sustain me on this journey. Maybe I should have asked for some of Raker's food.

It isn't just my lack of nourishment keeping me weak, I know. I'm resting every night, but not fully. I don't trust Raker. I don't trust this world. It's hard to completely slip into sleep out here.

This is the Questral. Of course I'm tired. Of course I'm hungry. These excuses won't matter when I reach the gods. I'll have to train myself through them.

I grip the hilt of my sword with both hands. My arms tremble as I lift my weapon higher.

Raker's voice cuts through my mind. *You are unworthy of any blade. Your sword is just as pathetic as you are.*

Rage simmers in my blood.

He's wrong. I am not pathetic. And one day, I will wield this sword just as easily as he does.

A growl escapes my throat as I lunge forward, cutting through the air, attempting even a fraction of Raker's speed. Instead of an elegant arc, the weight has me stumbling forward. Pain flashes through my biceps as I fight to keep it from piercing the ground.

Fuck, it's heavy.

It must be weightless in my hand if I'm going to fight with it. And that, I think, just requires practice.

Even a beast can be eaten in small bites, Stellan used to say. I would wrinkle my nose at the phrase, finding the idea of eating a beast repulsive, but, as the years went on, I understood his meaning. *Everything in life can be conquered in tiny steps.*

So, I start from the beginning, just like I had to when I was first learning to wield a sword. I begin with simply raising and lowering my metal for half an hour, until my muscles burn, trying to get used to its weight.

Then I attempt a simple cutting motion, one I've done a thousand times. This sword changes every detail and calculation. My stance. The energy needed. The strain.

I stagger forward—*shit*—then straighten. Shift my grip on the hilt, my right hand up against the guard, the other at its end. Grit my teeth. Try a second time.

And nearly fall on my face, the full heaviness of the weapon pulling me forward. I barely keep from dropping it.

Bent over my knees, I pant. *Get yourself together.*

Again.

Again.

This is the focus I find in the forge, and in early-morning training sessions with Stellan. I sink into a rhythm, and the world washes away, taking all my problems with it. It's only me and this sheet of sparkling metal. Nothing else matters. Nothing else gets my attention.

I shift my approaches, learning, then adjusting, until finally, I can do the move without compromising my stance. It's a simple victory, but pride seeps through my chest. I hold the sword in place, chest rising and falling, sweat sliding down my brow. *I did it.*

I'm just about to set it down when Raker emerges from the rotting trees. He has a creature on his back. I stare at him, breathing hard, forcing every bit of strength into my arms to keep my sword up.

He just strides past me, toward the cave up the hill, shaking his head, as though I am utterly ridiculous.

Screw him.

I continue, through the sounds of a fire being built, through the mouthwatering smell of roasting meat, through the crackle of the flames and the pattering of the crimson water. I train until my body is boneless, and the last shred of light fades away.

And then I drag myself through the bloodred waterfall and collapse into sleep.

I dream of a crackling hearth. Just beyond it, I can hear laughter, echoing through a full house. I smell burnt sugar and feel my sticky fingers curling around cards.

The fire burns out. The house is quiet again.

The darkness is thick as a blanket. The world is silent, and sleeping, and perfect.

All at once, it's burning.

Everything I've ever loved is up in flames, and I can't stop it, and I'm gasping, and coughing, and *everything, everyone* is—

I'm knocked out of my nightmare by a breath, right against my forehead.

I reach for my sword, but a firm hand is tied around my wrist, as if someone knew that was the first thing I would do.

Their other hand is covering my mouth.

I struggle, my scream muted, until I blink and see familiar gray eyes in front of mine. The rest of him is still cased in shadow. But the fact that I could feel his breath . . . it means he's not wearing his mask.

Raker's voice is a growl. "You were screaming."

He lowers his hand quickly, like touching me for even a moment is revolting.

It happened again. The nightmares.

I tremble against the ground, the remnants of that panic still running through my blood. I can feel the prick of tears in the corners of my eyes.

"You're going to get us killed," Raker snarls, before stalking away to his side of the cave.

LIKE RAKER'S MOOD, the rot worsens.

The ash-spun ground turns to mud. Every river, creek, and waterfall is red.

It isn't long before the juice from my berries isn't enough to quench my thirst. Raker drinks from the liquid in his pouch, offering none to me.

My throat aches. My head throbs. The sun beats heavily down on us without the veil of magic, scorching hot. This rot is a curse. All I can do is hope it ends soon.

We finally happen upon a forest, and my dry eyes search wildly for anything living.

Red. I spot large apple-like fruits and lunge forward, picking them—only to drop them. They're spoilt and teeming with insects.

I eat one of my berries, only to see that they themselves are starting to rot. It's as if this place has a sheen, a poison around us.

"We should go a different direction," I say, shaking my head. "This place—"

Raker ignores me.

We pass the carcass of an unrecognizable animal. I bury my nose in my shirt against the smell. Maggots crawl in and out of its skin, and its—its veins are dark, like that demon that tried to coax me out of the spring. Its flesh is gray.

Is this the God of Death's work too?

We walk for hours, without finding a suitable place to spend the night. Finally, we settle beside a rushing red river. We're not surrounded by water . . . but close enough to get in it, should we need to.

I really fucking hope we don't.

I won't be resting a moment tonight, anyway, remembering what happened the last time I fell asleep along a riverbank. Which is fine. I'm in no rush to return to that memory. Raker—bastard that he is—is right. Screaming in the middle of the night is a liability.

So is my very mortal reliance on food and water.

Training yesterday has only intensified my need for both. I'm so hungry that I find myself disappointed when Raker returns empty-handed. There's nothing to hunt anymore, I assume. Nothing that isn't poisoned.

I stare at my sad spread of food. I planned to save it for as long as I could ... but it's shriveling already. It won't last another day. I eat a good portion of it, the food grinding together into a dry paste in my mouth that I work to swallow.

Then I look up at the towering figure that is sitting on a rock by the red stream's edge, hunched forward. For once, his posture isn't perfect.

He must be hungry. Clearly, it takes a lot of food to keep a knight like him satiated.

He should have tried foraging. I'm sure he wouldn't turn up his nose at my berries and mushrooms now.

I eat another piece of fruit. I continue to watch him, trying to summon satisfaction and happiness at his current position.

I can't. Maybe it's because I know that him being weakened will only end up hurting me in the long run. Maybe it's because I'm not a heartless wretch like he is. Maybe I'm still hoping he'll train me.

You really are an idiot, I think to myself, before grabbing some of the mushrooms and berries and walking over to him.

He's sharpening his blade. Fantastic. His hands grip the sword and polishing stone and—they're huge. They're the biggest hands I've ever seen.

Why am I staring at them? These *huge hands* have killed hundreds. I should be disgusted by them. I *am* disgusted by them.

My eyes dip to his sword, wondering if I'll get another look at his mask in its reflection, but before I can, he lowers it, as if sensing my purpose.

"Here," I say, extending my hand.

He doesn't even look at me.

I scowl. "I know you're hungry. Are you truly too proud to take something from me?"

He doesn't say a word.

What? Does he think it's poisoned? I make a show of biting one of the mushrooms in half, chewing, swallowing, waiting, remaining very much *alive*, then offer the other half to him.

He turns away from me, as if the idea of eating something that has touched my lips is a worse fate than being poisoned.

I roll my eyes and offer him a different one. I wait a moment. Two. Fine. He wants to starve? Fucking *go ahead*. "You know what, I—"

He reaches out and takes it.

I'm stunned into silence. Slowly, his hand disappears beneath his hood and mask. I hear the faint sound of chewing. Swallowing.

"So, there's a face under there after all," I murmur to myself.

I'm shocked when he speaks again. Even more surprised when he reaches out and takes another mushroom from my palm, being careful not to touch my skin in the slightest. "As opposed to?"

I shrug. "A beak? A coil of snakes? A black hole?"

He makes a noise that sounds halfway between unimpressed and . . . and almost amused. "All of those would qualify as a face."

"True. Which means you still could look like a monster under there."

He doesn't say a word. He doesn't pull his hood back and remove his mask to assuage my curiosity. He just keeps taking mushrooms from my palm until they're all gone.

"I have more," I say warily, walking back to my things. As much as I hate him, I need him at full strength. And maybe this could be the start of a true partnership. One where I might actually be able to offer him something else of value, more than just the map . . . and he might, in turn, change his mind about training me.

I uncurl my leaves. All my food, out in the open. I sit in front of it. It takes a few minutes, pointed staring, and a long-suffering sigh from him, but—to my surprise—he joins me.

Good. This could be . . . good. We eat in silence, hands far away from the other's. But at least we aren't fighting.

Just when I think we might have formed a tentative truce, just when I think he might be capable of not being an asshole for just a few minutes, he says, "Why would someone like you be so desperate to go on the quest?"

My eyes narrow. "Someone like me?"

He takes a mushroom. Pops it into what I presume is, in fact, a mouth. "Breakable. Weak."

I should have let him fucking starve.

Fury boils beneath my skin. I have to remind myself why I'm working with him. Why I'm *feeding him*. "Excuse me, even though you have an *immortal ego,* you are very much human too. Just as *breakable* as me."

He tilts his head in a movement of utter arrogance, clearly disagreeing with that statement.

I roll my eyes. "I'm here for revenge," I say simply. "You?"

If his silence is any indication, my answer has surprised him. I suppose it would be shocking. Most people who make the journey are after the magic. He considers his answer for a moment. "You could say I have a similar purpose." He looks back at the spread of food.

I snort. "Who would be stupid enough to piss you off?" I ask, wondering if they've seen him with a sword.

Very slowly, his head tilts back up to me. I can feel his gaze locked with mine, even though I can't see his eyes. His voice is jagged steel against stone. "I don't know, Aris. You seem to do it quite often."

Aris.

He says my name for the first time, and my skin prickles. The way he says it . . . like his voice is both caressing it and mocking it . . . makes my pulse stutter.

But there's something else.

"How do you know my name?"

I've never told him. I'm not sure the Watchman ever even called it out. I'm certain he doesn't remember that day, two years prior, when we first met.

He says nothing.

I don't ask again. Instead, I give him a sugary smile, trying to ignore the stammer in my chest. "What can I say? I hate you. I'm sure I'm not the first."

He doesn't seem surprised by my hatred. He's probably used to having enemies all around him. He just continues to stare at me from the darkness of his hood, and I roll my eyes. "It's rude, you know. Keeping that hood on. I can't even see you glaring at me."

Raker just shakes his head and turns his attention back to the mushrooms.

We eat the rest in silence. When everything is gone, I carefully fold the leaf into a square. I look up and am shocked to see him offering something to me.

His water.

For a moment, I just look at it. I blink. I consider refusing. But in the end, I take it. Eyes fixed on where his must be, I slowly raise it to my lips. Take a sip. Try not to groan at how good the clean water feels sliding down my dry throat.

I offer it back to him, but he stands. "Keep it," he says roughly. And I know it's not because of generosity or care for me. I just know it.

I repulse you, don't I?

You have no idea.

He let me keep it because he doesn't want to drink from something my lips have touched.

We don't speak the entire next morning as the mud beneath our feet turns to dirt. Any hope of clean water withers as the crimson streams darken even more, to a thick metallic tar with an oily sheen. The sun is like an eye, staring me down, heat blazing. I make Raker's canteen last most of the day, then I'm thirsty again.

Mid-afternoon, Raker drops his pack by another riverbank and wordlessly slips away to hunt.

"I'm doing okay, thanks for asking," I say in his direction long after he's through the trees. I sigh.

If only I had literally any other travel companion.

My body is aching and spent. My legs want to buckle beside this putrid stream, but I slide my sword from its scabbard. I take a deep breath.

Then, I do the same slashing move I practiced before.

And I don't stumble. I keep my stance.

I keep my stance. I almost grin, realizing last time wasn't just a fluke. A jolt runs through the metal, striking my blood.

I tense.

I could be losing my mind. But I swear my sword just . . . congratulated me?

It could be the dehydration. Or the loneliness. Or my metal is really communicating with me. Whatever it is . . . it's the push I desperately need.

Time to see if I can do it while switching stances.

I can't.

I almost slice through my thigh actually, the blade careening forward.

Again.

My muscles burn as I shift my feet and legs, knees bending then straightening, yet every time my sword moves in its slicing motion, I lose my balance. It seems impossible to do both at the same time.

But I mastered it once, with a lesser blade, moving from wooden practice swords to metal, as a child with Stellan.

I can do it again.

I'm so focused on my shifting stances, that I don't even notice that the woods beyond the riverbank have gone deathly quiet.

I don't even see the glowing sword—

Until it's at my throat, casting a crimson light the exact shade of blood.

My breath catches. All my questions about how this sword is glowing come second to the fact that my pulse is currently beating against its metal.

I slowly turn my head to the side, only to meet a sparkling gaze. An immortal, whose skin is dry and split, like *this* is what happens to someone who spends too much time in this rot.

"Such a pretty sword," he whispers, in a strange lilt. "Lordship will love it."

I scream as loudly as I can.

Then, the glowing red sword's hilt smacks against my head, and the world goes dark.

18

I'm being dragged by one of my arms through the dirt.

My other arm is locked around something solid.

"Why the fuck is she still holding her sword?" someone new says as I come to a stop. My other hand is unceremoniously let go.

Another new voice. "It won't move without her. We had to play with her like a puppet to bring it over here."

Bile crawls up my throat. My temple aches where that strange glowing sword struck me.

The man makes an amused sound. "*Play* with her, you say?" A pause, and I can only imagine he's looking me over. "I hope you played a lot."

"Not as much as I would have liked."

It takes every ounce of willpower not to open my eyes and swing. But my head is still pounding. My senses are still returning. They have me more than outnumbered.

"It's a beautiful sword," yet another says. He pauses. I can hear the dirt shift around his feet. "We should kill her. Take it ourselves."

The same voice from before is back, with its distinct cadence. "*Silence.* Lordship will end her. Lordship will be grateful." He hums happily. "And we will be rewarded . . ."

"Let's throw her in, then," one of the men snaps, irritated.

Throw me in? Where?

"Not until he's summoned."

I hear steps moving away from me. Then more men speaking. Two of them, talking about my sword . . . then about my body.

"*Human.* Nice and warm," one of them says. A cold, bone-dry finger runs down my cheek. My hands are shaking, itching, pleading to kill him. "And soft." Someone tugs at a piece of my hair that's gone loose from its pins.

I wince in disgust, remembering a time years ago when men were also laughing, when they were *planning*. The hand stops. "Is she—"

A yell nearby. Boots thudding against compact ground.

"Stay with her," one of the immortals says as he darts away.

I open my eyes and find a man with the same dry cracked skin leaning down, as if he's about to touch me again.

I smile.

And my sword goes right through his gut.

Blood spurts onto me. I groan and sit up, throwing him to the side. Disgusting.

I look around. I'm in the rancid woods. Alone. I get to my feet and—I don't even know where I'm going. Did Raker hear my scream?

If he did . . . does he even care enough to go looking for me?

Probably not. I have to assume I'm on my own. I look up, as if to use the sun for direction.

A branch snaps behind me.

I spin and hardly get my blade up before it's meeting metal. The other sword shatters around us in shards of bronze, but the man is quick, pulling out a dagger. He lunges for my neck, and I twist away, my sword slicing all the way around his stomach with arm-trembling effort. More blood spurts, and I nearly vomit, now covered in dirt and gore.

The man falls, revealing a half dozen immortals behind him.

Fuck.

I swallow. Take a step back.

They all race forward.

"Stay still."

Stellan's voice is in my head. We're back in the graveyard where we used to train, because no one would ever bother us there. Only ancient, long-forgotten bodies are buried. Nowadays they're burned.

It's dark, but even if it wasn't, I can't see anything through the fabric he's tied around my eyes.

My heart races as I strain to hear his steps. My fingers tremble against the hilt of the blade.

"Your greatest enemy lives within you. It's fear. Kill it before it kills you."

I shift my weight. I take a deep breath.

His voice is right in front of me. "No matter what comes at you in this world, Aris, you stand your ground. You take a deep breath, and you focus. You make a plan, and then you do it. There is no fear. There is no indecision. Not for you. There's no time for anything but one steadying breath."

The darkness feels like it's caving in. I'm afraid of it, ever since that night, just like my sister used to be. I'm afraid of this place, where the wind sounds like whispers. I'm afraid of the fire I can feel just in front of me, the one Stellan has set.

"Kill your fears, Aris," he says. "Before they kill you."

Then he removes the blindfold.

A dozen men rush toward me, and I don't flinch. I dig my feet into the ground, sink into the stance I just spent hours practicing, lift my sword just like I did then, and take that *one steadying breath*.

Then I'm moving.

A sword comes at my neck, and I lean back, watching as he cuts off the head of the man behind me instead. Both hands firmly on the hilt, I swing my sword down in that slicing move I just mastered, right through bone and tissue, until he's just bloody tatters.

This metal is still too heavy, and I'm sore, but right now, fury ignites my strength.

These men . . .

They abducted me. They *touched* me. They plan to *offer* me to some lord.

No. I am not a thing to be taken and traded. If they want me, they will have me bloody and broken, because I refuse to go down quietly.

A battle cry sounds to my left, and I plant my feet, bend my knees, then turn and stick my sword through the immortal's stomach with so much force it goes through the man behind him too.

Another immortal moves in a blur, blade aimed at my arm, as if to cut it off to get my sword. So I let it go.

My blade dives forward, taking the impaled bodies with it, and I kick the immortal's legs out from under him.

He falls back, skewering himself on someone else's metal. But instead of bellowing with pain, he just closes his eyes in reverence as blood pours from his wound, puddling onto the dirt, and says, "Take it, Lordship. A gift, for you."

What the fuck?

I don't want to know what kind of *lord* wants blood. I need to get out of here. I pounce and take his sword, my fingers curling around the hilt and this—

This is bronze. This is familiar.

This, I can work with.

A smile inches across my face, just as an immortal's glimmering gaze meet mine. He frowns, skin splitting around his dry lips.

I lunge forward, slicing across his torso, his guts spilling out of him, smelling like rot, then duck out of the way of a gold blade, curved like a scythe. It whistles through the air, and I kneel, running him through, then rolling out of the way, before slicing the heels of the man about to put his weapon through the top of my head, sending him to his knees. I thrust my sword through his back. He falls face-first into the dirt.

It happens in a blink. One moment, I'm surrounded, and the next, all the immortals are bleeding out around me.

Fuck, it feels good to actually be able to use a weapon after weeks of struggling to even get my new one off the ground.

But I wouldn't trade mine for anything.

I rise, walking toward a final immortal who's trying and failing to pull my sword from the ground. My boots squelch over blood, but he doesn't even turn, he's so transfixed by my weapon.

No matter how hard he tries, it remains rooted in place, still buried in two men.

I reach behind him and slit his throat. He falls, and I throw the bronze sword at his body, reaching for my blade again. It slips out of the ground like slicing through butter. I lift my chin, feeling triumphant.

I only make it a single step forward before I'm slammed into a tree.

My head rings. The strange crimson glowing blade is at my neck. I thrash as much as I can, my skin brushing against the cold metal.

"Enough," the first man says, dirt and spit flying into my face. This close, I can see the cracks in his raw skin. "Lordship is arriving."

He doesn't waste another moment before shoving me to the ground. Metal still trained against my throat, he drags me by the hair through the dirt, past all the bodies. I fight against his hold, screaming, swinging my blade, but before I can get a good hit in, I'm being hauled to my feet again.

We're standing at the edge of a deep crater, lined in a strange pattern.

Before I can wonder how that happened, the dirt begins to swirl. And the hairs on the back of my neck rise one by one.

Somehow, I know this is the root of all this poison. I know that if he shoves me into this hole, I will never make it out alive.

The blade is still against my throat... but he hasn't killed me yet. He wants his lord to claim my sword. Not him. I take a risk.

I slam my metal through his foot, and he roars, loosening his hold.

He can't move my weapon. He's pinned in place. I use that to my advantage as I slip out of his arms and turn.

But his sword has magic. Before I make it far, my blood—

It stills.

And I fall to the ground.

How—

Without my own volition, my limbs start to move. They lurch forward... and I begin to stand. Even though it's the last thing I want to do, I stagger toward the crater. *No.* I grit my teeth, trying to fight it...

But the blade is like a thread pulled through my blood and bones, controlling my every move. Its crimson color flashes bright, deepening. *Reveling.*

I'm forced toward that swirling hole, and I fight every inch of the way, but it's no use. I keep shuffling toward my certain death. My jaw sets, refusing to give up, and I push back. With a burst of strength, I manage to turn my head to look at the immortal, and that's when I notice he and I might not be as different as I thought.

He's struggling to hold his blade too.

It's fucking heavy. I know. But he's supposed to be far stronger. I wonder if this rot has weakened him.

My own sword has him stuck. He can't fall into a better stance. His arms are trembling. I know what that's like.

He's going to lose his hold.

I keep fighting. My feet inch toward the crater, but I resist with every muscle, veins straining with the effort.

He does too. But it becomes all too clear that this isn't his sword. It belongs to someone far stronger. He's being allowed to use it.

Whose is it? The lord that's supposed to be appearing any second?

I don't ever want to learn the answer. I'm not going in that damned hole.

The mud keeps turning. The pit keeps deepening. My voice goes hoarse as I roar, battling the blade's vise enough to fully turn.

And take a step.

The immortal inhales sharply. His eyes narrow. His skin cracks as he trembles, yellowed teeth gritted, battling my will. But I think about all the gods have taken from me. And my fury?

It's deeper than this gorge. It could fill universes and galaxies and overflow the fucking ocean, and this immortal has no idea what he's up against.

Because I will not back down. Ever. Even if it kills me.

I take another step, bellowing.

He bares his teeth at me.

I bare mine back.

He tightens his hold.

I lunge.

He loses his grip.

And I don't hesitate. I rip my own weapon from his foot and thrust it through his chest in one smooth motion. He falls to his knees, taking me down with him. I reach for his blade—

But he reaches it first.

I wrench my metal from his ribs and retreat, panic gripping my heart. But instead of trying to kill me, he uses his final burst of strength to throw that sword into the hole. The dirt swallows it, before going still.

He slumps forward, dead.

Ears ringing, blood roaring, I stumble back, trip over a root, and hit the ground hard, knocking the wind from my lungs.

My muscles ache. I'm covered in blood and gore and dirt. I gasp for air, my pulse racing, late-afternoon sun scorching my skin.

This couldn't get any fucking worse, I think.

Then Harlan Raker fills my vision.

He peers down at me with little concern. He's not out of breath, from running to me. He isn't already holding his weapon. No, if anything, by the set of his wide shoulders, he looks almost bored.

My voice is a choked rasp. "You were—you were just standing there?" He didn't just *conveniently arrive*. No. He's been here for a while, hasn't he? I can almost imagine him leaned against a tree, arms crossed, watching as I fought for my life.

Doing *absolutely fucking nothing*.

Of course he ignores me. His head dips, and I feel his gaze like a brand as he looks me over. "How much of that blood is yours?"

"None of it," I spit, glaring daggers at him, still trying to find my breath. He studies me for another moment. Two.

"Good," he finally says. "Get up."

19

Harlan Raker is such an ass. I could have been killed. And then what? Would he have just shrugged, cut down whoever killed me, and continued the journey with two swords on his back?

Would he have jumped in and saved me, just to save the map in my mind?

I guess I'll never know, since I managed to save myself.

The grime all over me has hardened, weighing me down. The smell is awful, especially under the baking sun.

"His sword had magic," I finally say, the words rough from thirst.

"How perceptive of you."

I can't even find the strength to glare at him. It controlled my movements. It glowed. "How is that possible?"

Raker goes so long without answering that I've barely remembered what I said when he finally replies. "Godswords have unmatched magic. They're the only ones that glow with power."

Godswords? I've never heard the term. The immortal threw the sword into the hole. Was he throwing it to the God of Death?

He's the reason for the demons rising in the night. It would make sense that he's behind the rot too.

So why hasn't anyone done anything to stop him?

The sun sets, and we reach a cave with a sheet of onyx water covering it. Fantastic. I hold my arms over my head as I rush through it, wishing, more than anything, that I had a change of clothing.

I wouldn't be covered in blood and mud if he had helped me.

Raker is a cruel and merciless wretch. But I already knew that.

It almost makes me want to turn away the new pouch of water he offers. One he clearly stole off one of the corpses by the looks of the dirt on it. But I drink greedily. When my throat is smooth, I pour some on my face, washing off the dirt there.

Raker drops his pack on the cave floor and turns to me. "Your swordplay—"

"It's impressive. I know." *No thanks to him.*

"—could use some work."

I glare at him. "Did you miss the part where I killed all those immortals, or do you think they all ran into my blade?"

His voice is biting. "They were poisoned, undernourished fools."

My hands make fists by my sides. "Is there a purpose for your insults?"

A second of silence passes. "Will you draw the rest of the map for me?" I give him a withering look. With a slow shake of his head, he unsheathes his blade. "Then it's in my best interests that you don't get yourself killed."

I blink. "You're . . . you're going to train me?"

I remember his words in the woods, just a few days prior. How I *wasn't worth even a moment of his time.*

"I'm going to show you the very basics," he says, like he already regrets it.

I unsheathe my sword immediately. As insufferable as he is, I can't stop the excited thrill that runs through my veins.

He sighs, already vastly disappointed. "You're used to lesser swords. You can tell by the way you hold yours." He extends his own weapon, slowly demonstrating. "Like this."

I do exactly what he does, arms trembling with effort.

"*No.* Like this."

I slightly move my foot.

He sighs in a long-suffering way. He digs his blade into the ground, then takes a step toward me.

Gently, like he's trying to touch me as little as possible, his hand curls around my elbow. "Like this," he says, his voice a rumble just behind my ear.

He drops his hold like I've scalded him.

"Now shift your stance to advance."

I do. He makes a low sound of disapproval behind me. Before I can ask him what the hell is wrong with my form, both of his arms are around me.

I go very still.

His fingertips barely brush the fabric at my wrist as he gently twists my hold, then his long fingers uncurl, smoothing down mine, callused from battle, scraping my skin like a rough whisper, and a chill ripples up my spine.

I swallow.

His other hand shifts my hip, at the same time as his knee presses into the back of my thigh, using it to push my leg forward to where he wants it, leaving us—for just a moment—almost completely flush.

"Better," he whispers right into my ear.

My lips part. My every sense is narrowed on the places where he's still touching me. Against my hip. Against my thigh. Against my hand.

That *hand* . . . seeing it, the sheer difference in size . . . the way it so expertly holds a blade . . . it makes me think about what else his hands might know how to do.

What the fuck is wrong with me?

He's a monster. I could have died, and he would have just watched on, unimpressed.

I hate him.

But that doesn't mean something in me doesn't ignite, having his body curled around me like this.

I think back to how he looked in that grove, without his armor on. I wonder if he would put just as much focus and precision and stamina and skill into other acts . . .

My breath stutters at the thought. I swear I hear him swallow above me.

His hand flexes, right over mine.

Then he's on the other side of the cave. He's wrenching his sword from the rock and falling into his own fighting stance.

And now . . . now that he's pointed it out, I see the difference. The shift in weight. The easier grip on my metal.

Before I can blink, he's on me. All I see is a streak of silver and then I'm falling back with the force of his blade against mine.

He catches me by the front of my shirt, just like he did at the inn, but this time, his fingers curl even more, knuckles brushing my chest through the fabric. My skin feels like it's on too tight. My heart is racing. My eyes meet where his should be, and I can almost feel his irritation.

"Focus."

He drops his fist, and I stumble back.

Defiance lights up in my chest, smothering all those previous thoughts. I lunge, grip my sword with both hands, and strike with all my strength.

He moves out of the way quicker than someone his size should be able to, and I nearly hit the wall. I barely stop myself before tearing back around.

He isn't holding his sword anymore. No, it's dug right into the stone by his feet. He steps away from it.

I bare my teeth at him. "You're not going to use a blade?"

He lifts a shoulder. "It looks like I don't need one."

Cocky bastard. I swing, wanting to slice the inevitable smirk right off his hidden face, but he just moves to the side. He dodges as if he knows exactly what I'll do before I do it.

He clicks his tongue. "You're too predictable. Fool."

"Stop calling me that," I growl.

"Stop being one," he says, just as irritated as me.

I try again. Again. Every single time, he anticipates my moves, like he's a damned oracle. I exhale roughly in annoyance.

I move to dig my sword into the stone, just like he has a dozen times, but it doesn't pierce the ground at all. I try, and try, only managing to make my blood boil. My back teeth grind together, and I try one more time, before I growl in frustration. Raker just watches on, leaning forward against his own sword, his huge hands gripping the hilt. I can practically feel the arrogance coming off him in waves.

My head snaps up. "You're better than me. Happy? Is that what you wanted? For me to say it?"

He lifts a shoulder. "It goes without saying."

I glare at him. I hate him. But I need to survive the Questral. He has more training than I'll ever know. Even though I feel like flinging my sword to the ground and walking out of this cave, maybe all the way to the fucking gates, I swallow my pride and bitterness, and say, "Help me be better."

He just looks at me for a long time. Then he wrenches his sword from the ground. He falls into another stance and motions for me to follow. "Start with this."

Raker teaches me the proper way to hold my new sword over my shoulder, in a position ready to strike.

And nothing else.

After several minutes of insisting I'm not doing it right, then relenting that my feet are, in fact, in the right place, Raker gives a sharp nod, then walks away. He starts removing things from his pack, and I just stand there, still as a statue.

"Now what?" I finally ask. I know this position already. Of course I do. The heavier metal means more energy is needed. A slightly different stance—fine. I've learned it. Now I want to get to how to actually *wield this sword*.

"Nothing," Raker says flatly.

My eye twitches. "What do you mean, *nothing*?"

"Stay there, until I say otherwise." His tone leaves no room for discussion. Still, I open my mouth. Close it. His back toward me, he digs his sword into the stone. He removes some of his armor. He sinks to the ground.

And the bastard goes to *sleep*.

"Fuck," I breathe, halfway torn between flinging my sword at him in anger and staying here all night out of stubbornness.

This is clearly a test. He wants to see if I'm even worth training. If I can listen. If I can learn. If I have willpower.

Or maybe the demon has no intention of training me and just wants to make me suffer.

It doesn't take long for this simple position to become excruciating. My arms begin to tremble. My sword shakes with them, just inches from my neck. Damn it. If I cut my throat with my own blade, I don't know whether the blood loss or embarrassment will kill me first.

I breathe. I steady my core. I bend my knees slightly, using the rest of my muscles to offset the weight. To help.

Soon, my entire body is quivering.

This sword is a gift, I remind myself. It's an honor to have been chosen by such a blade.

I need to stop thinking of it as a burden. As something too heavy to hold. I need to start thinking of it as something to be worthy of.

My sword doesn't need to be lighter. I just need to be strong enough to carry it.

You believed in me, I think, apparently having reached a point of pain that I am *speaking to my sword in my head.*

If you didn't believe in me, you wouldn't have claimed me.

I must really be losing my mind.

Because through all the shaking, I swear I feel another jolt. A tiny spark, like a glimmer of encouragement.

You must have seen a shred of your strength in me, I continue. *I will find that shred and make it grow.*

I sink deeper into my stance. I will not fall over. I will not collapse. I will not stand down. Hard things prove my strength. I will be as unbreakable as my blade.

I repeat it over and over and over.

Just when I think I've reached the dregs of my strength, there is more. The well within me is deeper than I ever knew. I learn that only after hours of trembling, of *holding on.* Of standing firm.

And maybe, just maybe, that is what Raker is trying to show me.

It's still dark outside when his voice cuts through the silence of the cave. "Enough. Go to bed, Aris."

I nearly collapse onto the floor. Raker seems to know it, because I can hear his deep sigh.

My eyes are closed before my head even settles against the stone.

RAKER DOESN'T ACKNOWLEDGE me the next morning. Or during the hours we spend trekking through the sinking rot.

But when we arrive at our shelter for the night, he gives me a new position. Long guard. Extending my sword forward, in front of my body. With both hands, since I still can't lift it with one.

Then he leaves to hunt.

My arms are sore and aching from the night before, but my mind is stronger. My focus is unwavering. This time, I cycle through those ten memories. The ones I cherish. The ones where I was the happiest.

And that happiness . . . it is so much stronger than the pain. It is like Starside steel meeting lesser metal. Shattering everything in its path.

My mind narrows to them. To my purpose. To why I'm doing this.

I startle when I notice Raker leaning against a tree, watching me.

The sun has dipped low. I've been in this position for over an hour. I raise a brow in question. *Enough?*

He dips his head in a nod, and I thank the stars as I stumble forward. I drop my sword against the dirt in front of my boots and lean on my knees, panting. I only look up when he passes me, moving toward the mouth of yet another obsidian-blocked cave. "Nothing?"

He shakes his head. My berries are gone. The canteen he gave me is empty.

Inside the cave, Raker sighs as he drops his stuff onto the floor.

"Draw the map," he says. It both relieves and scares me that he sounds tired. If Raker is fading . . . if *he* is beginning to feel the effects of thirst and hunger, what chance do I have?

Arms still shaking, I carve the map into the stone with my sword, making faint scratches.

More of the same. Which I now know is just endless nothing.

Raker curses.

"We should travel north," I say. "Off the path. There are towns."

I expect Raker to ignore me. To stay silent while he comes up with his own plan, or to admonish me for wanting to veer from the quest.

But all he does is nod, before disappearing into the shadows of the cave.

THIS IS THE last time Raker is ever going to fucking listen to me.

The village is abandoned.

The rot has infected it like a disease, mold spores eating through the sides of houses, thorned vines snaking through windows.

"The map, it—" Is clearly outdated. Raker doesn't spare me a glance as he walks past me. My throat tightens. Is this the moment he realizes my memorization of the map isn't as helpful as he thought?

Seventeen days into the Questral . . . and we aren't even halfway to the Land of the Gods. If we plan on returning to the gates before the fifty days are up, we have to go faster. Or find a shortcut. We can't afford to make these kinds of mistakes. I come to a stop, half expecting him to turn. To slice me to ribbons and take my sword. But all he does is stalk through the town, to the other side.

I follow in silence.

He's going north. He must see what I do—that although this village was overcome, there are the faintest signs that the rot is lessening the farther north we travel. There are a few blades of grass peeking through the dirt, and the occasional sparse tree.

The Land of the Gods is northeast, anyway. We aren't going too far off the path. And we both know we won't make it there without food or water. We just need a lucky break.

After hours of walking, we finally reach a river that is only slightly clouded in color. Not clean enough to drink, though I'm almost desperate enough to try. I reach my hand inside, just to smell it—and Raker snarls at me. Begrudgingly, I remove my fingers.

There's an old bridge made of crumbling gray stone that curves over the water. It isn't wide. It isn't long either.

We're both exhausted, but still, he says, "Unsheathe your blade."

I expect another position. But Raker just stares at me, and says, "Again. Shoulders down, this time."

I do it again.

He shakes his head, reaches back. Then, all at once, his silver is in front of him. He's so fast, it becomes just a streak of metal. He sheaths it again. "Like that."

I grind my teeth. I didn't even fucking see what he did, since it was so quick. I try again.

He exhales deeply. Then, far slower than before, he reaches back again. This time, he uses both hands. It's for my own benefit, I know, since he only unsheathes his with one.

I watch the angles of his arms. His posture. His stance. I try again.

"Better," he admits, and I'm beaming.

"But you're so slow, your head will hit the ground before you even get your blade out."

I scowl at him, and try again, faster.

He shakes his head. "Dead."

Teeth gritted, I do it again, arms screaming.

"Still dead."

Irritation flares through me, and this time I'm so fast, I surprise myself with my speed. My blade blurs.

I'm panting, but the bastard still says, "Dead."

"You're wrong," I snarl, chest rising and falling.

"Am I?"

"*Yes.*" To prove it, I sheath my blade, then take it out again, and *this time*, I'm more than half a second faster than I was before, my metal arcing and—

It's still in the air, pointed toward the sky, not even in front of me at all.

And Raker's sword is at my throat.

His metal skims my pulse. "Dead without question," he says from the other end of it, his voice a rough whisper in the darkness. I swallow, his blade following the movement. All it would take is a millimeter less precision, and I would be bleeding out in seconds. My lips part.

Then, in a flash, his sword is gone, and I'm left burning in frustration. But instead of stalking off, like I expect, he says, "Again."

And this time, we do it together. He sheaths and unsheathes his weapon, so much faster than I am, but strangely, with him doing it at the same time, it pushes my limits. Makes me quicker than I ever thought possible.

"Good," he finally says, and I think I might keel over in shock. He notices my surprise and happiness, and makes sure to snuff it out by adding, "For you."

I glare at him.

The bridge is where we sleep, the stone so narrow we're forced to lie side by side, our blades between us. Raker's body almost makes it all the way across.

I drew more of the map for him, but he hasn't told me where we're headed. I open my mouth to ask, and he turns, giving me his back.

Right.

I stay on my spine, tired and starving. All that practice drained my energy.

How long can we go without food? Without water? I know how long I've gone without both on Stormside, but here? Carrying a sword like this? Traveling many miles every day? I try to do the math, to make the predictions, but my mind feels like ash in the wind.

This thirst, this hunger . . . it could kill me. I know that. It feels like it might. Like I could go to bed here, on this bridge, and never wake up.

Maybe that's why I open my mouth. Why I speak to a cruel warrior who clearly wants nothing to do with me. "Are you afraid of anything, Raker?"

I feel him stiffen beside me. But he doesn't answer.

That's fine. I'll answer my own question. "I'm afraid of the dark," I say, and I don't know why. He already thinks so low of me. Why add more to that list of weaknesses? Still, I don't stop.

"I used to hate the night. For many reasons." Like that guttering, ending, soul-shredding darkness when the fire that took everything from me finally extinguished. "Here, though . . . right now . . . looking up at these stars." I stare at them in wonder. They shine so much brighter. Diamonds tossed across the galaxy like skipping stones. "I think I could learn to love the night."

He doesn't say a word. But he doesn't tell me to shut up either.

"I'm afraid of water . . . and fire. You know the first one, I guess. Because . . . because I can't swim. Almost drowning helped that fear, a little. Because that death was almost quiet. Almost quick." The second certainly is not. My mind pulses with memories, and I move on.

"I'm afraid of dying in a stupid way, like tripping into my sword, or eating a bad berry, or dehydrating on an old bridge, next to the most miserable knight in existence." I turn my head toward him. "Are you afraid of anything?" I ask again.

"I'm afraid you won't stop talking, Aris," he says.

It doesn't hold as much bite as it could. I almost keep going, just to irritate him. I open my mouth.

I only manage to say something half sensical before being dragged into sleep.

IN THE MIDDLE of the night, I'm awoken by sharp stabs over every inch of my skin. I gasp and nearly choke—

Rain.

No. We aren't that lucky. But I swallow, and *yes.* Clean water. It washes away the grime on my face; it sinks through my fabrics, cleansing them of the blood and mud. The cold grips my bones, but I don't mind. I don't mind anything at all, because *finally.*

I rise to my knees, tip my head back, and drink. I run my hands through the messy braids, washing it of all the grime. Then I scramble to fill my canteen. My hands tremble around it, fearing the rain will stop, but it keeps coming. I wait until water is spilling down the sides. I drink the entire thing and then refill it, before I look up and see Raker doing the same with a new canteen. His back is to me. His hood is plastered to his head. If he turned, would I see his face, or his mask? I wait to see if the fabric slips . . . but it doesn't.

And neither does mine. It clings to my body. I lift my collar, trying to wash my neck the best I can, without exposing my throat. Not that Raker is looking. No, he's very pointedly still facing the opposite direction.

This is a gift. If I was most mortals on Stormside, I would be thanking the gods. I don't know who to thank, but I slowly rise to my feet and drink some more, feeling the cold water run through my dehydrated veins, until my shoulders finally melt, some of my tension releasing. We're still hungry, and moving too slowly across Starside, but at least we aren't thirsty anymore. This is a win.

I make to move, but suddenly my feet feel heavier. I look down. The riverbank is overflowing. The bridge is quickly becoming submerged.

I take a step forward—and slip. Only a hand locked around my wrist keeps me upright. Swirling black ink wraps down each finger, and I try to read the writing, the symbols, but I can't.

Slowly, I look up, wondering what I'll find, allowing myself hope that I might finally see him, but all I see is his mask.

And those gray eyes.

I blink, and I'm thrust back to that day, in a storm just like this one. Eyes hard and merciless as steel, staring me down. Hand gripped tightly around my wrist. Dragging me through dirt and mud as I thrashed and screamed.

I jerk back, and he drops my arm.

He turns wordlessly and stalks off the bridge. He doesn't stop. I know what he's thinking. If demons are so afraid of water, they won't surface in the rain. It's better for us to cover more ground.

Dirt slips beneath my boots as I follow Raker through the downpour, the scars on my lower back tightening—an ever-present reminder of why I can't trust him.

20

The rain continues all through the night, and into the morning. By the time it ends, I'm cold to the bone. But my canteen is full. My throat is blissfully smooth.

My clothes slowly dry in the dappled sunlight. By midday, we find a forest that isn't rotted, and my knees nearly buckle with relief. Especially when I find a single fertile bush bursting with berries. I pick every single one, cutting my fingers on the thorns, but I don't care. I'm so desperate for food that I shove the fruit into my mouth. I wordlessly extend a handful to Raker, and he takes it.

It's the only fruit for miles. I scour every tree, every bush, but there isn't so much as a single mushroom. The woods empty out into a wide plain. There's a stream running through it. It's almost clear, just a shade of gray—and our shelter for the night, by the looks of it.

I half expect Raker to leave me here without another word, but he slides into a defensive stance, showing me quickly. "Got it?" he says.

I nod. I slip into it, and he barks a few orders, a few fixes, then leaves with his things, ducking into the woods.

I hold the position for as long as I can. When hours pass without Raker resurfacing, I begin to alternate through all the stances he's shown me. The sword feels looser in my hand. More fluid.

Just as I think I could take on Harlan Raker himself, I stumble forward, nearly dropping the sword. *Fuck.*

A laugh sounds behind me.

I spin on my heel.

Two immortals—no more than children—are standing there, watching me. Tossing the coin I emptied from my pocket to train.

"Hey!" I yell, and they don't run, or set it down. No. They have the nerve to look *amused*. "That's mine!"

They don't even stop throwing it back and forth. It's as if I haven't spoken at all.

"I have a sword!" I bellow, lifting it.

One of the boys snorts. "Yes, and by the looks of it, you can't even use it." My eyes narrow.

Enough. I take off toward them, but they're across the clearing in a flash. They're *laughing*. Then they're tearing through the forest, fast as lightning, turning to look at me instead of looking ahead and still somehow avoiding the branches, while also continuing their game.

I'm short by most standards, but I'm much taller than them. I have longer legs. Still, they are *immortal*, and I don't have a chance of keeping up.

A growl escapes my lips as I listen to my coin clinking as it's thrown between them, glinting beneath the sun. I worked hard to get that coin. I need it.

They make a sharp turn, and I throw myself through the brush, needles stinging, leaves clinging to my sweaty face.

But their steps have stopped. I would have thought they had climbed into the trees if I didn't hear one of them say, finally, with a shred of shame, "We were just playing. We weren't really going to take it."

Raker. He must have caught them.

I lunge forward, feeling a little smug—then stop when I see another immortal standing at the center of the forest.

And she's not a child. No, she's a tall woman, with a bow on her back. My breath hitches.

With superior speed, her eyes meet mine. The sharpness of her expression has me stumbling back—but it's immediately replaced by a friendly, if not abashed, smile.

Still. She's immortal. I have no clue where Raker is. And, as this child very helpfully pointed out, *I can't really use my sword yet.*

I begin to retreat, my hands up, all but pleading that they please take my coin and have a very nice day.

"Don't be afraid, human," the immortal says.

I am still very much afraid, thank you. I take another step back.

She takes a step forward. "I apologize for my boys. They should never have taken from you." With brutal speed, she looks back at the children, snarling.

At that look, they mumble apologies, clearly more afraid of their mother than the sword slung against my spine.

I can relate. I am also, in this moment, afraid of their mother and the glorious set of arrows that she wears.

The immortal woman frowns. Then, as if to calm my fears, she places the coin on a branch. "Here you are. Sorry to have disturbed you." With another sharp look at the children, she begins to walk away. I watch her, pulse racing.

Only when she's on the other side of the forest do I creep forward and roughly pocket my coin.

I'm about to turn to go when she says, voice projecting from yards away, "That knight. He won't find much in these woods. We're too close to the rot and mists for any large game to come near."

She saw Raker. And she's still alive, which means she likely didn't try to attack him.

My stomach turns with hunger and sinking disappointment. So that's why he hasn't been back in more hours than usual.

Damn.

"We have food."

I slowly look up at her. She might as well have told me she has the gods themselves, tied up and ready for me to slaughter.

"The village isn't far. We could get you dinner for the night." My stomach lurches again. My mind becomes solely focused on the idea of something, *anything*, filling it, but still, I don't make a single move, and she continues. "It would be the least I could do. In . . . apology for my sons' actions."

Why would an immortal even care about her children stealing from a human? I'm about to refuse, hoping I can find another fertile bush, but her gaze flicks up to the sky and the gathering clouds there. "It's going to rain through the night. At the very least, let me offer you a roof. The local inn isn't much, but—" Her words are unspoken, but I get her meaning. *It's better than sleeping outside in the downpour.*

"Which way to the village?" I say.

We can't trust immortals. But when Raker finally walks through the trees and hears the same offer, he must know as well as I do that we are in no position to turn down food and a roof.

We follow the immortal and her children through the woods, and I hope this isn't just another mistake.

RAKER DOESN'T SAY a word during the walk to the village, even as the two boys zip around him, asking a thousand questions—about his sword, about his armor, about his size, about his hood and mask. His silence only seems to feed their fascination.

"Leave them both alone," the woman says, her voice tired, like this is a regular occurrence. *Them* is a generous term, because, other than my coin, the boys don't seem fascinated by me at all. They only want to see the *knight*.

"Are warriors not common?" I ask the woman, catching up to her pace. At the very least, getting information is better than listening to the boys and their endless inquiries.

She glances over at me. Her features are sharp—and pretty. She has deep tan skin and dark hair tied low. "They are," she says, mouth tightening into seriousness. "But the boys don't see them."

Interesting. I wonder what she means.

"Mother *never* lets us downstairs at night," one of the boys loudly complains.

"I shouldn't let you downstairs during the *day* if this is the trouble you find," she says through her teeth.

The boy rolls his eyes and goes back to antagonizing Raker.

"Are children . . . are children common for immortals?" I ask after a while.

"No," she says simply. "They are not."

I look over at her. At her weapon. "If large game isn't found near here . . . what do you hunt?"

"These arrows are not for hunting game," she says simply.

And with that, the hill crests, and I see the beginnings of a small village. There's a mill. Winding roads, and alleys, and buildings bunched together. But that is not what my gaze snags on. It is not what makes a lick of fear slide down my spine.

"What is that?" I breathe.

A forest sits just east of the village. At least, that's what I think it is. The weave of white trees is nearly wholly blocked by a thick wall of mist.

"That's the Bone Woods," the woman says, not stopping. I unroot myself, to keep up. She doesn't even look at it, and I wonder if it's because of fear, or disgust, or the indifference of familiarity. "With its mists."

Mists. One of the reasons she said Raker wouldn't find much to hunt so close by.

"And you . . . live on its fringes?"

"It didn't used to be so close," she says tightly. "Decade by decade, it creeps closer."

I would ask why she hasn't moved, but I understand, once we enter the village and a half dozen people nod at the woman and boys—before sharpening their gazes at us. They have a community here. A home.

The word hooks into a part of me and pulls behind my ribs. A mixture of sad and happy moments spill out from behind it.

I had a home, once.

I both mourn its absence . . . and celebrate the fact that I ever had one to begin with.

She stops in front of a small house with a painted wooden door that doesn't quite fit its frame. There's a large window, its glass glazed over by time. "Upstairs. Now," she tells the boys, who scurry off, with some parting words for Raker that he, of course, does not reciprocate.

She shakes her head and leads us down the street, stopping at another home, this one with a few additional levels. She slips inside, then returns shortly with two keys. "Dinner will be brought up to you."

Raker takes his key, nods, says his thanks, then slips through the door without another word.

"We really appreciate this," I say when she hands me mine, and, with a tight smile, she steps back onto the bustling street.

The stairs are so narrow I wonder how Raker even got up them. The wood groans beneath my boots as I step into a small, comfortable room. There isn't a tub . . . but there is a bucket of water, a cloth, and soap. I sniff it . . . and no, it doesn't smell anything like Raker's.

I carefully remove my clothes before smoothing the wet rag over my skin. Then I begin to wash my clothing, piece by piece, in the bucket. The rain got off most of the grime, but I take my time with the soap. Washing and rewashing until it's all clean. I hang them to dry by the fire, put one of the bedsheets on the floor in front of it, and lie down, luxuriating in its warmth. I stare up at the ceiling. The walls are thin. I hear everything—from moving around, to people relieving themselves to . . . guests very aggressively enjoying themselves.

For some reason, that makes me think of Raker. I wonder what he's doing in his room. Is it possible he's found someone in this town? I think about the way he cut those trees down, how it released some of his frustration.

Does he need a release in another way?

What the fuck, Aris?

I shake away the thought. Raker seems like he would gut someone for even getting near him. And even if he did find someone to bed here, that is none of my business . . .

A knock on my door has me jolting upright. By the time I open it, wrapped completely in a bedsheet, only a tray awaits. The smell of hot soup hits me, and I nearly fall to my knees. Bread. There's *bread*.

I drag the tray inside and waste no time sinking to the floor and eating my dinner there, too hungry for anything resembling restraint. My hands tremble as I lift the bowl to my lips and drink.

The moment the hot liquid hits my stomach, it lurches, but I keep drinking, hoping I don't make myself sick. I eat every bite of bread.

Then I lie on my back and enjoy the feeling of a slightly full stomach.

Hours pass like this, listening to the groaning of the inn, until hunger finds me again. I curse the fact that I don't have another set of clothing, before putting mine back on—they're mostly dry—and slowly making my way downstairs, coin in hand. I half expect to see Raker doing the same thing. I half hope to see him, just so I won't have to eat alone.

A warrior is staring up at me as I take the last step. But it's not Raker.

"Look what we have here," a deep voice drawls. "A human." He's sitting with an entire table of immortal knights, all in gleaming armor. A half dozen empty glasses sit in front of them. Just my luck.

I ignore him as I walk to the bar. I drop my coin, and the redheaded barmaid barely spares me a look before taking it, returning with a pile of unfamiliar carved metal, then a bowl of steaming soup. My mouth waters when its smell hits me. I could devour the entire pot. I begin to eat, as the chair beside me groans under the weight of a fully armored immortal.

Fantastic.

I keep my eyes on my soup. My inattention only seems to make him more interested.

"What is a mortal doing so far on our side? So close to the mists?" A thought seems to occur to him, and he slams his hand down onto the bar. "Right. The quest. It's about that time now." This close, I can smell the ale on his breath. He only gets closer. "Humans are so ugly. So blemished. But you . . . you're one of the prettier ones."

Wow, thanks, I think. I keep slurping my soup, hoping it will disgust him enough to leave me alone.

He doesn't. He just studies me closer, ogling my body. I see the moment his gaze finally lands on my back. And the sword there. It took him a while, like he didn't even entertain for a moment that I would have a weapon of value. His easygoing grin fades. "Say, how did a girl as spindly as you get a sword like that?"

I sigh.

This is the best soup I've ever had. And he's not letting me fucking enjoy it.

I gently place my spoon back into my soup. Slowly, I turn toward the annoying warrior. Voice sweet as honey, I say, "I won it when an immortal idiot interrupted my dinner."

The bar goes silent.

Shit. You know, I probably shouldn't have said that. But I did, so I lift my chin and don't let a hint of my instant regret reach my face.

A second passes. Another.

Then the grin returns. The immortal warrior puts his hands up, stands, but in his eyes I see the shadow of something like fury, that I would dare stand up to him. *Me, an insignificant mortal.*

Fuck. And I was trying *so* hard to be pleasant.

The bar doesn't return to its full swing of conversation. I feel eyes on me as I finish the rest of my soup. Even the barmaid is looking at me with a mixture of respect and pity that tells me I picked the wrong knight to talk back to. All I want to do is go back to my room, lie in front of the hearth and pass out, but the group of warriors is still there. Still glancing over at me. I don't want them to know which room I'm sleeping in.

So I leave the bar and slip out into the rain-slicked streets. I'm grateful when I don't hear steps behind me.

It doesn't take me long to reach the immortal woman's house. The light is on. Through the weathered window, I see her sitting at a table, poring over a book, reading by the light of a few scattered candles.

Before I can think better of it, I rap my knuckles softly against the glass.

Her head lifts immediately. Her eyes are fierce and protective—and they only slightly soften when they see it's me. For a moment, I wonder if she isn't going to let me in. She seems to be leaning in that direction. Then, with a sigh, she stands and walks over to the door. Opens it.

"Has there been trouble?" she asks. Her eyes flit up, toward where the boys sleep, and I know she's likely regretting potentially having brought danger to her door.

"No," I say quickly. There wasn't really trouble . . . I hope. "I couldn't sleep."

She frowns. "Right. I have something for that, actually, if you want to take it." With more than a little trepidation, she moves to the side and lets me in. The moment I step inside, the heat of the hearth hits me. My shoulders drop. Tension leaves me, in a rush.

This . . . this feels like a home. A place worn down by memories. I can see them in the scuffs in the floorboards, in the scratches on the walls, in the sagging of certain cushions on the furniture, in the drained color of the carpet left near the window. The house is quiet. The boys are sleeping. But as I walk through to the living room, I can almost hear laughter stored in between the floorboards. This house wears its memories. Just like mine did.

Glass clinks as the immortal woman rummages through rows and rows of vials. She searches with deft fingers, a fold between her brows, until she produces a violet liquid. "There," she says. She turns to me. "Open your mouth."

I blink at her.

She cocks her head at my hesitance. Her look says, *If I wanted to harm you, I could have done it a long time ago.*

It's true. She was armed when we met, after all. And though I lied about why I'm here . . . my inability to sleep isn't a lie at all. We have a long day ahead of us. My exhaustion could mean the difference between life and death.

I open my mouth. Two drops pierce my tongue.

Then she's putting the vial away. I'm swallowing something that tastes faintly like flowers. "You're . . . a healer."

She nods.

It makes sense now. Why she would see knights often. And, judging from the behavior of the ones at the inn, it also makes sense why she would want to keep her children away from them.

She sits back down in her chair, the wood gently creaking. Then, a bit warily, she motions to the seat in front of her table, a simple stool. "The elixir will take a little while to work. Sit."

Slowly, I do. She studies me. "You're on the quest, then?"

I nod. No use in pretending otherwise. She looks me over. I wonder what she's seeing. The undernourishment? The lack of any real, true muscle? The cuts already on my cheeks and hands?

"I assume . . . I assume you have a good reason" is all she says. *A good reason for throwing myself into near-certain death for a cup of magic* are the words she likely meant.

I can see in the shadow of concern on her face that she doesn't think I'll make it until the end. I can't blame her.

But she can help me. If she's a healer . . . if she knows about the mists, and the places beyond here . . .

"What is the Bone Woods? Is it dangerous?" I know the map. Now I realize what the lightly shaded area is. It's unnamed, and takes up a large swath of land. Going around it would take several days we don't have. Going through would be far easier . . .

"It's exactly what it sounds like. A forest made of bone. And yes. Very. The mist is a prison. Housing creatures even the gods leave alone."

The warm room seems to suddenly go cold. "Why?"

She lifts a shoulder. "They say they're as old as the gods themselves. Older, maybe. All I know is entire armies have gone into the mists . . . never to be seen again."

That sounds like a legend. I've learned by now that anything on this side is possible. But if she's right . . . What is powerful enough to do that, beyond a god?

"Why go in at all, then?"

She purses her lips. I can see she's weighing how much to say. How much to keep to herself. In the end, she must decide that I will likely die anyway, because she says, "There is a godsword in those mists."

Godsword. That's what Raker called the glowing crimson one, with the unsettling power.

"Which god's sword?"

She shakes her head. "That I do not know. But heirs of Great Houses, and even gods themselves, have sent countless people inside looking for it." She shrugs. "None of them return."

My next question is dangerous. "Why don't the gods go themselves?"

She just looks at me with her glittering violet eyes. I can see the simmer of something. She looks up. Not at the gods. At what she clearly cares about more—her children. Her words are measured. "The gods don't put themselves in perilous situations. Not anymore."

Not anymore? "Why?"

She shakes her head. I'm not sure if she's saying she doesn't know . . . or if she's telling me she won't answer. Not with her children in the house.

Does she think the gods can hear us? Can they?

There are various levels of commitment to the gods on Stormside nowadays. It's hard to worship something we know almost nothing about, but some of the most reverent believe the gods see all.

I think they have better things to do than listen in on a conversation in the middle of a distant, mist-addled town.

Still, I move on. "The creatures in the mists . . . can they be found in other forests?" I remember Xara's warnings about the dangers of different woods. Several more sit between here and the Land of the Gods.

She dips her head. "There are more there, surely, but yes. Deadly creatures can be found almost anywhere. Most of the ancient ones have been slumbering, or keep to territories like the mists, but others . . . wander."

Wander. I swallow, a chill blooming in my bones.

"What kinds of creatures?"

Her eyes meet mine. They are devoid of any humor, or anything but pure seriousness—and fear. "The kind that make even immortals wish for death. The kind that grind your bones with their teeth and suck the soul from your body."

I shift my weight in the chair. "How do you know so much about them?"

"Their venom is valuable. They can poison . . . but also cure. I trade with hunters who risk life and limb to hunt them down." Hunters. Xara mentioned them, back in Westwere. She stands and strides toward shelves that slump in the middle. Her long, smooth fingers brush a dozen spines before she stops. The book she takes out has a leather cover creased with age. Its parchment is yellowed. She flips toward the middle, then hands it, wide open, to me.

I take it carefully, the same way I would handle a sword in Stellan's forge. Like I'm dealing with something rare and valuable.

It's a book of beasts. The illustrations are meticulously made in various hues, the ink slightly glittering. I've never seen anything like it.

"Can I . . . can I stay and read this?" It's too much to ask. She's given me so much already. I prepare to be sent back into the rain.

But she just motions with her chin toward the hearth. A comfortable-looking chair sits in front of it. It has a cushion with a star stitched onto it. "Go ahead."

I gingerly take the book over. I sit. And . . . this feels like an indulgence, like the biggest luxury, to sit by the fire with a book.

I start at the beginning. I read quickly, to get through as much as possible, flipping through the pages, studying each image. Every description.

And I realize I don't know anything about Starside. Not at all. Because the greatest weapons here are not swords—

They are beasts.

And some have magic.

Few can use it. Most have it buried in their bones, or scales, or claws, ready to be extracted and smelted into swords or made into medicines. Those are the ones that are most hunted.

The others are the most feared. There are creatures that can turn into balls of flame, flying through forests, burning down entire woods in just minutes.

There are massive scorpions that can trigger earthquakes with flicks of their horned tails.

There are skeletal cats that can walk through objects, fading into shadows.

There are creatures like the immortal said, older than the seeds of this world, that can pry into minds and swallow souls.

Phoenix.

The word has my breath catching, remembering the last time Stellan called me one.

It turns out there are several types.

There are storm phoenixes that form only during the worst downpours, crafted from lightning and thunder and wind.

There are ice phoenixes that melt into puddles, only to rise again.
There are—
My eyelids suddenly feel heavy as iron. The words begin to blur. *The sleep serum.* It muddles my thoughts. Makes the letters melt together.

As my eyes slowly blink closed, I think that I have been traveling through Starside for weeks. I thought I saw the worst of it.

But this book has made it clear that I haven't yet seen this world's teeth.

A KNOCK HAS me jolting awake, gasping.

"It's just the rain," a gentle voice says. "Not to worry."

I'm still in the immortal's house. The book is open in my lap. A thickly woven blanket has been draped over my shoulders.

I sit up, blinking, feeling both rested and drained. Morning light is starting to filter in through the window. I slept here all night. The immortal is still working.

I'm not on the floor . . . which means I didn't have my nightmares. No. I slept deeply and calmly, for the first time in years.

Slowly, I get up. I fold the blanket and leave it on the chair. With a pang of sadness, I return the book too.

The immortal gives me a long look, before she ducks below her desk. Glass gently clinks together. "The lord here is strict. I can't spare much, but here." She emerges with a handful of vials. "For all you find and collect on your journey."

My throat tightens, knowing this woman doesn't expect I'll live much longer . . . but she's giving me something so precious all the same.

"I really am sorry about the coin," she says, as she walks me out of her house.

Rain whispers down the slanted cobblestones; it patters against aluminum rooftops. The rest of the village hasn't woken up yet. Only the faintest light peeks through clouds so dense, they look like another wall of mist.

I wrap my arms around myself as I make my way down the quiet road. I miss the hearth already, and the comfortable seat, and the book. Something tells me I'll never be that comfortable again. Certainly not during the Questral.

For a moment . . . for a moment, I could pretend like I belonged in a home like that. Like I had a home at all that was still standing.

Just before I take the turn to the inn, I pause. The hairs on the back of my neck go stiff. I look over my shoulder—but the road is empty.

It's just that book, putting me on edge with all its talk of dangerous creatures, some of which slink through the holes in cobblestone walls and follow travelers. But it's daytime. I have nothing to be afraid of.

Still, that strange feeling has me veering off the path, indulging my instincts. I go down a different alley instead, the rain masking my steps.

But not masking a voice.

"She just left. She should be here any second . . ."

A frustrated growl. "I've been waiting all fucking night. Cut her head off the moment she returns and be done with it. That sword . . ."

I step back, my veins like ice.

I shouldn't have left my room. I should have remained there, quiet and unseen until the next morning. I know that now.

And I never should have mocked the knight. Regardless of how good it felt to do so.

I can't return to the inn. I can't go to Raker, though with his silence and general apathy toward me, I'm not sure he would even interfere.

One hand still on the damp stone wall of a closed shop, I turn toward the woman's house . . . then stop myself.

They knew where I was before. They could easily follow me back. And the idea of bringing those knights to the immortal's home . . . remembering how she looked up at the second floor, where her children slept . . .

Remembering how I woke up with that blanket draped over my shoulders. That simple act of care . . .

No. I won't bring danger to her, so my only choice is to hide out somewhere else and hope they get tired of waiting for me. Hope Raker comes out of the inn sometime in the next hour, and I can reach him before the warriors reach me.

Using the rain as cover, I duck and turn down another road. The village is small. There aren't many places to hide. I try different door handles just in case, but all of them are locked. I look for sheds, hovels, anything—but there's nothing.

I turn another corner. There's the slightest scraping behind me. A boot against wet stone. I whirl around.

And there he is. The immortal warrior.

He grins.

I run.

My legs feel slightly boneless, as if they haven't fully woken up. *The elixir.* It must still be coursing through my veins. The immortal doesn't deal with humans often, I assume. Did she give me too much?

A wave of sleep washes over me like nausea. I grit my teeth against it.

Because I can hear them now. All three of them. All running after *me*.

"Raker!" I scream, beyond pride, beyond shame. The rain begins to pour heavier, as if colluding with those warriors. *"Raker!"*

The immortals behind me laugh. I get the feeling they aren't even chasing me with their full speed. That they are, in fact, *playing*, dragging out the hunt, as if it's a sport.

"Her fear . . . her desperation . . ." one says, his voice like velvet. "I smell it even through the rain. Look at her scream for help. Look at her realize no one is coming." The others laugh.

A pit forms in my stomach, knowing these immortals can sense my every shade of terror. And it pleases them.

My boots kick up water and dirt. I risk a look back—and they're right at my feet. Mouths pulled into grins.

At the edge of the village, I keep going, hoping they'll give up. But as my feet hit the mud, I hear them right on my trail.

They're immortal. Faster. *Better* in every way. The fact that they haven't caught me already is also likely evidence of the number of drained goblets that were on their table.

"There's nowhere to run, stupid human," one of them trills.

He's right. Up ahead is just a firm wall of gray. The mists. The Bone Woods. The fog is unmoving even under the downpour, sitting like an ominous cloud.

I run toward it, hoping its proximity will give them pause. And every inch closer I get, I feel it. An otherworldly coldness gripping my bones. Sliding through my veins. Freezing my blood, little by little. Clawing at my soul.

One of the warriors behind me curses, slows down, but the others don't.

And when I reach the mist, I turn sharply to run along its edge.

This close, I hear it like a whisper, like a beckoning. I feel its chill against my cheek, like a stroking skeletal finger. I feel its cut, like skirting a sword's blade.

"You can't outrun us," one of the warriors says, his armor clamoring as he sprints. His voice is too close. Right behind me. Almost at my ear. I look back and see him reaching for my sword. His hand is almost at the hilt.

His other hand is holding his weapon. It's nearly at my neck. I veer to the other side—only to gasp. The other warrior is there, sword outstretched.

The one from before is now in front.

They have me surrounded. Boxed in.

I turn toward the village, but there's no one coming to help. Raker didn't hear my cries, or he did and he didn't care. I'm alone.

"Look at that. Trapped like a rabbit in a snare. Nowhere to run," one of the warriors says, before swinging his blade back. I know that position well. I held it for hours. I know it's setting up for a brutal, killing stroke. He wants to be the one to claim my sword.

But he's wrong. There is somewhere to run.

Rain melts down my face as I turn—and throw myself through the wall of mist.

21

Cold spears my bones and settles in my marrow. More unnerving than that is the soul-withering silence.

The rain falls soundlessly against the ground.

My skin prickles with panic. I can't hear anything—even the warriors beyond the tree line. I can't see them either.

I unsheathe my sword as quickly as I did with Raker, ready for the possibility that they will run in after me. That perhaps the tales of the mist were exaggerated.

But there isn't a single movement. Even those immortal knights, armored, deadly, and likely centuries old, fear this place. My sweaty hands tighten around the hilt, in case I'm wrong. I keep my blade lifted high even through the lingering effects of the sleeping elixir, a testament to my recent practice. I've stayed in this same position for hours. I can stay in it for minutes.

I do. I count the seconds until ten minutes have passed, the quiet of the mist so unsettling, the thought of facing the warriors again seems almost like a preferable option. Hopefully, they're back in town. Or Raker's close enough that I can catch up to him. I take a steadying breath, then bolt back in the direction I came—

But I don't see the warriors. I don't see the village.

All I see is endless mist, as though I have fallen into an ever-changing labyrinth.

Fuck.

Dread trips down my spine as the immortal's words cycle through my head. Entire armies sent inside, never to be seen again. Ancient creatures that would grind my bones to dust with their teeth.

No. I can't stay here. Raker will be looking for me. Or, more likely, he will be leaving me behind. How long will he wait? Minutes? Did he even hear my cries in the streets?

Would he care if he did?

I run, right toward the village. It has to be there. There must be an end to this fog. I've barely taken a few steps. *I am not lost.*

I repeat the words even as the mist thickens. Even as the ground changes. Even as it becomes clear that this place is as deadly as the immortal said it was.

I open my mouth to scream—but even my voice is muted. It's hardly a whisper in the wind. I yell and yell, my neck straining, until my throat burns. The sounds I make are swallowed, as if I'm sitting at the bottom of a well.

No. This can't be happening.

Sword back in my scabbard, I start sprinting. In the direction I came, or the opposite, I'm not sure. Everything looks the same. Everything keeps repeating. My eyes burn. Terror clenches my chest.

My muscles begin to slacken.

That damned elixir. I can feel its magic slinking back through me, as if to smother my racing pulse. As if to lull me back to sleep.

No. If ever there was a place to fear sleep, it's this one.

I dredge up more strength, pushing my legs, my arms, to just go faster. To just find the edge of this mist. I think I see a parting in the trees, just as my foot catches beneath a root and the world goes sideways. My jaw hits the ground, and pain blinds me. My teeth crash together. My skull rings. As I grip the ground with trembling hands and my fingers find another root, I realize that the Bone Woods are, in fact, exactly what they sound like.

The trees are all crafted from bone—twisted, ancient, and fused together perfectly, as if someone took great care in shaping them. I reach toward one of the trunks, my finger running down long, sharp scratches several inches deep.

What has claws like this?

I don't want to fucking find out. Even though it feels like the mist is a heavy cloak over my shoulders, I get up and keep running. And the fog . . . it almost whispers against my skin. It almost stings, as if not sure whether to bite or caress.

I feel a thousand eyes on me, but everywhere I look there is nothing but endless mist and trees. I turn to run in the opposite direction, but it's all the same.

I stop. I turn again.

A crunch sounds behind me.

I pivot, unsheathing my blade in a flash. The metal's sparkle is dimmed. The pulse I feel from it has weakened. *Everything* is diminished.

There's nothing behind me, but I feel it. A prick against my neck. A breath against my ear. A metallic taste in my mouth as if all this side's glimmer has been concentrated into a copper paste. All at once, a sharp pain cleaves my mind in half.

And a silvery voice says, *Sleep.*

It's beautiful, like a wind chime. I turn—and only find the mist. It's moving now, curling around my ankles.

You know you want to.

My fingers tremble against the hilt of my blade. I walk backward, stumbling on another root.

A chuckle echoes through the forest, echoing in my mind.

Close your eyes. You don't want to see what comes next, the voice says.

The trees begin to shake as if something otherworldly is walking through them. Then they part completely, like a giant blade has cleaved the forest in half.

I stand very still, sword still up. If this is my fate, I will confront it head on.

Foolish child, the voice says.

Power spirals from the center of the trees in a flash of curling gray, hitting me right in the chest.

Sleep, it commands.

My head hits the mangled bone root, and I obey.

My skin is stinging. The back of my head hurts. I feel something faintly warm behind it, and I know at once it's my own blood. The warmest thing in this cold place.

This cold place.

I open my eyes and am met by a face made up solely of bone and teeth. I flinch, scuttling back, sword in my hand, until my spine hits a tree.

The man simply straightens. And in my soul, I know this is one of the creatures the immortal spoke of. An ancient presence. If I didn't know it from the fangs curling out of his jagged mouth, I would know it from the fear in my chest, an orb of fracturing ice, as if some primal part of me knows to *run*.

Looking at him, I know running would be useless.

He is nearly as tall as the trees. His fingers, reaching toward me, are made of curved blades, in a sparkling metal I've never seen before. They clash together in a pitch that makes my head scream. His mouth is lipless, opening slightly, to reveal several rows of fangs. His eyes are just guttered holes, with dancing silver flecks, like punched-out pockets of night. He wears the mist as a cape, without a hood, so I can see his entire smooth skull.

When he speaks, it is directly into my mind, the voice cutting through it like a knife.

Curious little creature stumbles into the mist . . .

My scream is a whisper as I fold forward, gasping with pain. Every syllable scrapes through my head.

With trembling arms, I manage to lift my sword again.

That only makes the creature smile, a fang-filled expression that sends fear spiking through my blood. He could rip out my throat with those teeth. Instead, he rips into my mind again.

What a pretty sword. Just like the one I hide.

I gasp from the pain. He steps closer, his foot peeking through the mist. It is just gnarled, twisted bone.

Have you come to steal from me?

"No," I breathe, the word hardly making any sound at all as I try to steady my mind, try to think my way out of this. Try to remember what the immortal said about these creatures.

The book said ancient beings make barters. If only I had anything to trade. Anything of value other than this sword, which I cannot part with.

My weapon is powerful. I struggle to stand as I lift it higher, to maybe have a fighting chance—

The being starts to laugh. The sound claws through my brain, scratching the inside of my skull, and I squeeze my eyes shut, my lips parting with another soundless scream.

That blade would break against my bone. I am older than the dawn of this world—alive before it even had a name. He stops himself, and I gasp for breath. *Or . . . perhaps it wouldn't. Are you willing to take that risk?*

He's in my head. It's not just his voice. I can feel him strumming through my thoughts with those metallic fingers, like he's flipping through pages of a book. I can sense how easily he could shred my mind to pieces with blade-like precision, without even needing to try.

How much can he see? How much does he already know? How much did he look while I was asleep?

"Get out of my head," I rasp. No use in considering ways to kill him. Not when he's hearing every one of my thoughts.

You're the one who entered my mists, girl. Did you not know what you would find?

I wouldn't have, if it hadn't been my only option. Though now I consider that I would far rather have faced the three immortal warriors than this being.

He circles me. His smile grows even larger, the bone fissuring.

Are you afraid? Disgusted?

I lift my chin, even as something deep and old in my brain is telling me to kneel and beg for mercy. "No."

He laughs again, and I double over, shoulder pressed to my ear in a fruitless attempt to block out the noise, but it's impossible. It's coming from inside my head. There's no outrunning it.

I can feel your emotions, girl. I can steal them, like sucking marrow from bone. I can drain you until you are just a husk, more bones to add to my forest. More blood to feed my soil. I've spent centuries tending to my domain. These are my woods, and I am its Gardener.

My brain swirls. I gasp. It's like he's turning my mind inside out like a pack, shaking out its contents.

Interesting. Your shade of fear . . . is perplexing. You are afraid . . . but not for yourself. Not really. You're afraid for your journey. How curious . . .

He pauses. A new constellation of silver flecks flicker in those dark eyes before guttering out.

Such sorrow. I have only felt such bottomless despair once before. Just now, actually . . .

His vise on my mind tightens, and I nearly pass out from the pressure. My eyes feel like they're going to burst. I can feel him sinking his claws into me, prying me open like a stubborn clam . . .

Until all at once, he's ripped out of my head, and I fall forward, onto my palms. My heart beats wildly. I'm panting, gasping for air.

That name in your head. What a dangerous name. What a curious name...

The look on my face must show I have no idea what he's talking about, because he speaks it right into my mind, carving it like a knife.

Vander Evren.

The name Stellan whispered as he was bleeding out onto the floorboards. The immortal I'm supposed to find.

He must be able to feel or see the hope surging within me, because he begins to chuckle, the sound raking through my thoughts. *Summoning Vander Evren would be a death sentence for you...*

"Summoning?" I manage to get out. "How would I summon him?" Can I summon him now is my real question, but of course, the immortal ignores me, moving on, studying me.

Curious little human, stumbles into my mists...

Unprepared. Naïve. Soul dripping rage and regret...

Each word slices into my brain. He says it like a poem. Like a joke. Like I am simply a plaything in his long, immortal life.

"What do you want?" I gasp out, tears slipping down my cheeks.

At once, he's right in front of me.

To feast on your flesh, to lick your bones clean, to swallow your soul, he says.

I take a shaking breath. I wait for those teeth to sink into me, but all he does is circle again, the mists spinning around him. "Do you like to play with your food before you eat?" I bite out, turning on my knees, refusing to give him my back. I lift my sword. I won't test it, but if he lunges at me, I will strike. Even if it's the last thing I do.

No. I'm so very hungry, I eat everything that enters the mists before they even have a chance to see me... The woods must be fed...

But the depths of your emotions... of your anguish... It makes me remember...

He trails off, as if he has been snared by another place and time completely.

Then, in a flash, his bottomless eyes are on me again.

Today is peculiar. So very peculiar...

He looks at me, and I can imagine how weak and insignificant I look to this ancient presence, but I don't drop my gaze. I don't cower.

My eyes remain locked on his. His next words are just the slightest bit gentler, the claws of his voice not sinking in as deeply as before.

I want to know why a starving girl has more courage than even immortal heirs.

I bark out a silent laugh. He can't be serious.

But he doesn't chuckle. His expression is firm. *You plan to face the gods, when even immortals have remained silent and complacent for centuries.*

So, he has seen in my mind. He has seen . . . everything.

And he still hasn't killed me.

Is he against the gods? Does he want to see them fall? Maybe I can convince him to let me go, to finish my quest. I answer honestly. "I don't have anything to lose. Everything I loved, I have lost already."

He hums, the sound rattling through my mind. *Yes . . . that loss . . . those memories . . .*

He turns his head with a crack. His night-torn eyes seem to ripple. I swallow. *You want to leave? You want to escape?*

I nod.

I want one.

I blink. "You—"

I want a memory.

I should feel relief at the chance to get the hell out of this place, but all I feel is crushing sadness. My memories are all I have. "Why?"

His cape swirls behind him, melting into the rest of the mist.

When I feast on flesh and bone, I feel but a ripple of your life. Then it fades. But if you were to give me a memory willingly, it would last . . .

Ten. I have just ten happy memories. I could offer up another, but I know he means *them*. I just know it. If my mind is a room, these memories are kept in the drawers. Locked tightly. Guarded. "No," I say, backing away.

He rushes at me, full force, that mist turning into a thousand claws and blades, all pointed toward me.

I gasp.

The mist settles, as if the weapons were never there at all. As if they could be summoned in half a second.

I grow hungry.

I can almost feel that hunger, as if the mist is an extension of himself, and it is also starving. I look around at the forest. Thousands of trees that must have been people at some point.

The creature is right. I'm not afraid for me . . . I'm scared I won't be strong enough to make it to the end of this journey.

Give me the memory, and I will spare you.

I don't want to. But if I don't . . . if I die here, in the mists . . .

All of this will have been for nothing.

"Fine," I say, my eyes burning.

He smiles, the bone of his face fracturing slightly with the movement. His longest metal finger reaches toward me, parting the mist. As he gets closer, that burning in my eyes intensifies, that sorrow distilling—until a single tear slips down my cheek. He presses his finger to it, the curious shimmering blade scraping against my skin. He pulls it toward him.

I jerk forward, hooked, then released, as something more than just a tear is taken. It sits on his finger, solid as ice, and as he brings it to his face, I can hear it. Laughter. Playing. Voices that I would give anything to hear again.

In a flash, the creature puts his sharp finger in his mouth, swallowing the memory, humming. Smiling. Tasting.

I collapse onto the ground, heart beating against the dirt. New tears turning it to mud.

It's . . . gone. That tiny, bright pocket in my mind is dimmer. The drawer in my brain has been ransacked.

"Thank you, Aris Godslayer," he says, before drifting away. Lost in thought. Lost in my memory. I look up at him from the ground, somewhere between cursing him for taking something priceless and thanking him for sparing me.

Before he fades completely, he looks over his shoulder. "I might be the oldest thing in these woods, but I am far from the deadliest. If you want to kill those gods . . . I suggest you run."

He disappears.

And all the sounds of the forest hit me at once, like a veil has been lifted.

Scratches. Growls. Right behind me. As if there were beasts waiting on the fringes, scared of the Gardener. But now he's gone.

I don't look. I just bolt.

The Bone Woods thicken, closing in, and I duck below branches, jump over roots, chest heaving. But even through my panting, I hear them.

Growls, echoing from every direction. Thundering steps against the dirt. Panic pounds through my blood as I count several. Whatever they are . . . there's a pack of them.

I push myself even more, not daring to look over my shoulder, hurling myself forward, but they're faster. I hear their snapping maws, just feet away. Their hunger—I can feel it, like a second mist, closing in.

I can't outrun them. They're going to mow me down any second. So, when I reach a tree with branches low enough, I throw myself onto it and begin to climb.

The bone is smooth beneath my fingers, as if well and truly licked clean, and I resist the urge to vomit. I haul myself up, groaning—

Just as a jaw snaps an inch shy of my foot.

Heart in my throat, I scramble higher, then turn. I brandish my sword.

And curse.

Saberwolves. I read about them in the immortal's text. They're three times as large as normal wolves, with two fangs that curl out of their mouths like curved daggers, sharp enough to shred their prey to ribbons and containing immobilizing poison.

Before I can even think about forming a plan, one of them leaps, and I jerk back, barely missing the brush of its fang. I cling to the trunk, my feet settling on a different branch. They can't climb. But I can't stay in this tree forever.

The saberwolves seem to know that . . . and their hunger makes them restless. Foam spills down their jaws. Their eyes are black. They snarl, revealing the full size of those massive teeth.

Shreds. I would be ripped to unrecognizable shreds by those fangs, by this pack. I wouldn't even become part of this forest; I have a feeling they would grind my bones to no more than powder.

There's nowhere to go. Nothing to do but hold my sword out in front of me—which is all these days of training have really added up to—and try to plan some sort of distraction. But there's no time.

One of the beasts takes a few steps back, then lunges. But not toward me. No.

Toward the trunk.

I hold on to the closest branch for dear life as the tree lurches to the side. If they can't reach me, they are going to bring me to them.

FUCK.

The wolf slams into the tree over and over and over, and I remember Raker's sword doing the same thing, how the leaves all came down. How he cut them in half. I am at risk of a similar fate as I cling to the trunk, my head banging against bone, my hands slick with sweat.

The wolf pulls back to go again. And the other two saberwolves glance at each other. That look is far too knowing, far too intelligent. One of them breaks from the group. It runs in the opposite direction, turns around—then rushes toward the tree. It jumps.

And uses the other one's back to launch off, right toward me.

I barely leap out of the way in time, clinging to another branch as the tree sways again. But this branch is lower. The third wolf leaps. I rush to pull my legs up—but not before its fang grazes my calf.

It's the simplest brush. But it cuts right through fabric and skin.

And burns like an inferno.

I scream, the sound echoing through the forest—before the pain is muted. And that's worse. Because I feel its venom slinking through my blood, until I can't feel my leg at all.

I'm so fucked.

Especially when the other wolf slams against the tree again, and I fall out of it.

22

I hit the ground with a sickening crack, and there's no time to run. Those saberwolf fangs are in my face a half second later, ready to rip me apart, rancid breath hot against my mouth, drool sputtering everywhere.

My mind is still spinning from the drop. I can't think. But I don't need to. The movement is instinct. I force my blade up, an echo of the memory of Raker's training.

Right through the wolf's neck.

Then the other wolves are on me. Shredding, ripping, feasting. Blood spraying, puddling, staining the woods. The smell of it pierces even the mists.

But it's not mine. They are eating their own, even as it's still taking its last breaths. Right atop me.

Are they that hungry? That quick to turn on one another when given the opportunity?

Arms shaking, face covered in blood, it takes everything in me to rip my sword from the saberwolf's throat and roll from beneath its corpse, before it crushes me.

I keep rolling. Keep crawling. My leg is wholly numb. I desperately drag it along. And hope to all the gods that the wolves are too distracted with their current meal to follow. The sound of those massive fangs tearing through flesh echoes through the forest, and my skin prickles with fear, anticipating the weight on my spine as they push me to the ground, as they gut me just like they did their pack member.

Blood roaring in my ears, dirt under my nails, I make it far enough away that their snarls of satisfaction are muted, and then I get to my feet and run.

It's more of a stumble. To make up for my leg, I push the rest of my body forward with all my might. I don't look back. I just keep staggering, hoping to find the end of this mist, hoping I get lucky and just fall out of it—

Silence. The sounds of thrashing teeth fade away completely. But I'm not that far, no. They're just done.

But not with me.

Those heavy steps are at my back in seconds. *Shit.*

I force my numb leg forward, gasping, clawing at the trees, using them to fling me ahead, but it's no use. I know that. Still, I can't just give up.

My limbs burn as I force myself forward. My neck prickles with awareness. A feral growl rumbles behind me.

I turn my head—and am met with razor-sharp teeth, nearly at my height. They're on my heels. A couple more strides, and they'll be on me. This is it. I stumble with a final push of desperation.

They leap.

The woods slope beneath my boots, the world spins, and I'm suddenly tumbling down a hill, gasping as my arms hit stumps of bone, as my vision turns to flashes of mist and soil, before I finally hit a tree with crushing force and stop.

I can't take a full breath. Everything hurts.

Cheek against the bone roots, I can't summon the strength to get up, even when those wolves crest the hill I just fell down. Even when their eyes lock on me. One of them snaps its powerful jaw, head falling back, emitting a satisfied howl.

It sits back on its haunches, preparing to bound down the hill in one massive jump. But before it can, it turns its head. Snarls. Lunges forward.

Toward nothing short of a swarm of winged, leathery bats the size of people. There are dozens flying in a wall. They open their mouths and emit high-pitched screams.

The two packs crash together, and it is carnage. Blood spurts. Flesh and fur paint the white bone forest, pieces getting stuck in its branches. Their shrieks and growls echo.

And it's like a call, awakening every monster in the mists. I can feel the forest rousing, almost rippling, like a stone being thrown into a lake, casting waves.

The fog goes still.

A sky-splitting screech has it *scattering*. What can shift even these mists? I have a sinking feeling I'm about to find out. For even though this pack and swarm are battling, more are joining in and they will all eventually turn their attention to me.

I cling to the trunk for purchase and push myself up, inch by inch. Stumble through the forest as more creatures barrel toward this stretch of woods, cries and screams and hisses turning the mists into a nightmare symphony.

Shredding. The unmistakable sound of ripping flesh fills the forest—something with rows and rows of teeth has joined the fight, and razed countless creatures. I need to get out of here. My breathing is too loud, my steps are too clumsy. My arm is hanging at an odd angle, and that's when I realize I must have dislocated my shoulder in the fall down the hill. *Fuck.* It's my sword-wielding arm.

I should give up. I'm lost, and defenseless, and in a hungry beast-riddled mist. It's useless to fight this hard, with so much stacked against me. And maybe that's what makes me a fool—refusing to stay down, even when the world tries to keep me there. Fighting, even when fighting seems useless.

Always rising, just like Stellan taught me.

Those roars are growing louder. Closer. As if the battle has spilled down that slope. As if it's coming right in my direction.

I turn to look back—

And a growl sounds right in front of me. I barely get my head back around, but I'm still rushing toward the monster, not able to stop myself before I crash right into it.

My scream is smothered.

By a hand.

I look up, eyes wide, heart battering my ribs, only to see a familiar hood.

A whimper of relief spills from my lips, and I don't even try to hold back the tears that streak through the blood and dirt.

"What are you doing here?" I try to say, but his hand only tightens over my mouth, choking the words.

It's no use. They've found me. I hear them, tearing through the forest. The swarms, the packs, whatever ancient creature made the mists *shudder*. All coming right toward us. Raker hears them too.

"Fuck, Aris," Raker growls, and I can feel the rage coming off him in waves. I deserve it. But if he's here . . .

He came through the mist to find me.

It's for the map. I'm sure of it. But the fact . . . the fact that he is *here*, means I will not die alone. I feel just the slightest bit of regret that I've dragged Raker into sure death with me.

Because the beasts are here now. The mist has scattered, as if even it is afraid. There's no time to run. No trees near enough to climb. None of it would make any difference anyway.

I reach back for the hilt of my sword with my non-wielding arm, still not willing to die without a fight. My shoulder is out of its socket. My leg is numb. I really don't stand a chance.

Raker seems to know that, because as I try to scramble from his grip, to face the beasts, he curls his arm around my waist and pins me to his chest. "You'll only get in the way," he spits down into my face, as that same world-shattering scream sounds right behind my spine, sending all the hairs on my neck rising. As those trees tremble with the force of the creatures about to crash through them.

He curses me again. Then, with me still pinned against him, his other hand reaches back for his sword—

And he lunges forward.

I can't see anything, pressed to his front like this. But I am nearly deafened by the roar of shrieks and howls behind me, louder than anything I've heard in my life, a wave of death crashing into us both. I manage to squirm enough to turn my head, cheek pressed against his chest, and all I see from this angle is his blade swinging as he fights the entire throng of beasts with just one arm. He moves so quickly, so expertly, it makes my mouth go dry.

Then I only see blood. Sheets of dark blood all around us as Raker cuts *through* the horde, his strength never wavering. The creatures never even getting close.

No marks on his armor.

If the rumors are true, then being pressed right against Raker's chest is the safest place for me to be. I pray his reputation isn't just rumor, and that he doesn't just have dozens of breastplates that he switches out, given that I am currently crushed against his. I cling to him, lifting my legs, wrapping around him like a tree, so that I don't get in his way. His arm remains unyielding as stone across my back. I tremble against his body, with cold, and relief, and pain, and fear.

One claw gets through him, and I'll be gutted. One bite from those massive fangs, or those shredding teeth, and my spine will be ripped from my body. I'll just be tatters strewn across this forest.

But absolutely nothing gets past Raker's sword. He keeps slashing and steadily moving forward, not yielding any ground. He advances like a warrior on the front line of battle. His blade sings as it hits its mark again and again. As Raker wields it with an arm that never seems to tire.

Until the woods go quiet.

I'm panting against his chest. My arms are wrapped around his neck as I cling to him, my ankles locked behind his back.

Then Raker unceremoniously shoves me off him. I manage to land on one leg, but the other gives, and I fall right on my ass.

I look up, baring my teeth—but the words die in my throat.

Raker is dripping blood. It rains from his hood. From his sword. Down every inch of armor. The only part of him that is clean is his front, where he held me, and now that I'm not frozen in terror, I can feel the thick layer of gore on the back of my body.

I can't see his face, but by his posture . . . by the way he grips his sword so tightly still, like he's considering plunging it through my chest and traveling alone—

"You're angry."

His growl in response has me swallowing.

I scuttle back on my hands and feet. "The warriors at the inn. They—they followed me, I didn't—"

"*I know*," he says, his tattooed knuckles whiter than usual as he grips his blade tighter.

Right. Of course. He must have seen them. My voice is just a ragged whisper. "You . . . you went in after me."

"I went through the mist for that sword," he snarls. My sword, he means. The one on my back, its blade still covered in saberwolf blood.

So, there it is. The reason he hasn't already abandoned me. Does he even need the map? Probably not. He wants my sword. Like everyone else.

I keep crawling back, on shaking hands. They almost slip in—blood. It's blood. Everywhere. It's creatures, shredded to ribbons, cut with such precise motions that the flesh doesn't hang off in jagged layers—no, the pieces are all clean and uniform. Like those leaves cleaved in half.

I don't turn to look at the extent of the carnage of the forest, but I can smell it. I can imagine that the white Bone Woods are now red with gore.

My knees nearly buckle as I rise to my feet. As I lift my sword with spent arms, the pain of my shoulder nearly blinding me.

I won't let him have it without a duel. Though, after seeing this carnage, I know more than ever that I don't have a chance.

"Why not kill me, then?" I demand.

"I don't need two swords on this journey," he spits, his voice pure fury. "I'd rather someone like you has it than someone else."

Someone like you.

So, I'm no more than a harmless mule, carrying a sword for him until he needs it.

That's why he's training me. Not so I can be protected . . . but so I have any chance of protecting this weapon.

He will betray me the first chance he gets. He will claim my sword the moment it pleases him. I knew that from the beginning, but . . . I thought . . . after so much time together . . .

Foolish of me to think he would feel any type of loyalty to me. The merciless warrior. The *monster*.

Everything I already thought about him has been confirmed.

"Demon," I say, voice shaking.

"Worse," he says. And that's when he prowls toward me. He keeps getting closer, and I stumble back. He's dripping blood. His hood and armor are soaked with it.

None of it is his.

He is the embodiment of a deadly warrior. He doesn't stop, and neither do I, until I trip over something and land on my ass again. A *head*. I tripped over the fang sticking out of a lifeless *head* that Raker single-handedly—literally—severed with his blade while I clung to his body.

And it's not the only one. Every single creature that hunted me in this forest is now in ribbons.

I look from the beast's eyes, up into the darkness of Raker's hood. He's standing right over me, like I'm cornered prey. I swallow. The blood dripping from his hood falls on my cheek, and I flinch. He leans in close, voice hard as the steel in my shaking hands as he says, "Don't raise your sword at me again, Aris, unless you truly want to lose it."

With that, he turns his back on me.

Monster. I should be terrified. I should be shocked into submission; I should follow his words and orders like they are law.

But instead of trailing him through the mist, I turn toward the head. Using my non-dominant arm, I begin to saw off the beast's fangs. They hit the ground with a thud. I reach for the vials next. Somehow, they didn't shatter in my pockets, even after that fall.

I poke a hole in the wolf's neck and begin to drip the little remaining blood into a vial.

"What are you doing?" Raker demands from across the clearing.

"I'm getting an antidote," I say, remembering the book. Often things are both their poison and their cure. The beast must be immune to its own venom, which means its blood is full of the medicine I need.

I pour half the vial on the cut in my calf then shudder. The blood steams, as if it's burning through my skin. Close to the same sensation as when it entered my leg. I squeeze my eyes closed.

Slowly, though, I start to feel my toes again. My calf.

And it fucking *hurts*.

The cut might not be bone-deep, but it's long. If only I had true healing liquid . . . but that comes from another creature completely. It takes a few moments before I can stand or walk without wincing. My stride isn't completely straight.

Raker waits for me to get close to him.

"Your shoulder," he says flatly.

"I know," I say, stumbling past him.

His voice is a frustrated growl. "You need to have it snapped back into place."

"No, thank you," I say, continuing forward, ignoring the pang of pain with every movement.

It takes three of his long strides to be in front of me. Then, there he is, blocking my path, the monster that cut down nearly all the beasts in the Bone Woods. His hands are in fists. It really must be so hard for him not to kill me. "You threw yourself headfirst into this fucking place, yet you're afraid of popping your shoulder back in?" he demands, seething.

I know why he's upset. With my dislocated shoulder, I can't protect his precious sword. I can't be the perfect *mule*.

"No," I say, in a sickly sweet tone I know he hates. "I'm afraid of *you* doing it, with your big fucking beast-destroying hands that don't care at all about my comfort or pain levels and hurting me even more." It's true. With strength like that, I wouldn't be shocked if my bones just snapped beneath his hold. I'd rather wait for a healer.

I must be imagining it, but I swear . . . I swear he almost flinches. Like finally I've nicked him in this ongoing duel of ours. I'm too tired and in too much pain to dig in further. I just step to the side, to keep going.

He steps in front of me again.

His voice isn't soft. I don't know if it's even capable of that. But it's as gentle as I have ever heard it when he says, "I won't hurt you, Aris."

My look is punishing. "Not yet, you mean?"

I don't trust him. Not at all. Even after he jumped through these mists and saved me. Because it's not really about me, is it? It's about the things I have that he wants. The map. My *sword*. He's practically *told* me he will kill me to claim it.

But right now, my shoulder really fucking hurts. And I don't stand a chance if I can't even hold my sword.

"Fine," I say through my teeth. I close my eyes.

He doesn't walk around me. No, his massive hands curl around my waist, and he turns me in a flash. His rough, callused fingers are surprisingly gentle around my wrist and my arm. Just like they were when he was training me in the cave. His head leans low.

"Please don't scream," he says, right into my ear.

Then he twists my arm to the side. He pulls it up. And I try. I really try not to scream. I grit my teeth.

As my shoulder slides back into its socket, though, my lips part—and those long fingers are on my mouth again. Smothering. He makes a tutting sound.

But it's done. And . . . he didn't shatter bone.

"Thank you," I say, when his hand finally releases my mouth, biting out the words. *Thank you for fixing my shoulder. Thank you for coming through the mists for me, even if it was for something I have, because without you, I would be dead.*

Raker takes a step back, but he's still close enough that I can hear his sharp exhale of incredulity. "Gratitude. From you. I didn't think you were capable of it."

Then he turns and stalks off through the mist.

And I follow.

For hours, there is nothing. Just soul-rotting silence. I keep the fangs clutched in my palms, instead of my sword. They're lighter, easier to use, and though my shoulder has been righted, pain still shoots down my arm every time I move it.

For an entire day, nothing emerges. I wonder if the mists whispered about Raker's fighting skills. Perhaps even these creatures leave a monster like him alone, after that.

We're both covered in blood. It hardens and reeks, searing the inside of my nostrils. I search for water, but there is none, and when darkness falls, we are unprotected.

But even the demons avoid the mists.

I left my canteen back at the inn, but Raker opens his pack the next morning and throws me a new one, with a little too much force. It seems he got provisions in the village while I was finding trouble.

The canteen is full. My throat works as I drink most of the water, then wash my hands and face. He seems to have known I would nearly drain it all, or lose it, because he snatches it back before I'm done, and puts it back with the rest of his things.

The creatures continue to leave us alone. We walk through the maze of moon-white trees in near silence.

Every once in a while, I hear them. The whispers at the fringes. Beckoning us off the trail. Creatures that don't slither or leave tracks behind. Beasts that are formless.

Every instinct within me tells me not to look into the trees. Not to search the distance. I just stare at Raker's back, his spine straight and his armor mirroring my reflection. I just follow him, like he's a guiding star.

Until I see someone join me in the mirror. I whirl around, fangs up. Nothing.

I see it, though, next to me. In the reflection.

A woman with long dark hair and deep green skin. Some sort of forest wraith. A blink—and she falls away, into a small puddle of water dark as night. I frown, about to open my mouth and say something, but just then the puddle ripples, and someone else comes rising out of it. An immortal in a fine dress, ready for a ball, her golden hair tied up into an intricate style. Her outfit is ornate, dazzling. The fabrics are like water turned to silk, stitched through with rare metals and diamonds. I blink, trying to get a closer look. What is this? An illusion? I step closer to Raker, lips parting to tell him, to *say something*, when suddenly, the puddle ripples again, and the woman turns into a warrior. In full armor. He lifts a sword.

Raker turns in a flash and throws his sword through the illusion. To my surprise, his blade pierces something real. The warrior. Whereas the illusion was invisible just seconds before, now it's solid.

It melts away, back into the dark puddle, and Raker's sword falls with it.

In a flash, Raker's blade is in his hand again, and he's stabbing through the puddle. It seizes—then slithers into the ground. Disappears.

"What—"

"It's a lusk."

"A . . . what? How . . . how do you know?"

He looks over at me. "Do you really think I came into the Questral as unprepared as you?"

Right. He knew about the pixie too. He must have sought access to one of those traveling storytellers, or maybe some of the king's own orators. Of course. I remember their conversation, in the castle, and think about what he told me later, about wanting revenge. Is it revenge for the king?

Or . . . revenge *against* him?

I swallow down my irritation, knowing details could help me in the future. As if Raker can anticipate my next question, he sighs, and says, "It has a faint sound, if you listen. A shimmering rattle."

I didn't even hear it. I was too distracted by the beauty of the illusions. Which, I suppose, is the point.

"If you look at it, it becomes real. It feeds off your focus, your energy. It gets stronger."

Right.

He starts to say something else but seems to think better of it and stops. He just shakes his head and keeps moving.

I keep following.

We walk for a few more hours, only encountering a handful of other creatures, each of which Raker quickly cuts to shreds.

Then, all at once, the mist is ripped away, and my jaw goes slack.

23

Beyond the mists is a forest of trees like giants.

"Skyquills," I breathe, only knowing the name through stories. Whispered legends about trees tall enough to scrape the sky itself. "Silver skyquills."

The trunks are thicker than both Raker and me combined. The needles are silvery green in the sun. I stop and look up. I just look, and look, gaping.

"What?" Raker snaps.

I shake my head. "Do you ever feel . . . utterly insignificant? In . . . in a good way?" Tears prick my eyes, stupid tears, because we almost just died a half dozen times, but this world . . . this world with claws and teeth is beautiful. I look over at Raker, only to see him looking at me. His stature says *unimpressed*.

"No" is all he says, before he turns around again.

Of course not. Harlan Raker, famous warrior, is anything but insignificant.

We made it through the mists. Part of me was sure I would die there, lost forever, like that hidden sword.

But slowly, the cold of the fog falls away, slipping off my skin, melting from my bones as I walk through the forest in quiet awe. Something about this place feels just like the Bone Woods . . . Ancient. Untouched. Yet instead of piercing, cold dread, all I feel here is steady warmth. It's not just the sun, which felt absent in the fog. No. The trees are so tall, they cast so much shade, that sunlight is shredded into glimmering ribbons, unraveling through the woods.

It's something else. A warmth from the nature, maybe. A pulse like a heartbeat.

We keep walking. Raker's posture never changes. But about an hour later, he stiffens. Turns. I hear it.

The gentle lapping of water. I don't even wait for him. My feet are snapping against twigs and kicking up dirt as I run toward the sound, and then suddenly, I'm kneeling by a creek. Perfectly clear water. *Finally.* I could laugh. I could cry. I take it by the handful, drinking from my palms, washing my face. My back is still crusted in blood.

The stream isn't deep, but it's enough water to bathe.

I turn toward Raker, who is approaching with far less vigor. He's covered in blood too. But none of it has reached his skin except for his hands, not with the armor, hood, and mask. I open my mouth. Close it. Decide it's not worth the trouble of asking.

But he's already reaching into his pack. I hear something break and nearly collapse in shock as he presents a piece of his soap. Before I can say a single word, he tosses it at me. It lands in my lap.

His soap. The one I like so much. I blink, not able to find the words. Not knowing how he possibly just did something that resembles a *kindness*. Before I can attempt to thank him, he says, "You need it."

Then he turns to leave.

Even his insult can't breach my happiness. I breathe his soap in, and sigh. *Mine*, I think. *All mine.*

When I can't hear Raker's metallic steps through the woods anymore, I begin to take my clothes off piece by piece.

The fabric sticks to my skin, bound by the dried blood. It peels off painfully. Raker's right. I stink. But with just a few scrubs with his soap, the blood clears. My hair is smooth again. I tie it back into my normal style, letting the braid hang down today, then I wash my clothes, before unfolding them to dry.

As I wait, I lie against the rocks, sighing into the stone, letting the shallow, gentle rush of the water smooth across my body. Across my markings. It's strange, being out in the open, with all of me showing. But Raker's far away. These woods are silent.

I need—I just need a moment to rest and remind myself that I am alive.

I survived. No, *we* survived. The last weeks are a haze, filled with thirst and hunger and pain and blood. So much blood.

I stare at the sky and melt further into the rocks. This world has taken bites of me. I can feel them. It has gnawed at my confidence. It has chewed through all my assumptions. It has punched holes through my fear.

I've only been here twenty days, yet I feel transformed. Like years have been folded into moments. Seconds of bravery, of skill, of foolishness that determined my fate.

I feel like those pieces at the forge, scraps of metal that Stellan and I would give a second life—smelt into a completely new sword. I'm not sure what I've turned into, but I know that I am not the same.

And some of those new pieces, some of those shards of strength I found in this world . . . they were forged by Raker. They were forged from flames that rose in response to the taunts, to the *figure it out*, to the moments he didn't interfere, forcing me to rise by myself. Forcing me to dig into the trenches of my soul and claw out the embers of my strength.

I curse him. I thank him.

I don't know how I expected to make it to the gods. But now, for the first time, I feel like I really could.

A flash of movement has me sitting up, breath caught in my throat, water parting around me.

I reach for my blade . . . and promptly let my grip sag.

I watch a glowing, translucent horse gallop through the forest—then disappear in a curl of mist.

I blink. Just when I've convinced myself I imagined it, the horse appears again, several feet in front of where it disappeared, sparkling silver trailing behind it, like a star-swept breeze.

Its hooves gently clop upon the forest floor, before it stills. It turns—and spots me. As its eyes bore into mine, I don't feel a single ounce of fear. Maybe I should. Especially as the horse canters in my direction, stopping only at the edge of the stream.

This could be another illusion, I think. Another beautiful thing I'm supposed to fear.

Slowly, I rise from the water. I keep my sword in my grip, just in case. I walk over toward the horse, expecting it to be spooked.

But as I get closer, it simply dips its head. And my silver markings glimmer beneath a stream of sunlight as I reach out to touch it.

It's cold as ice. Its mane is soft as silk. Its fur is coarse. I smooth my hand between its eyes, and it huffs out of its nose.

Beautiful. Before I can get a closer look, the horse takes off again, making a circle. I watch it go—then still, when it runs right toward me again. This time, it doesn't stop. Shit. I'm about to leap out of the way when the horse careens off the ground, flying above me, jumping over the stream. Landing.

Then becoming another curl of mist. It doesn't appear again.

I didn't read about those in the book. Both wonder and dread fill me as I consider that there are even more creatures out there, unreported or undiscovered.

Knowing Raker is probably sighing deeply and regretting ever giving me a shard of his soap, I go back to the stream. I twist my clothing, squeezing out any remaining water before putting them back on. I don't have time to let them sit and dry more. I really should see about getting more clothes, I think, as I step through the forest, looking for Raker. I doubt he went far.

In the direction he headed in, shrubs brush against the base of the Skyquills, their leaves coarse and pointed in various places. A sweetness pierces the air. It's hard to see anything buried in the thick, knotted green, but I carefully piece through the leaves, until I catch a flash of color. My eyes widen.

Huckleberries. Elderberries. I pick several, my fingertips staining violet, stick one in my mouth, and sigh deeply.

Yes. The fruit on Stormside—so limited and rare—is like ash compared to Starside. Everything here is heightened—the landscapes, the flavors, the colors—as if magic has touched everything.

I sink to my knees, and pick them all, eating a large fraction. The rest I stick into my wet pockets. I consider calling Raker over, to fill his pack with them.

I'm so happy, I hardly notice that a shadow has stolen all the light from the forest. And that the already quiet woods have gone deathly silent.

Until a sticky glop of something hits my shoulder and slides down my freshly washed clothes. I scrunch my nose. Sap?

I look up at the tree.

And stop breathing.

A bear larger than the trees themselves is on its haunches, looking down at me, fang-full mouth parted, drool dripping. Another stream falls directly on me, sliding down my entire body, but still, I don't move.

Until it throws its head back and roars, rattling the very foundations of the forest, sending me to the ground. Trembling hands clutching dirt, I watch its maw remain open. And from its mouth, a silver, glimmering stream of pure and utter power pierces the sky like a blade.

Magic. It has magic.

I scramble to my feet, and I fucking *bolt*.

This wasn't in the book. But if this creature is anything like the bears on Stormside, it'll have poor vision. It'll rely on hearing and smell. Its drool will mask my scent, won't it? And as for its eyesight, it won't be able to spot me easily through the trees . . . That's what I tell myself as I run for my life, heart in my throat, sweat spilling down my skin.

Then I hear those ancient, steady trees snap like they are no more than twigs, and any hope of surviving this beast turns to dust. I look over my shoulder, and the bear is on all fours, bounding through the woods with singular focus, cutting down everything in its path. Long needles erupt from its back, sharp as spears.

Fuck.

If this bear doesn't kill me, Raker certainly will. At the very least, he is never letting me use his soap again.

Why does trouble always find me? I was picking berries. Why couldn't it have happened to Raker instead?

The beast lunges—falling just short of me with such force the woods shudder. I scream as I'm hurled forward. From my knees, I watch as the bear opens its mouth again with a sickening snarl . . . and I know what that means.

I throw myself to the ground as another beam of silver light shoots out, pulsing with power, slicing through the forest like a scythe, cutting everything around us down. Those great trees fall. They fall and fall, snapping with ear-splitting cracks.

I see a chance for cover, and I run, heart in my throat, as all these glorious trees come down around me.

One crashes at my side, nearly taking me with it. Another blocks my path. I scramble over it and keep going. They keep falling. They're so large that some fall together, leaning, creating cages, and I run as fast as I can, knowing all it would take is one—one to fall on me and turn me into no more than a pool of blood in these ancient woods.

The bear does not stop. It crushes and splits these fallen trees as it hunts me, as the forest continues to break apart, and I run. I run toward a shard of light beyond the fallen trees, a clearing, a hole in the weave of this forest, and I launch myself through it.

Suddenly, he's there. Stepping out of the trees and into my path, on the other side of the woods.

Raker seems to sigh with his entire body when he sees me bellowing at the top of my lungs, clothes still wet, trees falling behind me, a massive bear at my heels. Sometime in the half hour I was bathing, he seems to have found time to clean himself, because his hood isn't covered in dried blood anymore. Neither is his armor.

The ground lurches. I can feel the beast's breath on my head. The trees I just ducked beneath now shatter into a thousand splinters. Some hit my back, piercing my flesh like throwing stars, and I gasp at the pain, but I keep going, right toward Raker.

He does not turn and run. He stands his ground. Pulls his sword from his back in a flash, as if he is going to cut right through the towering beast.

He doesn't get the chance.

From nowhere, an arrow the size of my leg slices through the forest—and sinks right into the creature's heart. It seizes. Gasps.

Then it falls. It falls and slides, dragging up dirt and stumps and roots, coming right toward me, eyes alit with that silver from its breath. I trip and am nearly crushed, before Raker yanks me to the side, out of its way.

"Fucking gods, Aris," he growls. His sword is still up.

An immortal steps out of the woods.

He's a man holding the largest crossbow I've ever seen. Its wood is pure silver, as if carved from a tree in the Land of the Gods. Just like the metal-tipped arrow currently buried in the bear.

He glances over at us, nods in greeting, then proceeds to climb the beast. He's muttering to himself, as if taking notes. He sounds excited. In a flash, he unsheathes a massive, glimmering saw and begins to cut the needles right off the bear's back.

I look over at Raker in question, but his gaze is still locked on that immortal. His grip is still tight on his sword.

I take a step forward. Another. I have the urge to sink to the floor, or retch, or simply curl into a ball and sob.

But I need to know. "What is that creature?"

The immortal glances down at me from his place high above. He looks me up and down for a mere moment, before grinning.

He has flame-red hair, tan skin, and bright, golden, glittering eyes. He has the body of someone who has done extensive fight training.

Perhaps for centuries. He's handsome. He tilts his head at me, in faint amusement, as if taking in my notice.

Then he turns back to the spines. I think he'll ignore me, before he says, "This is a steelclaw."

I glance down at the bear's claws and my breath hitches. They're each longer than my sword, glimmering in some ancient material that is decidedly not steel. The immortal seems to track my gaze, because he says, "Not really steel . . . but stronger than most metals. Melded into swords to make them stronger. Made into weapons itself . . ." He nods toward his arrow, and I notice its tip is made of the very same matter.

Interesting.

"And the spines?"

"Contain some of the most potent poison ever discovered."

I raise a brow at him as he unceremoniously collects almost all of them. "And you're what? A hunter?"

He flashes a white, perfect smile. "Precisely." He turns fully toward me. "Thank you, by the way. For drawing him out. I haven't seen one of these in a very long time . . . They're rare. They hibernate for centuries. Some thought they were all but extinct . . ."

My back teeth grind together. So, I was no more than bait. I remember what Xara said about hunters. How they're the reason some ancient creatures are all but extinct. I study this hunter, wondering if he's one of the ones she was referring to. "Steelclaws have an appetite for humans?"

He tilts his head at me, looking amused again. "No. They're aethervores."

At my blank stare, he says, "They eat magic."

Oh. I think about that glimmering silver beam it emitted. But that doesn't explain why it was chasing *me*.

I must look confused, because he motions toward my back. "Your blade."

"My sword?" He nods, and I shake my head. "It . . . it doesn't have magic."

He frowns. "I've never seen a beast chase an object with such singular focus. It most certainly does." At my insistence, he shrugs. "You're mortal. You can't activate it."

Both Xara and the book said scales and claws and bones from magical creatures can be melded into weapons, to give them a shred of their magic. Is that what mine has?

I reach back and trail a finger down its hilt. No wonder so many people are after it.

All at once, I remember the fact that this is an immortal. With a baldric full of weapons. If he wants this one, it won't take much effort for him to steal it from me. I take a step back. As if sensing the direction of my thoughts, he flashes that smile again. "Not to worry, human. I'm more of a bow and arrow man myself. Your sword would go for a pretty penny, I'm sure . . ." He purses his lips, considering. "But it would also likely cost me my head in the process. And I quite like my head." He winks at me. "You seem to like it too." I scoff. He just smiles wider before shrugging. "A blade like that isn't worth the trouble."

I look over at Raker. The other person who might steal this blade from me. But he doesn't spare me a glance.

The immortal looks over at Raker too, then seems to pale. His smile dims. "Especially when you're guarded by that," he says simply.

I almost keel over at the thought of Raker being my *guardian*. Someone who has practically promised a death at his hands.

I want to laugh, but I don't. Better the immortal thinks Raker would protect me.

And . . . I suppose he does. When he wants to.

"What else is valuable about the beast?" I ask, looking it over.

"Well, its saliva has healing properties. You must feel them."

I look down at myself. I feel sticky. Disgusting. But I turn over my hands. The scratches . . . they're gone.

That's when I remember the half dozen daggers of wood sticking out of my back. I gasp, pulling one out and clenching at the pain . . . before feeling the wound heal completely.

The saliva will dry. Will its magic dry with it? I won't take the chance.

Jaw tight, I take all of them out, sealing my lips to keep from screaming. Until they are just blood-tipped shards of wood at my feet.

When I glance back up, the hunter is still cutting off spines. "You're lucky, you know. Few immortals have survived a creature like that. Let alone humans."

Lucky he was there with his massive arrow, I think.

I dig into my pockets, until I find an empty vial. I approach the bear, the vestige of fear still prickling across my skin, but I grit my teeth against it and climb up the beast's paw. Fist my hands in its fur and ascend until I'm high enough to reach its mouth. I wince at those fangs.

How close they were to cutting me to pieces. Slowly, I begin to collect the saliva still pooled below its tongue.

"Who gave you those?" the hunter asks.

"A healer," I say simply, not wanting to get the immortal in trouble. Perhaps it's frowned upon to share with humans. It's not like she ever told me her name, anyway, and perhaps for this very reason.

But he just hums in approval. "Those are useful. They don't shatter. Good quality."

When I'm done, I climb down and study the rest of the creature. I have little use for poison. Even the fangs in my pockets from those wolves seem almost useless now. They would have done absolutely nothing to slow this beast.

But . . . maybe not completely useless.

I turn toward the hunter.

"How did you get here?" I ask. That crossbow is enormous. He wouldn't have just walked all this way with it on his back . . . And he must have a way to transport all the spines he's collecting . . .

His eyes narrow. He lets out a high whistle.

Then another shadow casts across the forest. My bones clench, remembering how the bear towered over me. I take a step back.

And a dragon lands with a forest-trembling force right between us. It stretches out its wings, dappled light filtering through the sheer, forest-green webbing, before the claws tipping them sink into the dirt.

"You have a dragon," I breathe.

He nods proudly. "This is Invira."

Invira just huffs. The steam she emits is cold, like what I imagine a winter breeze is like.

I can't stop the questions spilling out of me. Especially when this immortal seems so content to answer them. "Did you claim her at the Beast Tree?"

He shakes his head. "I freed her from a snare when I was very young." He frowns, looking at a jagged scar on her foot. I notice she's missing a talon. "Not all hunters follow the same code," he says sadly.

"And the code is?"

"Don't kill anything that doesn't first try to kill you."

Interesting. It seems like a loose code, one with more than enough room to allow for an innocent creature to be hunted and sold in parts. Not that I can be too upset at the hunter, given he just saved my life.

I have a thousand more questions ... but I look up at the trees. Those curls of buttery sunlight filtering through the forest are weakening. It won't be long before the light is gone completely.

It's not just shelter from the demons I'm after. No, I want a way to travel quickly, to make up some lost time.

I pull the fangs from my pockets and show them to the hunter.

He raises a brow. "Saberwolf?"

I nod.

"Where did you find one?"

"The mists."

At that, the hunter looks us over again. Me, then Raker, who I can feel has shifted closer to my side but still hasn't said a single word.

"You're here on the quest, aren't you?" I nod. He frowns down at the fangs. "I suppose you want me to offer you passage?"

I nod again. That's exactly what I want.

He seems to consider that. "I don't trust either of you on my dragon," he finally says. "Not with swords like those." I frown and am about to open my mouth again when he continues. "But for those fangs ... I will procure a creature that will get you out of these woods. Save you three days' journeying, at least."

"Safely," I say.

His lips purse. "Fine. Safely."

Maybe I shouldn't trust the immortal ... but it doesn't seem like we have many options. If Raker opposes my plan, he doesn't say so.

"You have a deal," I say. I toss the fangs up, and the immortal catches them with breathtaking speed. He hangs them on his baldric. Then he turns back to the spines.

I wait just a few moments before saying, "Well?"

The immortal smiles at my impatience. "It will take a few hours to lure such a creature out."

A few hours? My eyes slowly rise to the sky. Back to him. I try to keep my voice as steady as possible, even as my hands turn to fists. "We don't have a few hours. The demons—"

The immortal looks amused. "You're safe here from them."

I stare at him, bewildered, and he just laughs. "You'll see. Night is not a dark place in these woods."

"But *water*—"

"Is not the only element those creatures fear," he says. I open my mouth, and he gives me a look, as if asking me if I really think I know these beings better than he does.

Fine. He doesn't make a move to mount his dragon as darkness descends, so I suppose it wouldn't be in his best interest either to be wrong about a thing like that.

I wait as the hunter continues snapping off the last of the spines. Raker is leaned against a tree, looking unimpressed with the both of us.

The dragon looks over at me. Its eyes are glimmering green, darker than those of the dragon I saw in the Prism Pass. A smattering of spikes adorns its back. Its scales are tough as armor. It looks rock-hewn. Strong. I take a step forward, pulled by a yearning for my own dragon. Do they know each other? Does she know where mine went?

The dragon sniffs at me. I wonder if she can sense my dragon. If any trace of her remains on me.

I reach out my hand to touch her scales, just as she opens her mouth—

And unleashes a torrent of water in a stream that hits me right in the chest and has me falling onto my ass. I slide along the ground until I hit Raker's legs. I sputter, spitting out water, soaked from head to toe.

I look up at the immortal through the water clinging to my eyelashes, and he just shrugs. "She's sensitive to smell. And you . . . well, you smelled human, what with the saliva and all."

My cheeks burn with mortification. It doesn't fade in the slightest when I look up to see Raker staring down at me, arms crossed over his chest.

I flip him off, and I must be imagining it—but I swear I hear him chuckle.

"Water . . . instead of fire?" I ask, trembling as I stand.

"Invira is a skyrend," the hunter says simply. And I imagine there are entire classifications of dragons.

I take a shaking step. Wanting to get away from all of them, maybe go curl up and die of embarrassment.

Without missing a beat, the dragon sits back and beats its wings in my direction, sending me back onto my ass with the force. My braid blows in the sharp wind, and my eyes water.

She doesn't stop until I'm mostly dry.

"Thank you, Invira," I say through my teeth.

WHEN THE HUNTER is done collecting everything of value from the beast, we begin walking through the forest.

His massive bow is tucked to his side, almost as tall as he is. He keeps a single arrow clutched in his other arm.

"Still hoping to catch something else?" I ask.

His smile is pure charm. "There are plenty of things to ensnare in these woods," he says. I roll my eyes.

I'm holding a frozen apple in my palms that the hunter tossed at me from his pack. It stings just the slightest bit and is smooth like glass. He said it would draw out the creature we're looking for.

I just hope I'm not being used as bait for a deadly creature again.

As darkness finally settles over the forest like a blanket, and the stars come out, I look up to the sky and stop in my tracks.

This forest is not a dark place at night.

The hunter wasn't kidding.

Fireflies make an entire constellation through the trees, orbs and galaxies. I inhale a shaking breath. My eyes burn, watching.

To my surprise, the hunter stops too.

I saw a single firefly once. It flew by my window, and I shook my sister awake. We both pressed our faces against the glass, marveling at it until it disappeared. We stayed up several nights after that, taking turns at our post by the window. But it never returned.

She would never believe this. Never believe there was a wood where thousands would gather.

"This world is a beautiful place," I say.

He nods. "It is." He sighs, and the sound is deep. Resonant. "That's why I like what I do. I get to see the quiet places. The pockets of this world where the beauty has not been disturbed."

For a moment, the blood, the fangs, the fear, it all falls away. It's like staring at the night sky, seeing only the stars and not the darkness.

I stare so long that they become nothing more than blurs of light. A part of me, a wall inside, shifts.

I used to hate fire. I used to hate flames.

But I cannot hate this.

There is beauty even in monstrous places. Even in monsters themselves.

One of the fireflies dips low, close enough to touch. I reach up, and the hunter grabs my hand in a flash. His touch is gentle as he sets my arm back down.

"Careful," he says. "They're poisonous. Deadly to a human."

I spin to face him, perplexed, and he just laughs. "Learn this. Some of the most beautiful creatures in this world are the deadliest."

I look over at Raker, but he's not looking at the fireflies. He's not looking at the stars.

He's looking at me.

I stare back.

I can't see his eyes, but I feel his notice, piercing me. Our gazes are like blades between us. Skimming. Dueling.

The hunter keeps talking. "There's an elk, for example . . . we call it a florisfang. It has five rows of teeth, but you would never know it. It's beautiful. It usually has flowers in its antlers, like a crown . . ."

Raker tilts his head just the slightest bit, a whisper of a motion I wish I couldn't interpret, but from traveling together this long, I can.

I glare at him in response.

And there it is. That sound again, resembling a chuckle.

". . . you wouldn't believe how long their claws are. They're retractable. So, you don't know until it's too late, I guess," the hunter finishes. And I'm not sure if he's talking about the elk or another animal entirely. "Anyway. Best to keep moving if you're going to find that horse."

"Horse?" I say, whipping around. "I saw one earlier. It . . . it disappeared into mist."

He looks impressed. "I should keep you around a little longer," he says. "You bring out the best of the forest."

"And the worst," Raker says as he brushes by my side. I glare at his back.

The hunter doesn't seem to hear him, too lost in his own talking. "That's exactly the creature we're trying to draw out. A skyhorse. They're known to run through these woods. They seem to like the feel of them."

"Are there many types of horses?" I ask.

He nods. "Just as many as there are dragons. With just as many variations and specialties." He shakes his head and huffs. "The types of horses I've seen . . . you wouldn't believe."

I have the sudden urge to know. To see. To learn. I stamp that ember out, because that's not why I'm here. This is not my world.

Though, sometimes, the traitorous, selfish part of me wishes it was.

As we continue through the forest, a galaxy of fireflies threading through the trees, a second sky of stars, I think again, *This world is beautiful.*

24

The hunter manages to catch a creature called a hellice—about the size of me, covered in spikes, that rolls through woods, mowing down everything in its path.

"Lucky this one wasn't in a pack," he says, as he pulls out his arrow. "They're menaces. They kill countless creatures on their way to their prey."

"Which part of them is valuable?"

He shrugs a shoulder. "I just figured you both were hungry. And their meat is always tender. I wouldn't mind a bite."

That's how we end up sitting on the forest floor, the fireflies moving in glittering currents above.

The hunter gets a pile of logs together, then reaches into his pack. I expect him to produce a flint rock. Instead, he unveils a shard of brilliant orange and red. He uses his knife to slice off a small piece.

The moment he throws it onto the wood, it ignites.

Beside me, Raker makes an unimpressed sound, and the immortal notices. He must think the hunter lazy or weak for using magic instead of making the fire himself.

I, on the other hand, am very impressed. I stare at the luminous rock in his hands, lips parted, and the hunter grins and says, "I thought you'd like that. Want to hold it?"

I nod, and he throws the stone to me.

It's like hardened flame. And, as much as I've hated and feared fire, just like the fireflies above, I can't help but admire this rock. It's smooth. Slightly warm to the touch. "What is it?" I ask, handing it back.

"That's fireglass," he says. He shrugs. "I use it when I feel lazy . . . or when I want to impress a beautiful human."

I blush, because no one but my family has ever called me beautiful. It's stupid, really. He's just flirting, he's just being nice. He's immortal. Still, the compliment makes me feel warm.

Raker makes a sound of distaste next to me. He clearly doesn't share the immortal's sentiment.

The hunter looks over at him warily as he begins skinning and preparing the meat. "What's with the hood and mask?"

Raker, of course, doesn't respond.

"He's sparing us all of his glowering," I say lightly.

That makes the immortal laugh. It's a pleasant, musical sound. I find myself smiling. Raker doesn't say a word, but I can almost feel his eyes on me.

"Tell me about the creatures you've hunted," I say. "Please." Time is always running out on this quest, but right now, as we wait for the horse to make an appearance, as the hunter roasts this meat, I can get answers.

The hunter smiles. It's like he's been waiting his entire immortal life for someone to ask about all his conquests.

He tells me. He tells me story after story, face alight with excitement, like he's reliving every moment, every brush with death, every chance encounter.

He tells me about the hunter's guild. About the rarest beasts he's ever seen—and some that no one has ever been able to capture.

He tells me his biggest customers are typically heirs of Great Houses, who have the means to pay the most, and who are always desperate to have better resources than their counterparts.

"Especially lately, with courting season arriving," he says, rolling his eyes. I wonder what he means. But I have a more pressing question. The hunter seems to deal with various immortals from across Starside.

"Do you know . . . do you know someone named Vander Evren?" Stellan did tell me to find him. The Gardener's mention of him has me curious.

That curiosity only grows as the hunter pales. His easygoing smile fades completely. "How do you know that name?"

I'm not going to tell him about Stellan. I'm not going to answer him at all.

But I am going to wonder why a man who just single-handedly took down a beast as large as these trees, who hunts monsters for a living, is afraid of a *name*.

I say as much, and the hunter just shakes his head. "Some heirs spill more blood than these beasts. Vander Evren is one of them. Do not call upon him unless you want to be next in his long line of deaths."

He's an heir? Why would Stellan have known the name of a lord of Starside? And why would he tell me to find someone this dangerous?

"So, he's powerful?"

He huffs a laugh. "He is power itself."

He looks over his shoulder. As if someone could be listening. Watching.

This is the second time someone has said something about being able to summon Vander Evren. "How would I call upon him?" I ask.

"You don't," the hunter says, his voice firm. "If you want to live, you don't want to. Trust me."

"And if I do?" I press.

He sighs. His gaze flicks to my sword. "Then you summon him for a duel in the ancient way. By drawing blood, piercing a great blade into magical ground . . . and calling his name."

I swallow. Summoning an immortal lord for a duel seems like a sure way to lose my sword and my head. So why would Stellan tell me to find him?

Clearly looking to change topics, the hunter pulls a satchel of spices from his pack that he's collected across Starside, seasons the meat, then serves it. I take a hesitant nibble, and my tongue ignites in flavors I've never tasted before, varieties of salts and dried garlic. I eat every bite, listening as the hunter continues recounting his various adventures.

When the fire is put out, the skyhorse finally appears. It approaches my apple steadily, and this isn't the same horse I met before. No, this one is so tall, I have to hold my arm up just to offer it the fruit. It sniffs the frozen apple. Huffs.

Then takes the whole fruit in its mouth. It chews, ice shattering against its strong teeth. After a few seconds, it spits the core onto the ground.

The translucent fur deepens before my eyes, darkens to the most glorious silver-blue, until it's fully solid. It huffs, its breath cool against the top of my head.

"Keep feeding it apples, and it'll keep going, for as long as it can," the hunter says, handing me a simple satchel full of the frozen fruit, from the larger pack Invira carries.

Raker steps to my side. I try not to let my worry reach my face as I stare up at the horse, but he reads me immediately.

He scoffs, and I can almost hear his voice in my head saying, *Of course you can't fucking ride a horse without a saddle.*

It's not like there were many opportunities to learn. I've only ridden a horse a handful of times—always with a saddle—and one of those times was during the Culling.

Raker shakes his head. Then, in half a moment, he's gripping my waist and hauling me up onto the horse, as if I weigh absolutely nothing.

My shoulders hike up. The horse is freezing. I lean forward and run a hand down its neck. I scratch behind its ears, and it makes a pleased sound.

I tense as Raker climbs on behind me. Of course. There's only one horse, and two of us. I knew that, but still, I didn't really consider what it would be like until he was right at my back.

As if sensing my discomfort, Raker says, voice far too close to my ear, "Would you prefer I ride in front?"

His voice is acid. As if he knows I, of course, would not prefer to cling to him for the entire journey.

"No," I say, just as terse.

The hunter comes into view. "It was a pleasure meeting you, Aris," he says. "May our paths cross again." He tips his head in goodbye, at me, then Raker. Invira breathes out a puff of cold air.

All Raker does is kick the horse's sides—and the skyhorse jolts forward.

The forest becomes streaks of gold and silver and green as the horse runs faster than the wind. My grip loosens and I fall back with the speed, crashing into Raker's chest, head banging on his armor. I nearly slip off, but his arms are on either side of me, keeping me on, his own hold steady.

And now . . . now there isn't a single inch between us. Our bodies are completely flush. My ass is between his legs. His thighs are bracketing mine.

It shouldn't make my skin prickle. It shouldn't make it hard to breathe. I have seen what this body can do—I should fear it, but I don't. I hate him.

But that doesn't mean I am blind to his attractiveness.

I wonder if he senses at all that my heart is racing, or that I can't even form a single coherent thought, my muscles tensed, my entire awareness narrowing to the feel of him. Apparently, he can.

"Breathe, Aris," he says, deep voice piercing even the wind, and it does absolutely nothing to slow my pulse.

He shifts back, as if to put some space between us, as if *knowing* that's why I've suddenly revealed myself to be a statue, but we're going so fast, I just slip right back between his legs.

He's in armor. I know that. I'm just feeling metal. But we're so close. And I'm so cold, but he's radiating heat. I'm leaning back slightly to get closer to it. I'm wondering what it would feel like if he wasn't in his armor. If he was in fabrics just as thin as the ones that now are brushing uncomfortably against my heated skin.

I must be losing my fucking mind.

Especially when Raker lets go of the horse with one hand and uses the other to take my hair in his fist.

I lose the ability to think.

"It's getting in my face," he says, his voice a rough whisper in my ear, as if he's leaning down so that I can hear him, and I swallow as he twists my long braid around and around his wrist, turning it into a knot. Pulling just the slightest bit.

"Alleged face," I breathe, in an attempt at humor at a time when my skin feels like it's on fire.

He gently tucks the knot of my hair beneath my collar, and I feel the faint brush of his rough fingers against my nape.

THE SKYHORSE RIDES through the night, so quickly its hooves hardly touch the ground. Looking too closely at the rushing woods makes my eyes hurt after a while, so, after I give the horse her second apple, I close them.

Sometime later, I jolt awake, gasping. Only to find that I'm completely, shamelessly slumped against Raker. He's the only thing keeping me on this racing horse. My body is draped against his chest. His arms are on either side of me. To hold me still, his large body is curved around me.

I'm sure he's not fucking happy about it.

I can't imagine it's been comfortable not being able to move at all in the—I look up at the faint light filtering through the treetops—*hours* that I was asleep.

"I'm—I'm sorry," I say, trying in vain to scoot away, straightening so at least I'm not plastered against him.

"You're too thin" is all he says, bitten out like an insult.

I bristle. "Most of us don't exactly get enough to eat, unlike the king's guard."

He says nothing.

I sit like that, firmly upright, muscles tired, until the horse begins to slow, and the world falls into focus again.

We're finally out of the woods.

Light rain hits us all at once. The sky is gray, sun almost wholly blotted out. A storm is coming. A bad one.

The horse kicks down the side of a small rockface, and below sits a circle of water dark as night. At the center of it is a small piece of land. And at the center of that is a castle.

It's small. Abandoned. Part of it is just a pile of ruins.

But some of it is still standing. The idea of shelter, after days spent in the mists and forest, makes my posture finally fall forward with relief.

That's exactly where the horse takes us, riding the storm winds, galloping atop the water as if she is gliding on it.

She stops right in front of a half-crumbled door.

Cold bites my cheeks. I start to wonder how we're going to make it back across the water, but I quickly spot a small beached boat. Across the lake is another one. As if someone paddled out and left the house behind.

Why?

The horse begins to lose some of its form. I start to scramble off, swinging my leg over, sliding—only for hands to grip my waist. Help me down. Immediately retreat. I turn toward Raker, but he's already unsheathing his blade and stepping inside the ruins.

The horse huffs above me. She's rapidly deteriorating. Some of the rain is going right through her now.

"Thank you," I say, handing her the last apple. She takes it—but doesn't bite. As if she's saving it. Then she takes back off across the black water, until she's just another wisp of storm wind.

I wait for Raker outside in the freezing torrent, thinking he's gone to check if it's safe . . . but he doesn't return. When I see a faint curl of smoke coming from one of the few remaining chimneys, I walk through the door.

This must have been a beautiful place, once. Now it's hardly standing. Most of the ceiling is gone. Rain falls through large holes that look almost shredded by massive talons. Nature grows up the walls, and across the floor. Deeper into the home, the damage is worse. Some rooms are just piles of collapsed stone. Others look like everything inside has been sucked out. But I follow the warmth, toward one room that is almost fully intact. At the back of it sits a hearth.

Raker is crouched in front of the logs. His armor is in a pile on the floor. He's back in that light material, along with his hood.

I crouch next to him, and he visibly stiffens.

Carefully, I reach my hands toward the flames, burying the flash of unease that always forms when I'm near fire.

"Thank you," I breathe, closing my eyes, this warmth melting through my bones. I didn't know how cold I was until I felt this heat.

Raker grunts out something next to me.

When we're both warm, I turn to him. "My next lesson," I say, reaching for my blade. My shoulder feels normal now. I have the bear's saliva to thank for that. And Raker.

He stands. "I'm not training you anymore," he says.

A fold forms between my brows. I rise. "What do you mean?"

His voice is sharp. Quiet. "It would be a waste of time."

This again? "You said you'd teach me."

"I changed my mind."

I blink, and I . . . I don't understand. Just hours before, he was speaking to me. Making a sound that almost resembled a laugh.

Where is this coming from? Why is he suddenly being so cold again?

"But—"

He turns, fast as lightning. "You want a lesson, Aris? Don't run into fucking deadly mists. Don't approach deadly creatures. Don't look in wonder at something that will not hesitate to rip your throat out. Don't say that this world that will kill you in a thousand different ways is *beautiful*."

I stare him down, and he stalks forward, so I'm forced to tilt my head up to keep my gaze with the inside of his hood. He does not speak to me. He never does. But it seems like now he can't stop. Now he needs to let me know exactly how he feels.

"You are the most reckless person I have ever met. Danger is drawn to you. And you run right toward it. It's like you're courting death. It's like you're trying to take me down with you." I didn't think it possible, but his voice gets sharper, colder. "Every day, I think you can't get any more foolish, and every day, you prove me wrong."

I flinch like I've been slapped. "I have survived this far."

He just laughs. And it is mean. It is cruel. He steps toward me. "You are only alive because my blade has stood between you and death. And I'm fucking tired of it, Aris. I am not your savior. I am not your *guardian*." I frown. Is that it? The words from the hunter got under his skin? He looks me up and down, and I can imagine that beneath that mask he is sneering. "You want to die? Fine, keep going. But I won't be watching. Not anymore."

I open my mouth. Close it. I want to say a thousand things, but my throat tightens. The only thing that comes out is "You need me." He needs my map. He wants my sword.

"I need you?" He laughs again, that cruel sound that makes me feel like I am no better than dirt. "*You?* The reason behind every trial, every problem, every attack we have faced?" He shakes his head. "No map is worth this. I'm better off without you," he snarls.

My eyes burn. I feel a tear slide down my cheek.

And that only seems to anger him more. He steps right in front of me and says, "You are weak. You are foolish. If you want to live, turn around. Leave your sword. Give up. You don't have what it takes to survive this. You never did." I don't want to—*I don't fucking want to*—but I start to cry in earnest. A sob escapes my lips. He just shakes his head. "Go home, Aris," he says. Then he walks past me, past the fire, and out into the rest of the ruins.

25

The boat is heavier than it looks. The pebbled dirt crunches beneath its hull as I drag it to the edge of the starless-black water, the sound swallowed by the rain.

It must be afternoon, but it looks like evening, the sun still smothered by storm clouds. Raker is sequestered in a room on the opposite side of the ruins. He hasn't surfaced in the hours since he left me by the hearth.

My time with him is over. That's clear. He's given up on me. He's decided I'm not worth the map or being a fucking mule for the sword he has already claimed in his own mind, and I won't wait around for him to kill me and take it for good.

In this storm—I have a chance to run. From Raker. From my own shame and guilt.

Because he's right. I've been the cause of so many dangers. I could blame my sword and the notice it brings me, but Raker has a weapon just like mine, yet he hasn't gotten in a fraction of the trouble I've found myself in. I need to be stronger. Better.

Without him.

I keep looking over my shoulder, expecting to see that hood, to see the glimmer of that mask or glorious blade right before he cuts me down. But there's nothing but a wall of rain and wind.

I can't believe he thinks I would just give up my sword. Just leave it on the floor and crawl back to the gates with my tail between my legs.

Fuck him.

The ground finally gives way beneath the boat, and I exhale sharply as it surges into the water. Carefully, I crawl inside. There are paddles by my legs. I've never done this before—Xara's boat maneuvered itself—but I understand the basics. It takes a few tries, a few times the paddles nearly fall right into the dark lake, but I finally figure it out. Then, with the same strength I've attempted to build for wielding my sword, I paddle.

Rain pierces the water all around me in pinpricks. My boat and paddles cast ripples. I peer into the onyx lake, imagining a creature will come crashing up from the abyss. A chill slides through my blood, as if I'm locking eyes with something ancient, something my weak mortal vision can't see, just below the surface. But nothing breaks through.

My arms quickly start to burn, still I don't slow, lest Raker notice I'm gone and that I didn't, in fact, leave my sword behind.

If he really wants my blade, at least I have a head start.

And I have the map—an advantage. I know what landscapes await. Which is why I really fucking wish I didn't have to go through this alone.

Though it's so easy to hate him, he's been a steady presence by my side for weeks. He's been a hand in the dark places, begrudgingly helping me through them. An ember of sadness stirs at the thought of never seeing him again. It's quickly snuffed out by all those words he said. He clearly hates me almost as much as I hate him.

He'll probably be relieved to see me gone.

I paddle and paddle, until that small island and castle become just smudges in the rain. Until the boat roughly washes onto shore. Until my boots crunch against rocks, and I'm climbing a cliff face.

Until I'm through the trees and away from Raker for good.

I GUESS I'VE found the fucking Storm Woods.

On the map, it looked peculiar. A simple patch of forest with a few added whorls.

In real life, I'm being brutalized by leaves flying in vortexes, roaring winds, rain like hellfire, and branches intent on stabbing me through.

Every step takes enormous effort. I grit my teeth and push against the current, and it's like pushing against a wall. I feel my energy unspooling.

Shit.

I should find shelter or take my time . . . but I can't. Soon Raker will realize I'm gone. And if he really wants this sword, he'll chase after me.

I'm surprised he didn't steal it, back in the ruins. Did he think I was too weak to actually make a run for it? Too cowardly?

Did he really think I would just leave it?

It doesn't matter now. No, what matters is getting the hell away from him.

Sword in hand, I push my way through, eyes alert, looking for any sign of the many beasts that thrive in storms—the ones from the book that are awakened by claps of thunder and energized by spears of lightning. I don't see any movement beyond the trees being ripped apart by brutal winds.

But I smell it. The metallic, biting taste of magic. I duck behind a trunk still standing. Peer around it, and am struck—

By a smattering of giant leaves. They smother my face, and I gasp in shock, only serving to tighten them around my nose and mouth. I try to pull, but they fasten to my skin as tightly as a mask. *I can't breathe.* Panic pounds through my blood, and I claw, scratching up my face in the process, before finally peeling them off. I suck in air, head spinning. They could have suffocated me. It was almost like they *tried*.

Something is seriously wrong with this forest.

As if in response, thunder rumbles, rattling the woods, rattling my teeth. *Fuck. This.* I stagger through the tangle of trunks, until they end completely.

I've stumbled upon a dirt road through the woods.

The rain is heavier without the cover of treetops, but there's also less debris for the storm to kick up.

I remember that one ancient road, with the Masks. Are they here? Would they be out in such weather?

I look back at the forest. Then at the path. Time to make a choice.

A lick of fear running down my neck, I take off down the road, desperate to get out of these woods as fast as possible. It's only when I nearly trip over an errant root that I see the faintest pattern in the dirt. I duck and squint.

They're hoof marks. Dozens of them, in a line. Some have been washed away by the rain, but others are still perfectly shaped. Fresh, then.

Which means many, many horses were just on this road.

I must have just missed them. Are more coming? I look to either side. Strain to listen. But it's impossible to hear much beyond the onslaught of weather.

I should go back into the woods . . . I glance at the trees, at all the brush flying through them, and don't move a single inch.

Another ground-shaking roll of thunder makes the sky shudder. It's immediately followed by another roar.

This one comes from right ahead.

My veins turn to ice. There's a gust of wind hurtling down the road, dredging up all the dirt in its path, stealing peels of bark forming a face spun from roots and leaves and moss and spears of wood as teeth, rushing right at me.

Well, fuck.

I guess the book really didn't include everything.

Terror clutching my chest, I jump out of the way with only feet to spare, sheath my sword, then cling to a wide trunk. My feet lift off the ground.

And the world splits around me.

I scream as the surrounding trees are ripped away, the wind a bellow that turns into voices telling me to let go, pulling at my heels, pricking my fingers, shaking the trunk back and forth, trying to throw me off of it. My braid whips my cheeks, branches pelt my body, but I don't release my grip, using the strength I've been training to hold on, until, finally, the wind settles, and my feet hit the ground again.

In a half-mile radius, there's almost nothing left. My knees buckle. I'm covered in dirt. The rain is falling sideways, the large drops blinding me. My skin is cold as ice.

I have to get out of here.

On unsteady legs, I race through the plundered forest, boots sliding in the mud as I weave around the remaining trees, some just trunks without branches, their limbs ripped clean off.

I veer to the side to avoid a pile of trunks stacked like kindling—and step right into the path of a wind spout like a fallen tornado. Before I can retreat, I'm soaring. I land with a sickening crunch, hoping to all the gods it's branches snapping beneath me, and not my bones.

There's no time to assess any injuries. I roll out of the way and run like hell, turning in a different direction, only to be met with another mangled face, formed from the forest itself. Headed right toward me.

Its body is a tunnel of violent wind tearing everything in its path to form scales of wood it wears like a storm serpent. It opens its jagged mouth with an ear-splitting howl.

Shit.

My chest feels like it's going to explode with panic, but I wait. I wait until it's just a breath away, then I dive out of its path and roll, hitting rocks and roots, bruising everywhere, before I come to a stop.

I'm soaked to the bone. Cold, and trembling. I think of that fire Raker made. How good it felt to put my feet by it.

Gods, I wish I was back there. I know why I snuck out, but right now . . . I fucking regret it.

Especially when a startling flash of lightning spears across the sky, and I'm thrust into a memory.

A clear blue day, hunting wildflowers with my sister. Going way too far outside of town. Laughing. Chasing each other in circles. My sister in a cornflower-blue dress that she loved. The one with a wide white ribbon that tied in the back. That ribbon whipping wildly in the breeze as she ran from me. As she looked over her shoulder.

The storm came from nowhere. That bolt of lightning spiraled right at her. And I remember that fear. Pure, soul-shredding terror.

I—

A gasp rips me back into the present. It is no ordinary gasp. No . . . it sucks all the air out of the forest, leaving only muted quiet. Just like in the mists.

That smell of magic is all that's left, searing the inside of my nostrils.

I get to my feet. Look around. I'm alone. The storm serpents are gone. There are only endless sheets of rain in front of me.

Another flash of lightning—

Illuminating a woman.

Her hair is bone-white and clinging to her face. She wears a thin white robe over an elegant dress, with a hood and a long train. It drags behind her, whispering over rocks and twigs and fallen branches. There are just sockets where her eyes should be, with long scratch marks around the holes, as if she clawed them out herself.

In her hand, she carries a velvet pouch. It's drooping with weight. It's embroidered with glimmering gold.

I swallow. The lightning disappears, and the woman with it. Thunder roars.

I don't dare breathe. I can't see her anymore . . . but the forest is still far too quiet. The metallic smell is everywhere. My eyes search the woods wildly for any trace of her. Nothing. She's gone.

I lean against the trunk behind me, finally taking a breath. I can feel my pulse beating against its remaining bark.

Another flash of lightning brightens the forest.

And she's right in front of me.

I gasp. Her lovely mouth parts—

And a scream splits my mind in half, like the lightning has pierced right through my skull. My teeth clench painfully. My hand reaches toward my sword. Somehow, I know this metal would go right through her. Especially when the light disappears and she's gone. So is the scream.

No . . . not gone. Just not corporeal. I can feel the chill of her breath on my cheek. I can feel her searching . . . smelling . . . for something.

I remember what Raker said about that puddle in the mists. How it gained strength from my attention. From my fear.

I will not feed it. I will not be afraid.

I close my eyes tightly, and I don't think about the creature in front of me. I don't think of the storm.

I think about one of those nine remaining memories.

The day the tree in our lawn—the one my mother had nursed and cared for over several years, the one that many generations had given up on, but my mother never did—bore fruit for the first time.

Our neighbors came to celebrate. Wearing my longest dress, and fabrics that covered my throat, I joined them.

No one had much, but everyone brought something. Jam. A loaf of bread. A rare pheasant, caught by the local huntsman.

My mother carefully cut each fruit, and everyone got a piece. Its skin was deep violet. It was swollen with juice. I remember biting into it and feeling pure and utter joy. Especially when I opened my eyes and saw everyone else smiling.

There was so little to smile about on Stormside. So little to covet. But that one moment . . . it felt like a rope, tying us together.

That night, I asked my mother why we would share the fruit from the tree. Why we always shared everything we had. It was ours.

"Because what's the point in having anything if you don't share it?" she said.

I didn't really know what she meant. All I knew was that it had felt good to see my neighbors happy. It had felt good to share, even though I only got a small piece of the fruit for myself.

As the years passed, I understood more.

I understand now.

I can feel the moment the screaming woman releases her hold on me, as if I have lost her interest. As if, unlike the creature from the mists, she does not relish happiness.

The creature passes on. I feel the brush of the end of her robe, hear it murmur against the dirt and grass at my feet, until it vanishes completely.

The sound of the storm and woods rushes in again, and I fold over, fighting for air. For some reason, I'm sweating, as if what just happened took great energy.

Rain slips down my body. I lean back against the tree, trying to catch my breath. Wondering what the hell that being was.

Then I hear it. The snapping of a twig. I move in a flash—

And an arrow pierces the tree I was just leaning against. *Cadoc.*

No. I recognize this arrow. When I look up and squint through the rain, I see her in a tree.

Valen.

Her bow is already set again. There's the twang of the string releasing.

I lunge out of the way as another arrow slams into the place I just occupied.

"What the fuck?" I scream through the storm. As if I haven't faced enough. As if this tempest isn't enough of a danger.

I haven't seen another competitor since Raker and I started working together. I can't help but feel like Valen's appearance is this world telling me that I should have stayed with him. Or maybe that I should have listened to him and gone home.

Was she tracking us, to get my sword? Or did she just get lucky and run into me?

A tree in the distance shakes as she leaps into it. I don't even hear the snap of the bow this time.

Pain sears through the skin just below my ear. An arrow buries into the tree just behind me.

I reach up and—blood. That's blood. A small adjustment, and it would have gone through my throat. She's making killing shots.

Why? Is it truly for my sword?

There's a wider tree just a few feet in front of me. I throw myself behind it, using it for cover. I pant, frost coating the inside of my lungs, burning through my chest.

I feel a thud in my spine as one of her arrows burrows in the bark behind me. It traveled far through the wood. But not all the way. Not enough to pierce me.

Another tree shakes as she moves closer.

I'm a sitting duck here. But if I move away from this protection, I'll be wide open. The next tree is several yards up, and it's thin. I won't make it.

"Why?" I yell through the downpour. "I'm not your enemy."

She's a skilled archer. My sword would only weigh her down. Besides, she has her own blade. An elegant, small one, decidedly easier to carry. I saw her claim it during the Culling.

I'm surprised to hear her voice. It's deep and smooth. Straight to the point. "It's nothing personal," she says. Another arrow strikes the bark. This one with more force. I can feel it almost reach my spine. Leaves tremble as she jumps into another tree. Closer. "Cadoc and his group caught up to me a while back. They managed to stab me before I got away. It's infected now."

What does that have to do with me? I want to scream.

Another arrow. This one has enough force to go right through the tree, and I lurch forward, out of the way of its point.

Another jump. "I won't make it to the end like this. I was offered another chance. A goblet of magic without making the journey. You see . . . there's a bounty on your head."

I frown. A bounty?

I startle as another arrow pierces the tree, going all the way through and then some, its point sticking out right above my skull. If I was a little taller, it would be the end of me. She's so close. She won't make another mistake.

Maybe if I keep her talking . . . maybe if I convince her—

"I—"

She's done speaking. There's the rush of air as she jumps. I brace myself for an arrow through my head.

A snap sounds. Followed by a blood-curdling scream.

Hands trembling, I grip the bark and peer around it, just enough to see a body sprawled on the ground. Valen. Her bow is on the forest floor, just a few feet away—

From her arm that has been crushed by a branch so thick it might as well be a trunk. Other branches lay splintered around her.

Her limb is twisted at a gruesome angle. It's ruined.

She keeps screaming. "No. *No.*" Her entire body is trembling. I take a step closer. Another, until I see her face is flushed with fever. There's a bandage wrapped around her middle, where she must have been stabbed.

"Just kill me already," she snarls. Her face is contorted in pain. I'm not sure why she's on the quest. I'm not sure why she needs that cup of magic. It doesn't matter, I suppose. We all have our reasons.

When I don't move an inch, she thrashes like a beast. "Kill me. I'd rather a blade across my throat than to be picked apart by whatever lurks in these woods."

I wonder if she saw the woman. I can almost hear the whisper of that long white cape, as if she has turned back around, having sensed suffering.

Valen must hear it too, because she lets out a whimper.

And I am so very, very foolish. I can almost hear Raker's voice in my head telling me so. Because I walk over to her side, then squat. Grip the end of that massive branch crushing her arm, pinning her to the forest floor. Then, with a groan, I begin to lift.

"What are you doing?" Valen demands.

"Just roll out of it," I manage to get out, my voice tight with strain. I lift another inch.

With a bellow of agony, she rolls herself from underneath it, and I drop the branch, heaving.

Her bone is shattered. It's sticking out of her ripped, bloody skin. Her muscle is flattened.

"It's no use," she scrapes out. Her face has gone pale. "I'm dead."

She's right. I can feel that spectral woman getting closer, her hunger an endless well that can never be filled, her misery bleeding through this forest. And she's not the only starved creature in these woods.

"Who is after me?" I say.

Valen gives me a scathing look, as if I am a villain for not letting her die in peace. She's clutching her arm, as if it would do any good. Finally, she says, "I don't know. Some immortal told me about the bounty. I was told to bring you to a cavalry, if I caught you."

My heart stills, remembering the hoof marks on the road. "Cavalry?"

She nods. She gasps with pain as that bone sticking out of her arm moves. "I followed them here. They seemed to know you were in the area. They—they're not only after you. They're after . . . after him. The head of the king's guard."

Raker.

My throat feels tight. "Why?"

"I don't know," she growls. She grits her teeth. I can imagine that right now death would be a mercy.

Those hoof prints were headed directly for that black lake. Could they really know he's there?

I remember the curl of smoke from the hearth. The one I didn't put out before I left. The one Raker set for my benefit, given that he stayed in another room entirely.

A rush of guilt seeps through my chest.

I try to ignore it.

Valen is still glaring at me, as if she didn't, just minutes ago, try to kill me. I have no doubt that if she could reach for her weapons in her current state, she would try again now.

Still, I reach into my pocket. And I admonish myself for being so very stupid as my fingers curl around the vial of steelclaw saliva.

I need this. It's invaluable; it could save me. But I can't leave her here to die. I know it's foolish, I know this is what I signed up for . . . but I just can't.

I open the vial and pour it onto her arm.

Valen seizes. Opens her mouth to scream. But before she can, the bone lurches and rights itself. Her skin crawls together. Everything goes back to the way it was. She's panting with pain. I can't imagine that was pleasant.

A fold forms in between her brows as she looks at her arm with wonder. She turns toward me. "How—"

"Magic," I say simply. "Now show me that wound of yours."

There's the slightest pause, in her wariness. Maybe she's weighing whether she should reach for her bow in a flash and shoot an arrow right through my forehead.

Then she scrambles for the bandages on her stomach. Pulls them off. I pour the rest of the vial over the infected mess and watch it melt away, until the gaping wound is no more than skin.

I get to my feet. Step around her, toward the rest of the forest. The wind has lessened the slightest bit. Here's my chance to make up some time.

Valen's voice stops me in my tracks.

"Why?" she says, still on the forest floor. Looking at me with a mix of confusion and trepidation.

I shrug. "You've come too far to be taken down by a tree."

Then I turn back toward my path.

The storm rages on. I just keep running.

I make it another mile before the knot in my chest tightens. I remember Valen's words. There's an entire cavalry after us. There's a *bounty*.

I saw their marks on the road. They might not know exactly where Raker is, but he doesn't even know they're looking for him. He could run right into them. And he . . . he's the best fighter I have ever seen, but even he would fall against an entire cavalry.

An image flashes of that fate. Of a blade going right through his spotless armor. Of that magnificent sword belonging to anyone else.

Fuck me.

Fuck my weak, bleeding heart.

Fuck the sense of loyalty I feel toward someone who has told me they won't hesitate to strike me down.

He called me reckless. Foolish. He told me I wasn't strong enough for this journey. I should not care. I should *not*.

But I suppose I'm just proving him right as I curse through my teeth and turn around.

Rain batters the top of my head as I run through the woods I had carefully prowled through earlier. Running right *toward* the very warrior I had fought so hard to escape, facing every single danger a second time.

Because even though he has made me feel small, even though he has called me pathetic, even though he has pointed out all my flaws, again and again . . .

He went through the mist for me. I don't even care if it was for my sword, because if it *really* was, he would have taken it then. I know how easy it is for him to kill anything, so there is a reason he has kept me alive, beyond using me as a mule, beyond the map. I won't pretend it is care, or loyalty, or companionship.

I won't pretend there isn't a high chance he'll kill me if he ever sees me again.

Regardless of the reasons, he has saved my life countless times.

Regardless of the execution, he has forced me to become better.

And maybe I just can't bear the fact that someone like Raker would be crept up on by a group of immortals. Not after everything.

The scars on the bottom of my back pull and burn, the tissue stinging in the storm, the way it does whenever it rains. It's a reminder that I should leave him there to die, because he did the very same thing to me.

But I am not Raker.

I am loyal, I have mercy, and those might be flaws in a place like this, on a quest like this, but they are traits my mother taught me. So they can't be wrong. They can't.

It's the reminder of her, the reminder of everything she gave me, that has me sprinting through that forest without stopping. That has me ignoring the pull of every wicked thing lurking within it.

And the reminder of him. Of the relief of seeing him in those mists. Of the awe as he cut everything that was about to gut me down.

I'm heaving by the time I reach the cliff that looks out over the black lake.

There it is. The ruins. It's undisturbed. A wisp of smoke is still curling from the chimney.

They haven't found him yet. The rush of relief I feel at that is surprising. It's too strong, like a current that could sweep me off my feet.

It's quickly smothered when I notice a flash of light on the other side of the water. Panic clutches my chest.

A wave of knights on horses is advancing out of the valley, right toward the lake. There are *dozens*. All armed with swords.

Raker. My eyes find the boat upon the rocks. The one I took, leaving him no way of getting to shore. Not without swimming in that ominous water. I've just made it easier to get to him. They will use that boat, and the other one that was already there, to catch him unawares. They will surround the lake, making escape impossible. Guilt pierces my heart as I look from the advancing cavalry to that ruin. To that fire that we sat in front of together.

They're after both of us. It is foolish. It is ruinous.

But before I can think about every way that I'm about to seal my fate, I take a deep, rattling breath, bring my hands to the sides of my mouth, and open it to scream across the lake—

A large hand smothers my lips, pulling me forcefully back against a hard chest. My skull bounces off armor.

And a blade settles against my throat.

I GO VERY still. And I don't know whether to weep in relief or weep for myself for being so damned stupid, because I know that sword.

A voice dark as night says, "You didn't go home."

His blade is still against my neck. "No," I whisper, my pulse beating against its metal.

"You . . . turned back," he says, like it's the most idiotic thing in the world. Because it is.

"To warn you," I manage to say, the foolishness of that endeavor hitting me with full force as he presses that blade harder, right at the base of my jaw, metal against flesh. I wait to feel the sting of blood. To suffer the consequence of this very stupid decision that I almost certainly deserve. I inhale sharply.

"Fuck, Aris," he says, and the cold metal is ripped away. Sheathed.

I whip around to face him. He's soaking wet, water dripping from his hood, and down his armor. He swam through the dark waters.

Was it to hunt me? Or did he hear the cavalry somehow?

All I know is he just had every opportunity to end me for good and take my weapon. But he didn't.

We just stand there, staring at each other. I'm still panting from the running.

"There's a bounty on our heads," I finally say, through all the heavy breathing.

His head turns slightly toward the cavalry behind me. I hear the splash of water as the warriors begin to wade into it. "I figured."

"Do you know why?"

"Our swords" is all he says.

Right.

My sword is a gift—but it's also a death sentence. Apparently it's special enough that powerful people on Starside want it. It must be one of the heirs. Only they could command such forces.

And if they're here . . . someone gave us up.

Was it those knights from the village who alerted their lord to it? Someone else who caught a glimpse of us? Was it the hunter?

Either way, it doesn't matter. Raker knows about the pursuit. He's safe.

Of course he is. Did I really think I would be the one to save him? *Stupid.* I never should have turned back. I just lost hours. My body is aching with all the energy it took to get here so quickly.

He's made it clear I am a burden to him. He doesn't want to work with me. Shame heats my face, shame that I came back, and that I am all the things he called me.

"Good luck, then," I say tightly, trying to maintain any shred of self-respect. I make to move past him.

His fingers graze my wrist. They're still burning hot, even in the freezing rain.

Slowly, I turn to face him.

Is this the moment he demands I give up my sword again? Or finally takes it from me? Or does the honorable thing of challenging me to a duel, one I know I won't win?

I wait for his next move, chest rising and falling quickly, and he just stares down at me. He stares, and stares, and all I see is a shadow. A glint of a mask. A demon.

Finally, Raker drops his hand, like my skin has burned him. "You can follow me," he says, his voice a deep rumble.

I blink, shock rendering me speechless. It takes a few moments for the words to sink in. When they do, I'm immediately furious.

"Fuck. You" is what I want to say. I want to scream. I want to tell him how much his words hurt me, and see if I could ever hurt him back. But this isn't personal. There's nothing between us.

This is a quest of survival. And if the snarls and stomps of the dozens of horses below us are any indication, this journey just got much harder.

I can't trust him. I know that. But I won't make it to the end of this alone.

I raise my chin. Rain spills down my cheeks. If I'm going to work with him again, I need assurances. "Are you going to kill me? Are you going to take my sword?"

A second of consideration passes. Two. Three.

"No," he says simply.

"Which one?"

He doesn't answer me.

And that's just as well. Because I can't promise I won't do either to him.

"Lead the way," I say, my voice as cold as his. He turns.

I look back at the cavalry one last time—and a shard of light spears through the storm clouds. It illuminates one of the shields hanging off a saddle.

I don't know that crest. But by its color, I think I know who it belongs to.

"It's not a lord after our blades . . ." I say, my voice quiet. Raker has turned around. I watch his body tense as he reaches the same conclusion.

This entire time, we've been on a quest to reach the gods. I've been on a journey to hunt them down.

And now it's clear . . . the gods are hunting *us*.

26

"Why would the gods want our swords?" I say over a flickering fire.

We headed north through the woods, away from that main road, for a full day, until we reached where it turned into a stretch of mountains. When Raker managed to catch a wild boar, I didn't object. I sat and watched him set the fire with his stone. Roast it.

And hand me a good portion of it.

By going back for him . . . it seems a rock in the wall between us has been removed. His mask still hasn't. There are still secrets thrumming between us. I can feel them.

But there is also the start of a different type of partnership. One with a push and pull. I hand him a smattering of nuts I found a few hours ago. He takes them without a snide remark. I hear them crunching in his mouth.

"Mine's pretty nice," he says.

And there he goes again, proving just why I want to throttle him.

I nod. "What a relief," I say, chewing on the meat. Swallowing. "You were starting to be a little too tolerable for my taste."

He makes a huffing sound that isn't quite a laugh. He finally answers my previous question. "The gods hoard power. Haven't you noticed?"

I have. But I just thought it was being hoarded on this side. I didn't know . . . I didn't know they were keeping so much of it from the immortals too.

Now I've seen the truth. The villages are better off than the ones on Stormside, of course, but not by much.

The nature here is beautiful, the fruit and vegetables are plentiful, but the land is too dangerous to cross. The roads are full of perils. What good are all these resources if most can't access them? The God of Travels has outlawed maps and stationed Masks at each major trail. Now it all makes sense.

The gods want to keep the immortals weak and reliant on them. They want to keep them separate, lest they form an uprising.

"The gods were supposed to protect us," I say.

Raker snorts. "The only thing you can ever count on is your metal, Aris."

I suppose that's what he thinks. Is that why he hides himself behind it? Is that why he hides at all?

"Can I see yours?" The question spills out of me before I can help it.

He tilts his head at me.

"Your sword," I clarify.

He just stares at me, and my cheeks heat. It sounds so stupid. I've obviously seen his blade before. I just had it pressed against my fucking throat. But I've never been able to actually examine its details. "I work in a forge," I try to explain. I shake my head. "Never mind, I—"

In a flash, he stands, unsheathes his weapon, then, carefully, warily, places it flat in his hands, holding it up for me to study.

I blink too many times, shocked. A moment later, curiosity has me scrambling to my feet. I've admired and hated this blade in equal measure for years. I've only ever seen it when it's being used or standing proud in front of him.

But up close . . .

It's magnificent. Its cross guard is made up of sharp pieces of shattered metal, expertly melded together. Its blade is long and broad, sparkling and smooth, perfectly straight, with a fine edge. It's so big, it's a wonder he can fight so effortlessly with it. My hands drift toward its steel.

"May I?" I ask, glancing up at him, only to find him staring down at me. Just when I think he'll refuse, he nods.

My fingers lightly brush the metal, and Raker shudders.

With anger? With disgust that I'm touching his blade? I smooth my fingers down it, all the way to the hilt, studying the detail, taking it in, and all the while, Raker is tense and silent in front of me. I might be overstepping, but I curl my hand around the hilt, just to see what it feels like, not even able to get my fingers all the way around, and—

Just as fast as Raker drew his sword, he sheathes it.

"Now you know what a real sword feels like," he bites out.

I glare at him. "I have a real sword."

"Maybe. But forging weapons and even claiming them doesn't mean anything if you can't use them."

"Then I guess I should get to work," I say through my teeth. I don't spare him a glance as I creep to the mouth of the cave we've settled in and cycle through the different positions he taught me. I won't beg him to train me again—but that doesn't mean I still don't need training. My own knowledge is better than nothing.

Raker puts out the fire, leaving me just the moonlight. For once, I know his action isn't out of malice. The flames are too much of a risk, knowing we're being hunted. On horseback, they're faster than us. They could catch up at any moment.

The storm is still raging. Rain reflects off my metal as I move my sword up and down, fighting an invisible opponent. I go through my memory of battling the split-skin immortals, repeating my motions, then changing them to be better. Envisioning myself in another duel.

I train until my muscles are sore. Only then do I creep past Raker. He's facing the wall. But his breathing—it isn't steady. If he's awake, he doesn't turn around.

Slowly, I lie down on the stone floor and stare up at hanging rock, sharpened into fangs. Each piece is just slightly glowing, with hidden crystal. Beautiful—with an edge. Just like our swords. Just like Starside.

His deep voice echoes through the cave. "Your footwork is sloppy."

I roll my eyes. "Thank—"

"Your back foot. When you retreat, make sure it moves first."

Oh. I didn't realize I was doing that.

"Thank you," I say, my voice losing some of its bite.

I go to bed turned toward the cave wall.

THE THUNDERING OF a hundred hooves wakes me. The ground shakes. Rocks fall from the ceiling, stabbing into the stone floor, shattering.

They've found us.

How? We only had the fire lit for a few minutes. Maybe they haven't found us at all. Maybe they're just going into the mountains, like we are.

That theory all but dies when the horses stop.

And I hear voices.

Raker is pulling me up in an instant. "We need to go." Still half-dazed from sleep, I stumble forward, grabbing my sword.

"Go where?" Heavy metallic steps sound just beyond the cave's mouth. If we go out there, we'll run right into them.

Raker isn't going toward the mouth, though. He's going in the opposite direction, deeper into the mountain.

It's early morning. Only the faintest curl of light follows us as we run straight into the darkness.

The ceiling slopes down and loses its glimmer. Raker has to duck, maneuvering around mounds of sharp rocks dripping like teeth. I follow the slight shine of his armor. We run for several minutes without slowing.

The path is wide, but instead of moving forward, he suddenly takes a turn. He rushes toward a dark corner. I'm about to ask what the hell he's doing when he says, "There's a hole. Another level, below."

Without warning, he's gone. I blink—and can barely see the trace of a circle on the ground. A gap in the rock.

I stand very still.

The light from the mouth of the cave has been all but ripped away. The entrance has been wholly blocked.

Fear roots me in place. Because—because I can't go down there. I know that.

The memory grips me.

Flames guttering into pure and utter darkness.

Screams melting into silence.

A starless night, like even the galaxy was closing its eyes, like even it didn't want to see what had happened.

Only my sobs, because everything that I loved, everything that once burned so fiercely, all of that *was* burned, and it was all my fault.

I'm alone. In the dark. Screaming.

Alone forever.

A metallic step echoes from the other side of the cave. It won't take them long to get here.

"Aris, you need to jump." Raker.

His voice barely reaches me. How far is the drop? I blink, but I can't see anything. Not anymore.

Just like that night.

Clutching ash. Trembling in it. *Smeared* with it. Gasping—

"Aris."

"I'm scared," I say, my voice quivering. My eyes burn as memories from that night blind me. As they echo through my mind just like those metallic steps through this cave, getting closer. *Closer.*

Then him again. "I know. I know, Aris," he says, and his voice is devoid of its usual cruelty. He says my name almost like a caress.

"I'm afraid of the dark," I gasp, and hearing it out loud . . . how pathetic it is . . .

"I know," he repeats. "You told me."

I did. Beneath the stars, I did, in the same breath that I told him that I could learn to love the night. But this isn't night. It is a dark, cold place.

"You need to jump, Aris," Raker says, his voice harder now, like he can hear them coming. "I'll catch you."

I shake my head. No. I can't trust him at all. I can't trust *anything* in this place. Especially when he's saying my name like it's something to savor. The Raker I know would never be this patient. Maybe Raker left. Or maybe he's dead, in a heap below. Maybe this is an entirely different beast speaking to me. I'm reaching for any excuse I can not to jump into that dark hole as I say, "How do I know you're not a demon? Or a creature like that man in the mists?"

A pause. "You saw the man in the mist?"

I blink, momentarily distracted from the approaching steps. The yells as they find the remnants of our fire. "Did you?"

I think about what the Gardener said. That he had only ever met one other person with as much suffering . . . *just now.*

He couldn't have been talking about Raker. *Heartless, cold* Raker.

He doesn't answer.

Instead, he says, in a frustrated growl, "You snore in your sleep."

I rear back, shock melting away some of my fear. "What?"

"When you're not waking up half the world with your fucking nightmares, you're keeping me up with your snoring."

Do I?

"That doesn't prove anything," I say.

"Why would a demon care about your sleep habits?" he demands.

"Why do you?" I hurl back.

"Aris, *just fucking jump*," he says.

Just as a boot echoes right behind me—I do.

And he catches me, just like he promised. Before dropping me right on my ass. "Fucking *hell*, Aris," he snaps, before he drags me back into the shadows.

There's murmuring above. I don't dare breathe. I don't dare move.

Then there are steps as the warriors keep going, right past the hole. They'll find it eventually. I hear calls for torches.

It's more than we have.

I tense, fear like ice in my veins as I realize we are beneath a mountain. In pure and utter darkness.

My breath hitches. I feel around for anything I can, which is mostly Raker. I get close to his hood, and he rears back.

"Your fear, Aris?" he says, that cutting voice back. Any hint of patience is gone, like it never existed in the first place. "Get over it."

It's said like an order, a general telling his warrior to do something, without any room to argue.

I swallow.

He's right. I'm not going to make it out of here if I can't even get a full breath.

I remember what I did in the forest when I encountered that screaming woman. My memories were a tether. A light through the darkness. I can do this. I have no choice.

"I will," I say.

"Good." He turns. I hear his steps, getting farther away. Desperately, I stumble forward, trying to follow in the direction he's moving, not wanting to be left alone again. My pulse picks up when I can't reach him, when I don't know where he's turned. I hear a deep, rumbling sigh before he grabs my arm.

Together, we walk through the darkness.

Walk is generous. He all but drags me, because it's almost impossible to walk quickly when I can't see even an inch in front of my nose.

The tunnels are narrow. I know that, because the wall scrapes my arms every few seconds. My breaths echo. The air is stale. It feels like—it feels like I'm trapped.

But I focus on the steady heat of Raker's long fingers around my elbow. I focus on his and my breath merging. I use his strength to steady myself, for even though my strides are cautious and unsure, his are not. He walks just as smoothly as he does in a field. He is like a blade cutting through everything, bending the world to his will.

I cling to that strength, try to let it call to my own. If he is not afraid, then I will not be. I slow my breathing. I steady my steps.

Then I pluck one of those remaining memories I covet.

I think about the time my father told my sister and I the story of how he and my mother fell in love.

They were neighbors. They had known each other their entire lives.

His father died young, so my father had to help his mother take care of the family. He would travel far away, to where thicker trees still grew, cut them down, then drag the wood back to the village in a sled. There wasn't time to play in the streets, like the other children, but he would watch them as he cut that wood. He admired my mother from afar. He said she was the most beautiful girl he had ever seen. He said he liked the way she threw her head back when she laughed. She was doing it that day, as she and the other children played a game.

The wolf came from nowhere. Its ribs were visible through its flesh. It was starving. It grabbed my mother by the back of her dress and dragged her through the streets, all the way into the forest, a patch of trees that were sickly and half-rotted. She screamed.

The other children ran away, but my father grabbed his ax and ran after her. He ran right into the woods.

Before the wolf could take a bite out of her, he chopped the fabric from her dress, freeing her.

And—as my mother added—it wasn't the fact that he saved her that made her fall in love with him. No. It was the fact that he did not kill the wolf, even though he had an ax in his hands.

Instead . . . he brought it food.

It came back. And my father fed it again. And again.

What my father loved about my mother was that she forgave the wolf. She had mercy for it too, and she found flowers with soothing properties, to mend the scrapes on its paws. Little by little, the wolf became a friend.

Of course, the first thing my sister said after the story was over was that she wanted a wolf as a pet. And that, if one attacked me and she saved me, could we keep it?

I still remember the look our parents gave each other. Like maybe they shouldn't have told us the story after all.

And I'll never forget the love in that expression—like an entire lifetime of memories was trapped in that one look.

I blink, and the darkness is just as deep as it was a few minutes ago. But it has lost some of its weight and teeth.

"Can you see anything?" I ask, wondering how Raker is walking so assuredly.

"A little."

"How?"

He waits a few moments before answering. It's like every word has to be dredged out of him. "We trained in tunnels sometimes."

I frown. "I didn't know there were tunnels on Stormside."

"There are several."

I suppose there's a lot about our side that I don't know. "And what . . . what was the rest of your training like?"

His voice is sharp as a scythe. "If you're looking for a distraction from your fear of the dark, then this isn't it, Aris."

I don't know why the bottom of my spine curls every time he says my name. Even if it's with irritation, like just now.

It's been weeks of this, though. Just like he sees right through me, to my weakest points, I see right through him.

I exhale heavily. "That bad?" Is that . . . is that the suffering he endured? The one the Gardener spoke of?

He huffs a cruel laugh. "You don't know what *bad* means, Aris." His fingers tighten against my skin. "You don't know what fear means. Or pain. You don't know *any*—"

"You don't know what I know," I say, my voice coming out so sharply, it cuts him off. He doesn't say anything in response.

Silence. For several moments, it's just silence.

Then curiosity overtakes me, and I break it. "How many people have you killed?"

He doesn't hesitate. "I lost count a long time ago."

"Hundreds?"

A pause. "More."

I take a stuttering breath. So many lives . . . gone at his hand. This same hand that is now steering me through the darkness.

I shouldn't be shocked. I know his reputation. I have seen him in action.

"The only way you get good at killing is *by killing*, Aris," he says.

He's right. And maybe that's been my biggest flaw all along, the biggest threat to me reaching the gods and getting my revenge.

I am not as heartless as Raker. I can't just turn off my emotions. And . . . and it makes me reckless.

"Have you ever been anything else?" I ask quietly. There is nothing but our voices in this tunnel. "Anything beyond the killing?"

I can't imagine him as a child. Laughing. Carefree. Hell, I don't even know if he has a *face*. I don't know if he's badly wounded, or monstrous, or anything at all.

Did he have a family? Was he born into one of those orphanages where the children are trained to fight from the time they can walk? Is that how he joined the king's guard?

I want to ask. But—but I don't want to ask anything I won't answer, if he turns it on me.

It doesn't matter.

That's the question that quiets him, and turns into miles and miles of walking in endless silence.

And I can't help but wonder why.

We walk in darkness for a full day.

The tunnels groan and shift around us, as if constantly being shaped with magic, and Raker guides us through different paths. He's our compass, moving assuredly, and I really hope he knows what he's doing.

I start to fear we're traveling deeper underground. That maybe there is no ending, and we're forever lost in the maze of the mountain. Maybe we've just been walking in circles. In this darkness, I'd never know it.

Even my memories can't keep cold terror from settling in the pit of my stomach. Or, after a day without rest, my legs from wobbling.

They finally give out, and Raker only plucks me from the ground and drags me along again. "I can't," I say, blinking away dust. My voice is just a rasp. My body is spent.

"You can" is all Raker says.

And the fight in me that rises at those words, that wants to scream at him . . . it is enough. It is enough for me to dig into that pit of strength again and find more.

His hand is still splayed against my spine, where he fisted the fabric of my shirt and pulled me to my feet again. It's a large steadying presence, keeping me upright. His fingers are long across my sword. But he doesn't take it. He just keeps his hand there.

"How are you not tired?" I ask.

"I am," he rumbles.

He doesn't sound it. He doesn't feel it. That hand is radiating strength, and I am taking it, as if leeching some of his years of training.

I take a rattling breath. "My third fear," I say. "Of . . . of dying in a stupid way . . . I—"

"You are not dying in these caves, Aris," he says, with so much credence that the next words die in my throat.

"Okay," I say instead. I believe him. And I steal some of that confidence too. I focus my mind not on if I will make it out of these caves, but when. I imagine rays of sun spilling into these tunnels of darkness.

And I keep walking.

Hours later, I finally see it.

Sunlight. It hurts my eyes, after all this darkness, but I keep looking. Everything in me wants to run toward it, but I don't need to. It's . . . getting closer, like it's barreling toward us.

I frown, and that's when I feel something else. The bite of magic, just like in the Storm Woods, an energy pulling all my senses toward it, begging me to give it my full attention . . .

I don't think. I grab Raker and shove him against the wall as hard as I can. I press myself against him.

"Don't look," I say. I close my eyes tightly.

Then, all at once, there's fire at my back, the suffocating heat of this demon, or whatever it is, begging us to look. To make those flames grow so large, they might flow right through these tunnels.

Look, it whispers, its voice calling to my blood, to my wants, as if to pull them out one by one. *Everything you desire, I have it. Right here.*

It feels like it does. I can almost taste the whisper of everything I've ever wanted right behind me, so close I can see it in my mind. So close, if I just look, it will be mine.

My body trembles with the need to turn around and have everything I'm envisioning. And it's not just innocent wants that it has pulled from me. No, treacherous wants sear along my skin in flames so hot they draw a whimper from my lips.

I lean harder against Raker, to get farther from the flames . . . but also, for other reasons.

And instead of pushing me away, like he always has, Raker curls his hands around my hips—

And pulls me closer. I draw in a ragged breath, in pure shock. I don't know if it's an attempt to hold me still . . . or if he actually wants to touch me. But no one's ever dared, and I've never even gotten close to this, what with my markings. And in this darkness, with our eyes closed . . .

All these buried wants are clawing out of me, and I'm trying to stop them, but part of me doesn't want to. My palms are against his armor. Our chests are flush—and his is rising and falling just as rapidly as mine is. His breaths are labored. His body . . . it's trembling, like he's fighting something too.

Slowly, my hands slide up to his neck, giving him plenty of time to stop me, but he doesn't. My fingers brush against his pulse . . . and it's racing. I need more. I—I need to keep touching him.

"Raker," I say in a strangled whisper, lifting to my toes, to be anywhere near his significant height.

Like a seal has been broken, his fingers slip beneath the hem of my shirt, and my blood ignites.

27

At that first brush of Raker's callused fingers beneath my shirt, my nerves catch fire.

I don't know if it's this demon's heat, or maybe I'm just this touch-starved, but my skin prickles everywhere, and it's like a new sense awakening. Raker's gone very still in front of me. I wonder if he feels it too, this fire in his veins, this deep, pulsing *ache*.

The quest is a distant thought. The fact that he's been my enemy for years doesn't seem important. No, right now, I feel raw and needy, and when he finally drags his rough knuckles up my spine, slowly, like he has all the time in the world to discover me in the dark, the flames behind my back expand, strengthening, unleashing a toe-curling, blood-smoldering desire that nearly brings me to my knees.

His name spills from my lips again, in a shameful whimper. "Raker—"

"*Don't speak,*" he bites out.

He's trying to fight it. His hand flexes against my skin, fingers going still as if he's using all his restraint to keep from touching me. I hear him swallow hard.

The pause clears my head a bit. I hate him. We shouldn't be doing this. I fall to my heels, then try to pull back, put some space between us . . . but he doesn't let go. His hold is light. I could easily slip out of it.

But I don't want to.

Fuck it.

I lift to my toes again, slide my hands up his armor with a possessiveness that doesn't make sense at all, the silver spotless and smooth, not a single mark marring it, until the metal ends, then I slip my fingers beneath it, feeling the strong muscles of his upper chest, touching as much as I can and—

Fuck.

That's the word Raker growls, right before his other hand dives below my shirt.

He strokes up my sides, calluses scraping my sensitive skin, and my blood turns molten. He's the head of the knights I've feared my entire life, given what they hunt. Right now, he's touching silver and he doesn't even know it.

Who he is should smother this flame in me, but it doesn't. I lean into him, desperate for him to touch more, to go higher, and when his rough knuckles gently trace the heavy underside of my chest, I tense, readying myself for a flash of pleasure. But before he reaches where I'm aching, his hands retreat, settling on my waist. His grip is loose, his fingers trembling, almost like he's afraid to touch me. Like he thinks he might break me.

But I need more.

And I'm done waiting.

Consumed by this flaming want, I lift even higher on my toes, loop my arms around his neck, then drag my chest against his hard armor, desperate for friction, my nipples tight with need. He groans, a rough tortured sound in the back of his throat, and his hands drop away.

He's going to finally put a stop to this madness, I think. It's probably for the best.

But then he grips the hems of my shirts.

And tears them both over my head.

Shit.

I gasp, flooded with panic, heat kissing my bare skin. *My markings.*

But his eyes are closed. I know that, because opening them would seal his fate. The fabric falls to our feet, and any doubt falls with it. All that's left is this blazing desire that's growing by the second.

His hesitance is gone too. I know that for certain when he roughly pulls down the fabric band I wear around my chest—and palms my breast.

Fire explodes behind my eyelids, nerves tightening and effervescing.

Fuck.

We both inhale sharply at the same time. I don't even try to pretend it doesn't feel good, and when he drags his thumb over my nipple, I moan, the sound echoing through this tunnel. Raker growls in response, then does it again. He makes circles, kneading, as if trying to make me unravel just by this alone.

It fucking feels like I could. My thighs are clenched tight against this growing heat, and he can tell. I know, because his other hand slides down my side, until his thumb hooks the waist of my pants and underwear.

I don't think I'm breathing.

He makes a low sound of need as he feels the material, a scrap of silk from the castle's wardrobe. Then, in a desperate flash, he pulls them both down my hip. Heat floods through me in a fiery wave as he strokes the sensitive skin there with his knuckle, back and forth, so close to where I need him, and he seems a second away from taking it all off, maybe just ripping the fabric to shreds, and *I want him to*. I want him to give me everything I've never experienced right against this wall.

Just when I think he might, he lets go of the band of my pants.

Then, before I can feel a hint of disappointment, he curls his hands beneath my ass, and lifts me to his height, holding me up like I weigh absolutely nothing, and—

He's right there. For the first time, we're level, and I can hear his breaths coming out hot and labored beneath that mask. Now more than ever, I'm tempted to open my eyes, pull that silver layer away, and see everything he hides beneath, but that's something he'll have to show me himself. I don't know what I'm doing, just that I need to be as close to him as he'll allow.

So, heart racing, blood pounding, I lean forward blindly—

And press my lips against the cold metal.

Harlan Raker has single-handedly slayed entire battalions. He's the greatest warrior in Stormside's existence. But that one move makes him *shiver*.

Our lips are so close, separated by just a thin sheet of silver. *I need to feel him*. My fingers dive into his hood, and he lets me, and they rake through hair and—

It's soft. His hair is so soft, and not too long, and he groans as I run my hands through it, the sound rumbling beneath my lips, and I wish he wasn't wearing a mask, I wish he wasn't wearing armor, because I need him.

It seems like he needs me too. Hands still curled under my ass, he pins my hips to his, and I suck in a sharp breath. Closer. I want us closer. I wrap my arms around his neck, crushing my lips to his mask harder and then my bare chest is pressed against his cold armor, in complete contrast to the roaring flames behind me. I've almost forgotten about this demon crafted of towering fire, trying to get us to open our eyes, but I don't feel afraid, not at all. There isn't room for anything else, beyond knee-buckling want.

And I want *him*.

My lips slip down the curve of his mask, toward his bare skin, and when my nose brushes against it, I tense.

He smells like his soap.

His fucking amazing soap.

I groan, and I can't help it. I kiss up the side of his neck, needing to taste him, and he *shudders*, a tortured sound leaves his lips. I would think he hated it, I would stop, if his hand didn't immediately lift to curl around the back of my head—and pin me to him.

He wants this. I do too. He tastes so fucking good, and I stroke him with my tongue, then suck against his pulse and—

"*Aris*," he growls, my name like a curse and a prayer.

"Raker," I gasp against his neck, and that's the word that snaps any sense of self-control. The hand still gripping my ass and holding me up starts to move me on him, knowing what I need, rubbing me against him, and—"*Oh my god*," I moan as liquid fire rushes through me, pooling between my legs, right where he's working me against his metal. He goes harder, and I don't think, I just roll my hips against him, helping, trying to get more of this delicious friction, my sensitive chest dragging against his armor with every movement.

Nothing else matters. Only this. A ruinous pleasure racing down my spine that's all-consuming, blazing, awakening a primal need only he can satiate. My nails sink into the back of his neck, using him to move faster, and he just threads his other hand through my hair, keeping my lips against his skin. He's burning up, pulse racing, and when my teeth graze his throat, he chokes out my name, and the sound nearly does me in. I'm burning from the inside out, nerves gleaming, pressure building inside me as I hurtle toward the edge of this cliff.

This feels so fucking good. But it's not enough. I don't want to feel metal; I want to feel *him*.

"Please. Take this off," I beg, clawing at his armor, wondering if I'm leaving marks. He doesn't seem to care. He nods. He's going to do it. But first—

I reach up to his mask. My fingers skim its edge. I give him plenty of time to stop me, but he doesn't. So slowly, slowly, I grip both sides. Lift it.

That's when he drops me.

Before my feet even hit the ground, he unsheathes his blade in a flash, and blindly slashes right above my head, so close, I feel its whisper against my hair. If he didn't know my exact height, I would be missing the top of my skull.

The fire dies. The cave is plunged back into cold darkness.

I open my eyes—

And gasp as Raker shoves me against the opposite wall, his boots sliding through the ashes of the demon he just slayed.

I groan, still trembling with the remnants of this desire, as his hands find my hips. As he pins them to the wall. I part my lips, wanting his hands to slide up and down my body in the darkness, across all the places I'm still aching.

But his voice is a growl. "This was nothing. *You* are nothing. Don't get close to me again," he snarls.

I open my mouth in shock, not even knowing what to say, but he doesn't give me the chance. Before I can speak a single word, he turns and leaves me panting against the wall. Flushed with want.

The moment he's gone, all that desire falls away. It turns cold.

It was the demon, then.

He doesn't want me at all. Not really.

I know that now. He made himself very clear. But he doesn't have to pretend like I was the only one influenced by this desire. We both acted on it. And I *saved* him. I'm the one who sensed the demon, who pulled him out of the path.

All that's left now is sinking shame. My cheeks burn with it and fury as I struggle to find my shirts in the dark, and blindly pull them on, eyes stinging.

Of course I don't want him. Of course he doesn't want me. That fire demon would have made me want *anyone*.

I keep telling myself that as I stumble through the darkness, in the direction of Raker's heavy steps. Fuck. Him.

I'd wanted to. *A lot.*

And that's the fucking problem.

I stay far away, trying to erase those last few moments from my mind, letting that hatred of him build up again, like a wall between us.

28

When I finally step out of the underground, my knees buckle. I close my eyes against the burning light and finally breathe in fresh air after the staleness of below.

Raker's a few steps ahead, but I don't even acknowledge him. Not after—

No. I won't think about it. He's right. It wasn't real. Raker is incapable of wanting anyone, least of all me, someone with traitorous secrets across her skin. If only the head of the king's guard, a knight trained to kill or capture anything silver, knew what he had been touching.

Even in the dark . . . that was reckless. *Stupid.*

On the other side of the gates, I don't doubt a glimpse at my bare skin would have him dragging me straight to the king himself, which might as well be a death sentence.

Yes.

Fuck. Him.

Finally, I get to my feet, eyes on the horizon, dread curling in my gut. The land in front of us has been razed. There's no green. Just an empty crater sits where a lake once must have.

My eyes burn. I would cry if I had the liquid to spare.

I expect Raker to stalk off ahead, but he waits, back toward me, until I'm closer, and then he takes off, a wall of metal.

When dusk falls, we can't find a cave with water, so we make camp by the remnants of a stream, no more than a few puddles of misty water we lay in the middle of. It's not ideal. Not even a little bit. But I would sleep on a bed of nails right now.

I collapse against the ground, and I don't even have the energy to dream.

W E TAKE OFF at the first sign of sunrise. We don't speak, and I'm grateful. Anger and hurt still churn in my chest. I'd be happy if we spent the rest of this journey in silence.

It's been more than two days without food or water. My heart is beating too quickly, like a last burst of life, a final, desperate push. Nausea roils through me. It's an effort to take every step, but my body moves anyway, knowing very well that I will die if I stay still.

It's not just me that's affected. Raker is moving slower than he ever has. I want to suggest he take off the armor, leave it behind, but after having said those words underground—in a desperate plea—in very different circumstances . . . I decide to keep my mouth shut.

The land slopes like it's melting. I ready myself for more desolation, for more thirst.

But there's something green ahead. A forest? Hope surges through me until we reach the putrid waters.

A bog.

A scraping sound escapes the back of my throat, a weak little noise that Raker ignores.

My veins feel dry. My breaths are shallow. I can't keep going. *I must keep going.*

Because there is clean water close by. If this journey has taught me anything, it's that there is always an end to the turmoil. Always an end to the rot, and the mists, and the darkness.

I just have to keep walking.

Thick trees abound, half rotted and wrapped in vines covered in thick barbs. The waters are various shades of murky gray. There's no way around, only through.

One moment of frustration.

Then I follow Raker into the water.

It reaches his knees. At my height, it reaches my waist. I keep my distance, watching him move, to make sure the water doesn't deepen.

It doesn't. It's still and steady, and it smells disgusting. My body lurches with a retch, but there's nothing in my stomach to vomit.

Insects buzz around us, the sound spiraling through my mind.

Thick, black moss covers sections of the water. I push through it, frowning at its grittiness. I slide my feet against the ground, kicking hard objects out of my way. Strange. My mouth opens when I feel something new. A caress against my leg, like a piece of fabric.

I pause. In front of me, Raker keeps going, parting the waters with his broad body. My voice is hardly more than a rasp as I finally break our silence. "Do you—"

I'm pulled beneath the swamp's surface before the rest of the words reach my lips.

This time, I don't gasp. I don't fill my lungs. I've learned that much. My eyes open instead, stinging in the acidic water, and my body goes rigid.

Glinting metal. Everywhere. The bottom of this bog is covered in swords, and chalices, and other priceless prizes.

And bodies with shriveled skin that have somehow been preserved in this stinging water.

Not all of them are dead. My throat constricts as the creature that pulled me under finally comes into view. It has the pale face of a man, but it—it doesn't have a mouth. Its eyes are milk-white. Sharp bones erupt from its skull in a crown; each spire covered in ashen flesh. Tattered rags with gold stitching hang off its bony limbs, a glowing spot of crimson in the center of its chest is visible even through the fabric. Terror spikes through me.

Skelmire.

It was in the book. Legend has it they were once royalty consumed by their greed. Now they keep everything that stumbles into their bogs. I should have remembered before I stepped foot in one.

Fuck.

The skelmire leans forward, and its flesh . . . it begins to peel off its limbs in long ribbons, leaving behind only bone. A spindly hand reaches toward me—

In a flash, those ribbons of flesh uncurl, pinning me to the bottom like shackles.

I thrash beneath its hold, lungs constricting. Everywhere it's touching me burns.

It bows its head, so I'm only facing its crown of flesh. It gets closer, as if it's about to stab those bone-sharp spires through my skull—

Before it can, it's gone. I'm freed.

I crash through the surface, sputtering, head pounding, only to see the creature standing right in front of Raker. Without a head. But it's still lifting a sword.

"Its gem!" I sputter out, remembering the book.

"What?" Raker demands.

"There's a gemstone inside its chest. It keeps them alive even after death. You have to—you have to take it out to kill them!"

Raker's fist busts through the skelmire's rib cage, cracking right through bone. I swallow at that raw strength. His hand emerges holding a glimmering ruby.

The creature breaks apart, bones scattering before sinking into the bog.

Raker looks back at me, and by the tilt of his head . . . he almost looks impressed.

Not pathetic. Not nothing.

That's what I say through my glare as I pant, relief settling my blood.

But before my heart can return to a normal cadence, the still gray water all around us breaks. And dozens of skelmires slowly emerge from its depths. All holding swords they must have fished from the bottom of the swamp.

Raker and I share a look.

We're surrounded. I'm exhausted. I want to sink to the bottom of this bog and give up. I want to let this swamp *win.*

But just that look . . . I can't see his face, but I can feel the intensity of his gaze. It's like a promise. We will fight. We are tired, and fading fast, and I fucking hate him right now, but we will *fight.* "Keep that elbow up," he says, voice like ground stone.

I nod. I unsheathe my sword. It glimmers.

The skelmires lunge forward.

My blade swings widely, cutting off three heads at once. And I do manage to keep my elbow up. Energy pounds through my dehydrated veins, every last shred of strength rising, *fighting.* I can't break their bones with my fists, not like Raker can, but when they stand still, I plunge my blade through their chests, cutting the precious stones out.

Rubies, diamonds, sapphires, and emeralds all spill into the water as the skelmires go down, one by one.

Each body that drops is soon replaced. Ancient swords shatter against my own, but the skelmires reach down and get new ones.

I turn, fighting them off, and catch a glimpse of him.

For a moment, I forget myself, I forget I'm surrounded by swamp creatures, I forget my thirst. I just stand, unable to do anything but watch as Raker's blade carves through the air in perfect arcs, every movement precise, like he and the sword are one.

One hand holds his weapon, and the other keeps breaking into ribcages, over and over, splitting bone like snapping twigs. He takes down ten creatures in mere seconds.

A dagger glints in the side of my vision, and I barely turn in time, distracted. I cut another creature down, then steal its stone. "Is that all you have?" I growl.

As if they understand me, two of the skelmires slowly drift closer. Closer. Until they're touching. Until the bones within them begin mingling, cracking, reforming, and they merge to create a beast double the size, with four arms. Two weapons. Two gems.

"Fuck," I say, watching helplessly as skelmire after skelmire emerges, uniting into one monstrous beast now wielding a dozen weapons.

"Run," I breathe. I turn and sprint, before I hear the creature following, upending the bog, a torrent forming from the force of it, nearly pulling me under.

The skelmire horde is faster. Its ribbons of skin shoot out. Sheets of flesh wrap around my arm, dragging me back.

I scream, my body roaring in pain where it's touching me, like my bones are melting beneath my skin.

I see the flash of metal right above me, a blade coming down, and I bring my sword up at the last moment, just barely blocking it.

The weapon shatters, and I cut the flesh around my arm, but another thick ribbon of skin replaces it. Another. Until the creature is lifting me out of the water. I gasp then choke as one wraps around my neck.

A dozen faces study me, flesh pulled thin over smothered screams. My strength has nearly left me. My legs are numb. I'm tired. *So tired.*

But with one last flash of resolve, I cut the skin holding me up in one smooth motion.

I drop into the swamp, my head banging on the bottom, the water barely cushioning my fall. The back of my head pulses. If I'd landed on a chalice, or a weapon, I would likely be dead.

Vision spinning, I rush to my feet. When I rise, I don't see Raker. I blink away the blurriness, searching wildly.

I'm still looking when the horde lunges forward, right at me.

I raise my sword, knowing it will do little against this thunderous beast, especially when it wields several swords, and my knees are already ready to buckle. Even so, I stay firm.

Both hands curl tightly around the hilt. I clench my teeth, waiting for the impact.

But before the horde can reach me, Raker emerges right beneath it, his sword flying out of his grip, soaring, cutting right through the creature, through every gnarled bone and sheet of flesh that lashes out, until it is halved.

For a moment, there's just silence.

Then, a dozen gemstones fall around Raker, spilling into the water. And there are two thunderous splashes as both halves fall on either side of him. His sword is still in the air, floating, glimmering. He reaches toward it.

Right behind him, another skelmire silently rises from the depths of the pale water, ancient sword gripped high. It swings right for Raker's head.

I throw my blade through the air with all my power, and it buries itself right through its glow, knocking the stone out of its chest. It goes still.

Raker turns to see the blade half an inch from his neck. He looks from it to me.

The skelmire collapses into a pile of bones, and we just stand there, staring at each other. Chests heaving.

Slowly, I take a step forward, and he doesn't stop looking at me. Not as I bend into the water and retrieve my blade. Not as I sheath it. We're both panting, wrung out, and *exhausted.*

"Not nothing, after all," I say, before turning my back on him and the bog.

THE BOG TURNS into woods. The trees are hardly standing. The forest is bare, like it's been ransacked. There are no streams. No berries. No mushrooms. *Nothing.*

It's been too long without water, without food, without rest. Fighting the creatures took too much energy, which we didn't have to spare, and something about that bog still sticks like a film to my skin.

Poison.

I try to deny it, but the cold slowly sliding through my veins becomes too noticeable to ignore. This was left out of the book, but I can feel its effects.

Raker must feel it too. Their skin touched his when he defeated the horde.

Our steps slow. We don't speak. My eyes open, then close, and I have to catch myself from falling multiple times.

There's nothing to do but keep walking, hoping somehow our starved bodies are able to fight this.

Sun rains down through the sparse trees, but I barely feel its warmth. My body has gone numb and cold.

The gray is ending, I think. Just a little longer. I grip that hope and will it to keep me moving, knowing that all bad places end, but—if there is a good place after the bad, I don't think I'm strong enough to reach it.

"Raker," I say, the word just a whisper.

I'm fading, it says. *I can't keep going.*

"Aris," he says, and it's ridiculous that my body still has the energy to form a chill. The word is quiet but filled with a strength I don't currently possess. Filled with *keep going*. Filled with *don't fucking quit now*.

I stumble on a vine, and a hand reaches out to steady me. His fingers wrap around my arm, keeping me upright. His hand doesn't drop, as if he knows that if he lets go then I'll go down.

My legs are boneless. My thoughts become muddled. My feet drag against the increasingly fertile ground, pulling me forward.

Just a little longer—

No matter how badly I want to keep going, to swallow down the pain and just keep moving, I can't.

Flashes of green and brown and fading sunlight blur together until I hit the ground. It's cool and soft beneath my cheek. There's no movement. No one next to me. It's only then that I realize Raker must have already fallen. Or he left me.

If I close my eyes now, they'll never open again. I know that. Body quivering with the effort, I turn onto my back so that I can see the sky.

One last try.

With a final scrap of energy, my fingers crawl into my pocket. There, I grab something I stole from the bottom of the bog. An emerald, large as my palm.

I hold it up to the sky, arm shaking. "Eat," I say, the word a croak. "Come to me. Come to eat. *Please.*"

I repeat the words until they are just rasps.

Then my arm drops. My eyes close.

The moment they do, something gleams above me, so bright I can see it through my eyelids. It's getting closer and closer, like a falling star.

It feels like the hardest thing I've ever done, but I force my eyes open, just to see it, just to know what's so bright that I can see it with my eyes closed.

My dragon?

No. A woman with a crown of stars, in a silver dress, the fabric glowing, liquid, curling behind her. A woman with golden hair floating right above me like a cloud.

She looks like an illusion, but no. There's a force around her, an energy. My sword hums against my spine.

I blink away the darkness as she turns her head, studying me so carefully, it's like she sees through me. She frowns.

Then she reaches a gleaming finger toward me. I use every last piece of myself to reach back. Between our hands, something like a star forms, blinding me.

When I can see again, she's gone. My hand drops against the dirt, spent, and from the finger she touched, silver roots spiral across the ground, through the forest.

Somehow, I know it's a road. I know it's a gift from this mysterious woman. She won't save me . . . but she'll show me the way.

Just when I think I've reached my limit, there is *more*. More strength waiting.

Slowly, knees shaking, I get to my feet. I take one step. Another. *Raker.* He didn't leave me. He's just a few steps behind, sprawled out on the dirt. Only poison could have brought him down.

"Get up," I say roughly, the way he did to me not so long ago.

He doesn't move.

I reach for his mask, and his hand stops mine just an inch away.

"Get up," I say again. "I know the way."

Raker doesn't question the silver. Maybe he can't see it. But I can, and I follow it, with desperation scraped from the very bottom of my soul.

And he follows me.

My body is aching. It's pushing beyond itself. But I never, not once, doubt the silver stranger. For the first time on this quest, hope and peace bloom in my heart. This path is leading somewhere, I know it. I just have to be strong and patient enough to reach the end of it.

I stumble through the forest, fluttering through memories, my mind not strong enough to smother them.

I see my parents. My mother, with her long, brown hair and freckles across her cheeks, and her lips red as cherries. Her dark blue eyes she gave me. I see my father, with his wide smile and the lines around his eyes, because he smiled with his whole face, and laughter poured from him like song.

I remember.

"I remember you," I whisper to the forest, which might be listening. "I remember, and because of that, you're not dead yet. You're with me."

You're with me.

I feel them here, helping me take every step. Pushing me forward, like I'm being carried by a wind of all our memories. My mind plays the ones I have left, and they're alive in my head. Always.

My eyes burn, my limbs are trembling, but I keep going, for them. *For them all.* For Stellan, on the floorboards.

For my sister.

For my parents, who never left, never gave up trying to save us.

Until the forest begins to twist together.

It starts with the roots. They join like ribbons. Then the branches. They unite in embraces across the forest floor. It keeps going until the woods tangle into a knot that ends at an arched set of gates, twisted from the trees.

Raker falls.

I try to last one more step, for the both of us. My arm reaches toward the doors.

But as I fall, my fingers don't even brush the lock.

29

"Her hair is in a hopeless tangle." My head jerks to the side as a comb is run through my braid, trying to unravel it.

"She's human, Gallie," says a soft voice. "Be careful."

Am I dead? Is this some sort of hell?

Something clamors against a table. "Hopeless, see? We're better off cutting the knots out." Movement, right next to me. Rummaging.

"Don't—don't touch me," I say feebly, hoping they didn't already take off my clothing and see what's underneath. "Please."

A pause.

I open my eyes to see two stunningly beautiful women. Their tan skin is glimmering, like they've been brushed by starlight. Their eyes are like freshly cut emeralds. Unlike mine right now, their hair shines, tied into perfectly smooth waterfall braids running down both sides of their heads, before meeting in the back to form an intricate shape. A blooming rose, for one. A bow, for the other. They're wearing gleaming, otherworldly fabrics, one in pink, the other in purple. I blink, confused, unbelieving. The last thing I remember is gates, crafted from wood. Were we saved?

The silver woman, she—

"She's awake!" the one in purple says. *Gallie, apparently.* The one who wanted to cut my hair.

"We won't," the one in pink says, in response to me.

If my dirt-crusted discomfort is any indication, they didn't try to change me out of my clothes, whoever *they* are. I look down to see I've ruined the perfect, silk-soft linens they placed me on.

It makes me think of someone else who would be just as dirty as I am right now.

"Where . . . where is he?" I ask warily, a pinch of worry forming in my chest. I remember the poison. How we both collapsed.

Gallie smiles mischievously. "Just down the hall. Growling at anyone who goes anywhere near him."

Yes. That sounds exactly like normal Raker behavior. Relief runs through me, far sharper than expected.

"He's handsome," Gallie says, smiling.

I frown. "You saw his face?"

"No," she says. "But I can tell. Just by the way he walks." So he's up and walking? I don't know who these people are . . . but clearly, they healed us. I swallow, only to feel my throat smooth again. As if they somehow fed me water while I was sleeping.

The one in pink shakes her head in a long-suffering way.

"He's a demon," I tell Gallie.

She shrugs. "Demons can be handsome."

"And how would you know that?" the one in pink snaps, exasperated.

I blink at them. They seem friendly, but what if they're not? "Who—who are you?"

The one in pink smiles. "I'm Este. This is my sister, Galice."

Sister. I feel the familiar pang of sadness, seeing them together, remembering what I once had.

"I'm Aris," I say slowly.

Then, suddenly, I feel a rush of panic. Something is missing. "Where's my sword?" No one is supposed to be able to move it.

I'm still alive . . .

Did it choose someone else? Did it abandon me?

Gallie blinks, unfazed by my alarm. "The blacksmith took them. Weapons aren't allowed here."

"How—how did he move it?"

Este's voice is more understanding. "Blacksmiths have ways with metal. They can move any sword, even claimed ones. Even ancient ones. It's their power."

My first instinct is to not believe her. I don't believe any of them. She's immortal. She's *glowing*, though faintly.

But when she puts her hand on mine, I see something in her. Something that reminds me of the mysterious woman who led us to safety.

"The Elders will explain everything." Este rises, offering her hand. "Come. We've drawn a bath."

I blink. I should run out of this room. I should find my sword, and Raker, and get the hell out of here.

But I'm still exhausted. And . . . they clearly helped us. Trust, I think, must sometimes be worth it. So I follow her through the ornate, strange room and into another.

The bath is a massive sparkling geode filled with steaming water, with flower petals and sprigs of lavender swirling on the surface.

"These will help with your pain and injuries," she says, motioning toward the nature. "The plants have healing properties. We already put some on your forehead while you were sleeping." So that's why I feel strong enough to stand. It must have counteracted the poison somehow.

"Here you go," Gallie says, offering an entire tray of different soaps. "Use all of them. *Please.*" There are roses and valerian woven through the thick pieces, but even then, they don't smell half as good as Raker's. "And this." She places vials of oils and liquids on the lip of the tub. "You need to wash your hair like twelve times," she says, before Este shoots her a look. "What? She ruined my comb. It was from a siren!" She holds up what looks like snapped sea glass.

I don't know whether to laugh or scoff, but Este grabs her sister by the arm and drags her through the towering bathroom doors. They whisper shut.

And then I'm left alone.

I look around the room. It's made of bark, leaves covering the walls, ivy crawling across it.

There are no windows. I lock the doors, just in case.

Then, carefully, I take off my clothing.

My skin is raw and dry. Dirt has crusted around my ankles and wrists. I slowly lower myself into the bath and tense, before sighing in relief.

Este was right. The bath does help. I pour what looks like honey into my hand and smell it. It's sweet and rich, a nectar that glides across my skin effortlessly. There are a thousand sparkles inside. It makes my body gleam.

The next is purple, like Gallie's dress. I put it in my hair, sliding my fingers against my scalp, then washing every strand.

Another smells like the sea. It's a thick paste, with salt and dark sand. I use it to get the dirt off. I scrub and scrub, and for a moment, I *enjoy*.

This journey is not about pleasure, but right now I let myself sit back and breathe. I'm alive. I'm here in this mysterious, glittering place. I've made it this far.

Another brush has been left by the tub. I comb it through my hair, starting at the bottom. It takes several minutes, and winces, but finally, under the oil's command, it goes smooth again, the knots forgotten.

I mourn the bath the second I step out of it. A cloud of a towel is waiting on a stone surface. It wraps completely around me, like a blanket, and is as soft as one. Only when I frown at my pile of dirty clothing do I wonder what I'm going to wear.

I don't wonder for long. The door creaks slightly as I poke my head out into the room, relieved to find it empty.

A pile of dresses is stacked on the bed.

Este and Gallie must have noticed the modesty of my clothing, because all of them are long-sleeved and high-necked, unlike theirs, which showed plenty of skin. A warm seed forms in my chest at that notice. At that consideration.

My hands run through the fabrics with wonder. They feel liquid. They glow as if drenched in moonlight, almost as brightly as the ones the woman who saved me wore.

Who was she?

I choose a dark blue one that molds to my form but feels like I'm not wearing anything at all. It's a balm against my tired, aching skin, and puddles at my feet. I decide to go barefoot, not in a rush to be in my cramped boots so soon. Instead of braiding my hair back into my typical style, I shrug and keep it down to dry.

The moment I step out of the room, Gallie and Este stop speaking. They've been waiting there.

Gallie blinks. "Wow. The oils work *wonders*."

Este squeezes her arm. Her face brightens. "You look vibrant, Aris. You always did, but now . . ."

"I'm not covered in dirt and mud?"

She smiles. "Exactly." She motions me forward. "Come. They'll want to see you."

Right. The mysterious Elders she mentioned before. I follow the sisters down bridges that cut through trees and are suspended with dangling vines.

I see him first.

Raker, his sword on his back despite the rules. I almost smile, imagining his fury when he woke up without it. I pity the blacksmith.

His hood is still up, of course, mask still on. His clothes are washed. His boots aren't covered in mud anymore. I can see by the set of his shoulders that he's on guard and irritated. He's very noticeably turned away from the two people next to him.

Este and Gallie bow. "Elders. May we present Aris."

A man and a woman turn, and I'm momentarily stunned by their brilliance. Their skin is smooth as stone. There's a soft silver glow around their bodies, and their hair and clothes float in a gentle wind reserved just for them.

The man wears a suit of silk, with glowing leaves accenting his shoulders. His buttons are made from acorns. His skin is dark, his eyes a searing amber. The woman is wearing a dress of glimmering, slightly transparent gossamer. It hardly covers much. Pink roses are stuck on the fabric and on her moon-white skin. She wears several layers of glittering necklaces around her neck.

She smiles, and it's like a ray of sunshine. "You were asleep for a while. We were starting to worry."

By *we*, I suppose she means her and the man next to her, because I don't see a hint of worry in Raker's posture. If anything, he looks angry.

She picks a flower from the plant next to her and offers it to me. It has a long green stem and curved, bulbous, light pink petals, shaped like a goblet. Inside sits slightly silvery water. "Drink," she says, her voice slightly resonant and drawn out. "It will help the thirst and hunger."

I've never drunk from a flower before, but I bring the petals to my lips, and they're soft as velvet. The liquid smells sweet.

I tip it back like a cup, and the moment the nectar hits my tongue, sweetness melts through my mouth. It's not just the taste. Instantly, I feel the balm in my bones, the energy through my limbs. It's as if I've slept a full month and eaten a feast.

I throw my head back, draining every last drop. When I finally put the flower down, the Eldress is smiling. "Better?"

I nod, then look around, my vision sharper than before somehow. "What is this place?"

"For us, it's home. For others . . . it's known as the Traveling City." The paradise that is constantly moving, appearing in various woods. The one Xara spoke of. The place Kira's sword came from.

"You're the faelings," I say, looking at them with even greater notice than before.

The Elders both bow their heads in confirmation, the diadems they wear sparkling beneath the moonlight.

Moonlight. I look up, only to be greeted by a blanket of stars. Panic grips my bones. "It's night. Shouldn't we—"

The Eldress studies my brow, the fold in it, as if worry is unfamiliar. "Ah. The demons." She shakes her head. "They can't come here. The light keeps them out." She motions around her. There's a shimmer over everything, like a dusting of stars. There are tiny puddles of it, between the crooks of trees, and smeared along branches. Orbs of the light are threaded through some of the treetops, larger versions of the strings she wears around her neck.

"Starlight. We're descended from the stars themselves. Their glow is in us." She takes me in with curiosity . . . and a bit of hesitancy. "A human hasn't found us in centuries."

I lift a shoulder. "I can't take credit for finding you. I was led." I can almost feel Raker's questioning gaze on me.

At the Eldress and Elder's obvious interest, I continue. "There was a woman. She came to me, almost like a dream. She . . . could fly. She floated right above me."

There's a sharp inhale, followed by shattering glass. I turn around as Este apologizes, picking up the pieces of what looks to be a vial.

"Is . . . is something wrong?" I ask, searching their faces for answers.

But the Elder and Eldress simply share an unreadable look before he says, "What was the color of her dress?"

"Silver," I say.

The world seems to go silent. I do too, remembering the worst night of my life. Remembering the woman wearing silver. *Silver.* The color of the gods.

But this woman's hair was blond. And her eyes weren't hardened with cruelty.

"Was she a god?" I ask.

"No," the Eldress says. "That was the Astral Queen."

I blink. "Is she . . . one of you?"

She shakes her head. "She belongs only to herself. She's older than these lands, than any of us, than many of the gods." Her brow furrows. "She must want you to complete your journey. Helping a human . . . how curious." She looks at the Elder. He nods gravely.

"What—"

"You must leave. If the Astral Queen is helping you, then the gods are against you." She's right.

My chest fills with dread, thinking about that cavalry and bounty. And leaving in the darkness would be a death sentence—

"Eldress, Elder," Este says, stepping forward. Her eyes are fierce, but her voice is polite. "We certainly can offer the mere basics of hospitality." Her head dips. "They did find us, after all. Even with help . . . the gates appeared to them." Pure and utter gratitude for Este smothers any lingering bitterness at the fact that her sister wanted to cut off my hair.

It seems there are rules, or traditions, as old as the Traveling City that must be adhered to. The Eldress lifts her chin. She looks over at the Elder, and I hope they both don't decide to change the rules now.

"Very well. You can stay until first light. Then, you must go." Her voice softens only slightly. "Tonight . . . rest, eat. Dance, if you'd like."

I don't think she understands how far away Raker is from ever dancing.

"Enjoy all the city has to offer, as our . . . esteemed guests." She says that last part with more than a little reluctance. Then, she lifts a hand, and glimmering stardust falls from her fingers. "Welcome to the Traveling City, home of wonder and whimsy."

She turns to go.

"My sword," I say, stumbling forward, knowing I'm pushing my luck. "I'd . . . I'd like to speak with the blacksmith, if that's okay."

The Elder's eyes move from Raker back to me. "He is currently . . . *recovering*. He should be able to see you tomorrow, before you leave."

I glare at Raker.

The Eldress and Elder bow in unison before finally leaving us.

"Come," Este says, still looking a little haunted. "Let's get you some food."

As much as I want to eat an entire feast, after consuming just a few fruits and vegetables, my stomach twists, as if it's still adjusting to having something fill it. I excuse myself from the meal early and lie in bed, trying and failing to find sleep.

Hours later, I finally get up. If I'm not going to rest, I might as well explore this famous Traveling City. Maybe I can find something useful for either killing the gods . . . or speeding up our quest.

The stone floors, cold and smooth beneath my bare feet, are long shards of different shades of marble, like a giant mosaic I can't fully see. The wooden railings are carved in legends, stories of battles long fought and won. The windows don't have glass; they're just gold arches that look out into a courtyard of trees brimming with endless flowers of every shade.

The palace is quiet. Most faelings must be sleeping. I should be sleeping too, I think, especially with the Eldress's warning and her insistence that we leave first thing tomorrow, but instead I wander down the stone steps, and out into the night, knowing I'll likely never get this chance again.

I walk down roads lined in thick oaks, so wide that houses have been carved into their trunks. Up above, strings of starlight glisten like an extra sky, draped over bridges that dart through the trees in half a dozen levels, each one looking like a completely different market. I imagine they house the world's rarest, most coveted relics. Specks of silver cover most surfaces, making everything gleam like a galaxy.

Home of wonder and whimsy.

No wonder so many people try to find this place.

I keep walking until I reach the golden tree that sits in the center of the Traveling City. It has an energy. A force. A *feeling*. I reach out to touch one of its weak branches, hanging like hair. It's surprisingly sturdy beneath my fingers. And the leaves—

They're pure gold. My thumb runs across one of them in wonder.

"It's a gild willow. Their bark is coveted. So is their nectar." Este.

The faeling steps next to me, running her fingers over one of the branches. "Look," she says, dropping it against another. It emits a high-pitched, beautiful ringing. "In a strong breeze, it'll play a song."

A song. My mother would have loved to see this tree. She would have loved every single thing in this Traveling City. So would my sister.

"You lost someone," Este says, knocking me from my memories.

I turn to look at her.

She lifts a shoulder. "It's the eyes. They're hardened, like they can't ever light up again. I lost my mother." She nods and repeats herself. "You lost someone."

I shake my head. "I lost . . . *everyone.*" I drop the branch, and the full note it emits is completely at odds with the hollowness of my heart.

"I'm sorry." Este studies me. She must have guessed I'm on the Questral. "Pain is a powerful motivator, I suppose."

I shake my head. "No. Pain is paralyzing. Revenge . . . revenge is galvanizing."

Her mouth tightens.

"What? Judging me?" I strum the branches again.

She shakes her head. "No. I'm afraid for you. Revenge ruins. It corrupts. I've seen it." I wonder what, exactly, she's seen. Is she hundreds of years old? Thousands?

However old she is, she's right.

I know that. I've always known. This rage is choking; it's all-encompassing. But it doesn't matter. *I* don't matter.

"How does it end?" she asks gently. "Your quest?"

"With death," I say simply, dropping another branch. It rings.

And Este takes a shaking step back. Her eyes are wide. She looks startled, like she did a few hours ago when I mentioned the woman in silver.

"What is it?"

She opens her mouth. Closes it. "I—Sometimes words . . . they crystalize. Harden, in my mind. They—" She shakes her head, and her expression is replaced by a tight smile. "I—I should go." She turns and runs off. I watch her pink dress and rose-styled hair shift wildly before she disappears.

It's only then that I notice them—wings on her back. They're hanging limp, spilling down her spine in thick gleaming strands, like sparkling ribbons. What—

"Already scaring people away?"

Raker.

I turn and give him a pointed glare. "If only."

He takes a few steps toward me. "This place—"

"Is wonderful."

"—is ridiculous."

I reach down and run my fingers through the silver glitter that coats everything. Without losing eye contact with the shadow beneath his hood, I smooth my fingers up his armor, smearing the glimmer toward his hidden face, until his hand reaches up, fast as lightning, and stops my wrist.

I try to move, but I might as well be battling stone.

"*Don't*," he warns.

Fine.

He releases his hold, and I flick my fingers, glitter exploding into the darkness of his hood. He propels himself away from me, coughing and sputtering, as if he's been poisoned. It's then that I realize he must not be wearing his mask. Did he take it off to get some fresh air?

I can't see anything, though I try.

"Oh no. The pile of snakes beneath your hood is now covered in sparkles. What a shame."

"Witch," he says.

"Demon."

He takes a step forward, anger radiating off him. "Fool."

"Bastard."

Another step. "Weakling."

He's right in front of me now. I tip my head up, and in the dark, with that hood, I still can't catch a glimpse of his face. "Is that all? I'm disappointed."

"Duel with me," he says, not missing a beat.

I blink. "What?" I say, shocked and breathless.

His head lowers. "Your words are weak. Your blade isn't. If you're going to fight with me, then *fight with me*."

It sounds as much like a threat as an invitation.

I swallow at his proximity. He's right there. Blocking everything. He's so close, I can smell him, and—he smells like his soap. Like he used it instead of the ones here. I breathe it in, fighting back a groan, burying the shameful memories of my lips against his throat. "My—my blade is with the blacksmith."

He shrugs a shoulder. "Then get it."

I don't even know where the blacksmith is, but I make to step around his body, mostly just to get away from him and the confusing thoughts that bloom in his presence, but he takes a step and cages me in.

"You said—"

He tilts his head at me in a clear challenge. That's when I remember the times he called to his blade—how it spiraled into his grip.

"I can't do that."

"Try."

I think back to before, when I almost lost it and attempted the exact same thing. *"I have tried."*

His voice is unimpressed. "So that's it? You try something once and are done with it?"

No. Asshole.

He takes a step back, as if he has all the time in the world to stand and watch me fail at this.

I don't want to fail. I want to wipe what is a no doubt smug expression off his coil-of-snakes face.

"Fine."

I dig my feet into the ground as if I'm about to fight. I take a breath. I clear my head. I remember watching Raker do this, over and over.

I extend my arm to the side with every ounce of force—

Nothing.

"Call to it," he says. His voice is right above me. "Like you're calling out a name."

"My sword doesn't have a name," I say through my teeth.

"Every sword has a name."

I frown. Was I supposed to name it? Suddenly, I can't think of a single word to save my life. I don't know—

Breathe. Sometimes, I just need to remind myself to take a full breath. I do, and then I imagine vines digging through my feet, rooting me in place, keeping me in this moment. I imagine a wave washing through my head, clearing it of any worry or pain.

Then, I think of my sword. Of its patterns. Of the moment I first gripped its hilt, and the sound of silver shattering against it. I imagine it in my mind's eye, and then, out of the darkness, out of the quiet—

A voiceless command. A word, written into my mind, with a different sense. I can't see it or hear it—I just *know it.*

Stellaris.

I don't know if that was always its name. Or if its name merged with mine, though the pronunciation is different, sounding like the words *are* and *is* combined. Or if I—*subconsciously*—named it as a tribute to me and Stellan.

But I whisper it into the night, and it sounds like a spell.

"Stellaris."

Glass shatters. Branches snap. Chaos erupts. There's a high pitch as metal cuts through sound and space.

Then something heavy crashes into my hand, threatening to break my wrist or send me stumbling back.

But I stand strong and wrap my fingers around it, holding my blade with one hand for the first time. It glows for a moment, as if it's speaking. As if it's recognizing me, the same way I've recognized it.

I fall into my fighting stance and face Raker.

For a moment, he's very still, watching. I've never wanted to see his face more, if only to see if he's pleased, or surprised, or anything at all.

Then, a moment later, his blade is against mine.

Stellaris hums, and both blades glimmer for one startling second. I don't give in to the distraction. I move, slicing my metal down his, turning, almost meeting flesh.

But he's fast. He's fast as if he's spent every waking minute fighting. Armies have fallen against his sword, but mine is strong too.

Now that I know its name, I can feel its presence. Its energy. Its desire *to win*.

It pulses in my grip, as if pushing me forward, and I move. The flower's healing nectar running through my veins, I lunge with strength I've never known, with conviction and trust in myself and my metal.

Another clash of weapons echoes through the city center, seeming to rumble the surrounding trees and the homes built into them, and the bridges that span several hundred feet above, intersecting one over the other in ethereal crosses just like our blades.

Raker turns, aiming for my side, but I block his metal, then immediately strike, sending him moving. Again, again, again, this is forgetting, this is bantering, this is playing, this is my mind emptying for a moment and my instincts taking over. Because nothing—*nothing* but being in the forge has ever felt like this.

This is clashing, gasping, heart-thundering, metal-pulsing, exhilarating *madness*.

And it's not just this way for me. I can tell, by the way Raker's moving. By the way he's actually *trying*.

"You're enjoying this," I say, breathless, turning, brushing strands of the tree with my body, the gold clinking together in its haunting song.

His voice is annoyingly steady, reminding me that if he really wanted to end this, he could. "Winning? I can't say I hate it."

I whirl around and feel the clash of our swords in my teeth. No. It's more than that. "You asked for this. Why?"

Another strike. He goes for my gut, but he did the same move last time we practiced. I remember. His metal meets mine.

"I've never been able to duel before," he finally admits.

I blink as the realization sets in. His sword. It's always been more powerful than the rest. He's never had a fair rival.

"Met your match, then?" I ask. I go for his side, and he turns quicker than I can see. By the time my mind rights itself, I'm being slammed up against the tree and his blade is settling against my throat.

"Hardly," he says, right above my mouth. Then, he just stays like this.

I can feel his gaze traveling down my body like it's casting flames. That's when I realize he's never seen me in a dress. Or with my hair down. His stare is like a brand. He moves the slightest bit closer, until he's just inches away. So close . . . that I can see his jaw. It's a strong one. Then, he dips his head, and I see the shadow of his mouth.

And his mouth—

"Blue," he breathes, like he didn't even mean to. He's looking at my dress. Slowly, his head lifts. I can almost feel his gaze snag onto mine, like a key fitting into a lock. "Just like your ridiculous eyes," he murmurs.

Irritation flames through me. Of course, he would make my favorite part of myself seem inferior. I raise my chin. "My eyes are not ridiculous," I spit in a harsh whisper.

He doesn't respond. He just reaches up . . . and takes a strand of my hair between his fingers. It's dry now, in loose waves that curl messily around my face. My heart is racing. My chest is rising and falling deeply, almost reaching his. He pulls the piece of hair the slightest bit, and chills erupt down my skin. "This is dangerous," he says.

He's right. This . . . *is* dangerous. This heat spreading through the core of me is fucking treacherous.

But he's talking about my hair—it's a liability in a fight.

"I'll put it up before we leave," I whisper.

He leans in. I stop breathing. He's so close, curved over me against this tree. His fingers are still tangled in my hair.

I don't understand him. He told me not to get near him again, but here he is, pressed against me. Worse, I don't mind it. No. I want him closer.

He doesn't have his mask on. Those lips . . . they could be against mine in half a moment. My back arches slightly, meeting him halfway there.

"Pity," he finally says. I barely hear the word. Then he drops his hand, sheaths his blade in one smooth motion, and turns away.

30

At first light, I visit the blacksmith. He's a tall, regally dressed man with perfect posture, dark skin, and long, lean limbs. Just like everyone else in this magical place, he emits a subtle glow. He eyes me warily, though that might be due to the hole in his window. And the matching one right next to it.

His forge is built into the base of a massive tree. Swords with clear, crystal blades cover the walls. Silver speckles float within them like trapped stars.

"You don't use metal," I say, my lips parting in disbelief. "You don't actually . . . forge." I look around and barely see any of the materials that were crucial to making blades back home.

"There are different ways to forge weapons," he says smoothly. "And various strengths to different materials."

He motions at the wall. "Faeling swords are made of pure, distilled starlight."

Incredible. I would have never thought something like that was even possible.

"How does one forge starlight?" I ask, marveling at the material. In response to my wonder, he motions toward his worktable.

There, at the center, sits an anvil. It glows more than anything in this Traveling City. Beside it sits an equally stunning silver hammer.

"My bloodline is one of only two blacksmiths blessed by the original god," he says. Original god? I've never heard that before. "I claimed these tools—and they claimed me—just as your sword claimed you."

His skills must be incredibly valued. I can feel the strength radiating off the starblades.

I rub my fingers over the strange material, and the specks of silver stir beneath my touch. "And those?" I ask, jutting my chin toward the opposite end of his workshop.

One wall isn't filled with blades at all—but with various objects. Bones. Feathers. Sheets of strange metal. Crystals. Gemstones.

"We are the keepers of many of the most powerful materials on Starside. Those who come upon us often leave us with their most treasured possessions. The ones they don't want anyone else to find."

It makes sense. I stop in front of a long feather made up of shades of red, orange, and yellow, like a slice of sunrise. "What is this?" I ask, though I already know.

"That's a phoenix feather."

My soul snags on a hundred memories. All the times I was called that very creature, by someone I cared for very much. My voice is rough with emotion. "They're real, then?"

The blacksmith nods. "Real, but rare. One hasn't been seen in a long time." He runs a finger down the middle of the feather. "Which makes this all but priceless. And dangerous, should it be forged into the center of a sword." Right. Because bits of powerful creatures can create weapons that draw from their magic.

"So a sword made with this would have powers?"

He dips his head again. "If it's forged correctly, then yes. Blades that possess magical abilities are called skylarks. It means they are more than just their metal." *Skylark.* Even the word seems to contain a whisper of power.

I want to ask him a thousand questions. I want to stay here and shadow him, the same way I did Stellan. But light is beginning to fill the forge. My time is up.

I present my blade. "Is this . . . a skylark?" The hunter hinted as much, but I need confirmation from an expert.

He gently takes it in his hands, and it's strange to see anyone else holding my metal. But he's careful, turning it slightly. I imagine he's already studied it, when we were first saved.

"No," he finally says.

Oh. I feel a rush of disappointment, for some reason.

"This is a godsword."

The world around me goes very still. My breath gets caught in my lungs.

Then, everything breaks. My mind, my assumptions, my framing of this entire journey.

No. I must have misheard him. There's no *fucking way* a godsword claimed *me* . . . a mortal hellbent on slaying the gods themselves.

But as his words sink in, it all starts to make sense.

The bounty. The cavalry.

Golden rays pour through the broken windows. I could stand here and refute his words, remain in denial, but I don't have time to doubt. I just need answers. "What does that mean?" I say in a whisper.

"It once belonged to one of the original gods. It holds their power. It's the greatest type of sword—and, of course, the rarest."

No. I haven't seen this blade have any abilities other than its metal . . . but I remember what the hunter said. Since I'm mortal, I can't access its power.

My head is racing, thoughts tripping over themselves, but I manage to ask, "Do you know which god my sword belonged to?"

"No, I can't be sure. But one might know. The other blacksmith from the original line. The oldest blacksmith among us."

"Where is he?"

He shakes his head. "He might as well be dead."

"Where is he?" I ask again, pleading. And—this shouldn't be important. This is not part of my journey. But I need to know what I'm carrying.

The blacksmith looks up from my metal. "He is known as the Great Betrayer. He left our people to work for one of the Great Houses."

He hands the sword back to me. "Godswords hold great power . . . and great power is a poison. People will be drawn to it . . . and you. They will risk everything just for a chance to claim it."

I remember the Masks in the woods. The warriors. How they were pulled toward it by an invisible force.

"This sparkling steel," I say, brushing across the flat top of my blade with my fingertips. "What is it? What do you call it here?" I'm guessing it isn't called Starside steel.

"You mortals have your high metals and low metals. Immortals have an additional tier of sparkling metals. This one is the rarest, most powerful . . . and most dangerous, strong enough to contain limitless magic. It's only found where the gods live. It's called paladian."

The Eldress walks into the forge then. Her eyes go from my sword to the blacksmith. Worry flutters across her features, before they settle. "I trust you got the answers you wanted?"

I suppose I did. The most I could hope for, anyway. I also have far more questions than ever before. She motions for me to follow, and I thank the blacksmith, then leave the workshop, blade sheathed against my spine.

It holds an entirely different weight now.

A *godsword*. Why would a godsword claim me? It doesn't make any sense.

All I want is to reach the end of this . . . and now I know for certain the gods won't stop until they get my weapon.

Fuck.

Dread settles in my bones. The end of this quest is going to be far harder than the beginning of it.

And I only barely survived that.

The Eldress looks over at me as we walk past tree-homes, long oval windows propped open, letting in the crisp pine and mint-swept breeze. Above, the bridges sway slightly with featherlight faeling steps.

As if she can sense my stirring thoughts, she says, "The Astral Queen hasn't been seen in centuries. This is a sign."

The dread in me tightens and twists. I fight to keep my voice casual. "A good one? Or a bad one?"

"I'm not sure yet." She quickens her pace, her movements lithe and impossibly elegant.

I glance at her back—and there they are. Another set of limp wings, long down her spine, mixing with the ethereal fabrics of her dress.

"You can fly," I say.

"*Could* fly" is all she says.

A pinch forms between my brows. "They're . . . broken?"

"Something like that." She does not elaborate.

We pass a rock face, part of the palace. There are carvings along it. I slow to study them, mouth opening, then closing. "Are these—"

"Dragons."

Hardened into stone. Asleep. I think back to mine with a sinking sadness. Is this what she looked like, hidden below, before she saved me? Is this what she looks like now?

"They're slumbering. We haven't needed them in centuries."

I frown. "There's been peace for that long?"

"There's never been peace," she says flatly. "But long ago, we learned not to meddle in affairs. We keep to ourselves. It keeps us safe."

My eyes narrow. "And the rest of the world? Do you not think it's a crime to be complicit?"

The gods are not the only ones who forgot about us.

She must sense the anger in my words. She studies me, curiosity written across her features. "We must prioritize our own survival. It's how we have remained, when so many other ancient beings have long been extinguished." She tilts her head. "Tell me, Aris. Do *you* care about the rest of the world?"

I grind my teeth. I'm not here for the magic; I'm not here to *help*. I'm here to hurt. I'm here for my own selfish reasons. She seems to know it too.

She continues walking toward the gates.

There, Raker, Este, and a grinning Gallie are waiting. She keeps shooting looks in Raker's direction, but I'm not even sure he notices. His sword is dug into the ground in front of him. He clutches its hilt with both hands. His mask is back on. Of course, it is.

As much as I liked the dress, I had to leave it behind. Finally, though, I'm in new clothing. Fitted pants, fortified at the knees. A long-sleeved shirt, tight enough to make fighting easy, without constricting my breathing, with a high collar, that I suspect was specially made after the faelings noticed my preference in style. A large pile of new undergarments that I keep in my newly gifted pack.

"The Astral Queen has blessed your journey . . . and so will we," the Eldress says. I raise a brow. This is a change from yesterday, when she was about to kick us out into the demon-riddled woods in the middle of the night. I keep my mouth shut as she takes one of the many strands of her glowing necklaces—and places it around my neck. It's made up of hundreds of tiny glass orbs, each containing a small flicker of light.

"The night creatures won't harm you with the starlight."

Relief rushes through my veins. *We can travel at night.* It will help our pace . . . and help us avoid enemies, since no one else would dare be out after sunset. This couldn't have come at a better time. We're twenty-four days into the Questral, and, according to the map, close to the Land of the Gods. We could actually reach it, and make it back to Stormside, especially now.

"Go," the Eldress says. "Travel quickly. Avoid the Great Houses at all costs. They all have dangerous partnerships with gods. I hope you find what you're looking for."

I nod my thanks. Raker does too. Then the wooden gates creak open.

Before we can walk through them, I feel a light hold on my wrist. Este. I turn to see her looking conflicted. She stares at me, eyes searching for something . . . before finally saying, "There is no such thing as a starless night, Aris. Silver breaks through darkness. Every single time." In her look is a quiet determination, hard as the strongest metal. A fierceness that does rival the stars. "If you need help, just reach for it." Her gaze is on my necklace. I don't know what she means . . . but she doesn't elaborate. She just steps back into the line. The Eldress gives her a sharp look.

Birds chirp in front of me, pulling my notice. The forest beyond the gates is blossoming. Shards of morning light are piercing through the treetops. I turn to get one last look at the Traveling City—

But it's gone. As if it never existed.

31

In the daytime, my necklace offers a faint glow. Hours later, when we're still trekking through the woods, and the sun begins to fade, it grows into a crown of light.

"It feels strange, being out in the open," I say, remembering how many nights we spent hiding behind water. Or running.

Raker grunts. That's the extent of his reply.

"You know, I was starting to get worried that this journey would get boring with the starlight protecting us. But your rousing conversation is definitely going to make up for the lack of danger."

He ignores me.

This again. I roll my eyes. Let him be miserable. It's the only state he's ever known in his life.

The forest is dangerous, even during the day. But the necklace seems to offer us protection from more than just the demons.

There is rustling in the trees occasionally, but no creature or immortal ever approaches. We walk in silence.

Until the middle of the night, when the stillness is pierced by something completely unexpected.

My brows come together. "Is that—"

Music. Voices. *Laughter.*

We look at each other. Are these demons? Is this another illusion?

The starlight casting a wide protective shield, we unsheathe our blades. It gets louder as we approach. Pots clang together. Conversation spikes.

Then . . . the smell of something recently roasted. The faelings fed us, but my stomach is already twisting in hunger. It smells *good*. Well spiced.

We walk through the trees, into the clearing—and everything goes silent.

More than two dozen heads turn to look at us, stopping their lively conversations. At the center of them sits a fire... no, an *orb* shining just as brightly as my necklace.

Trapped starlight.

They're all immortals. But they aren't warriors. They're dressed in modest clothing. Most don't even carry swords. Some look like children.

Whispers begin the moment they see the light encasing us. All eyes turn to my necklace.

A man steps forward. He has long braided hair tied back, dark brown skin, and a friendly face, which is rare for immortals, who often look perennially unimpressed. "You wear the light, traveler," he says, motioning toward my neck.

I turn to Raker. He's standing perfectly still, as if he's still assessing the situation.

I gently rub the miniature orbs between my fingers. "You—you know the faelings?"

More whispers. Excited trills. The man shakes his head. "No, no—but that's where we're headed."

His meaning hits me. "You're trying to find the Traveling City," I say, looking around at them. There is a cheeriness, a sense of hope, among the group.

He nods. "We have the light to guide us," he says. "We found it. It's our destiny to find the city. We have been traveling for a while now, looking."

In this land of immortals, I imagine a while could be years. Decades? Guilt flutters through my chest, knowing we just left the place that these people seem so desperate to find. But I remember how it disappeared once the gates closed, already moving again. Maybe it's still nearby. Maybe they'll find it, if they're meant to.

"Why?" I ask.

A woman with a long scar down her pale cheek says, voice full of excitement, "If we find the gates... if we knock... they must let us in. Those are the ancient rules."

I remember Este's insistence, like there was a code. I want to tell them that the Eldress also *insisted* we leave. It wasn't a permanent invitation.

"Have you . . . have you seen it?" someone asks. A woman with curly hair and light brown skin. Her voice is edged with desperation.

I open my mouth—

"No." Raker's voice is absolute. I turn slowly to face him. He doesn't even look at me. More whispers from the group. Now mostly directed at Raker, who must look like a demon to them in his armor and hood, magnificent sword at his back.

"You are welcome to join us in our search," the man says, motioning toward the group. "We're just about to take off again. The more time we're traveling, the better," he says, smiling.

I can almost sense Raker about to refuse. My hand clutches his arm. I feel him tense completely.

"That sounds wonderful. Thank you so much."

The man nods. "Take a serving, if you would like," he says, motioning toward the roasting meat. "There's plenty to go around."

A few others get to their feet and start cutting some slices off, eager to offer them to us. I think of Stormside, where no one eagerly gives anyone *anything*. Starving people rarely share. But immortals . . . they don't really need food the way we do. It's an indulgence.

It's a welcome departure, I think, for them to be so focused on the light around my neck and not the fact that we are human. Though some in the group look more eager to have us join them than others.

A plate is presented to me, and I smile, taking it with thanks, before retreating back to where Raker still stands at the edge of the clearing. Immortal hearing is superior to ours. I wait until the conversation picks up again to whisper, "I really think we should travel with them. Until we get out of the forest, at least."

"Of course you do," he says, his voice as grating as ever.

My eyes narrow at him. "The gods are after us. There is a bounty on our heads. With them . . . we'll blend in," I say, meaning more me than him, since I don't think Raker blends in anywhere. "Plus, it seems like they know their way around these woods. We've been lucky so far, but we don't know what other dangers we might come across."

Raker doesn't say a word. He just shakes his head as he walks past me, likely off to go sharpen his blade or some other very *him* thing to do.

"You didn't take your plate!" I yell at his back, but clearly he doesn't care. Fine. More for me.

I sit down on a large rock, eating the spice-coated meat, groaning as the salt hits my tongue. Flavor hasn't been a priority for many years now. But I remember a time when food tasted good, even on Stormside. When my mother had a collection of spices, passed down through generations, said to have been from here. I always thought it was a myth, or a lie, but tasting this food . . .

It tastes like that.

"You're human," someone says. I look up to see a woman with light skin and pink cheeks peering down at me. All immortals look young, but she looks especially so, maybe even younger than me.

I blink, feigning shock. "I am?"

That earns me a wide smile. Her teeth are glimmering white, just like the rest of them. "I didn't know humans could be funny."

I snort. "Funnier than immortals, I would think, given our constant edge toward mortality."

She seems to consider that. "What is it like? Knowing you'll die so soon after birth?"

I smile between bites of meat. "For us, it doesn't feel short." I shrug. "What's it like knowing you'll likely live centuries? Millennia?"

Her lips purse. "It's terrifying." In a flash, she pinches my arm, and I gasp. She nods. "Your skin is softer than ours. Less smooth, less durable. But we too can die, especially at the other end of a blade like that . . ." She looks at the hilt of my sword.

"Is dying common?" I ask.

"During war, it is," she says, sitting down next to me. "But during relative peace . . . communities typically stick to themselves. Everyone is so *cautious*. So afraid of another war. So afraid of the gods and their wrath . . ." She turns to me. Her heart-shaped face is covered in freckles. Her hair is the color of hay. "That's why I left. I ran away and joined this group. Because I hear in the Traveling City, there is nothing to fear. Death rarely happens there."

I think about Este and that she lost her mother. Now I wonder how. I want to tell this immortal that death happens everywhere, but I keep quiet.

"I'm Daphne," she says. "Do you have a name?"

I scoff at the fact that she thinks humans might not. "Of course. Aris."

Her eyes narrow. "That sounds like a name from here," she says.

I grit my teeth, wanting to remind her that our lands didn't used to be divided. The gates didn't always exist. Humans and immortals lived together once, all beneath the gods.

Instead, I just offer a tight smile.

There's clamoring as everyone stands. Pots and blankets are packed up. Daphne turns to me. "Watch," she says, excitedly. "He's about to choose the next leader."

Leader?

The man who offered us a spot here steps forward. He walks around the crowd looking at hopeful faces before stopping in front of a tall man with long hair tied back into a single braid. "You," he says.

The tall man smiles, steps forward, and carefully picks up the orb.

"It's an honor to be at the front of the line, holding the light," Daphne explains. "I've been picked twice before already. The light . . ." Her glimmering blue eyes drop to my neck. "It's unlike anything I've ever felt before."

I feel it, against my pulse. An energy. Magic. Daphne's eyes don't lift until a drum is beat, and then she stands. "Welcome to the group, Aris," she says.

The drums don't stop. Behind the tall man wielding the bright orb, three people play instruments. The music is beautiful but quickly becomes tiresome. I can't see his face, of course, but by Raker's stance, he is thinking of ways to kill me for putting us in this position.

But I don't regret it. Because right after sunrise, we pass a group of Masks, waiting in the trees, clearly searching for their next targets. Though I would expect them to want to steal the orb, they keep their distance. Does their god not want conflict with the faelings? I'm not sure. But we pass without notice or incident.

Daphne finds me in the line soon enough. She stares up at Raker. With her height, I imagine she can see the flash of silver beneath the shadow of his hood.

"What's the deal with the mask?" she says, speaking to me as if he's not standing right there.

I shrug a shoulder. "He's embarrassed by his face. He doesn't have one." I give my most sympathetic look. "It's just . . . it's just a coil of snakes under there."

Daphne's mouth parts in horror. She nods understandingly, readily believing that all humans might not look like immortals.

I can almost *feel* Raker glaring at me. It makes me smile.

Daphne bows her head before him. "I apologize for your . . . for your *affliction*," she says, voice dripping with pity. Then she quickly moves down the line, as if Raker's coil-of-snakes face could somehow be contagious.

I'm still smiling to myself when Raker says, "You think you're funny, don't you?"

I lift a shoulder. "I think I'm hilarious." I turn to him. "One of us has to be."

"And if I really do have a coil of snakes as a face? Will you feel bad about mocking me?"

I blink, stunned to hear anything resembling teasing coming out of his mouth. I press my lips together, considering. "No," I decide.

"No?" He seems shocked.

"No. You're too much of an asshole for me to feel bad for you."

He makes a derisive sound. "And you're perfectly pleasant, Aris."

There it is. My name again, sounding like an embrace. I ignore the chill working its way down my back.

"Thank you," I say sweetly. "One of us has to be."

WE TRAVEL FOR two more days with the group, only stopping for a few hours every night. That's when I realize this might have been a mistake.

Immortals don't need sleep the way we do.

They stop just to play music, and to eat, and to tell ancient stories about the Traveling City, most of which don't match what we saw at all. It's nearly impossible to sleep, but I do, until a peel of laughter wakes me up.

I blink my eyes open, only to see a group of children circling Raker, holding wooden swords up, all of them pointed right at him.

Shit.

I rush to stand, worry gripping my bones, ready to save them from Raker and his perpetual bad attitude, when all at once, he slides his towering blade from his spine.

My eyes widen, my lips part—

I'm too late. There's a crack as his blade meets one of those wooden swords.

But he uses such little force, the oak remains intact.

I blink. He doesn't break the blades with his bare hands, the way I know he could with little effort. No. Instead, he play-duels with them, battling all six swords at once, letting some of the kids get a few hits in.

The boys scream with delight, closing in, and he hunches over, pretending to be injured, until they're nearly on him. They make to tackle him.

Before they can, he stands to his full height, lifts his sword high, and roars.

The children scatter in a mess of giggles and gasps.

I'm standing with my mouth hanging open, wondering if I'm still dreaming, because there's *no fucking way* Raker just played with those kids.

Slowly, sword still up, he turns right toward me.

He just stares and stares. Neither of us break our gaze. Then, he steps forward, sword up, just like he did with the children.

I don't run. I take several steps forward, until I'm right under him and his sword.

"I'm not afraid of you," I say casually. I tilt my head. "But I *am* a little scared I died in my sleep, because there's no other explanation for what I just saw."

He huffs a laugh, returning his blade back into his scabbard.

"Do you . . . do you have siblings?" I ask, wondering about the life he left behind when he decided to go on this quest. The idea of him having a family feels odd. Wrong. He's a deadly knight, with a reputation. I can't even imagine him . . . sitting at a dining table. Laughing at a joke. Bringing a mug to his lips.

No. I can only see him as he is now, fully armored, wearing a mask, ready for battle.

I watch his body tense beneath all that metal.

"I did," he finally says.

And then, he turns around again.

I did. I stand very still as the group begins to pack up once more. Those two words haunt me.

I frown, remembering what the Gardener said in those mists. Harlan Raker is a demon. There's no doubt about that. He has hundreds—if not thousands—of kills on his blade.

But never did I once consider that often monsters aren't born . . . they're made.

The line is moving. I find Raker and stagger behind him, trying to keep up. My eyes are dry and red. My legs still feel stiff.

"This was your idea, remember?" Raker says from in front of me, as if he can hear me struggling. His voice is rough. I wonder if he attempted to sleep at all.

"How could I forget?" I say, taking a swig from one of the many water pouches the group has offered us. "You keep reminding me."

Excitement blooms toward the front of the line. The youngest in the group, one of the immortal boys that was playing with Raker, has been chosen to hold the orb.

He's traveling with family. They cheer him on at the front. The music is livelier than normal.

The stars are so bright here, a blanket above us. I look at them, fighting to stay awake. "Maybe . . . maybe we veer off after tonight," I say. Behind Raker's back, I consulted with one of the older immortals, drawing parts of my map in the dirt during one of our breaks. We've been heading in the right direction so far, but they plan to make a turn soon. If we keep going straight, we'll be out of this forest in three days, and into a desert.

Miles and miles of sand are all that sits between us and the Land of the Gods. Reaching it sounds almost easy.

Then I remember what I learned in the Traveling City.

Even in this jovial group, with music spilling through the woods, I can't help but feel the whisper of danger prickling the back of my neck.

Wondering if the gods are watching us now, readying their attack.

They aren't going to stop until they get my sword. I just hope I can face them in person.

They can have my blade.

Covered in their silver blood.

I almost trip, and Raker's hand steadies me. He drops it the second I'm on my feet again. The roots are thick here, snaking across the powdery dirt. I have to step over them every few minutes, and my knees ache with the effort.

We're moving too slowly, thanks to me. The rest of the group passes us in the line, chatting with excitement.

I'm surprised Raker isn't telling me to hurry up, or leaving me. I know he can walk faster, even with the lack of sleep, and all the armor.

We should have taken more of those flowers, I think. The ones from the Traveling City. I wish I could ask Raker to carry my sword, but of course I can't. I wonder if he would be able to take it from me. I think about the blacksmith's warning.

If Raker knew it was a godsword, would he kill me, map be damned? Even after everything?

Wait. Is *Raker's* blade a godsword too?

A sharp gasp drags me from my thoughts. I hear it, even at the end of the line.

It's followed by a sickening crack.

Everyone ahead lurches to a sudden stop. The music cuts off on a shrill note. The boy must have tripped.

He dropped the orb.

And shattered it.

In a flash, silver light races to the sky in high-pitched shrieks, as if the previously contained stars are eager to return home. It's a brilliant brushstroke of blinding starlight.

Followed by darkness.

The line goes deathly quiet.

The only remaining light is around my neck. But it isn't large enough to cloak us all. Not like the orb.

One second of silence. Two.

Then the scraping begins, as if the demons have been crawling along the fringes of the light, waiting. *Waiting.*

My heart hammers as that slicing continues. Closer. The carving is closing in.

Then—the first mind-splintering scream echoes through the woods, followed by the sounds of ripping flesh and splitting bone. An immortal is being torn apart.

Chaos erupts.

My head jerks back as someone grabs my necklace. I gasp then choke as the immortal tries to rip it straight through my neck.

"Human bitch," a voice I don't recognize shrieks. "Hand it here. Your life is worthless, anyway." Other hands, clutching. Ripping. I hear Raker's blade unsheathing.

Before he can strike anyone, the grip goes limp. Gasping for breath, I turn to see Daphne standing there, knife in hand. She plunged it through the immortal's back.

"Run!" she says, and I grip her hand, pulling her into the safety of the light. "They're beneath us!"

I squint at the ground. Shit. She's right.

Onyx blades are stabbing up through the dirt. Bone-white claws are breaking through, grabbing anyone they can. An immortal runs right into that grip—and is dragged through the dirt before I can even try to help.

Fuck.

"Stab through the ground!" I bellow, plunging my sword in and out as I go, but it's too late. And so few have weapons. They had blind faith in the starlight. They thought it would keep them safe.

Screaming. So much screaming.

We sprint as fast as we can, and I try to pull more people into the light, but one by one, they're dragged away. We all need to get to higher ground. At least there, we wouldn't have to worry about being taken from below.

Daphne has the same thought. "The cliffs!" she yells.

Then, her hand is ripped from mine. An immortal has grabbed it, in an attempt to be saved from attack. I stop and turn, lifting my sword.

Blood spatters onto my face as Daphne is torn in half by teeth sharp as knives.

"No!"

Roaring fills my ears. Fills the forest.

I stumble back, screaming, into a strong body.

Raker.

He's fighting them off, one by one. A demon emerges a few feet away, outside the crown of light, and Raker's sword gleams as it cuts the beast in two. But there are too many.

They're everywhere.

Hundreds of them. As if they've been called.

And the demons might not be able to pierce our light . . . but the immortals can. Bloody and desperate, a woman who served me food lunges for me, reaching for my throat, trying to rip the necklace off.

My back hits the ground. My head cracks against a root.

The immortal is clawing at me, reaching for the orbs.

"I can—I can help you!" I say, knowing there's room for a couple more people. Wondering if I can break the necklace so more can use its light. Trying to keep her from choking me.

But it's like she doesn't hear me or doesn't care. And there are far too many to even fit anyway. I hear the rest of them rushing forward, toward the bright glow.

The woman's sharp nails scratch my cheek, and blood streams down my face. "Please stop," I say, not wanting to hurt her.

She doesn't. She reaches again, and I push her away, until her legs are out of the light.

And she's immediately pulled into the ground. A blood-curdling scream pours from her mouth, and she manages to grip a root, keeping herself outside. I can't just sit and watch. I lunge forward, trying to drag her out, but strong arms band around my middle, pulling me into the air. My legs thrash as I'm lifted away. *Raker.* He unceremoniously throws me over his shoulder.

"Let me go!" I say, watching from over his back as the woman disappears beneath the dirt in a spurt of blood.

Raker doesn't. He's running toward the cliff face.

"Climb," he snarls, turning me in the air and hurling me against the rock with brutal force. Ears ringing, head pulsing, I grip on to the stone and climb all the way to the closest ledge, a sheet of jutting stone with just enough room to stand, planning on helping the rest up. On showing them the way. But when I turn around to help, Raker is there, pinning me to the cliff.

Screams pierce the night.

"We need—we need to help them," I say, shaking beneath the cold of his armor.

Raker is silent.

"They'll die!" I say, raising my voice so he can hear me through the yells for help.

He doesn't move a muscle.

"Fine. Stay. I'm going." I try to push against him, but he doesn't budge. He's as firm as the stone behind me. He's pressing me against the rock face, his body shielding mine, not for protection . . . but to cage me. I can't move without him moving first.

Their voices become more desperate. Their *begging*. My mind goes back to a time when I was helpless. Those screams are like knives through me.

"*Please*," I say, my voice breaking on the word. Tears slip down my face, sliding against his armor. I can't stand here and not help. I can't live when everyone else doesn't. I *can't*.

Not again.

He doesn't say a word. He doesn't move an inch. Not as I push. Not as I scrape with my nails. Not as I beg. He just stands there against me, body firm and all-encompassing and unyielding as the screams grow louder.

Then—

As they go quiet.

"Bastard," I say, voice shaking in a sob. "Demon. You . . . heartless, merciless monster." For hours, I call him every name I know. I curse him over and over.

But he seems to have endless armor everywhere, even over his heart, even over his feelings, because his body does not shift in the slightest. He is not moved. He does *not move*, even when I dig my nails into the skin of his neck, even when I plead.

Only when the sun rises, and all traces of the demons are gone, does he budge. He shoves off the rock and lands on the ground. I land in front of him, legs nearly buckling from exhaustion.

The forest is carnage. Skin hangs off the trees. Blood spatters the ground. I fall to my knees and retch.

When I finally look up again, he's just staring at me, his hood and mask covering everything. But I imagine if I could see his face, it would be as smooth and expressionless as the cliff we just clung to for our lives.

I get to my feet and stumble toward him. I stab my finger into his chest and say with every smelted inch of my soul, "I hate you, Harlan Raker."

He just looks down at me for a moment. His gaze dips to the finger still in the center of his chest and then back up at me.

"Good," he finally says.

And then he turns around, back toward the path.

But I'm not fucking finished.

I really don't know what I'm thinking. Maybe I just want to get a scratch in that spotless armor, maybe I just want to show him he's as fallible as us all.

Blinded by my tears and fury, I unsheathe my blade as fast as he taught me and hurl it through his back.

Or I would have.

If he hadn't unsheathed his sword so fas. It flies through his fingers, into the air—and then is caught behind his spine, perfectly blocking my hit, while the rest of him still faces the opposite direction. He sheathes it again in the same second.

Shit.

He turns in a flash, and then he's right in front of me. *Furious.*

"You hate me?" he demands, spitting the words.

"*Yes,*" I reply, falling into my stance. The one he helped me perfect.

"Prove it."

Then his sword is hurling toward my neck.

I lift mine, blocking it, the force of his hit nearly enough for me to drop my weapon, but I don't. I spin, then lash out, slamming my steel against his, over and over, spilling my fury and sadness and *rage* into every single movement. He takes it, for just a few moments.

Then he meets me stroke for stroke, harder, forcing me to stumble back with every strike, my jaw clenching as his hits get rougher and rougher.

Our metals crash together, and I feel their joining in my teeth, it rings through my blood, ripples down my spine.

Raker isn't even using a fraction of that famous strength, and it's still nearly enough to bring me to my knees.

My body rattles as it takes another hit. My sweaty hands barely keep their grip on the hilt. Air rushes through my lips with the force of him.

He must see that I'm about to collapse beneath the weight of his strength, but that doesn't make him back down, no. It makes him *furious.*

He swings his blade ruthlessly, snarling as I stumble, like this is a test I'm failing, like he wants me to fight back. I try. I groan as I give him every bit of resistance he's giving me, and he doesn't hold back. He pushes against my metal until I'm sure it's going to break. Until my entire body is shaking. He's just a wall of metal, closing in.

Fuck. Him.

"*I hate you,*" I spit into his face, my bones screaming against his pressure, our swords clashed between us.

"Hate. Me." He pushes against my blade. "*Harder,*" he growls.

Then his blade pulls back and slams against mine with such force, my back hits the cliff face. A gasp spills from my lips.

Our metals meet again, and this time he just stays there, pushing down, edge skimming mine, sinking toward me inch by inch, steel scraping, his masked face getting closer and closer. When he's just a breath away, he thrusts hard, trying to make me fall apart. I almost do.

Then I bare my teeth and push against him with everything I have, my senses shredding at that sound, of two blades made of the very same metal, both refusing to yield. I manage to hold my own.

But he's stronger. And his sword is getting closer to my throat.

He's so close I can see those steel-gray eyes, buried beneath his mask. Hard and heartless. I glare at him with every piece of myself, every shard of my hatred, sharpened over many years, every unforgivable thing he's ever done echoing through my mind. I wield it like a second blade.

And I guess I'm just as stubborn as my sword, because I don't drop my weapon, I don't admit defeat, even as my arms tremble, even as sweat spills down my brow, even as every muscle burns as he presses harder. *Harder.*

No. I spit in his face, and even though it lands on his mask, his eyes flash with fury.

He pulls back, to release his final blow, and again—I must really have a fucking death wish. Because instead of trying to strike him with my blade, I throw my weapon to the ground.

And launch at him with enough force that I actually manage to knock him down.

The air rushes out of his mouth as he lands hard, me atop his armor, and he could have his blade through my heart in a second, but I don't care. I want to mark him. I want to rip his armor to pieces, I want to make him bleed, I want him to feel the fraction of loss and hurt that I do.

I swing at him wildly, pounding my fists against his chest, his mask, scraping and scratching, not even knowing if I'm reaching skin.

He lets me.

"They're dead!" I scream, and all I'm doing is hurting myself, my knuckles going bloody, but I can't stop. I don't even feel my arms or hands anymore, just this growing hole of despair in my chest, and I—I can't. I can't keep it in any longer. *It's too much.*

Any light that I found on this journey has been shattered and snuffed out, just like that orb. Just like waking up in a pile of ashes. I see flashes of it now, merging with the blood all around us.

Not again. Not again.

I'm breathing so hard, but I can't get a full breath, and I can't even see, the tears are blocking everything out, but I keep swinging, keep raging, until finally, he reaches up and takes both of my bloody hands in one of his, and says, *"Enough."*

Just like that, the fight leaves me, and I collapse against him. And then I'm sobbing into his neck, trembling against his armor, and he doesn't move. He remains very still, until finally, he gets up, me still atop him, has me retrieve my sword, and carries me out of this patch of woods.

Out of the bloodshed.

32

I don't know how long Raker carried me, just that when I finally look up from his neck, sun is pouring down into the forest, right above us.

My body is curled tightly against his chest.

There's a mess of vines blocking our path, and he shifts my weight to one arm, pulls his sword out with the other, slashes the vines to pieces, then sheaths it again. All in one smooth motion. Then both his arms are holding me again.

"Raker," I say, and his focus doesn't budge from in front of him. He's alert and ready, just like he must be all the time on the battlefield, fighting countless rebels.

"Aris," he says, the sound like ground stone.

I swallow. I still hate him. I hate that he didn't even *try* to save those people.

Maybe we would have died, trying to go back, or trying to help more. I don't know. I will always regret not at least giving them a chance.

But I also regret how I reacted. I don't want to be as bad as him.

"I'm sorry I attacked you." The words are forced. I'm sure he can tell.

He finally looks down at me, sun glinting off the metal of his mask, as if he's shocked that those words seriously just left my mouth.

I think he might be about to answer.

Then, without warning, he lets go of me, and I stumble before managing to catch myself, even though my legs are still numb with sleep.

He summons his sword in a flash. "And I'm sorry you were so fucking bad at it," he says.

Right. Stupid of me to think Raker could be tolerable for more than a few hours.

For a second, I wonder if he's just going to finally get rid of me, but then he falls into his stance and says, "Try again."

I blink. He can't be serious.

He nods at my incredulous look. "Try *harder* this time, Aris."

Hate. Me. Harder.

I reach back for my blade. Pull it from its sheath. Fall into my stance.

"All that rage?" he says. "Make it mean something." Then, he's on me again.

Our swords clash and skim and join and tremble against each other. And without the rush of anger, my head is clearer. I frown in focus, remembering every time I've watched him fight. Every little movement. Every detail. My memory is my advantage.

And I've been watching him.

Maybe too carefully.

I know his favorite moves. I know how I've reacted to them in the past. So, when he goes to shove me against a tree, lifting his blade to press it against my neck—

I duck around him, kick the back of his legs, use his own momentum to my advantage, and shove him against the trunk instead.

My metal is at his throat.

I'm panting against his chest. The sword is shaking in my grip.

Shit. I . . . I did it.

He's not even winded. I'm not sure he was even fully trying.

His mistake.

A win is a win.

I lift to my toes, and lean in, very carefully, luxuriating in this rare moment I never thought would fucking happen. "All this metal slows you down, Raker," I whisper, as close to his ear as I can get. "Hiding behind it might just be your downfall." My lips curl into a smug grin.

I let the metal graze him for just another moment.

Then, I go to drop my blade, but his hand reaches up, stopping me. His long fingers curl over mine, swallowing them. "No," he says. "Go ahead. Follow through with it."

I frown. What?

"Come on, Aris," he drawls, his voice a rasped challenge. His rough thumb gently brushes against my pulse, and my treacherous heart stutters. "You know you want to."

The sword trembles even more.

But his grip doesn't loosen. No, massive hand gripping mine, he guides my blade's edge closer to his throat. Together, we dig it into his skin. Harder. *Harder.* Until blood drips down his neck. There's a line of it, a thin mark on his previously unmarred skin.

My eyes widen, watching the crimson, horrified.

"There," he says. "A memory of my weakness."

Then, he drops his hand.

I stumble back, his blood on my blade.

A sight I never thought I would fucking see.

I open my mouth. Close it. Still unbelieving that I actually bested him, and that he *marked himself* with my sword.

"Good job, Aris," he says as he walks past me, not even bothering to wipe away the blood.

DUELING BECOMES A daily event.

I never get close to beating him again, but that's because he's finally trying. Finally treating me—consistently—like a worthy opponent.

Even though he doesn't know it, he's training me to have a chance against the gods. It's why I don't mind the break in our journey, the few hours it takes for us to get all our frustrations out with our blades.

After one of these sessions, I draw the map for him, and together we decide to go north, to avoid the desert completely. It adds a few days to our travels, but I'd rather be in woods lush with berries and mushrooms and game, than in a sea of sands.

Thanks to the starlight, we can travel more hours of the day than ever. We sleep whenever we must. And instead of the old nightmares, I have new ones. I hear the immortals' screams. The ones we *ignored.*

I look at Raker, and I see mercilessness.

But I also see the knight that carried me until I woke up. That has trained me, every day since I marked him, like he wants me to be able to do it again.

I don't pin my hair up anymore, tying it into its two braids at the sides that become a long one down my back, using it as a cover over my eyes at night, to sleep while wearing my bright necklace.

But tonight, I just stare up at the stars. According to the map, we're almost to the edge of the forest. Almost to the Land of the Gods.

This is what I wanted. It's why I'm here.

But for some reason, my mind is filled with all the things I'll have missed out on if facing the gods leads to my death.

"I've never seen the sea before," I say, staring up at the sky. I don't even know if Raker is still awake. We've been camped out here for over an hour now.

He doesn't answer. Of course he doesn't.

Still, I turn to my side to face him. "Have you seen it?"

His hood is still on, just like his mask. I'm used to talking to fabric, but I have the strange urge to see his face. To see if he is truly the monster he acts like.

"I grew up by the sea," he finally says.

I'm shocked into silence. It takes a few moments for me to say anything at all. "Was it . . . was it beautiful?" I ask, knowing all on Stormside has rapidly degraded since the gates.

"It used to be," he says.

And that's it. But now that he's given me another tiny thread of his life . . . I want more. I want to know how this man became the most feared knight on Stormside.

"How did you claim your sword?" I ask.

By the tensing of his shoulders, it seems my question is a surprise. And, perhaps, unwelcome.

Right. Foolish of me to think he would be interested in having a lengthy conversation.

"It's fine," I say, scowling, turning back around. "I don't know why I thought you'd—"

"I killed its wielder," he says simply.

Of course. It makes sense. Still, I swallow. "Its wielder must have been powerful."

He lifts a shoulder. "Not more so than me."

I roll my eyes. "At least you're humble."

He turns toward me. His voice sharpens. "Should I lie? Should I pretend to be a simpering weak fool, the way you do?"

At that, I bristle.

"I saw you, at the Culling," he continues, sitting up. I do too. "Shrinking into yourself, playing weak damsel until you got close enough." He makes a derisive sound.

I saw you.

My back teeth scrape together. Never in a thousand years would I have imagined Raker had been watching me.

It makes sense. He was getting a good look at his supposed competition.

And he's right about me. I do it often, on purpose. There is nothing stronger than a woman underestimated.

But his pointing it out, his *knowing* it was an act, makes me strangely furious. "You're one to judge," I say, getting closer, so I can say the words right at his face. "You've never been starving, you've never been without a family, you've never been imprisoned, and tied down, and *tortured.*"

"You don't know *what* I've been," he says sharply, ducking his head, just inches away. Wind howls around us. It blows my braid back. I just stare up at him, and that glimmering silver.

"You're right," I finally say. "I don't know anything about you. I don't even know *your face*. Tell me. Does building a wall around your heart make it hurt less?"

He stares me down. And his invisible gaze feels like a weapon itself. His sharp voice feels like one too. "I wouldn't know. I don't have one," he says, perhaps recalling all the times I've called him heartless.

"Well, at least you're honest," I say. "At least you know you're a monster."

That word . . . it makes him flinch.

And I'm still so angry about what happened in that forest that I want to dig in that knife and twist it. "Yes. That's what you are," I say. "You *are* heartless. You *are* a monster. You *are* merciless. I'm sure you wear those words with honor."

"Mercy will get you killed," he says, his voice rumbling just inches from my mouth.

I laugh without humor, remembering when he was merciless to me. "Is that what you tell yourself to sleep at night?"

He shrugs. "I'm not the one with the nightmares, Aris," he says.

Bastard.

I open my mouth—

And lightning flashes across the sky, illuminating everything, followed by a knee-wobbling crack of thunder.

I remember.

How soft the small patch of grass was beneath our fingers. How quickly the storm came rolling in.

How wide my sister's eyes—

A hand locks around my arm. "Come on," Raker yells, and that's when I notice it's raining. Badly. Out of nowhere, like the sky was just ripped open at the seams. "Let's find somewhere dry."

I open my mouth, trying to recall the surrounding landscape, then freeze.

It's not just the skies. The ground is thundering.

Fuck.

Hooves. Horses, grunting.

The cavalry has found us again.

We start to run.

And the rain pours down harder. I don't know if it's to our advantage, or not, all I hear is those dozens of horses, getting closer.

"The *light*," Raker says, looking over at me. I look down. It's like a beacon, leading them right to us. Even through the rain.

I know he probably wants me to leave it behind. "But—"

He rips it over my head in one smooth motion.

"That cave, up in the mountains. You go there," he yells, motioning northeast, to the faint shape of a mountain I can barely see through the rain. He says it like a general ordering his forces. Then, without waiting for my response, light clutched in his hand, he runs in the other direction.

I realize what he's doing immediately.

Shit.

I try to run after him, but he's so much faster, even with the armor. It doesn't really slow him that much, not really, no matter what I said.

He disappears in the blur of the rain. I stay rooted in place, listening to those hooves as they change course. As they chase *him*.

Raker is the best warrior I've ever seen. He also doesn't really give a shit about me. This isn't some sort of noble sacrifice. This is him telling me I'll just get in the way.

He's going to be fine. That's what I tell myself as I take a breath and start to move, sprinting to the hill, and the cliff carved into its side.

My boots slip and my knees crash against the rock. Dirt gets lodged beneath my nails. But I finally make it to the mouth of the cave. A curtain of water is spilling over it, runoff from the top of the hill. I dart through the entrance, and finally, I'm dry.

I didn't realize how cold the rain was, until now. My skin is pebbled. My teeth chatter.

Arms crossed over myself for warmth, I stand there, for a few minutes. Then, almost an hour, just waiting.

Waiting.

Raker doesn't return.

Dread starts to crawl through my blood. Should I—should I go looking for him?

No. I think about when I bolted through the Storm Woods, believing I would save him. He's the head of the king's guard. He'll have had a plan. A way to distract them or lead them away.

I sit. And wait.

Drip. Drip. Drip.

Quiet.

Scrapes echo against the stone like nails scratching a wall. I groan, turning over, realizing I fell asleep waiting for him.

A step sounds close by.

Raker.

Relief slams into me. I open my eyes, blinking away sleep, only to see a creature with a skull-like face reaching toward me, with claws of glimmering steel. They scrape against each other gently as they stretch out. Fear grips my chest.

Demon.

Without moving, my gaze travels to the mouth of the cave, where the rain has stopped. The water that was like a door in front of it is gone.

I don't dare breathe. I don't dare blink.

The claw goes right toward my face, sliding against my cheek—not stopping until it reaches my sword, still on my back, the metal peeking up from behind me. My hands tremble against the stone ground.

The creature seizes. Stops. Then it throws its head back and screeches, revealing rows of sharp, mismatched teeth.

That's when I strike. I kick it with all my strength, and when it staggers back, I reach for my sword, fast as ever. It recovers quickly, and lunges forward.

I put my blade up to block it, both hands gripped tightly around its hilt. Entranced by my metal, the demon launches forward, claws of steel extended, reaching.

It hits me with the force of a wagon, slamming me against the wall with blinding speed. My head hits the jagged rock. My vision spins.

Those claws reach past my blade and wrap around my neck.

I gasp.

Before they can shred my throat to ribbons, the demon is pulled back by its protruding spine.

Raker doesn't waste a moment before putting his blade right through its skull.

Raker.

Relief washes over me in a wave. Not just because he saved me from the demon. But because he's . . . alive.

Chest heaving, I grip the wall for purchase. I shoot a look at the mouth of the cave, and the water that's no longer there, but mercifully, it seems we won't need it any longer. The entrance begins to be bathed by the first signs of day.

But Raker isn't looking at the sunrise. He's not looking at the dead creature. No, he's looking at me.

At my throat.

He takes a step forward. Am I bleeding? The cuts can't be deep or I would be dead. I reach a hand up.

And that's when I feel it. The long tears in the fabric. I swallow.

"What. Are. Those?" is all he says.

"Nothing," I say, voice sharp, as if I could command him to forget this.

Instead, he takes a slow step toward me. Another. I can hear the intensity of his breathing. "They are very clearly not *nothing.*"

I turn to leave, but his arm juts out, blocking my path.

I could stab him. I don't know if it would do me any good. He's seen them already. There's no taking that back.

The fear, the shame, the guilt of these markings . . . it has consumed me like a poison. Now the truth is out. It can't ever be locked away again.

"*What. Are. Those?*" he asks again.

Instead of shrinking away, I lift my chin.

Fuck shame. Fuck hiding. I've been through too much—this *body* has survived too much to be ashamed of itself.

I rip my shirt over my head and throw it to the ground. Only the tight band of fabric around my breasts remains. He sees it all now.

Silver. Thin roots of silver, faintly sparkling through the remaining darkness.

The exact color a knight like him has trained to hunt and kill.

He doesn't say anything. He's staring. I can feel the heat of his eyes on my bare skin. Panic races through my blood, years of fearing knights and getting discovered rushing through me. I want to run.

But *enough*.

I stand very still, spine straight.

And he shakes his head. "Impossible," he breathes. Then he lifts his gaze slightly. I can almost feel his eyes boring into mine. "How?"

I don't want to tell him. I want to keep this secret for the rest of my life—but all the people who know this story are dead. The truth of that slams into my soul, and my eyes burn.

I have the sudden urge to tell someone. Because maybe . . . maybe that would lessen the shame. Maybe I wouldn't feel so alone.

The words come out in a whisper. "When I was eight, my sister and I snuck out of the house. We went to a nearby cliff, to the only remaining patch of grass. We wanted to steal a few pieces. We thought we could bury it in our backyard and make the green grow. We . . . we were hoping to find wildflowers too. Out of nowhere, the sky changed. The storm struck. I could feel it coming. Right toward my sister." I swallow. "I pushed her out of the way, and the lightning struck me instead."

I take a shaking breath.

"My sister was just a little kid, but she pounded on my chest for hours. My parents eventually found us, in the rain, and my father didn't stop trying to get my heart started again. He never stopped. He never gave up on me. None of them did. Until it worked. My eyes opened. And the red marks from the lightning turned silver."

I don't tell him that it's my biggest regret, pushing my sister out of the way. That if it had hit her instead, maybe she would still be alive, after what happened later.

"Lightning," he says roughly.

I nod.

Slowly, so slowly, he reaches toward me. He gives me more than enough time to stop him, but I don't. I just watch as his long fingers get closer and closer to my bare skin.

Then his rough thumb is gently trailing down my neck over the markings, and I gasp. A chill rains down my spine. No one but him has ever touched me there. Anywhere, really. His thumb is callused, but his touch is featherlight, just like it was in the cave. He strokes my pulse, then across my collarbone, before following the markings down, touching me in a path, like he's tracing a constellation. Down my chest. Farther still, until he reaches its center. His large hand splays out, his fingers curling over my breasts. My skin prickles.

Out of nowhere, he stops, ripping his hand away.

Then, without another word, he turns and leaves the cave.

"They're silver, Jesper."

"I know they are." My dad sounds tired. My sister and I have our ears to the door. I sink low and peer at my parents through the keyhole.

My mother's face is in her hands. "What are we going to do?"

My father places his palm on her back. "We're going to protect her, at all costs," he says, his voice steady. "We'll never let them take her away."

My mother shakes her head. "Never," she promises. "If they find out . . . they'll never stop chasing her."

"Who?" my sister asks from up above. I shush her. I don't really know. The king? He's known for his greed. Perhaps he wishes he was silver.

"His knights will come for her," my mother says, her voice now steady. "One day, they will all come, and they will try to take her. They will . . . they will try to destroy her."

My father's voice is as firm as I have ever heard it. I feel the strength of it in my bones, distilled from pure anger and determination. "Let them try."

Just when I thought we had formed a tentative truce, we're back to silence.

He knows about my markings. That one fact makes me feel bare, exposed, at a disadvantage. It's one of my greatest secrets. For my entire life, I've hidden away, afraid that someone would find out about them and take me from my family.

Especially the knights of the king's guard. Let alone its damned leader.

I feel shame crawling across my skin for what I am, all that confidence in tatters. The way Raker stormed out doesn't make me feel any better.

For nearly an entire day, he doesn't talk to me. He doesn't even *look* at me. It's like I'm invisible. Or disgusting.

Am I that strange? That repulsive? I haven't seen many people shirtless, but my markings don't seem that noticeable. Or maybe they are.

We reach a long field with grass that shines and curls like ribbon. It's beautiful.

I can hardly notice that beauty. Inside, my emotions are battling. We've been through countless obstacles together. Traveled side-by-side for weeks. After all the stones taken down from this wall between us, I refuse to let it build up again.

I stop walking. Raker keeps going. Of fucking course he does.

"If you're going to kill me, just do it already."

I unsheathe my blade. I stand my ground.

At that, he pauses. His shoulders stiffen.

"Kill you?" he says from up ahead.

"*Kill me*," I say. "Or capture me. Or whatever else the king does with the silver he collects."

He still has his back to me. His voice is a snarl. "You think I would hand you over to the king?"

I keep my hands tight on my blade, knowing his metal could be against mine in a flash. "You serve him."

"I serve *no one*," he spits.

I scoff. "That's very interesting, considering you're literally the head of his *guard*."

He doesn't say a word.

So, I keep speaking. "I heard you talking to him, promising to bring something back. What is it? The magic? Is that why you're on this quest? For him?"

Raker makes a derisive noise. "I'm not on the Questral for anyone but myself." I remain rooted in place. Blade up.

"So, if you're not going to kill me . . . why . . . why won't you look at me?" I take a shaking breath.

And I feel stupid for even saying the words. But I can't stay silent.

Once his apathy was expected, but now . . . after everything . . . it feels like a betrayal. It *hurts,* and I know that rudeness and cruelty is all I should expect from Raker, but damn it, it feels like the least he can give me is his respect.

"I've been ashamed of my markings since the moment I got them," I say. "You don't—you don't have to make it worse." My voice cracks, and I fucking hate it, but I keep going. "You might find me ugly, and that's fine. I don't care. But you . . . you are the only person alive who has seen them, and you, of all people, should know what it's like to keep yourself hidden. To show yourself. And . . . and then to be *shunned* . . ."

I hate that my eyes are stinging. I hate that I'm speaking at all, that I think he even cares.

"You say I don't know you, and you're right. Because you haven't told me anything. All I know is you're a warrior who grew up near the sea, and once had siblings. All I know is you hide your face, and you hate mercy, and you wield a blade better than probably any human in history. Now you know one of the worst moments of my life. You know my greatest secret. I have laid myself bare to you, and you . . . you might as well be a stranger, Raker. I guess you're just a knight . . . and I'm silver. We were always meant to be enemies. Stupid of me to think any different."

He tenses, but he doesn't turn around. I stand there, regretting ever opening my mouth. Ever caring. I look at the ground.

Then he speaks.

"There is nothing to know about me," he says. "Nothing I can give you. Nothing I can offer. I am nothing but rage and vengeance, Aris. Nothing but countless kills on a blade. There is no home. No family. Nothing to look forward to. Nothing to covet. Don't waste your time trying to figure out a person that doesn't exist. I am nothing beyond this."

I swallow. "I—"

He keeps walking. He doesn't look back.

I remain in place, watching him, the broken pieces coming together. The shards of his life. The way someone turns into Harlan Raker.

He has nothing and no one, just like me.

Maybe . . . maybe we really aren't as different as we both like to think we are.

I sheath my blade, and finally, I start to move again, eyes on the grass. My skin still prickles with shame.

He doesn't need to look at me for us to continue this journey. His notice doesn't matter. We aren't friends. We aren't anything but unlikely and begrudging companions. After we reach the Land of the Gods, we'll never see each other again. That, I'm sure of.

And I don't know why that thought makes my stomach twist.

I'm so lost in my head, that I don't even hear the hissing, not until it's so loud, it's impossible not to notice.

I squint. I take a step forward, reaching back for my blade, only to stop in front of a long, coiled snake with sparkling silver scales.

It reminds me of the one in the maze. The one that looked at me, with far too much awareness.

This one does too. Its forked tongue flicks out, and then it rises, inch by inch, until it nearly reaches my height. It stares at me with bright silver eyes, rimmed in red. I inhale sharply. I know those eyes.

I've seen them before.

A flash of memory shocks me still. Silver-red eyes, burning through the fire. Silver hair, floating as she—

Far ahead, Raker has turned.

"Aris," he yells. "Aris, don't—"

Whatever he says fades away when the serpent lunges—and bites the place between my neck and shoulder.

A rattling, otherworldly pain fills me. I gasp, then seize, falling to the ground, my limbs going numb.

There's the slice of a blade, and the hissing stops.

White-hot agony blinds my senses. It's unlike anything I've ever felt before.

Everything—my nerves, my voice, my skin, the world—is *screaming*.

Then, like blowing out a candle, it all goes silent.

33

I wake up soaked in sweat. And I'm *moving*.
Strong arms are encircling me.
I tense, and look up, only to see Raker's hood.
"It *bit*—" I say, my voice raw, like it's been dragged across a rock face.
"You'll live," he snaps, with more than a hint of regret.
Was he able to find a cure? Did my body overcome the snake's poison? Raker won't answer any of my questions anyway, so I close my mouth to conserve my voice. It's only a few minutes later that he drops me onto a cave floor.
"Sleep," he snaps at me. And then he disappears through the entrance.

I WAKE UP with a pulsing headache, but better. Able to move. There's a pile of berries next to me and a mound of mushrooms next to that. A pouch of water is right by my head.
Raker. He must have foraged for them while I slept. I look around—
And that's when I see him. Slumped against the wall.
Somehow, I know he's not sleeping. I know something is wrong.
"Raker?" I get to my feet, losing my balance for a step as I fight off a wave of dizziness. In a moment, I'm on my knees before him.
He doesn't look up at me. He only reaches up, as if to keep me away from him. His hand brushes against my shoulder. "Go back to sleep, Aris," he says.
But his *hand*.
I take it in mine before he can stop me, and—"You're *burning*." He's hotter than should be possible. I'm not sure how he's still conscious.

And his veins . . . they are the same red as the snake's eyes. Did he get bitten too?

I think about how quickly I recovered without medicine. I reach up to touch the place the fangs pierced me, only to find the skin a normal temperature. My own veins are not this color. I'm completely healed, as if—

I swallow. No. No—he *wouldn't*.

"Did you—did you suck the poison from my neck?" I ask, my voice just a whisper.

He doesn't say anything.

A strange feeling tugs in my chest. He *sucked poison from my blood*. He . . . saved me. Now here he is, burning up, the poison having reached his heart.

His enormous hand is still in mine. I weave my fingers through his, as if to cool it.

"What a stupid thing to do," I say, my voice a whisper.

At that, he tilts his head up, only slightly. I can imagine he's glaring at me. His voice is rougher than usual. "Saving your life? Stupider than you can possibly imagine."

So he did.

"Yet you keep doing it," I breathe.

"Someone has to," he says, echoing my own words back to me. As if . . . as if he was listening. Remembering.

I raise a brow. "I've saved your life too."

He makes a sound. "Hardly. All you've done is made my life a fucking nightmare."

Keep talking, I think, worry crawling through me. *Don't fall asleep. I don't know if you'll wake up.* "Yet you sucked the poison from my throat."

He sighs. "I need you alive."

"Right. For the map." Though he hasn't asked me to draw it in days. "Yet—yet now you're dying."

He doesn't deny this either.

"Well . . . well, you can't," I say.

He shifts his head an inch, his body seizing, as if even moving hurts. "I would have thought my death would please you," he says. "Given how much you hate me."

I nod. "Normally, yes, but . . ." I shrug a shoulder. "It would just be embarrassing," I say, "being the Warrior Without Marks on His Armor and then dying from snake venom."

He makes a sound that almost resembles a laugh.

"Also, I don't think that snake could lift your sword, so your death would really be a waste."

There it is. That rough sound of amusement again.

I wish I could see it. I wish I could see if demons can smile.

His breathing is slowing. It makes something rise within me. Worry? Panic? Poisons either need antidotes . . . or they need to be fought. He cannot succumb to it. I won't let him. I need to keep him talking.

"Did you always want to be a knight?"

"Want?" He says the word like it's foreign. He shakes his head. "I became a knight to survive."

I frown. "You . . . you were starving?" I remember how fiercely he told me I didn't know him at all. For some reason, I can't imagine Raker ever not having anything. He just seems so capable of taking it.

"*We* were starving," he says. "My father was a fisherman. My mother was a seamstress. One season, all the fish washed up dead. We were out of food by winter. My siblings were little more than flesh and bone. Against my parents' wishes, I enlisted as a knight in the king's guard. The stipend kept them fed." I don't miss how he uses the past tense when it comes to his family. I think about all the assumptions I made about him.

Shame sinks through me. I don't know why I just assumed the opposite. It's the tale of many warriors. The king provides them and their families with food. So many of them often die, in training or in war. It's a brutal sacrifice.

"And you were just . . . really good at killing?" I ask.

"I was good at doing whatever I needed so they survived," he says. His voice is deeper. Rougher. "The more I advanced, the more food they got, so I became the best."

"And did it work?" I ask, wondering if I'm prying. Wondering if he's going to just stop talking. "Was all of it . . . worth it?"

His breathing is more labored now, as if his body is fighting. *Good*. If his experience with the poison is anything like mine, his heart will be racing. His head will be pulsing in pain. A distraction. What he needs is a distraction.

"No," he says, and it's the only time I've heard even a sliver of emotion in his voice.

I can feel it in him. Barbs rising. He might as well have his sword between us. I've poked at something sensitive, and I know how much easier it is to build walls than to break them.

"I lost my family too," I say softly.

I think he might tell me he doesn't care. Or to stop talking. But he doesn't. He just sits . . . like he's listening.

"It happened in one night." I swallow the emotion in my throat.

"The nightmares," he says, his voice ragged.

I nod. "That's what I dream about. Every time I reach deep enough sleep. That night, when everything changed. I was the only one who survived." I take a rattling breath. "And I wish it was me who died."

"Reaching the end will help you get your revenge?" he asks. He must assume I'll use the cup of magic for something in my plan.

I nod.

"And you?"

He nods back.

I sit down against my heels. "So, we have that in common. Dishonorable intentions." I tilt my head. "Though I expected nothing less from the king's most brutal warrior."

He just stares at me from within the darkness of his hood.

"I know it's selfish," I say. "Our side is dying. People are suffering. But—but ever since that night, there's been a hole inside me. It's grown, devouring everything. Every shred of empathy or kindness . . . I feel it withering. I don't want to care about everyone else. I cared about *them*, and they're gone, and this world is worse for it." My eyes burn. I smile weakly. "I know it's wrong. But I would trade every single person in this world for them. Without flinching." I shake my head. "It's wrong, but it's the truth."

"I understand," he says.

"Of course you do," I say. "You're a demon."

He makes that half-amused, half-frustrated sound again. It's faint . . . but there. I stare at the darkness. He stares back. I wonder what he sees. I can feel the heat of him, of his feverish skin, right in front of me, as I lean slightly closer.

That's when I realize he's not wearing his mask. Only his hood.

My voice is barely a whisper. "Well . . . since you're dying." I swallow. "Your face. I want to see your face before then. You know, in the interest of coils of snakes and all." He has seen my markings. He has seen me. We have fought back-to-back and survived countless dangers.

He doesn't say anything. So, I raise my arm. My hand trembles as I reach for his hood, slowly, so slowly.

I give him time. Space. Opportunity. But this time, he does not stop me. His breathing seems to become even more labored. My fingers brush against the edge of his hood, and I swear I can feel him shiver. Perhaps it's the poison. Or it's the fever.

With a rush of curiosity, I push the fabric back, and there he is.

And the world isn't fair, not at all.

Because Harlan Raker is a monster, but he doesn't look like one.

He is painfully beautiful.

His skin is pale, his cheeks are sharp, his hair is dark and curled around his ears. Just looking at him makes my blood heat. He looks like he was carved by a merciless god, one that wanted a weapon people would run *toward*.

He's like a blade. I know if I touch him, I'll bleed. But I want to, anyway.

I can't help but be enraptured. I stare, even though he's watching. I open my mouth, then close it, unable to find the right words.

"Why hide?" I finally ask.

"Why did you?" he says.

"But you—you didn't have a reason."

His voice is sharp as a scythe. "Neither did you."

That isn't fair. Especially coming from the very person I was taught to fear.

I study him for far longer than is acceptable, and he just stares at me, eyes narrowed, almost as if he's *glaring*, but I can't stop.

"You—" I say, my voice just a breath.

"Are not a coil of snakes," he says.

I shake my head. "No. Not at all." Maybe it's the shock, or the remnants of the poison, or because I've finally lost my fucking mind, but I say, "You're beautiful, Raker."

He raises a brow at me. "You think I'm *beautiful?*"

"On the outside, yes."

He sighs in that long-suffering way I've heard before, but to see it . . . to see the way his eyes close in irritation, the set of his perfect jaw . . .

He winces, as if pain has lanced through him again. For some inexplicable reason, I want to make it go away; I want to distract him.

"You must be filled with regret . . . dying for someone so insignificant," I say, my voice light. Trying to make him laugh again.

But his own voice is serious. "Aris," he says, my name a deep whisper that scrapes against my bones. "You are irritating. And reckless. And an idiot."

"Thank you—"

"But you are not insignificant."

You are not insignificant.

It's barely a compliment. Barely anything at all . . . but for some reason . . . it means something. I feel a rush of warmth.

For a moment, we just look at each other. His gray eyes . . . they're like steel in the darkness. Like the magnificent metal of our blades.

"You're nicer when you're dying," I whisper. "You should do it more often."

And that is the moment I first see Harlan Raker smile.

My chest tightens, my breath stolen away. It's just a small movement, not a full expression at all, but I can't stop looking. His teeth are straight and white. His eyes crinkle at the edges.

"What?" he demands, that glorious smile now in ashes.

"You smiled," I breathe. "I'm waiting for the world to stop turning."

He shakes his head, the corner of his lips twitching almost imperceptibly. "You're funnier when I'm dying," he says, dropping his head against the stone wall behind him. His eyes close.

"It's because I'm so happy."

"Are you?"

"Yes. I can't wait to get that sword in my hand."

At that, his eyes open. "You wouldn't know the first thing about handling a sword that big," he says.

"Now that sounds like something else," I say.

I don't know if he's about to scowl, laugh, or frown. He doesn't seem to know what he's going to do either.

My cheeks flush. I can't believe I said that. "You're dying," I say, definitely making it better. "You won't remember this." It's almost like I'm trying to reassure myself.

Even if he doesn't die, with this fever, everything is going to be a daze.

I hope.

"If I'm dying," he says, voice strained, "and you're so sure about it, and *so thrilled* . . . then tell me why you're doing this."

His breathing is slowing. His eyes are closing, then opening. I smooth my thumb across his wrist and feel his pulse. It's not as strong as it should be, but it's there. Maybe he needs to rest.

Or maybe he's actually dying.

He looks at the place I'm touching, then back at me. I drop his hand before he demands it.

"You want to know?" I ask.

He nods.

I lean in close. He's staring at me just as carefully as I studied him, even though he's seen my face countless times in these past weeks. He's staring like he might never see me again.

When I get close to his face, he stops breathing. I'm practically in his lap. I lean in even more to whisper my secret right into his ear. "I'm going to kill the gods," I say, my lips brushing his skin.

And that's when he goes very still.

"You'll die," he says flatly.

I can tell he's fighting the sleep that's coming. He's fighting to stay awake. He tries to shift himself to be more upright, but his eyes are blinking closed. He's losing consciousness. I pull back, so I'm right in front of him.

I shrug a shoulder. "It's okay. I'll be with you," I say, meaning it as a mocking threat.

It's the last thing he hears before he goes under.

RAKER SLEEPS THROUGH the entire day, but he's still alive. I know. I check often, worry for him twisting my gut.

His pulse beats weakly but steadily against my fingertips, and relief rushes through my chest. I press my hand to his forehead, assessing his temperature. Still burning up. Yet still living.

Please keep living, I think.

Fingers still against his feverish skin, I marvel at him. He looks like a sculpture. Immortals are perfect, but he . . . he has a dangerous, striking beauty. It's a shame he hides it behind a mask.

I can imagine he hates his face. He hates being called *beautiful*. He must have hated it most when it came from my lips.

He has to live. *He has to.*

But his fever is getting worse. If we don't get help, he's going to die.

There are herbs that help with fevers. My mother used to steep tiny, dried pieces of it, kept safe in a tin over generations, when my sister and I were sick. I don't know if Starside has the same variety . . . but I have to try.

I quickly fill the pouches from the running water covering the mouth of the cave, then set off into the forest.

This final stretch of the woods isn't as plentiful as the others. I weave through the foliage, searching for those long, pointed leaves, cursing as the minutes tick by.

Raker might not have much time left. Panic races through my veins as I search wildly. I'm just about to enter a grove, when I hear voices.

I stop, pressing myself to the closest tree.

"Look. Footprints," someone says, with the smooth tone of an immortal. "They must be close."

Raker.

I take off in the other direction, going around, running so fast my heart burns with strain, before finally shooting into the cave. Fear grips my chest—then loosens when I see Raker still sleeping undisturbed. But not for long.

They're faster. It'll take them just seconds to find us.

I shake him gently. Then more firmly when he doesn't stir. "Raker," I say. "Raker, you have to get up. They're—"

A boot echoes against stone.

I freeze. Slowly, I turn to the mouth of the cave, where a tall, sinewy-muscled immortal is leaning against the wall. He looks amused.

He's not part of the cavalry, as I first suspected. Yet here he is, having clearly tracked us down.

"Well, well, well. What do we have here? It was almost too easy to find you."

I unsheathe my sword as I rise from the ground. "What do you want?"

"You, of course," he says. He takes a casual step forward. "Everyone's after you. There's a large bounty on your head." He tilts his head. "And what a pretty head it is."

Me? No. He must mean my godsword. Though Valen said the same thing.

I grind my teeth, trying to think, trying to come up with a strategy. "Who wants me?" I demand. "Which god?"

His eyes glimmer with hunger. "The God of Death, of course."

The God of Death. The reason behind the demons. Possibly behind the rot. The god stealing brides. What does he want with me?

"You . . . I could possibly bring in alive . . . *him* . . . he wants him dead."

I shoot a look at Raker. He's still asleep. He's still far gone . . . feverish. Weak. This isn't about our swords, then. It's about us. Why? I take a step back, studying the man's footing. His motions. All things I would normally do before a duel.

But he's immortal. Even with this blade, I don't stand a chance. I talk, to buy myself time to fucking *think*. "Why would someone want me?"

A slow smile crawls across the man's wretched face. He takes his time looking me up and down, and bile slides up my throat. "I can think of a few reasons." His eyes meet mine again. "As for why someone wants you dead?" He shrugs a shoulder. "As long as the money is good, I don't ask questions."

He lunges forward in a flash, and I barely get my sword up in time.

He's fast. Strong. I gasp as his metal slams against mine. Only the tiniest crack forms across his weapon.

His sword is good. He must have stolen it off someone powerful.

But mine is better.

With a growl scraped from the center of my chest, I aim for his neck, using a move Raker taught me, only for the immortal's blade to get in the way at the last moment. Another fissure forms, spiraling all the way to the hilt. Just a few more hits, and he'll be without a weapon.

I try to raise my sword again, to aim for his side, but he's too quick. He rams his weapon down against mine with such a force, it knocks me to the ground—

And my sword out of my hand. It goes flying, clamoring against the other side of the cave.

The man smiles. "I'm sure I get extra for the blade. Or maybe I'll sell it to a different god," he says.

No. My head is spinning from the fall. I can barely concentrate on the words, but I reach my hand out.

"Stellaris," I say.

"What was that?" the man says, taking a step forward.

"*Stellaris*," I hiss, desperate. My blade trembles but does not fly into my grip. I try to focus my energy, my mind, but it's scattered. It doesn't hold.

The man reaches his sword up over his head for a clean cut. His metal arcs through the air toward my neck. I reach my arms up over my face on instinct, my eyes squeezing shut, my muscles seizing.

One moment passes. Another.

I slowly open my eyes to find the immortal still in the same position, only with a gaping hole through his chest.

Behind me, Raker has his hand open. His sword is in it. His blade went right through him.

"You're not dead," I breathe.

I hear the man hit the floor, his metal echoing against the stone.

"Sorry to disappoint," Raker says, echoing my own words back to me, before putting his hood over his face, erasing the beauty.

He stands, takes one step forward, then pauses. He's still recovering. I race to help his balance. "We have to go. Now. There are more of them in the forest."

He takes another unsteady step before his entire body tenses, like pain has stabbed through him. His knuckles are white, curled tightly around the hilt of his blade.

"Stay here," I say, making a decision. "I'll leave. They'll chase me. I'll—I'll come back for you, with medicine."

Raker ignores me as he takes another step, then another. He moves almost smoothly. I race to get my sword and follow him.

Voices. There are others, and not far. Raker raises his sword, ready to fight, though I don't miss the tremors going through his body. I can see them even through the armor.

Then—

Hooves. The cavalry. They've found us.

Fuck.

Fuck, fuck, fuck.

I turn to face Raker. I know he can feel it, how close they are. In less than a minute, we'll be surrounded.

He looks at me, his hood falling back. It seems like he doesn't have the strength to straighten it. "Go," he says, like an order, like he *always does*. "I'll buy you time—just go."

I don't budge.

He bares his teeth at me. "For once, would you fucking *listen*, Aris."

I shake my head.

In a flash of fury, he steps toward me, as if he's about to throw me over his shoulder again, as if he's about to fling me into a tree or force me to leave him.

But before he can do anything, his body finally collapses.

I rush to his side. His face is burning up, worse than before. His veins are bright crimson. I don't know how he gathered the strength to summon his sword or even *stand*.

I rise, watching as he tries and fails to sit up, powerful arms shaking.

"No," I say, my voice a resolute whisper. "Unfortunately, I'm not leaving you."

The hooves are like a roar. The trees are moving wildly. The cavalry is here. They're coming from all sides. There's no way out.

I remember all the warnings. *Stay away from the Great Houses. Summoning him would be a death sentence.*

But the ground is trembling, and Raker can't even stand. He sucked the poison *from my blood*. We're surrounded.

Before I can talk myself out of it, I swipe my blade across my palm, dig it deep into the soil, kneel by its glimmering silver, and whisper, "*Vander Evren.*"

At the sound of his name, the forest stills, as if even it is afraid of him. The hooves stop.

"*No,*" Raker growls. He crawls as if to stop me. But he buckles under the effort.

A step echoes through the woods.

I can hear my own breath, the beating of my own heart. The hairs on the back of my neck rise, as if my body can sense danger.

I swallow, looking in every direction, hand still curled around my sword, blood dripping into the dirt, trying to see where the steps are coming from. But I can't.

I rise and turn—

And meet one of the most beautiful men I have ever seen. Even standing tall, he towers over me, every part of him imposing. His hair is silver, cut shorter than Raker's, the same color as his intricately detailed armor.

Silver. A color typically reserved for the gods. How powerful can this immortal heir be to have been born with hair that shade?

Every single warning about him skitters through my mind.

And they were all right.

He looks every bit the ruthless immortal warrior, especially as he frowns down at me, unimpressed. Then he turns to Raker, who is now motionless on the ground. His gaze stops at the blade I've buried in the dirt.

He raises his own without hesitation.

I've summoned him for a duel, using the ancient method. He's the heir even immortals—even the Gardener—fear. He's about to strike me down.

He's about to win my sword.

I raise my bloody hand, as if that will do any good, and the words tumble out of me in a single breath. "Stellan said you would help me."

His sword stills just an inch from my palm. A small fold forms between his brows. "Stellan sent you?"

He knows him. A prickling forms behind my eyes, to meet someone who did.

I swallow. I have a feeling he would know if I was lying. "Not exactly." The sword races forward again. "But he knew you would help me all the same! He told me to look for you."

Vander frowns, considering me. Considering my words. Considering the warrior just feet away. "And where is Stellan?"

Stellan.

The image rises of him stiff on the floorboards, eyes wide and unblinking.

"Dead," I say. At the crack in my voice, his eyes narrow. They are searching, and brutal, studying me as if he can see into my deepest thoughts and emotions. As if that one word could tell him even a fraction of the memories Stellan and I had together.

I don't drop that piercing, clawing gaze. I stare into his eyes, the way Stellan would have wanted me to, unflinching.

It's he who looks away. He curses.

Then, just when I think he'll leave me here, or cut me down, he outstretches a hand.

Warnings still echoing through my mind, I take it. It's cold as ice and smooth as bone.

"Leave him," he tells the guards that have begun spilling in from the forest, out of nowhere, wearing the same crest that is carved into the hilt of the blade now sheathed behind this immortal's back.

I rip my hand away. "No. I'm not leaving him here."

He frowns, as if disgusted that I've spoken back to him. "I am not allowing an unknown warrior with a sword like that into my castle." He looks over at me and my own sword. "The only reason I'm allowing you entry is because of Stellan."

Panic spikes through me. "Fine. Don't let him in the castle. Keep him in the stables for all I care. But I'm not leaving him here."

Vander's eyes narrow at me. At my nerve. Finally, he sighs, as if deciding that the struggle isn't worth it.

He motions his warriors toward Raker. It takes five of them to lift him to his feet. His head lolls, as he's still unconscious. I wince, hoping he'll last long enough for me to find him medicine or a healer.

Vander reaches for his own blade, which glows bright violet. A *godsword*.

He digs his blade into the ground, and the forest vanishes.

34

I land on my knees. My bones rattle, and my stomach drops. I clutch the dirt for purchase, then look up at massive gates and the castle behind them. We were in the forest a moment ago . . . and now we're in front of a sprawling estate. I blink.

"You—you portaled us?" It isn't a word I've ever used outside of the context of my mother's passed-down stories, or when my sister and I would imagine opening a door and entering another world entirely.

"The blade did," he says sharply, before walking through the gates, which open at his approach.

I look around. Raker is nowhere to be seen.

"He'll be in the stables, as suggested," Vander Evren mumbles from up ahead. I swallow. He's going to be really fucking unhappy about that when he wakes. *If* he does.

Panic is like ice through my blood.

Raker needs medicine. This immortal I was warned never to summon is our best bet. I just have to convince him to give it to me.

Vander Evren's castle is crafted of glimmering light gray stone, with tall arching windows, and over a dozen gray-blue turrets with blade-sharp points. It sits like a beast, taller than that massive bear in the skyquill forest, with spires that brush the lowest clouds.

I can imagine a ball taking place here just as much as I can imagine it becoming a fortress.

I follow Vander down the pine-lined path, through a courtyard, up stone steps, and past towering silver doors.

The ceilings are impossibly high, sculpture carved into the corners. There's a front room, then a glorious double staircase, hewn from pure marble—white, infused with silver veins like bolts of lightning.

Vander looks over at me, gaze snagging on my dirt-crusted clothes and still-bloody hand. "Attendants will see to your needs. Then dine with me." He turns and makes to go upstairs. I know I'm supposed to wait here, for his attendants. But I take a step after him.

It's a risk. He could kick me out of his estate for disobeying him, or—more in keeping with the fact that the hunter seemed to fear even his *name*—slay me where I stand. But Vander just sighs. He grips the marble banister so hard that his already-pale knuckles get whiter. By the tense set of his wide shoulders, he looks one moment from either cutting me down or simply snapping at me.

Luckily, he picks the later.

"What—"

"I need medicine," I say quickly.

He frowns, looking over at me in a cursory way. His brow raises. "You're sick?"

"Not for me."

That makes him pause. I see a shadow of interest pass across his face. "You care for that knight?"

My laugh seems to startle him. "I care about making it to the end of the Questral."

I get the sense that Vander's patience and attention are as thin as needle thread. His eyes are sparkling light blue, the color of the sky here on the clearest day, but they hold no warmth. They're as cold as ice as he looks me over, as if I've already wasted enough of his time. "Dine with me. Then we'll discuss the medicine." He turns back toward the stairs.

Ordering me. All these people, always fucking ordering me. I should probably be thankful for it, I should just shut up and listen, but I have met enough powerful men to know that they are all capable of steamrolling right over a woman's voice the moment they think she won't speak up for something.

"And if I don't want to?"

That makes him go predatorially still. When he turns around again, he looks not only angry but also genuinely confused. "I am heir of the most powerful house on Starside. It is an honor to dine with me."

I laugh. I can't help it. "Wow. Most powerful house on Starside . . ." I shake my head. "I'm sorry, was I supposed to bow?"

Silence.

The entire house seems to go still, as if the stone is listening.

Maybe, on second thought, it wasn't a good idea insulting the *heir of the most powerful house on Starside* in his own home, while I'm in need of medicine and Raker is at death's door.

What would he do? He certainly wouldn't cower before this immortal.

Confidence I didn't have before holds me still. Keeps me from backing down. I hold his gaze, waiting for his next move, hoping it won't be reaching for his godsword.

But Vander simply frowns. "What a strange human," he says.

I glare at him. "What a proud immortal."

He takes a step down the stairs toward me. "Stellan didn't teach you many survival instincts, did he?"

My chin lifts. "He taught me not to bow before bastards."

At that, the ghost of amusement plays on his lips. "Stellan would never bow before anyone."

He's right. The fact that he knows that makes a strange mix of pain and comfort run through me. Like part of Stellan is here. Like I've finally met someone who knew him as I did. "And neither will I."

"I didn't ask you to."

I snort. "Your attitude practically commands it."

I can see my pushing has limits when a flash of irritation passes across his expression. His eyes narrow. "I don't think you understand how lucky you are to be alive. I could sense at least five different creatures and warrior sects in those woods, all headed toward you. Not to mention the cavalry." He studies me again, as if searching for what could possibly make me that special.

His gaze is piercing. I feel the power around him in my very marrow.

He's right, of course. But just like any predator in the wild, he will sense my fear or hesitance and take it as weakness. I try my best to look casual and unaffected. He can't know how desperate we are for his help. How Raker will die without his medicine.

I shrug. "What can I say? Apparently, my head is worth a lot." My own eyes sharpen. "Is that why you saved us? Are you going to turn us in for the reward?"

His lip curls in disgust. "I don't need a *bounty*."

"Right. Heir of the most powerful house on Starside. I almost forgot. It's a good thing I'm sure you'll be constantly reminding me."

He sighs in a long-suffering way. But he hasn't killed me yet. All because of Stellan. They must have—somehow—become friends, during the quest. His eyes shut tightly, and I'm sure he regrets ever responding to that call in the forest. Finally, in a manner that suggests it's almost impossible for him to get the words out, he says, "Will you dine with me?"

He opens his eyes when I don't immediately respond. They are fierce, and confused, as if saying, *I just gave you what you wanted. Now respond the way I want you to.*

I have a feeling that being here will be filled with winning and losing battles. This, I think, is something easy to agree to.

"Yes," I say. "I'm starving."

He sighs again.

"But at least give him tea for the fever. Please." I'm not sure Raker will make it even a few hours without it.

His eyes narrow. "Fine."

I try not to show my knee-wobbling relief.

Then, Vander shifts his grip on the hilt of his weapon, and I tense, but a moment later, an attendant walks through the door, as if called. By his sword?

"Ethel. If you would please show—" He frowns, turning back to me.

"Aris," I say.

He frowns even more after hearing my name. "*Aris* to the guest chambers."

The woman looks like she would rather do anything else, but she bows and strides forward. She practically drags me away from Vander, past him, and up the stairs.

"I can walk myself, I assure you," I say, yanking my arm back after her nails sink into it.

She just huffs at me. I wonder if Ethel is this unpleasant to everyone or if I have somehow already made her dislike me. Perhaps she heard my conversation with Vander.

His castle, I admit, is commensurate with his ego. It is enormous.

The halls are made of marble as cold and pale as its owner. We stride down a grand hall, and the immortal woman turns toward me, eyes narrowed. "Your insolence will not be tolerated," she spits.

I raise a brow at her. So, she did hear our conversation. She seems unconcerned by the blade on my back. Her glare, I think, is practically just as sharp.

My silence only makes her angrier. "Do you know anything about the lord?"

I snort. "Do you really call him that?"

"Of course we do. He's the greatest heir of the last millennium."

I roll my eyes. "So I've heard. Have you even been alive a millennium?"

She bares her teeth at me. "Lord Evren is the only reason any of us is alive. He does not make us call him 'lord,' but we do, because he has given every part of himself for us. In ways you could never understand."

Interesting.

"He was about to leave me for dead," I offer.

She lazily looks me over. "You're human. How much time do you have left, anyway?"

My glare casts flames. She doesn't look at me again, but turns down another hall, then opens two towering double doors with more force than necessary. "Here," she says, before turning on her heel and leaving me, grumbling something about already being busy enough with preparations for a houseguest.

I've spent nights on cave floors, in cold waters, in ethereal woods, against a rock face with a ruthless warrior pressed against me. I've seen magnificence.

Nothing compares to this.

It isn't a room—it's a *wing*. I walk through space after space, all crafted out of white and silver-speckled marble.

There aren't many attendants, at least from what I've seen. If this castle is full of rooms like these . . . it would be impossible to keep them maintained.

The bed is a monstrosity, with columns and sparkling fabrics cloaking it. The windows are enormous, showcasing a garden that is manicured to perfection. Right now, at dusk, the statues and ponds and shapes are shrouded in darkness. I wonder what they look like in the sunlight.

The bathroom is almost as big as the main room. A white claw-foot tub sits in the center of it.

Another attendant must have been in here, I think, as the tub is already full of steaming water. It doesn't have flower petals like the one in the Traveling City, but there is a sparkling dust like crushed diamonds swirling on the water's surface.

I turn and am almost shocked by my reflection in a mirror. Wow. I look *awful*. I almost want to go to dinner like this, reeking of dirt and blood, but I take a bath because Raker is dying, and it would be in my best interest for that to *stop*.

When I'm done with my bath, I look inside the wardrobe and frown. It's clear a woman hasn't lived in these quarters for a long while. There are only two dresses, and they're made from thick, scratchy fabrics.

I open the drawers instead, and find them mostly empty, save for corsets. I search them once, then again, desperate to find anything more wearable.

Pants. I must have missed them on the first pass. They're made of a soft material, and are tight against my body, far more so than the ones I've been wearing throughout the quest. I must be losing my mind, because next to the pants I find a tight long-sleeved shirt of the same material. It goes all the way up my neck, and the sleeves are long enough to cover my hands.

"Perfect," I say to myself, hardly questioning the outfit that was not there the first time but then *was*, before taking my sword and slipping out into the hall.

VANDER IS SITTING at the head of a table so long, it starts on the other end of the room. The moment I enter, his blue eyes click up. I feel his gaze slide down me. "You don't like dresses?"

"No, I love dresses," I tell him. "Your dresses are hideous."

He frowns. "Are they?"

I nod helpfully.

He scowls. "Is that all you do, human? Complain?"

"I have a name," I say, walking toward the end of the table. The place on the opposite side of his has been set. I linger by the chair but don't sit.

"Yes, and careful who you tell it to. Names have power. Sword names, most of all."

I lift a brow at him. "Are you telling me I should be afraid of you?"

At this, he grins, revealing teeth that look particularly sharp. "You should be running for the gates, human."

He's not completely kidding. I can see some vestige of a beast of prey in his eyes, the way they sparkle like I have something he wants. All those warnings echo through my mind, before I silence them.

I lift my chin. "Stellan trusted you. He would have never told me to seek you out if he didn't."

At the mention of Stellan, his gaze softens just the slightest bit. I take my opportunity.

"The medicine," I say, my thoughts annoyingly crawling with worry about Raker in the stables. I haven't seen him. What if he's dead? What if he's thirsty? What if Vander didn't get him the tea?

Panic squeezes my insides.

The hardness in his eyes is back. "Eat," he says firmly. "Then we'll talk about the demon you're traveling with."

I bristle. "You don't order me."

He doesn't even look up from his food as he stabs a piece of his meat and eats it. "I just did."

Battles. I have to choose them. Without medicine, Raker will definitely die. If Vander has it . . .

I sit down slowly. He looks far too pleased that I listened.

"How did you get that sword?" he asks, as I set it down next to me, within reach.

I steal Raker's line. "How do you think?"

He gives me a look that says he doesn't believe me for a second.

I glance at his own sword, leaning against the wall feet away, as if he doesn't fear at all that anyone will try to claim it. "How did you get yours?"

"How do you think?" he says, words full of mirth.

I reach for the goblet in front of me. A golden liquid sparkles inside. *Wine.* "I think it was handed to you, just like that seat, just like this house, just like that silver hair. I think you were born with all of it at your fingertips."

Someone drops something behind me. Another attendant horrified by how I'm speaking to *their lord*, no doubt.

Vander Evren's own wineglass was halfway to his lips, but it stills. All at once, the force of him fills the room, power like an invisible, crushing wave, searing through my skin and bones, as if the entire time, he's been holding it back. Ice-cold fear grips my chest. That's when I realize, perhaps for the first time, the immortal I'm dealing with.

The supposed greatest heir in a millennium. The warrior that quieted the whole forest. That even the *cavalry* stayed away from.

Maybe he's right. Maybe I don't have any sense of self-preservation. I swallow.

All at once, that power is ripped away, as if taken back. I rock forward, released from its hold.

He sets down his glass with unnerving gentleness. "You don't know anything about me, or what I've done." He looks me over. "I could tell you, but you'd be dead of old age before I got to any of the good parts." He looks bored. "I won't waste my breath. Eat."

The word is a brutal command, and after that wordless display, I heed it. Gaze not leaving his, I slowly pick up my fork and stab at something orange. I bring it to my mouth.

And try not to let my face reveal how *extraordinarily delicious* it is as I chew some type of vegetable that is sweeter than any honey.

Vander watches me eat for several moments, until half my plate is empty. Only then does he speak again. "Who was Stellan to you?"

The question hits me right in the chest. Every twisted shard of guilt and sadness that I buried pokes through my ribs.

I take a sip of the wine, the sweet nectar slightly burning down my throat but not doing anything for the knot in it. My voice is tight. "He was—he was my savior."

Vander nods. His gaze touches the table, then me. "That, human, we have in common."

I blink. He must know I'm wondering how Stellan, a mortal, could possibly be an immortal's savior.

He leans back in his chair, looking every inch the powerful warrior heir.

"Half a century ago, he saved my life. I gave him a piece of rare metal in thanks and hosted him on his journey." I don't breathe, remembering the sparkling silver. The most valuable item Stellan owned and turned into a gift for me.

The dagger he died for.

"He learned about my people's . . . suffering. He finished the quest. Instead of going for the gates, he came here. He gave the magic to me, and to my people." My eyes widen. *That's* where the magic went. Confusion grips me. Why would Stellan help immortals who have so much . . . instead of our own neighbors?

Vander looks me over. "He was a friend to me at my worst, a friend to all immortals, when he had little reason to be." His gaze hardens. "That friendship and sacrifice are the only reasons I answered your call."

My eyes burn. Stellan—he was a friend to me too. He *died* because of me. And, even in those final moments, even as he called me a fool, I know he didn't regret taking me in.

I blink, and a tear escapes. It runs down my cheek. Vander turns his head, studying it, as if it's something grossly unfamiliar.

He stands. A blur, and he's right in front of me, fast as lightning.

Slowly, he reaches forward and brushes away the tear. His skin barely touches mine. He's entirely focused on the liquid.

He rubs it between his fingers. He frowns.

His arm extends in a flash, and his magnificent blade is hurtling across the room, into his hand. It's against my neck in an instant, glowing wildly. Yes, definitely a godsword. He's right in front of me, and his face—it's transformed.

It's become a mask of cold rage.

"Why so guilty, human?" he growls. "Did you kill him?"

I can't even find it in myself to feel fear. All I feel is knee-wobbling sadness. And yes, guilt.

How could he know? My emotions? My tear?

More are falling now. I shake my head, my pulse brushing the shining metal. "No. But I might as well have. I . . . I *should have*." I sniff. I should fear this angry immortal, who could end me in a moment. But being with someone who knew Stellan makes me want to be honest. "He wanted me to. But I wasn't strong enough." I take a rattling breath. "He's dead because of me."

Vander just studies me. Top to bottom, he studies me, and then he frowns, and I can almost read his disappointment, seeing that *I* am what his friend gave up his life for.

"Everything in me wants to kill you," he says. He sounds like he means it.

Then, just as suddenly as it was drawn, his sword is back against the wall. He sighs. "But if he died for you . . . I won't let it be in vain." His eyes meet mine. They are harsh and fierce. "Why are you making the quest?"

My answer is immediate. "Revenge."

He looks surprised at that.

"On who?"

Telling him would be a risk. The gods are revered on this side. Even the faelings told me Great Houses are associated with them. Though I haven't seen any hints of reverence in the castle.

But Stellan trusted him. If I'm going to make it to the end of my journey, I need to trust him too. "The gods. I'm going to kill them."

Silence. The world stills.

Then a slow smile spreads across Vander's face. "Now, human, you're getting interesting." He looks toward the door and, as if commanded by his mind, it flies open. An attendant is waiting. "Get me a vial of healing elixir."

The immortal rushes out of the room.

I lift my brow. "You're helping him?"

"I'm helping you. This is only the first step. We'll discuss the rest tomorrow."

The attendant returns with a vial. He hands it to Vander, bows, then leaves us alone again.

Slowly, Vander turns back to me. "You say you want to kill the gods?"

I nod.

"You don't stand a chance."

I frown. "I—"

"Alone. You don't stand a chance alone." My skin brushes his as he hands me the vial, and my shoulders spike at the otherworldly cold. "You're staying until I say otherwise," he says.

Then, he passes me by, and leaves the room, glowing sword hurtling after him.

RAKER'S EYES FLY open.

They go right to me, standing on the other side of the barn watching him. Then they go to the chain fixed around one of his wrists.

He looks up at me, bored. "Really?"

"They're afraid of you," I say.

He glares past the sweat spilling down his forehead. He isn't wearing his mask. His hood is down. "Then at least not everyone here is a fool."

I throw the vial at him, and he just manages to catch it before it hits his face.

"Take it," I say.

"Poison?"

I give him my best smile. "No. When I kill you, it will be with my blade."

"I would expect nothing less, Aris," he says, before uncorking the bottle with his teeth, then downing it.

I take a shaking breath. I still haven't gotten used to it. Matching that ruinous voice with an equally ruinous face.

As beautiful and deadly as a blade. I feel like a fool watching it, like being mesmerized by the shine of a sword right before it stabs me through the heart.

"What?" he demands, eyes narrowing at my focus on him.

I swallow. "You look disgusting," I say, hoping saying the words might make them true.

"Lovely words, Aris," he drawls. He looks me up and down with a curl of distaste on his lips. "But that's not what you were saying yesterday."

My cheeks burn. He does remember, then. "Forget the vial," I grumble. "Maybe I'll just let you die."

At that, he chuckles. I'm momentarily stunned by the sound, by the way his lips curve. I must be losing my mind. It must be a side effect of the poison that was in my body for just a few seconds.

I turn on my heel and leave, before he can see the blush spreading across my face.

In my room, I stare at myself in the mirror. Now that I'm clean, I can see more than I did before. I look . . . different. Still too thin. Cheekbones just a little too sharp. But there's a hardness to my eyes. A fierce determination.

There are cuts down my cheeks. I wash them, then turn my attention to my hair. After my bath, I put it in my single braid, that I now unravel. There's a brush. I take my time combing through it, and blink, a memory taking over my reflection.

My mom, brushing my hair.

"Why, Aris, are there so many tangles?" Her voice is playful, but I can see the worry in her eyes. I'm not supposed to leave the house. Playing outside, with my markings, is a risk.

"It was just for a moment," I say. "We—we just played with the neighbor boy."

My mom sighs. "You are not like other children."

My lip trembles. "But I am. Only these make me different. And they— they don't mean anything."

My mother looks at me, and in her eyes, for the first time, I see fear. "Aris," she says, and the way she says my name sounds like home. "They mean far more than I hope you'll ever know."

My hair snags, pulling me from the memory. Quickly, I braid my hair into a crown, the way my mother used to before bed. I haven't done it in years. I'm surprised my fingers remember the movements, but they do. *They do.*

An attendant must have walked in without me noticing, because there's a dress waiting on the bed. It has long sleeves and is long enough to touch the floor. I frown, wondering why I would need a dress to *sleep in,* before I touch the fabric.

It's thin, and soft as a blanket.

It melts against my skin like a lullaby. In the drawers, I find a scarf, which I wrap around my neck, just in case another attendant decides to walk in without knocking. I crawl into the cloud of a bed, through the silky curtains. I lay in the center and tuck my sword in next to me.

I fall asleep wrapped around it, trying not to think of the poisoned demon in the barn.

I FAIL.

Late into the night, I'm still tossing and turning, thinking about the way he collapsed from the poison. The way he *sucked it from my skin.*

We hate each other. This is an arrangement.

So why am I crawling out of bed and opening the door? Why am I intent on checking to see if the medicine is working?

In the darkness, the castle is truly like a beast. I can almost hear it breathing. Whispering.

I run a hand along one of the halls as I move down it, and it's almost like the silver in the stone is moving with me.

Through nothing short of a miracle, I find the kitchens. Mercifully, they're empty. I put as much food as I can in a large napkin, then wander until I find the center staircase. It's only then that I realize I've forgotten shoes.

I curse and turn back toward my room, before something glimmering catches my gaze. There's a pair of silk slippers by the front door. They must belong to an attendant.

They're beautiful, with ribbons as ties, and they somehow fit perfectly. I push on the door, expecting to find friction, or that it's locked, but it creaks open, letting in a shard of moonlight.

We're safe on this estate, according to Vander. Still, I grip my sword in my hand as I creep to the barn.

Raker isn't sleeping either. He looks up the moment I enter. Now both of his hands are tied in manacles, his arms chained above him on either side. I wonder what he did to earn that second shackle.

His sword is still on his back, but he can't reach it. I wonder if he can still call upon it, locked up like this.

His eyes sear into mine as I step forward. They slip down my body with little interest, even though I do find my new outfit *interesting*.

"It's soft," I tell him about the fabric, knowing he doesn't care at all. I smooth my hand down my leg, to convey my meaning.

"I'm glad you're nice and comfortable," he says, voice grating.

Right. I'm in a castle, and he's here . . . in a stable. My nose crinkles. A stable that smells horrible.

He sighs. "Why are you here, Aris?"

"I—I wanted to make sure—"

"I wasn't dying a brutal death? How thoughtful of you. I am, as you can see, perfectly alive."

"Right." I nod. "I—I brought you this."

I'm about to toss the food at him when I remember the restraints. There's a full cup of water a few feet away from him, clearly left as a taunt.

This demon deserves to starve, to thirst, but—that poison should also be mine. Even though he did it for his own selfish reasons, he took pain from me.

Slowly, I bend down to get the cup of water. He watches me with narrowed eyes, eyes of precision, someone who is used to sketching and enacting battle plans. Used to predicting all his enemy's movements.

Right now, I'm moving toward him with the cup in my hand.

He's so tall, even sitting down. I sink to the ground and—this isn't going to work. He watches as I slowly lift onto my knees to get anywhere close to his height. He just stares at me, his gray eyes even more piercing this close.

Our faces are almost level. I lift the cup.

"What are you doing?" he demands through his teeth, eyes still narrowed, as if trying to ascertain my ulterior motives.

"I'm helping you, you cranky bastard."

He glares at me. But when I slowly bring the cup to his lips, he drinks.

I watch his throat work with far too much interest. Everything about him is enormous. Muscled, but lean. I wonder—I wonder what—

I realize the water is gone and I've been ogling his body when he says, voice echoing into the empty cup, "See something you like?" I drop the cup. It thuds against the dirt.

His voice is cutting, full of brutal mirth. My cheeks burn.

"I could never like anything about you," I say.

He tilts his head. "And here I was, thinking we were becoming friends."

Friends. At that, I have to laugh. I want to turn and leave him here, the way I did before, but his face is still too flushed. "You're feverish," I say, leaning closer, feeling his heat.

"Poison will do that to you," he says.

I sigh. Carefully, I reach my hand out, until the back of it touches his forehead. "So foolish of you, to save my life."

"I'm regretting it more and more every second."

His fever has gone down; the medicine is working. I feel a flush of relief. Still . . . he's warmer than he should be. It must be uncomfortable, especially in the heat of the stables.

"I'll be right back," I say, rising and turning on my heel. I saw ice in the kitchens. I return with it minutes later.

"This will help," I say, avoiding looking at him. I hold the ice to his forehead, until my own hand goes numb. Until it's dripping down his heated skin.

"Interesting," he finally says.

"What is?"

He lifts a shoulder. "Nothing. You've imagined a thousand ways to kill me. I would think you'd be happy to let me rot."

I frown. "How—"

"You talk in your sleep," he says. "When you're not screaming. Or snoring."

My cheeks heat. I wonder what else I've said.

I try to find all the nonexistent composure I have and say, as casually as possible, "You can die after the Questral is over."

"Right," he says. "Tell me. What do you want, Aris?"

"What?" I say on a breath, far too aware of his proximity and the heat of his body. At how close we are. At how I'm in front of him, on my knees.

"Why do you want to kill the gods? What do you want? What are you hoping to get from your revenge?" He studies me. "Why do you want it in the first place?"

Oh.

His words are a bucket of ice over my simmering thoughts. I look away. "Don't pretend to care, Raker. You'll lose some of your villainous sheen."

At that, I swear I see him smile from the corner of my eye. But when I turn back again, he's all the same broodiness I've come to know well.

His voice is flat. "I don't care. If I survive this, though, our fates are tied until we reach the end of this journey. I want to know that your motivations are clear. That you will do anything needed to reach the end."

"Have I not proven that?" I ask, my voice sharp, remembering everything we've had to do just to make it here.

His head tilts, considering. "The ends of journeys are always the hardest."

I lean forward so he can hear my every syllable as I say, "I will do anything to reach my revenge. *Anything.*" I hope he can see the intensity in my eyes. I hope he can hear the unspoken words. *I'll do anything—even kill you.*

The ice in my palm has practically melted against his heat. The drops are now snaking down his neck, disappearing beneath his armor, and I watch—I watch with far too much interest. I watch, lips parting, suddenly overcome with thirst.

When I look back up at him, I see he's watching me too. His eyes are burning, like he can sense my longing. Like he knows very well that I'm lying to both of us when I deny that I *see something I like.* Slowly, his own gaze drops down to my lips, then to my neck, then to my chest. It snags there, lingering.

I follow his eyes and gasp, leaning back, dropping what's left of the ice. The material of this dress is thin. The ice—*it's cold.*

His eyes snap back up to mine. Nothing short of anger twists Raker's face as he says, "Don't visit me again, Aris."

35

Breakfast is waiting in the foyer of my quarters. It's set on a silver tray, atop intricately painted porcelain plates. The pastries are still warm, stinging my fingers as I pull them apart, steam curling. Butter melts across my lips and I groan as the sugar-crusted top scrapes gently against my tongue. I recognize cinnamon—a rare spice my mother let me try once, from her coveted collection. It's folded in between the layers of this bread. There's another similar pastry with orange-blossom icing that sticks to the top of my mouth.

I eat every single one, accompanied by a cup of steaming lavender-colored tea.

What must it be like to wake up every morning like this? My thoughts drift to Raker, hungry in the stables, but then I remember the fury in his gaze and force myself to forget him.

He took the medicine. His fever was already improving. He'll be fine.

When I'm done with every single crumb and every drop of tea, I sit back in the chair, slumping against the pillows. That's where I am minutes later, when there's a knock on my door.

Vander is standing there, looking as though he's already been awake for hours. He doesn't bother with pleasantries. He just says, "If you don't have a creature—you need alliances."

A knife twists within me as I remember my dragon. I frown. "Alliances? How will that help me?"

He turns to stride down the hall, and I slip on those shoes I found downstairs, then follow. "How much do you know about swords?"

"I know how to make them," I say. He nods, an understanding between us that Stellan taught me what he knew. He was a blacksmith even before the quest. "I know how to summon mine now."

"You knew how to summon me."

I nod, remembering how the forest had stilled. Remembering that, no matter how much Stellan trusted him, I cannot. Not fully, at least.

We turn a corner. The halls are empty. We only pass that same woman attendant—Ethel—who glares at me and bows to Vander before hurrying away, in a rush. I remember her mentioning being too busy with something else to host a guest.

"Not every sword can summon," he says. "Not every immortal can hear a summoner's call." He turns another corner. "All swords can make oaths."

I think about the king, asking for oaths on the blades he provided his challengers. I wonder how many of those challengers are still alive.

At my silence, Vander continues. "Oaths bind to the blade itself. If the oath is broken . . . so is the sword. And depending on the connection . . . so is the wielder. You see, after much time, a wielder and their blade become almost one. The bond is just like riders and their creatures. Especially for great swords like ours."

"Okay. How will oaths help me?" I ask, as he finally leads me into a room.

I go still, taking in the rows and rows of books. We've entered a sprawling library. In the middle sits a long table made of ancient wood. I can almost feel its history, its power.

Without a word, Vander plunges his sword into the center of the table, and a map spills from its metal.

A *living*, silver map. It has all the places I know now from memory. The Prism Path. The Beast Tree. Some places we haven't reached yet, like the City on Fire. I reach out and can feel the heat of the burning city. I swallow. If Raker ever saw this, he would leave me. I know that. *He's told me.* It's a good thing he's locked in the stables.

I look over at Vander in question.

"On foot, it's a long journey still," he says, trailing a finger through the metal, all the way from his home to the Land of the Gods. Vander's estate is in the center of Starside, to the south. We've gone backward more than two weeks' worth of travel in just portaling here.

Fuck. Even if I expected to return to Stormside before the fifty days are up . . . now, it seems impossible. It might even be impossible to reach the gods in time.

Vander seems to have a plan, though. He points out various homes that sit between his and the archway where we're heading.

"The Great Estates," he says. "From the Great Houses of Starside." There are far more than there are left on Stormside. They had the magic necessary to keep and hold their power. "They are all enchanted and connected. If you're able to get an invitation to a Great House, your sword can take you to its gates."

Portaling across this much land . . . it would make a huge difference in our journey. It would almost make it *easy*.

"My sword . . . could portal me?"

He nods. "But invitations are forms of oaths and are rare, of course. They aren't given up lightly. An heir of a Great House swearing on your blade would be at great risk." He turns to face me. "But there are those among us who would like to see the gods dead." He frowns. "To what lengths will you go to get your revenge?"

"Any length. I'll do . . . anything."

He looks pensive. His expression grows serious. "Think about what you might promise these heirs. It's your choice."

Dread settles, knowing his meaning. What would I offer? Would I truly do anything?

"How would I even meet them in the first place?"

"You're in luck." His eyes glimmer, but I don't miss the shadow of a frown. "There's a ball happening in four days. Here, at my estate. It's been planned for a while now." The attendant's preparations—that's what she must be working on. "Heirs of most Great Houses will be in attendance."

A ball. The way he says it, with irritation, makes me think it might be more than just a grand party. Still, if what he says is true . . . it offers an incredible opportunity.

He tightens his fist on the hilt of the sword, and the map retreats into its metal in a glimmering wave. He pulls the blade out of the table and makes to turn, but I whirl to face him. "Am I losing my mind?" I ask, remembering the bath, and the clothes that weren't there at first, and the shoes by the door. "Or is your estate . . . is your house. . . . *alive?*"

I know Great Houses have magic. But this is something more. It's like a consciousness. It's like eyes are buried in the walls.

His lips pull up with near-amusement. "Something like that," he says. "Don't antagonize it." Then he frowns, scowling. "It can get an attitude." He looks at me. "I'll leave you to your plotting," he says, before he strides out of the room.

EACH GREAT HOUSE has a crest, just like the gods.

According to Vander's endless texts, they were formed by sons and daughters of the gods were strong enough to claim the first skylarks. Some also bonded with creatures who wielded magic.

Over millennia, some of the swords were lost, won, or—most interesting—*combined* with other swords to create even greater weapons.

Each have names. They are famous. I trace their illustrations, marveling at their designs, techniques and carvings that seem impossible to create, with human hands, at least.

Family trees are helpful.

So is Vander. He comes to visit me the next afternoon, his sword dripping blood.

He cleans it off and says, "Every time a head of House dies, there is a duel, which decides which heir will claim the blade. The heir is thought to be the strongest of the line, and they become the head. It's often a bloody affair." He points to the family trees. "Age doesn't matter. The one with the star is each generation's heir."

"Which are expected to attend the ball?"

He sits. "I suppose I should tell you it isn't simply a ball," Vander says, finally cleaning his blade with an equally bloody rag. "It's the beginning of a long and tedious courting ceremony." I remember the hunter mentioning the start of courting season.

I blink. "Are you—are you auditioning *wives*?"

Vander flashes his sparkling teeth. "Why, human? Are you interested?"

I give him a look, and he chuckles. "Not just me. Every eligible heir and heiress will be here for months, to make matches. All staying in this castle."

"Sounds fun."

"Sounds *tedious*," he says, clearly not looking forward to it all. It almost makes me smile, seeing an immortal so annoyed.

Until I realize what he's saying. What I can *promise*. "You think I should . . ."

"I think you should dance with them. Talk to them. See what they want . . . and if you can give it to them."

I open my mouth. Close it. There are a million things I have to say to that, but the one that comes out is, "I don't know how to dance."

At that, he rises. He offers his hand.

It's covered in blood. I raise a brow at him, and he takes off his gloves. Tosses them onto the ancient table will little care.

"Come on, mortal, I don't have all day. And I don't particularly enjoy dancing with anyone, let alone a clumsy human."

"How charming," I say, taking his hand. He only grins.

"Here are the steps."

It's been two days since I've visited Raker. I mean to forget him, the way he so clearly wants me to, but at the last moment, I make a plate at dinner and sneak it out to the stables.

Raker is there, of course, still chained. I don't even bother with insults as I stride over and touch my palm to his forehead. He hisses at my touch. "I told you not to visit me," he snarls.

"And I told you to stop ordering me around," I say, happy with his progress. His fever is gone. "Better. Here."

I pick up one of the pieces of meat on the plate, then pause, frowning. I should have brought a fork or something, I think, as juices drip down my hand. Too late now.

Raker's eyes are still narrowed and locked on mine as I press the food to his lips. He takes it with his teeth, and I swallow. I don't know why I swallow.

He chews. I watch him. In silence, I feed him, and we're both glaring at each other, as if to communicate how much we hate this.

Then the food is gone. I lift the cup to his lips. When it's empty, I leave without another word.

I eat breakfast with Vander, who between bites tells me tidbits about this world, before heading off to whatever mysterious duties heirs attend to. The ball is in just two days. I spend all the daylight hours in the library, that night practicing the dancing steps, and then when everyone is asleep, I sneak food to Raker.

He isn't sick anymore.

We don't talk. Every time I get an urge to say something, to let him know what I've discovered, I stop myself. I can't trust him. We are contingent partners, nothing more, nothing less, and if he knew my plans, I worry he might try to make alliances on his own sword, all by himself.

Maybe *I* don't need him, I think, if I'm able to actually get oaths on my metal. Maybe this is where we part ways.

I ignore the sinking feeling in my stomach at the thought.

The next morning, just one day before the start of courting season, Vander stands from breakfast and says, "You'll need a dress. Heartfall is full of dramatics." That's the name of the months-long courting ball, I've learned. He rolls his eyes. "A person's clothing signifies their importance. You are human . . . already lowly. You'll need to show your strength in your outfit." He looks at my weapon, considering it. "One that will showcase your sword."

I think about all the hideous dresses in the wardrobe. Those won't do.

He seems to hear my thoughts and frowns. He sighs. "There's a room."

I raise a brow. "I'm listening."

"A dress . . . can be made for you there."

Does he have tailors? I nod happily. Then the rush of excitement dies when I think through exactly what that might entail. "I don't . . . I don't like anyone seeing me naked," I say quickly. "I could take my own measurements."

"That won't be a problem," he says.

Relief floods through me. "Okay. I'll need something . . . that covers. Covers everything but my face."

He looks like the last thing he wants to be talking about is a gown. "Also not a problem."

He motions for me to follow.

The room Vander spoke of is small and rounded. It's in one of the turrets of the castle. Besides large, open windows, with long, sheer drapes, it's empty. But not completely.

There's a magic to this room. A force. I can taste it on the tip of my tongue.

Vander frowns as he presses a hand against the stone. "A dress that covers everything but her face," he tells the room. "In any color other than silver." Of course. Silver is the color of the gods. "Don't be too fussy."

Then he turns and closes the door.

I blink, dumbfounded. Am I supposed to wait? Is something supposed to appear?

After moments of silence, I walk slowly to the center of the room, toward the drapes that curl gently in the wind. They reach out, tickling my ankles before they blow back toward the wall.

A whisper sounds close by, followed by more. It could be the breeze, but no . . . these are words. They have a rhythm. I listen as closely as I can, but I can't make out anything specific. The tone changes, though. It sounds a little like an argument. Many voices, weaving together, until it melts into one single sound.

The wind blows harder. The curtains lift higher, brushing my arms. Smoothing against my skin.

Then, all at once, they violently uncurl, whipping toward me with a crack. I gasp and stumble away, but they wrap around me like arms, tightening, until all I see is fabric. The whispers have returned, and they're louder now. Many voices, locked in a debate. I don't breathe, trying to listen, but I gasp as something tightens around my waist. Then fabric is torn. I feel the breeze upon my bare skin for just a moment, before it's erased, and the curtain become a flurry again, ballooning around me.

Then the drapes settle, and the room goes quiet.

I blink, not knowing whether to thank the room or cut its curtains with my sword. But then I look down and decide on the former.

I'm wearing the most stunning gown I've ever seen. It's deep blue, with delicate white stitching, a tight bodice, a high collar, and a silky-smooth skirt that just barely kisses the floor. I admire myself in the reflection of the partially open window, blinking, questioning if this can even be real. If I could even *look* like this.

I've never—I've never felt beautiful until now.

The door opens, and I see Vander leaning against the doorframe. He nods. "That will do."

IN THE LAST few hours, I've visited the room more times than I can count. Vander hasn't stopped me. And the room . . . I think it's starting to like me. It's made me all sorts of dresses that I know I'll never wear, but I like to look at them. I like to pretend, even for a few seconds, that this life could be mine.

It isn't. I know that. It's just a break from the endless hours spent researching in the library.

That's where Vander found me a few minutes ago, far after midnight. He asked me if I would join him for some tea, and here I am, sitting on a thick balcony, knees pulled to my chest, overlooking the gardens.

"Your house is magnificent," I say, glancing at Vander.

He looks at me curiously. "They don't have homes like this on Stormside?"

A pang of sadness hits me. "They did, once." I swallow. "The ones that are left . . . they're nowhere near as grand as this."

Vander Evren might be slightly terrifying, and have a massive ego, but he has shown me kindness. He has told me more than I thought the heir of a Great House would. I turn to him. There's something I've been wondering for days now. "Have you ever been to the Land of the Gods?"

Vander blinks, as if pulled from a thought of his own. He shakes his head.

I lift a brow at him. "You are the greatest heir alive, *as you and everyone in this house has reminded me*." I roll my eyes. "Why not journey there yourself during the quest? Why not try to get the magic?"

"The gifts of the immortal cup are unpredictable," he explains. "It's the same reason humans often don't drink it for immortality. Few are strong enough to survive the Turn. For our kind, drinking the cup can lead to greatness . . . but it can just as easily become a curse. There are horror stories throughout the years that keep most of us from trying." He lifts a shoulder. "We immortals value our lives more than you do. When you live this long, death isn't an inevitability . . . It becomes something to fear." I remember when Daphne said something similar. *Daphne*.

"I didn't take you as one to be afraid, Evren," I say.

A ghost of a smile plays on his lips. "Not for me," he says. "I don't have an heir. If I fall, the future of this house and my people is uncertain. They rely on me to protect them." I get the sense he's going to have to find a match at this ball. I wonder who will be enough for this impatient, prideful immortal heir.

"Protect them from what?" I ask.

His head tilts. "So many questions, human."

Yes. So many. He doesn't answer more of them as we walk back to the library. I expect him to leave me here, as he usually does, but he walks to the center of the room. The map pours from the silver of his sword again, melting across the table. "This is the farthest I've gone," he says, pointing at a stretch of desert far east of here. The bottom of the sands Raker and I chose to avoid. "I made it all the way here . . . and turned around."

"Why?" I ask, not imagining this immortal warrior turning away from anything. Especially so close to the Land of the Gods.

He rubs at his jaw. "There is a creature there that is deadlier than all the rest. It makes men their own worst enemies."

I don't know what that means. With the expression on his face, I know Vander won't tell me. He looks haunted. Wounded.

"Why are you helping me?" I finally ask. Yet another question that has stirred in my head in the last few days. I know it isn't just Stellan. As Vander said, he's responsible for much more than just himself.

"Because the gods took something from me too," he says. "And I'd like them to pay for it."

The door whispers closed as he slips out of the room.

THE MORNING OF the ball, I'm in the library when Vander says, "Not him. He's a snake. Try *him*." He points at the list of Houses I've made.

I jump. "I didn't even hear you coming," I mumble under my breath, cursing his immortal speed and quiet.

His eyes sparkle with amusement. He offers his hand. "Let's see what you've learned, human."

I oblige him. While we get into the steps, he says, "Why did you take House Rodin off your list?" I know why he's asking. It's the house closest to the Land of the Gods.

"It serves the God of Death, according to your books," I say. "He's the god after me."

Vander seems to consider that. "Put him back on. House Rodin historically has served the God of Death, but secretly, the last few centuries, he's been working against him."

"You think he'll help me?" I say.

"If it means opposing the God of Death he hates so much . . . then yes." I nod.

And we dance. In the middle of these books, in the muted light, we dance. Vander adds some variations, but I know the pattern well by now and adapt. That seems to shock him.

"Impressive. For a human," he says.

I give a poisonous smile. "Kind. For an immortal," I say, as he twirls me. I see his sword, leaning against one of the shelves. He doesn't ever carry it unless he has to. I wonder why. I also wonder about something else.

"How can you make that map, with your sword?" Is it something I could learn with mine?

In response, Vander uses our joined hands to summon his blade. It floats right above us. Then, in mesmerizing slowness, I watch as the metal turns liquid.

The paladian peels apart, and long silver curls begin to swim around us, sparkling and casting light like they each contain galaxies.

"This is a morphblade," he explains. "A sword that can change properties." All at once, the metal melts into a half dozen daggers. Then, a mess of throwing stars. Finally, it fuses again, forming a sword, and glimmers as Vander makes its blade longer, curving it into a scythe.

"It's also a godsword," I say, and Vander's brow raises. He doesn't ask where I learned that.

"Correct. A blade can be more than one thing, Aris. They can be just as multifaceted as people, gaining skills and powers over time."

We continue our dance, with his blade still floating above us. "Just like people?" I say. "Is this you trying to convince me you're misunderstood? You're *not* the monster everyone whispers about?"

His lips twitch. Mouth already open in retort, he gently turns me for my first spin.

But whatever he was going to say dies in his throat.

He's still gripping my hand. I turn back toward him, smiling, before I see that his gaze is fixed firmly on my wrist. And the sleeve that has ridden up over it.

I pull my arm back, stumbling. His sword is still gleaming above. I've seen how easily he can bend the metal to his will.

There's no escaping him, but I try. Slowly, I step away, until my spine hits the books. My heart hammers in my chest.

Vander just looks at me. A moment passes.

Then he takes a slow step forward, with all the smooth gracefulness of a creature happening upon easy prey.

"Don't be afraid," he says, as if he can smell my fear. "If I wanted to kill you, you'd already be dead." He says it so matter-of-factly, I swallow.

He reaches toward my hand again. I should *cut his damn hand off.* But his sword is just as good as mine, and I have nowhere to go.

I don't dare breathe as his fingers grip my sleeve.

He hesitates. "Is this okay?"

No. No, it's not. It shouldn't be. Still, I might be afraid . . . but not of him. Not anymore. I nod.

He lifts my arm, so it's right between us. I close my eyes as the fabric slowly rips, down my wrist. Lower. Lower. Cold air spills across my bare skin as it's revealed, inch by inch. He stops right above my elbow. And I hear a sharp inhale.

"*Silver*" is all he says. It's enough.

I open my eyes, and he's staring at me like I'm not some lowly street rat, or thief, or blacksmith's apprentice. He's staring at me like I am something to marvel at, in this castle where everything is ancient and priceless.

"Now you see . . ." I say, my voice raw and brittle. "Now you see why I need to hide. Why my dress . . . why my dress needs to *cover*."

"No," Vander says, with pure conviction. "You don't need to hide. You never need to hide, Aris. If you want to survive, you won't hide at all. You will show them exactly what you are."

I take a shaking breath. His eyes are still on my wrist. "And what is that?"

His rough fingers gently scrape down my pulse, down my knuckles, down my markings, and I gasp. No one's ever *seen* me and marveled.

He leans down, and I can feel his breath right against my pulse.

"Magnificent," he says.

Then he pulls away. "I'll have something sent shortly." He walks out.

And I'm left gripping the wall, wondering if I've just made the biggest mistake of my life, trusting an immortal heir.

36

Hours before Heartfall, Vander has a dress delivered that is barely a dress at all.

It's clear, liquid fabric that does exactly what he intended. It shows every one of my markings, and my sword tucked against my spine. Thicker fabric barely covers small places, hardly keeping me decent.

I stare at myself in the mirror, at all the silver, glimmering through the gossamer. For as long as I can remember, I've avoided looking at my naked body. It's been a source of shame. Of sadness. Of fear.

Now I look. I *look*, and for once, I am not disgusted. I might not have had enough to eat for many years, but I am strong. This body has gotten me this far. I am capable, and maybe Vander is right. Maybe these silver markings are not a curse.

Because I'm silver, just like my dragon. Just like my sword. And they, I think, are *magnificent*.

Maybe I could be too.

I take a steadying breath, running my eyes down my dress again. Down my skin. I am *not wrong*, I think to myself. I am sky-touched.

And everyone in this castle is about to know it.

THE FESTIVITIES ARE about to begin. The estate is full of attendants who are running around, putting the finishing touches on the decorations. The gates, usually closed, are now wide open. Dragons and other majestic creatures have started landing outside them, making the ground lurch every few moments.

I walk into the stables, careful not to get my heels in the mud.

Raker's head is hanging down, his wrists shackled above him. "Tell me that awful music is going to stop," he growls, referring to the violinist who's been practicing for the last hour. I think it sounds lovely. I roll my eyes.

"Of course you don't like music."

His head snaps up. "I don't like—" His eyes widen, then narrow as he takes in the sheer dress.

"What the fuck are you wearing?" he demands.

I lift a shoulder, and the fabric shifts. "It's a dress," I say through my teeth.

He frowns. "All I see is *you*." He says it like that fact is horrifying.

I lift my chin, refusing to let him make me feel anything but beautiful right now. Anything but strong. "Vander gave it to me. He said everyone would like it."

"Did he now," he says slowly, deep voice rumbling. Even chained, he sounds fearsome. I might be afraid of him if I hadn't known him for weeks.

"Yes. Not everyone finds me as repulsive as you do."

His lip curls in disgust. Something flashes in his eyes, something I can't read. "Is that it? You've become enamored with the immortal?" He laughs, like I'm a fool.

I don't even deign to answer his question. I just take a step forward, watching his gaze slide up my dress, up my body, until his eyes meet mine.

In a flash, I produce my sword. I dig it into the ground between us and sink to his level, both hands clutching the hilt.

I don't know how this works, but I have a feeling Raker does. He's had his sword longer than I have. He has royal training.

"Swear on my sword," I say. "Swear you will help me reach the end."

Seeing the map in Vander's castle has shown me just how precarious this alliance is. Raker could betray me at any point. I need an oath.

I was right. He doesn't look shocked at all. If anything, he looks bored. He lifts a brow. "Someone learned a new trick." Fury rises. He manages to always make me feel like a fool.

I lean forward, until I'm just a breath away from him. "*Someone* is chained to a gods-damned *stable wall*. Swear on my sword."

He just blinks. "Don't trust me yet? I'm wounded."

"You would be dead if it wasn't for me."

"Same to you, Aris."

"Swear it." Spit flies with the intensity of my words, landing on him. He looks at me with nothing short of contempt. Then, his gaze shifts to my hair. It's down, loose waves to my waist. His frown deepens.

He leans forward to say right into my face, in a voice that is brutally quiet, "This might have worked, Aris, if you didn't need me. You won't survive the rest of the way without me." He says it like it is fact. He says it like an insult. He looks me up and down in a way that has me burning with anger and shame. "I've never sworn upon anyone's sword, and yours will not be the first."

We stare at each other for a moment longer.

"Fine," I say, rising and pulling my sword out of the muddy ground. I clean it on his armor, making him bare his teeth at me. "You're not the only one I'll be asking to swear on my sword. After tonight, I might not need you at all."

Then I turn around and leave him chained to the fucking wall.

VANDER EVREN KNOCKS on my door minutes to midnight.

He's wearing silver armor that matches his hair in its brilliance. Up close, I can see delicate lines carved into it, ancient symbols and sweeping designs. He gives me a quick glance that doesn't linger.

"Perfect," he says.

I've never been called such a thing in my life. He offers his arm, and I take it.

The music is getting louder as we stroll down the empty halls. Everyone is already inside. Vander told me to wait until he came to my door, to make the best entrance. I've been hearing footsteps, quiet voices, and attendants for hours. Apparently, the festivities will last well into the morning.

Nerves flurry through my stomach.

"Immortals . . . they marry, then?" I ask. He nods. "Do they . . . do they take oaths? On their swords?"

Vander does something completely unexpected—he laughs.

"Oaths are sacred," he says matter-of-factly.

"So are marriages," I say, remembering my parents' own. They didn't swear an oath. There was no ancestral sword, or weapon, to swear *upon*.

He tilts his head at me in curiosity. "Most are not" is all he says.

I can hear all the strings of the song now, a violin weaving together with other instruments I don't recognize. It's like a glimmering pulse, making my own heart quicken as we get closer and closer to the ballroom.

"Don't be afraid," he says.

"I'm not," I insist quietly.

He snorts. "I can hear your heart racing. It's a bit concerning."

I clench my jaw. Sometimes I forget how different immortals are from us. How much more powerful. And I'm about to put myself in the middle of a room filled with the worst of them. I'm about to show them the secrets across my skin. I'm about to rely on them to make it to the end of the quest.

We reach the main doors, and my chest locks up. What if I can't do it? What if I came all this way only to fail?

Vander looks over at me. "The entrance is important. Many heirs and heiresses have entire demonstrations to show their worth."

My eyes widen. "I—I don't have anything planned," I stammer, nerves spinning, making me feel light-headed.

He lifts a lazy shoulder. "You're arriving on my arm. That's enough."

I take a breath as we both face forward again. I straighten my spine. I might not feel completely confident, but I must look it. "You think highly of yourself."

"Yes," he admits. "But I'm also right."

The doors open.

And everything goes quiet.

We're standing at the top of a long marble staircase, leading into a grand ballroom. Below, hundreds of hungry, glimmering eyes are on us. Most are widened.

Even the music has stopped. With a sharp look from Vander, the musicians start again.

I stiffen. "Everyone is looking at me like they want to kill me," I murmur.

He makes an amused sound. "No, just some of the women. Most of the men are looking at you with a very different purpose."

My cheeks heat, and he smiles. He reaches down and lifts my chin, so my eyes meet his. "You are silver. Marked by the gods themselves. They should be doing nothing short of going down on their gods-damned *knees*."

I swallow. It almost hurts. "I don't see you kneeling, immortal," I say.

His smile grows. "Soon enough, human," he says. "Soon enough."

Then we start down the stairs.

I've never seen so many beautiful people in my life. These immortals are dressed in their very best, an array of dramatic fabrics that melt into a sea of glimmering color. One gown is made up of giant rose petals, the edges beaded in lilac, the rest slightly sheer. Another is made of purple gossamer that glows ethereally, as if made with those star-woven fabrics from the Traveling City. Another immortal has only a band around her chest and a flowing skirt—expertly illustrated metallic paint upon her body covers the rest. Yet another dress is made of high metal chain mail cut into an elegant form. Another is made up of a mosaic of shining onyx dragon scales.

The fabrics are like a map of Starside, showing the rarities from every corner. It's not just the women—some of the men are also dressed ornately.

Vander was right. All of these are statements, outfits crafted from rare materials to show worth and wealth, like the guests themselves are weapons to be desired and claimed.

"These are all heirs?" I say, frowning, remembering the family trees.

Vander shakes his head slightly. "No. But they're all nobles. Heirs and heiresses are preferred matches, but there aren't enough of us. Other nobles might have something advantageous to offer. Relics, perhaps. Mines. Skills in war."

I snort, earning me a horrified look from a woman in a dress made from the scales of what must be a rare, luminous fish. "So marriages are just alliances."

He looks over at me. "Precisely."

When we reach the bottom, he takes my hand and bows. Just like we practiced.

The rest of the couples give us room. There are whispers, and I hear pieces of them.

Silver, they all say, staring at my markings. Staring at my *sword*.

Human.

Silver human.

Vander and I circle each other, two hands touching, then switching. Soon, the others start to dance around us. It's dizzying, all this color everywhere. There's an emerald-green dress made up completely of gemstones. An orange one that looks like the flames of a phoenix. A blue dress of ice, the water flowing in waterfalls beneath a frozen layer. Another is violet, with cap sleeves and diamonds stitched into the fabric. The women twirl, their dresses moving with them, looking like flowers in a living bouquet.

Dancing is different with music. It's beautiful. So very beautiful. Every part of this is like a dream.

Crystal orbs of light are strung across the room, in long glimmering strands, floating above, knotting together to create chandeliers in some places, forming constellations in others. Flecks of silver light like shredded stars float around the dancing couples, like a celestial snowfall.

Glorious. This is all beyond any of my wildest imaginations for what a Starside ball might look like.

In this room, for just a few moments, I am disconnected from the rest of the world, and all my problems. They all melt away in a mesmerizing flurry of light and magic and music. I feel every step, every twist, every strum of the song. I look around, memorizing everything, promising myself I'll never forget.

For those few minutes, I'm not just surviving, I'm living. I'm *enjoying*. I'm smiling.

When the song ends, Vander's expression turns serious. He pulls me in for the last move and whispers in my ear, "Now your game begins. You have your list?"

I nod. It's all in my head.

"Good. Remember to look at the crests. Get your invitations, Aris. Your quest depends on it. I've done all I can, for Stellan."

Then he's gone. And I'm alone.

So, it begins.

The fear of not finding another partner vanishes when I immediately spin into another's embrace.

His crest is clear on his suit. So is the blade at his hip.

Heir of House Ashcroft. They have a sprawling estate in the south, surrounded by woods. He killed four of his siblings in duels to win his sword.

There are four heirs on my list. Four houses that stand between here and the Land of the Gods.

His is one of them.

"Human," he says, marveling at my hand. At the heat of it. His gaze lingers on my body. "I haven't had a human in a while."

I don't know whether to retch or reach for my sword.

Remember your purpose, I tell myself. I'm supposed to find out what he wants.

"Perhaps we can remedy that," I say, trying for my most flirtatious smile. I think he'll see right through me. That he'll read the distance I'm keeping between us more than my words, but he doesn't. Of course he doesn't. He pulls me close to him, and I swallow.

"Perhaps we can," he says. "You're on the Questral. You're *silver.* You might survive the change to immortal, should you drink the cup." His eyes drop to my chest. "I'd like to have you before and after . . . See the difference."

Oh my gods I want to vomit, but instead I say, "Help me reach the end, then."

His eyes glimmer. "You want an invitation to my estate, human?" He laughs. His eyes slide down my body again. "Perhaps I'm inclined to give it to you."

That's when I realize that he doesn't fear me . . . He just wants me. He doesn't think I'm truly capable of causing any damage . . . My access to his house doesn't bother him.

Good.

"Find me at the end of the night," he whispers into my ear, his pale hand stroking down my dress. My skin crawls.

Then I'm spun away, into another grip.

The heir to a great mine—but not a Great House. He's polite enough, but his steps aren't smooth, and I find myself almost losing the rhythm of the dance. When he spins me, I look around, searching for my targets.

I find one across the way. House Harlow. His crest is recognizable—covered in stars. I turn back to the immortal, smiling, slowly leading us in the other heir's direction. By the time the song ends, I spin, shamelessly cutting another woman off, landing in my target's arms with a gasp, as if I really didn't mean to.

If he sees through my strategy, he doesn't show it. His smile is warm.

Unlike the other two, this immortal holds me with the gentlest touch. He's tall and handsome. His skin is light brown. His eyes are kind.

The facts about him and his house flitter through my head. Only child. He inherited his sword. His house is protected by a goddess, given a temple built on its grounds.

"You are very beautiful," he says, his eyes on my face instead of my body. I smile, genuinely.

"I'm very human," I say, because my looks don't compare to any of the immortals around me.

"Yet, here you are. With these markings . . . with this sword." He gazes at my shoulder, and the blade behind it, before finding my eyes again. "I'm Magnus. What is your name?"

He's the first to ask it of me. "Aris," I say.

At that, his eyes light up. "An ancient name. A strong one."

"Is it?"

He nods. "It's fitting. Tell me, Aris. What do you seek from the quest?"

He doesn't assume I want immortality, not like Lord Ashcroft. "I want revenge," I say.

His face goes solemn. "Against the gods."

I blink, shocked. "How do you know?"

His smile is sad. "Why else would you be here? Who else has caused such destruction?"

"Destruction?"

He looks around, as if the gods themselves could be among us. "In this, humans and immortals aren't so different. The gods rule above us all, with an iron hand. They use us for their own bidding. We've lost many because of them." I know. I've now seen proof of it.

"And you never tried to overthrow them?"

His smile grows, reaching his eyes. "Your courage is refreshing. But . . . perhaps misguided. Anyone who has ever tried to face the gods has been killed, along with their entire bloodline. Or . . . worse." What's worse than death?

My throat tightens. It might put more fear in me if any of my family was left.

He studies me carefully. "I can see you're firm in your conviction."

"I am."

"And you've made it this far."

"I have."

In a flash of crystal, he unsheathes his sword. It's clear and glimmering, like the ones in the Traveling City. The light is slightly different, though. More white than silver. Slowly, he kneels before me. There are gasps around the room as everyone watches. He doesn't seem to care, or notice.

He grips the hilt of his sword in both hands, the tip scratching the floor. "You are welcome at my home any time, Aris of Stormside," he says. "Consider this your invitation."

I blink. My eyes don't leave his as he rises to his full height. Clumsily, I reach for my sword . . . and press its metal to his. A jolt goes through it, as the invitation is given.

I sheathe it, unbelieving. *I actually did it. I got at least one.*

It was almost . . . too easy.

It's hard for me to trust anything. *Anyone.* Especially an immortal heir I just met.

He must see the questioning in my look, because he says, "Any human with more courage than an immortal has a friend in me."

He bows before stepping away. The song ends.

I'm thrown into another dance.

Seven partners. Each with various degrees of conversation. Some are kind and gentle, if not a little shy. Others try to touch me far too many places. Some aren't heirs. Some are heirs of houses I don't need.

I seek out the ones I do. I smile at them until they come to ask me to dance. I make my interest known. There's no time for nerves or wariness.

I'm here for alliances. I'm here for the quest.

But—for a few more stolen seconds . . . I *enjoy this.*

The glittering fabrics. The spins, all coordinated, all perfectly executed. The music, the food, the laughter.

I love it.

It is selfish, it is foolish, but I like these sparkling things. I like this glimmering, enchanted world. This is momentary, this is not my home, but right now I revel in this experience; I drink up all of it.

I genuinely laugh at something that my partner says, before a song is over. A bite of disappointment pricks at me, that our conversation has finished, even though he's not one of the alliances I need. He gently spins me away, smile still on my face, and I crash so roughly against a chest that my breath is stolen from my lungs. I fall backward.

A massive hand catches me by the front of my bodice. Callused knuckles smooth down my breasts, long fingers gripping the fabric, pulling me back up.

Right toward a devastating face that has become far too familiar. My eyes widen.

"Don't look so disappointed, Aris," Raker says.

He's not in the mud-crusted armor I last saw him in. No, he's not in armor at all. He's in formal wear that he must have stolen. And he's clean. He must have bathed.

My rush of surprise is smothered by anger.

I can hear the whispers. Feel the eyes on us. I can't let anyone know that anything is wrong, or he will ruin everything. I plaster a smile on my face and let him take my hand as we blend into the movements.

The demon knows his steps. He must have been watching for a while. We circle each other, my eyes sharp as the blade on my back. His glare is cutting.

It's like a duel. Instead of metal, our hands meet between us.

"How did you get in here?" I demand through my teeth as he spins me around. He dips me back with an ease that makes me breathless, and that's when I see one of the guards in the corner. His head falls to the floor.

I gasp as he pulls me up, right into his chest. "You are going to ruin my plan," I spit, worry bleeding through me. I shake my head, a lock of my hair getting in my face with the movement. "Everyone is looking at you."

"No," he says, his grip tightening on my waist and hand. His eyes slip down my dress, then meet mine again. "They're not."

They're not.

I swallow, his words skipping down each vertebra of my spine like a rock thrown onto a river, casting ripples. That's what he's doing. The way he's looking at me, eyes searing in what might just be anger but might also be something else, makes heat spread through me, nerves alighting at his touch. Especially when he carefully tucks that loose lock behind my ear.

"Why are you here?" I ask, my head spinning as we continue the dance. "And *how?*" He's been chained to a wall for *days*. The last time I saw him, the shackles were still locked.

At his silence, realization sets in.

"You could break through those chains this entire time, couldn't you?" I demand, thinking of all the times I *hand-fed him*. He must have enjoyed that in his twisted, horrible mind.

Why allow himself to be chained in the first place?

He ignores my second question. "I'm here to watch you play princess," he says, eyes full of dark mirth. "I can see you were enjoying yourself . . ." He tilts his head at me, and his gaze sharpens. His voice turns cruel. "Are you that desperate for attention? Do you like having eyes on your bare skin?"

I glare at him. "Not yours," I snarl as we move as one.

He grips my hand tighter, veins going taut like they do when he holds his sword, swallowing my fingers. He glares back at me. "I'm not a simple fool, distracted by something so ordinary as a woman's body."

Ordinary. My hold tightens on his shoulder, my nails digging in, which I hope is painful.

"So, none of these women have caught your attention?"

He blinks. He looks completely serious when he says, "There are other women here?"

Ridiculous bastard.

This is going to end the moment Vander spots him. The moment people realize the four immortal guards securing the perimeter are all dead. He's ruined it. I take a look around, at this beautiful room, at this beautiful place, at the music.

I can feel his gaze following mine. I hear his huff of disdain.

"Beautiful things do not belong to us," he says. *Us.* Humans. Questral challengers, fighting for drops of magic.

"I know," I say, meaning it. "But I like to look anyway."

Only then do I realize he has slowly been moving us toward the door. No one else seems to notice. Vander Evren is on the other side of the room, attention completely fixed on a woman in a stunning gold dress. He looks enraptured. And furious. His knuckles are white against his goblet. I almost smile, seeing him so angrily transfixed. I want to see more of this woman who has completely captured his notice, but Raker drags me into the hall.

"What are you—"

Before I can say a word, Raker has me in his arms, and there's the slam of doors behind us. We're in a crimson room.

I slip from his hold and am about to knee him in the groin when he grips behind my leg and spins me so my spine hits the wall.

"Cute," he says, glowering down at me, his hand still curled beneath my knee, pulled in an angle against his body.

To anyone walking in, we would look like a couple. A couple doing anything but glaring at each other, baring our teeth at each other.

"What are you *doing*?" I growl.

"He is parading you."

I scoff. "Do you think I care? Do you think I have any remaining shame?"

"You should."

"Why? I'll be dead soon anyway, right?" I say, throwing his own words back at him.

He doesn't like that. His eyes narrow. He leans in, opening his mouth to no doubt insult me further, but then he pauses. He ducks slowly, nose nearly touching my jaw.

Then, he goes rigid. "I can smell him all over you," he snarls. His eyes are alight with nothing short of fury.

"If I didn't know better, I would say you were jealous," I counter.

"Good thing you know better," he growls, our lips just inches apart. We're both breathing too quickly, both fuming.

Just at that moment, the doors fly open.

It's the heir of House Harlow. *Magnus*. He must have heard my protests. Or maybe he saw me get shoved into this room. His hand is on his sword. He's here to defend me.

It's almost endearing.

Raker will kill him without a second thought. And though I have no interest in him whatsoever, his is the only oath I've secured. Also, he did seem halfway decent, which seems to be a rarity in this castle.

We don't need the entire ball up in arms.

So I do what I think is the best solution.

I take Raker's face in my hands and pull his mouth toward mine.

His eyes widen.

Widen.

We have almost been ripped apart by demons. We have survived a deadly mist and bog, crawling with beasts. We have gone days without food or water. We have faced countless dangers.

Never once have I seen Raker seem this terrified.

His arm juts out against the wall, stopping my lips half an inch from his. He bares his teeth and glares at me.

Stubborn idiot.

My lips slip down his neck instead, and I feel him tense beneath me. "Pretend," I whisper against his skin, and if anything, he stills even more. But he doesn't back away. No. He moves closer.

I groan, pretending but also not being able to help myself, as I breathe in the fresh smell of his incredible, intoxicating soap. I'm going to need to ask him what's in it, if we get out of here alive. Whatever it is, it's my favorite.

I blame the soap for what I do next—which is to lean in very slowly, making my intent known. Waiting for him to pull back. When he doesn't, just like in the underground under the fire demon's influence, I press my lips against his throat and suck against his pulse.

Fuck. His soap is like a drug. I want more. His heartbeat races beneath my tongue. In anger, I'm sure. I hear a sharp inhale, and ready myself for Raker to rip away, to take a step back. To not, in fact, *pretend*.

But then his hand touches my spine, ever so slightly, pulling me toward him like a beckoning and I shamelessly taste him, stroking his heated skin with my tongue, nipping and sucking, until my head is spinning. Heat floods through me. This is too far. I pull away, miming, but not touching, not anymore.

Until I feel his fingers curl tighter around the back of my knee. My leg is still up. I don't know what's wrong with me. Maybe it's the wine. Maybe it's the glittering dizziness of this night. Maybe it's the soap? But I arch my back against the wall, leaning into him just the slightest bit.

He leans in too, caging me in. Pressing himself against me, right between my legs. And that's when I feel it.

He's hard.

My eyes fly back up to his. He's pinning me with his gaze, as if *daring*, just *daring* me to say anything. I don't. All I do is slowly drag myself against his considerable length, blood roaring at the friction, at his *size*, as both of us take a shared breath—

Steps sound across the room, and the doors close again.

Raker moves so quickly away from me that I have to grasp the wall for purchase so as not to slip down it.

Halfway to an insult, I freeze, then gently peel my arms away from the sticky wall. They're covered in crimson.

"Who would paint right before a ball?" I ask, frowning down at the dark red all over my dress and skin, the same red coating the rest of the walls and the hand Raker used to keep our lips apart.

"That's not paint," Raker says, staring at his palm.

Our eyes meet in an instant.

"Huh," Raker says. He almost sounds impressed.

"What?"

"Vander Evren is a bloodbane."

The click of a door has us both turning around.

Vander is standing there holding the head of one of his guards, the one that Raker so cavalierly slayed. "And what do you know about bloodbanes, human?"

37

I'm not breathing. Raker doesn't look shaken in the slightest. He shrugs. "I know that you're miserable creatures sustained by blood. You drink it. You paint your walls with it. You probably fuck in it. You have to be around it, all the time, or you'll go mad with hunger."

My eyes widen, looking at Raker as if he's just lost his mind. We are humans. Standing in front of an immortal *bloodbane*. A word I'd only ever heard spoken in legends.

Vander's grin is a mixture of amused and poisonous.

Raker keeps fucking going. "Mortal blood is preferable to immortals, isn't it? Not tainted by magic?"

I swallow, and Vander's eyes go straight to my throat. But he does not move a muscle. "As I said before," he tells me, "if I wanted to kill you, you would already be dead." The veins on his hands stick out more than usual. His face is severe; he looks almost pained. Like he's using every shred of his immortal strength to stand still. The words grind out of him. "If you'll excuse me, I need to feed. And . . . as much as I would like to keep you alive . . . whatever you two were doing in here has your blood *pounding*." He's looking at me. His eyes flash with nothing short of hunger as he stares at my neck. The skin there prickles. "Get out of this room, Aris," he rasps.

I don't need to be told again. Almost to the door, I hear him say, "Bathe. Change. Then we'll speak to the heirs."

It takes two baths and endless scrubbing to get the blood off my arms. Even then, I can still feel it on me.

I can't believe we didn't smell it before, in the room. I was too caught up with Raker's gods-damned *soap* to notice. Not just his soap, really.

Vander was right that day when he said I should be running for the gates. But he was also right when he said he could kill me in an instant if he wanted to.

I'm not going anywhere. Not until I get the invitations I need.

Vander didn't order Raker to be chained again, perhaps knowing it would be useless. He's waiting in my room when I walk out in nothing but a towel. I go still—but he doesn't turn to face me. He's looking at the walls, unimpressed. His gaze narrows on everything, as if he is finding fault after fault. I roll my eyes at him.

On my bed sits another gown. I smooth my hand across the wall in a silent thank-you to the mysterious powers of the house before slipping back into the bathroom to put it on.

This dress is lilac, just like the flowers I saw near the Prism Pass. Now that I don't have to hide, it has a low-cut bodice that's curved and pointed at each end like a scythe, and a silk skirt. I love it.

The only thing I don't love about it are all the ties in the back. I'm able to get the ones at the base of my spine, but then I can't reach any higher. I try for several minutes in vain to do it myself, before giving up. I walk out of the bathroom, only to find Raker still frowning at everything.

"I need—I need your help."

He doesn't move an inch.

I roll my eyes and turn. "Please, I just—These cursed corsets . . ."

His voice is punishing. "If you think I'm going to *tie your dress*—"

I sigh. "Fine. I'll ask Van—"

The name isn't out of my mouth before he's roughly tugging me back by the strings of my corset, squeezing my ribs, choking the words out of me.

I whip my head back to glare at him.

He's scowling. "Let's get this over with." He starts to tie the strings, muttering curses and something about why dresses are *so damned complicated.*

It almost makes me smile, then seize as he squeezes the air out of my lungs again. I laugh ruefully. "Famed knight can cut down an entire army without a mark on his armor . . . but can't tie a corset." I turn to see him glaring down at the strings as if they have personally insulted him. "I'm sure you've *untied* plenty of them."

At that, his eyes slowly drag up to meet mine. They are hard as steel. "Do you want me to untie it, Aris?" he asks, his voice a low rumble along my bones.

I stop breathing. I think about him pressed up against me. His length between my legs. How it felt to writhe against it. My throat goes dry, remembering. *Imagining.*

I'm dragged out of the thought by Raker roughly pulling on the strings with far too much force, choking me again, like he's taking out his frustration on them.

When he's done, he doesn't even look at me before striding toward the doors.

"Don't kill anyone," I say, still fighting for breath. Anyone *else*, I guess.

He looks over his shoulder at me. His eyes slip down my dress, gaze snagging on my chest, which I can feel spilling from the top of my bodice since he *tied it so damned tightly.* "Be happy if I don't kill *everyone*," he says, before slamming the door behind him.

VANDER HAS GATHERED some of the heirs in a room. He's picked the ones most likely to sympathize with my cause—including Magnus and the other three who I had previously marked, given the locations of their estates. I've already danced with all of them. The ball is still going. I can hear the trill of music and laughter just down the hall.

Raker and I stand in the room as the heirs argue. They keep going on and on about a *prophecy* without naming it. They keep talking about a *paladin that was promised.*

"What's the prophecy?" I finally demand. The room goes quiet.

Sixteen glittering eyes fix on me. Not one of the heirs speaks.

Finally, Vander sighs. "We can't tell you, human," he says.

I frown. "Why?"

"Prophecies are heirlooms, passed along and earned like blades. It would break the vow of our swords. Even if we wanted to tell you, we couldn't," Vander says.

"And we don't," Lord Ashcroft says lazily.

Fine. I don't care about a fucking prophecy. I just want to get an invitation to the closest estate possible.

"Why are you arguing about it now?" I ask. In front of us. I look at Vander, my eyes saying, *I thought we were trying to get me alliances?*

His eyes drift away, and that's when I blink.

"Wait. Do you think . . . I have something to do with it?"

I expect them to laugh in my face. To roll their glimmering eyes at the fact that some mortal thought *she* was the paladin that was promised.

But instead of ridicule . . . I'm met with silence.

I back up a step. I look to Vander, silently pleading him to tell me I'm wrong. Finally, he does meet my gaze again. But it looks sad.

Whatever the prophecy is, it can't be fucking good.

Still . . . it's apparently a good enough outcome for some of these heirs that Vander is bringing it up now . . .

As a reason to help me.

"We don't know for certain if it's about you," Lord Ashcroft finally says, as if he heavily doubts it. But that's confirmation enough.

They think there's a chance I fulfill this mysterious prophecy.

My blood goes cold. Is that why the gods are after me? The God of Death, in particular?

Do I actually have a chance at killing the gods, like I promised?

Lord Ashcroft shakes his head. "I don't believe it. The prophecy can be interpreted in different ways." With one last long, lingering look at me, he strides out of the room.

Vander looks at the door, shoulders tense. Then he turns back to the rest of the heirs. "If it isn't her, then why is there a bounty? Why do they want her dead?"

Magnus looks deep in thought. "The gods are thorough. They'll eliminate anything they believe fits. It doesn't mean it's her." He seems hopeful it's not. Which again, makes me *desperate to know what it is*.

There are murmurings of agreement.

"But if it is?" Vander's voice silences the room. "Do you want to take that risk? Not helping her now?"

More murmurs. More whispers.

More debate. One by one, heirs walk out of the room, one ignoring me, one shooting me an apologetic glance, one outright ogling, until only four remain.

One is Magnus. "You know where I stand, Aris," he says, saying my name just as gently as he held me. Then, he reaches into his perfectly pressed jacket . . . and pulls out a necklace made of diamonds the size of the town weaver's buttons. He offers it to me.

My lips part. It sparkles so brightly, my eyes hurt looking at it The cost of the silver chain alone—

"I—I can't accept this."

"Please," he says, his voice so tender it reminds me of dancing beneath strings of starlight. "I insist."

I nod, if only not to be rude.

"May I?" he asks.

I nod again, and he walks around me. His fingers lightly brush the nape of my neck as he clasps the lock. I don't feel anything at all. No chill down my spine. No flurry in my stomach. "There," he says, admiring me. "Now you shine brighter than the stars and the moon combined." He bows. "The invitation to my House is always open. I hope to see you again soon, Aris."

With that, he walks out of the room.

I frown, still dazed by the gift, wondering if it's some part of this Heartfall Courting Ball, when another heir approaches me. His eyes are dark as night, just like his hair. His skin is pale. Lord Rodin—the heir of the House Vander says is secretly working against the God of Death. *The one I need the most.*

He looks me up and down with relish. His blade has a black stone in its hilt, and its edges are slightly brighter than the rest of its metal, as if it's recently been sharpened. He buries it into the ground before me. "You have my oath, human," he says.

And my knees nearly buckle in relief as I press my blade to his.

I don't need any others now. His estate is the closest to the Land of the Gods.

I actually fucking did it.

Relief wins out against the revulsion of his heated gaze.

The last heir other than Vander is tall, and handsome, with light-colored hair and piercing green eyes. He's the heir of House Drake. Instead of a sword on his back, he wears a bow and a quiver of glimmering arrows, tipped with a glittering metal I don't recognize. He turns to me and bows. "I will offer my invitation . . . if you promise to visit me, should you survive the journey. And if you consider my hand."

My hand. He wants to be . . . matched. I can tell from the look on Vander's face that this is a big deal. An immortal heir . . . considering a human worthy of his House at all.

My brows slightly lift. He *is* handsome. I'm sure he would make an excellent match for anyone. But I can't offer anything resembling a future.

Still—I nod. Because even though I already have the invitation I need, the end of the quest is uncertain. I'll take as many promises as I can get.

His green eyes sear into mine. Slowly, very slowly, he lifts my hand to his lips, smoothing them against the silver markings. Then he buries his bow into the ground. It glimmers with the oath. I press my metal to his and feel it like a whisper through my blood.

He raises to his significant height and turns to Vander. "I'm leaving," he says. "She's the only one I want." He looks over at me, glance heavy but not ogling. "I'll see you soon, Aris."

Then he and his bow vanish.

I turn to see Raker still glaring at the place he left. That glare makes its way to me. "You didn't have to make every oath," he says.

I frown, shocked by his anger. "These oaths could make the difference between life or death." He doesn't look convinced. "They could be the difference between making it to the gods or not."

That doesn't do anything to dim Raker's fury. Of course not. He hates it here. He hates every one of these heirs. I can almost understand why. He's a warrior, from lowly birth. Seeing these heirs, perhaps he doesn't think they earned their armor and metal. Not the way he did, on countless battlefields.

"And you?" I ask, turning to the immortal bloodbane. "Ready to get on your knees?"

Vander smiles, recalling our conversation just hours ago. "In time, human," he says. "In time." He looks at my blade. It's twinkling with the new invitations. "You know how to summon me, if needed."

I nod.

Suddenly, Ethel steps into the room. She's holding a magnificent scabbard crafted of Starside steel. Stories have been carved into its metal, endless etchings that must have taken decades to make.

She gives it to Vander, turns her nose up in my direction, and strides back out of the room.

He hands it to me.

A pinch forms between my brows, and I don't even open my mouth, unable to find words, carefully taking it.

Vander smiles, sharp teeth gleaming. "No one, not even a blacksmith, will be able to summon your sword when it's in here."

It's invaluable.

"Thank you," I say, the words breaking. He's helped me more than I ever could have expected.

"Human," Vander says, the word spoken with a shadow of appreciation that wasn't there before. "As much as your attitude speaks otherwise, you are not immortal. Portaling with your sword will expend significant energy." He looks over at Raker warily. "Especially with someone else. Your invitations will grant you hospitality at the Houses you travel to. Eat. Rest. And . . . I hope you complete your quest."

"So do I," I say, nodding my thanks again.

"The other heirs will be ratting you out as we speak, to gain favor with their gods. Your journey will be more perilous than ever. Go."

We do.

As we get farther from the music, and the laughter, and the wonders of this mysteriously long courting ball, part of me, that *pretending part*, withers.

That isn't my life, I think, passing by the beautiful woman in the transcendent gold dress, the one Vander was watching so intently. It's someone else's. It's hers.

This beautiful moment will never be mine again.

As we fetch the rest of our things, Raker remains quiet.

"What?" I finally ask once we're outside, striding toward the gates, his silence unnerving. It's like he's slipped back into who he used to be weeks before. The knight crafted in stone, the monster behind the mask.

He doesn't say anything. Of course he doesn't.

We pass the threshold, where Vander portaled me in, and I can't take it anymore. I whirl to face him, throwing my hands up in frustration. "Clearly, you don't agree with my plan. Is it just because I came up with it? You're used to making the plans, not following them?"

My anger seems to call to his, because he finally speaks. "You give yourself away so easily?" he spits. "I would have thought someone like you would have a bit more pride." He says the words with clear derision. As if he has any right to judge me. As if he has any right to *me* at all.

"Why do you care?" I demand, yelling, my voice spilling through the empty grounds.

I can't see his face. It's beneath the hood *again*. His hands are in fists. His entire body is coiled tight.

Then, in a flash, he's pressing me against those open metal gates.

My mouth goes dry, remembering how he felt against me, without armor on. How he *glared* as his body responded to mine. How he hated it. How he leaned in just the slightest bit anyway. How his eyes seared into steel as I ground against every inch of him.

My blood pounds with need, remembering. Waiting to see that firm, well-practiced control snap once more, for good.

His hands are on my hips. He's staring down at me, curved low, and no. Now that I've seen him, I don't want to look at shadows. I reach up and tear his hood back—and he lets me. He's not wearing his mask. My heart stutters, just seeing his face. My voice is a whisper. "Why do you care?" I ask again, and I wait. I wait, and when he doesn't say anything, I place my hands on his, not knowing if I want to remove them, or just feel them under mine.

He grips my hips harder. My breath hitches. His eyes darken into ink, bleeding into mine. Slowly, they drop to my neck, and the diamonds sparkling there. "Take this off," he demands, instead of answering.

I scoff. "Are you back to ordering me again?"

"It means more than you are aware of." Again, I am reminded of my limited immortal education compared to a king's knight.

I lift my chin. "And what if I don't care?"

At that, his eyes blaze. "You should care about being claimed, Aris. I would have thought that was exactly what you were hoping to avoid."

Claimed? I rip the necklace off and shove it at his chest, pushing him away. "How convenient that you tarnish every shred of happiness that comes my way. Not everyone wants to be as miserable as you are, you know."

I nearly slip out of his grip, but his gleaming gray eyes keep me still.

"This?" he demands, holding up my jewelry like it's worthless and not valuable enough to feed villages for centuries. "*This* makes you happy? Shiny, pretty things?" He shakes his head in near disgust. His head leans low. His gaze slips down my dress and back up again. "I've seen you, beneath these fabrics. You don't need diamonds." My lips part with a gasp.

He must have heard what Magnus said—how the diamonds now made me shine "brighter than the stars and moon combined."

You don't need diamonds.

The words echo through my mind, and I hate him for it. Because he doesn't just get to decide to say something like that after insulting me.

We glare at each other, chests heaving. He gets closer, as if to say something else, something he wants me to hear clearly.

Then his gaze flickers to the side, toward the shining gates at my back, and I watch him shudder. *Shudder.*

I turn, wondering what could make a warrior as fearsome as Raker flinch, but there's nothing there. Nothing but his reflection.

"I wouldn't want to take away any more of your happiness," he says, dropping the necklace into my hands.

He turns to go, but my voice stops him. "I told you. The only thing I care about is reaching the end of this." I shrug. "And the promises mean nothing. I don't plan on living that long anyway."

"So you've said."

"So *you've said*," I say through my teeth. "Almost exactly." I tilt my head at him. "Or have you changed your mind about my chances of survival?"

He says nothing.

He doesn't need to. I did it. I got Raker medicine. He's recovered. I got invitations that will get us to the Land of the Gods in mere days.

I push off the gates, shaking away these feelings that are making it way too hard to focus.

The quest is all that matters. It must come first.

And now more than ever, I see a path to the end of it. Breaking up the portaling by going smaller distances might be what's best for my energy, but I don't care. I don't want to waste another moment. My mind is full of my purpose as I dig my sword into the dirt. Power pulls me down, as if something is being drained not only from my metal but from my very bones. "House Rodin," I whisper.

Raker's hand grips my elbow—and then we're gone.

If Raker is surprised by our destination, he doesn't show it. If anything, he seems pleased we're skipping all the Houses but one. In any case, I don't give a shit.

Not when he's been so unpleasant, even after everything. Does he think I want to beg these men for their oaths? Does he think it pleases me to make promises I almost certainly can't keep?

The black iron gates we landed in front of begin to part by themselves, emitting a high-pitched howl.

And it's immediately clear that this house is meant to honor the God of Death, at least in appearances.

House Rodin is crafted of pure dark obsidian. The walkway is lined in towering statues. All with the same subject. A man with every muscle imaginable, wielding a menacing sword.

Fear inches through my blood. This is the god that wants my head. The same one who is collecting stolen brides.

Is that really what he looks like? Or is it a generous rendering?

The moment we reach the palace doors, they open, just like the gates. An attendant is waiting for us.

The immortal's posture is stiff. She looks like she exists in a perpetual state of terror.

"Welcome to House Rodin," she says, bowing low. "It's been—it's been so long since we've had guests."

I smile tightly, unease already sliding through me.

"Are you hungry? There will be a feast, of course, but—"

"Feast?" I ask.

She nods. "As is custom for Great Houses. All guests are welcomed with the best we have to offer. Feasts. Gifts. Our most ancient wines."

It's still the early hours. I shake my head. "Just a place to rest would be good," I say. Raker is silent beside me.

"Of course. I—I will show you to the guest quarters."

The attendant hurries up a set of onyx stairs, looking back at the door as if waiting for the lord of the house to suddenly appear. He doesn't, and she rushes to show us to our rooms, which are right next to each other. I don't know whether to be relieved or disappointed. The moment she can, she scurries away again.

I turn to Raker, only to find him already striding down the hall, instead of going inside his room.

"Where are you going?" I snap. He doesn't respond.

My eyes narrow on his back as I follow. "Are we back to this? You ignoring me?" Apparently, yes, because he doesn't answer.

I sigh, following him. This castle is bathed in shadows. I find myself not rushing to be alone in my quarters. I watch as Raker tries door after door, peering inside, until he finally finds a room that holds his interest.

It's a library. For how desolate and dark this house is, the library is full of art. Shelves of ancient books fill the generous space. Tapestries line the walls. They all feature the same subject—the God of Death. Unlike the statues, these have color.

The God of Death is silver-haired, tall, and facing a swarm of monstrous creatures. His sword glows just as much as his hair does. Every tapestry is the same. The great God of Death on top of a pile of bodies, or surrounded by severed heads, or sitting on a throne of bones. A statue of him sits in the corner, towering and intimidating. Is it life-sized? I study it carefully, turning my head. My lips purse.

"You know . . . he's kind of hot," I say.

Raker shoots me a scathing look.

I lift a shoulder. "What? He is."

His hood is still down and I watch his eyes narrow. "Diamonds and death. That's what gets you going. What a remarkable pairing." He clearly finds me ridiculous.

I give him a sympathetic look. "Don't be intimidated by a statue, Raker. It's unbecoming."

He glares at me.

I slowly walk over to him, eager to ruin his day as he has ruined mine. "Or . . . are you afraid? Is that it?" I take another step.

"I'm not afraid of anything," he says.

I laugh. "You looked pretty terrified at the idea of kissing me." I remember how his eyes widened when I gripped his face. When he realized what I was going to do.

His look could make an entire field of wildflowers wither. "I don't kiss anyone."

I raise a brow at him. "As a rule?" I say it as a joke, but he doesn't reply. My smile fades. "You're not kidding." I frown. "You don't . . . you've never bedded anyone?"

He looks at me as if I'm stupid. "Of course I have. But fucking and kissing are two different things." He looks utterly revolted as he seems to imagine the act. "I would never let anyone get that close to me."

The corners of my lips twitch. "You act like kissing is more intimate than having sex."

"It is."

"You make it sound repulsive."

"Isn't it?"

I smile fully now. "It isn't so bad." Not that I have much experience. I only kissed one boy, once, as a teenager. It was fine, but not good enough that I ever rushed to do it again.

Raker's eyes narrow. He looks like he's about to say something, then thinks better of it and turns around, toward the table.

"The map," Raker says, clearly desperate to change the conversation. He points at a pile of parchment and pieces of charcoal. Still shaking my head in amusement, I begin to draw.

"We're here," I say, drawing the estate, then the desert, with the flaming city at the corner of it. *City on Fire*. Not far from a place that doesn't have a name, only endless bolts of lightning.

"We just have to make it through the desert. And hope the cavalry doesn't find us before we reach the Land of the Gods."

He nods. He doesn't look worried at all.

"Vander said a beast lives there. One that will make us enemies of ourselves."

He just looks at me. His gaze repeats, *I'm not afraid of anything.*

My glare says, *Cocky bastard.*

Then, I yawn. I didn't sleep at all last night, and Vander was right. Portaling with the blade has sucked away my energy. "Fine. We'll leave from the edge of these gardens first thing tomorrow," I say, pushing off the edge of the table. "I'm going to get some rest."

I LIED.

The blacksmith in the Traveling City said one of the Great Houses has a forge, run by someone who might know which god my blade once belonged to.

Lord Rodin's sword was freshly sharpened, evenly so, with precision, and limited scratch marks along the metal. By a grinding stone, I would guess.

A device found in a forge.

It's still a theory. I could be wrong. But something tells me the ancient blacksmith is here.

I just need to find him.

The attendants aren't helpful. The moment I spot a few and open my mouth, they scuttle away. You would think the God of Death himself roamed these halls, hanging anyone who dared look him in the eye.

Maybe he does, I think, as I creep down a set of stairs. A forge needs fire. So far, I haven't been successful searching the top floors. Maybe he's below.

For the first few flights, all I feel is endless chill. Then . . . the temperature changes. It becomes warm when it should be getting colder. I follow the mysterious heat, until I hear it—pounding metal. Like a melody.

"Pass me the iron, would you?"

I do. I'm only ten, and convincing Stellan to let me help him in his forge is the biggest accomplishment of my life.

He looks at me and shakes his head, frowning at my wide, curious eyes. "You'll be bored in a week."

I take not being bored as a personal challenge, especially when shadowing him becomes monotonous. I fill the silence between pounding metal with questions.

"Have you ever made a blade so big no one could hold it?"

"No."

"Have you ever poured honey into the burning metal, just to see what would happen?"

"What? No."

"Have you ever—"

"Here," he says, handing me his tools. "Why don't you keep yourself busy by trying all these ideas of yours?"

I blink down at them. My excitement turns to worry. "But what if I fail?" I ask. Would he let me back into the forge? Would he . . . would he put me out on the streets? I don't have anywhere else to go . . . I try to return the tools. "Maybe I shouldn't try."

He doesn't take them back. All he says is, "The only way you fail is if you don't."

I open an iron door, and a blacksmith turns his focus away from a blade to me. His brow furrows. Then his eyes light with that all-too-familiar terror. "Does he know you're here?" he asks, looking around.

"Who?" I say, even though I'm almost sure I know.

"Lord Rodin."

I think back to the man with the dark, oily hair. He didn't seem that intimidating, though I only interacted with him for a few minutes.

"I'm a guest," I say, but clearly that doesn't cut it. He stands as if to close the door in my face, when a tiny voice sounds nearby.

"Who is it, Dad?" Before the man can speak, a small child with hair black as night darts forward. He looks at me and tilts his head in wonder. "I've never seen you before," he says.

The man leans down and whispers words I can't hear. The boy unhappily walks away. Then the blacksmith looks at me. His eyes are full of irritation . . . but also fear. He's afraid for his son.

"You have to leave," he says, looking around as if the walls have eyes and ears.

"But—"

"Come back at midnight." His gaze lands on the sword over my shoulder, tucked in my new scabbard. His eyes sharpen, just at seeing the hilt.

I slowly ease it out of its sheath so he can see its metal. "Have you—have you seen my blade before?"

The immortal blacksmith's jaw works. For a moment, I don't think he'll answer me. Then, as if the words will cost him, he says, "I have."

Hope rises through my chest. I open my mouth.

"Tonight," he barks, before slamming the door shut.

38

Instead of a feast downstairs, trays of food are delivered to our chambers. It's almost as if the attendants saw us snooping and are encouraging us to stay in our quarters. I eat my dinner quickly, anticipation building in my bones. I marvel at my blade, the metal glistening.

"What secrets do you hold, Stellaris?" I say, running my finger down her metal. Her glimmer is like a wink.

The drawers are full of useful clothing, like pants and long-sleeved shirts better suited for the rest of the journey, which is good because I can barely breathe in this dress, especially after dinner.

"*Fuck*," I say, after my third try at getting it off. Raker tied it unreasonably tight. I could ask an attendant for help, I guess.

I peek my head out into the hall, but it's empty. Even if it wasn't . . . they all seem terrified. I doubt anyone will help me. My gaze drifts to the door beside mine.

This is a bad idea. I know it is. Still, the lack of air in my lungs wins out against my better judgment.

My knock echoes through the hall. My hand is still raised when it swings open, surprise forcing me still.

There he is. Hoodless.

Shirtless.

I swallow. I try very hard not to drop my gaze from his face.

He doesn't try at all. Raker's eyes slip down to my dress, and the way the top is hanging down from the few unraveled ties I was able to reach. He blinks slowly.

"I need help," I explain hastily. I turn around and show him the back, looking at him from over my shoulder. "You tied it so tight I can barely breathe."

With a sigh, he drags his massive hand down his face. That *hand*. Why am I admiring a *hand*? It's like a work of art, though. Callused in all the right places. Strong. Perfect for wielding a sword. Perfect . . . for other tasks . . .

I need to fucking get it together.

He shakes his head. I am clearly the biggest inconvenience he has ever come across. But instead of telling me to find someone else to help, or somewhere else to be entirely, he opens his door the slightest bit. An invitation.

I slip inside before he can slam the door in my face.

"Your quarters are much smaller than mine," I say, looking around.

"Are they," he says, not sounding shocked by that fact at all.

Raker's eyes drift across my neck, as if marking the absence of the diamond necklace currently on my bedside table. Something about his air seems entirely too pleased.

I give my back to him.

For a moment, he doesn't move at all. I wonder if I'll just stand here like a fool, waiting. But just when I'm going to look over my shoulder to see what's taking him so long, I feel his warm hands against my skin.

I go very still.

My entire awareness narrows to that one place. His moves are careful, like he's trying to touch as little of me as possible, but when his callused fingers finally scrape against my spine, all my nerves ignite in a rush. I hold my breath. Then, I hear the first stitch come undone.

Air kisses my back as the bodice is opened slowly, slowly. His fingers are long, battle-hewn, but featherlight across my skin. I'm breathing again, and it sounds too loud. Too labored. The fabric is brushing against my all-too-sensitive chest. This room feels smaller than it did moments ago.

His rough knuckles gently graze my back as he works intently on one spot. "It's caught," he says harshly, as if to explain why it's taking so long. And I've never been so damned grateful for a caught thread.

Carefully, he tries to undo it, every time his skin scraping mine. I can hear his breathing now. It's almost as loud as my own. He ducks to get a better view, and I feel the heat of his exhale on the back of my neck. My skin prickles everywhere.

He growls in irritation, and in a quick, frustrated movement—

Fabric tears. My lips part in a gasp. I look over my shoulder to see him glaring at the corset like it's an enemy across a battlefield. He ripped it by accident. I wonder if it was his strength or his temper that did it.

"It's ruined now," I say lightly, knowing I have little use for this dress during the rest of our travels. "Might as well rip the rest."

I didn't mean for my words to be so heavy, or to come out so breathy, but slowly, Raker's gaze slides up the bare expanse of my back, before crashing into mine.

And there's something in that look—something half crazed. Something dangerous. Something wanting.

This is just another duel. Another test of wills—of testing limits. Of seeing who will bend first, who will concede, who will win. But neither of us looks away. Neither backs down.

His hands grip the fabric.

Then, eyes never leaving mine, he tears the bodice right down the middle.

I suck in air. My hands fly up to catch the front, barely managing to cover my breasts.

That's where Raker's gaze goes, to the parts the fabric doesn't conceal. At the heat in his look, I let the fabric slip.

And his eyes go wholly black as he studies me hungrily, with a focus that leaves me breathless, until they finally meet mine—and they are *blazing*, brimming with emotions I can't even name. Slowly, achingly slowly, his knuckles slide down every inch of my spine, lingering, scraping, and my skin is on fire. My nipples are straining beneath my fingers. The want within me has turned into a wildfire.

Then, just when that heat has reached the center of me, just when I wonder how far he will go and how far I will let him, his hand stops. His brow creases.

He drops my gaze to look down at my skin. My awareness flares to life once more as he goes deathly still.

He stops breathing. The air seems sucked out of this entire room.

My scars. He's seen the twisted, mangled mess of them. I stare straight ahead, refusing to look at him.

His voice is hard as steel. "Who did this to you?"

So is mine. "You did."

Those two words sit between us, and I feel the air shift. I *feel* his confusion and wrath. His voice is pure fury. *"I did not."*

I whirl around to face him. "You might as well have." Rage pounds through my blood as I tilt my head. "You don't remember, do you?"

He says nothing. He's just looking at me, and the tear that has slipped down my cheek, and he has the nerve to look *outraged*.

He might not remember, but I do. I remember so well, I can practically taste the bitterness of the moment on my tongue.

"That day, it was raining. I climbed the fence to train, to use the guards' practice sets while they were inside. So that I would even . . . so that I would even have a *chance*." A chance at the Questral. A chance at my revenge.

My hands are trembling with resentment, remembering.

I was about to jump off the wall, to test my landing, when a hand fisted the back of my shirt and pulled me back.

My breath nearly left me as I was shoved back into a wall. A sword was at my throat. That glittering, beautiful blade.

"You're not supposed to be here," a brutal voice said.

I looked up and through the rain I saw two gray eyes set in a battle helmet, staring down at me with nothing short of hatred.

I remember being struck by the depths of that hatred.

He didn't know me at all. He didn't know me enough to hate me.

"I—I'll leave," I said, my voice barely making any sound. I knew what happened to trespassers. They were imprisoned—or worse. Stellan couldn't know what I was up to. If he suspected at all that I was training for the Questral, he would find a way to stop me.

His grip on my shoulder tightened, even as he sheathed his sword. He turned toward the training camp to alert his knights.

My hand jutted out in desperation and wrapped around his wrist. He jolted, as if truly shocked anyone would dare touch him.

"*Please,*" I said, willing to beg. "Please. Let me go. You'll never see me again, I promise."

His eyes locked onto mine for just a moment, and that hatred . . . it seemed to grow. I knew what he was about to do. I could feel it.

In one last attempt to stop him, I said. "Please. Have mercy."

Mercy. That simple word seemed to seal my fate. His eyes hardened of any emotion at all. He dragged me to the other guards himself.

They hauled me away kicking and screaming, the tips of my boots cutting lines through the mud.

I was thrown in a cell for two days without food or water. Then, on the third day, after I refused to take off my shirt for punishment, knowing what they would find . . . they sliced me through my clothing, with rusted knives. They pinned me down on my stomach as I screamed. . . . and carved me up like an animal. The only reason they didn't see my markings is by the time they got through the fabric, they were covered by my blood.

All their names. *Their names.* They carved them there, on the lowest point of my spine, saying something about wanting to see them while they had me the next day.

The only reason the next day didn't arrive was because Stellan did first. He found me half dead, offered new weapons for the guards in exchange for my release, and carried me home in his arms. I made some excuse about having been caught stealing. He never asked about it again.

I've never forgotten the hatred in Harlan Raker's eyes. The mercilessness.

It's the same hatred I see now.

I get the sense it isn't directed toward me. I wonder if he recognizes the names. He was head of the king's guard, even then, two years ago. They were *his* warriors. He backs away from me a step, expression shifting. "I—I didn't know they would do that to you."

No. I'm not letting him retreat. I'm not letting him not face this. I take a step forward. "Really? What did you think they would do?" Another step. "You knew you were leading me to my death. You knew, and you refused to have mercy. You refused to let me go."

I grit my teeth. My hands are shaking, so I curl them into fists.

I don't allow my voice to tremble. I don't allow any more tears to fall as I say, "So now you know. You *know* and you never won't. I hate you just as much as you hate me. And if for any moment, any *second*, I forget"—I slide my fingers across the raised markings, the names—"I have all these scars to remind me."

I don't even look at him as I gather my dress to my chest and leave his room.

That night, lying in my bed in the shreds of my dress, my mind replays those memories long buried. The laughs echo through my mind. The men jeering as I screamed, like every letter carved into my skin was an accomplishment. They cheered as they branded me, claimed me. As they planned to claim me further. I remember when the pain became too much and I lost consciousness, face against the dirt my blood had turned to mud.

He's the reason I was sent there in the first place. Even if he didn't mean for it to happen, *it did*.

If by any miracle this does not kill me, I will find those men, I think. I never saw their faces . . . but I have their names.

Carved right into my skin.

MIDNIGHT ARRIVES, AND I shed the tatters of my dress, replacing them with simple black pants and a long-sleeved shirt from the wardrobe. Then I open my door carefully, bones bracing as it creaks. I wait. But Raker's room is silent. Good.

I slip into the hallway. The castle is empty. With every step down the stairs, anticipation builds in my bones. What will I learn? What is this great sword that decided to save me?

I know it doesn't matter. Stellaris will not be mine for long. But part of me wonders at what I was able to claim.

Part of me wants to know that during this brief and brutal time in this world, maybe I have been more than my all-encompassing rage.

The iron door swings open at my approach, as if the blacksmith was listening for my steps. He looks behind me. "Are you alone?"

I nod.

He opens the door a sliver. The moment I'm inside, it clicks closed behind me.

And I see that he is not.

Traitorous asshole.

The forge is full of knights, wearing the crest of House Rodin. In the center of them stands their lord.

He smiles good-naturedly, as if we're meeting in the middle of a ballroom.

"I thought you were at Heartfall," I say smoothly, not willing to let him see anything but calm and confidence, though inside panic surges through me.

"And miss this? Never."

My eyes roam across the warriors. "Miss what?" I ask, my tone casual, my heart hammering.

His smile only grows. He looks at me like I'm a caged animal that hasn't realized it will never see the sun again. "Did you really think I would betray the gods for you? When they've been so good to me?" He shakes his head. "Oh, no. I've already alerted my patron god. He's on his way. I'll be looking forward to being rewarded."

My jaw locks. Vander was wrong. It seems House Rodin hasn't abandoned its god after all.

The blood drains from my face, and with it, any desire to pretend. "The God of Death . . . is coming here?"

"For you," he says. "He seems quite interested in you . . . perhaps more than the other gods." He smiles. "I'm sure he'll make great use of you."

Use. I don't plan to be used by anyone.

The blacksmith bows before his lord and—with a regretful look at me—exits the room. He leaves the door behind me open. The snake. *The Great Betrayer.* He's certainly fucking earned that name. Why did I think he would help me? Why did I trust him at all?

A shred of empathy breaks through the fury, though. He's protecting his son. Stellan would have done the same for me.

And maybe he's allowed me a chance at an exit.

I stare at the open door with a flint of hope. I could make a run for it . . . but they'll just follow.

No, I won't run. And I won't sit around and wait for the God of Death to arrive.

This is what I've been training for. Why I've been strengthening my muscles and working on my form and practicing with Raker. I unsheathe my sword in a flash of sparkling silver. Lord Rodin's eyes glimmer with greed as he studies it.

"An unmatched blade. Perhaps he'll let me keep it."

I don't even waste my breath on a response as I swing my metal at his head, using another position I've practiced countless times before.

He doesn't move. He doesn't reach with immortal speed toward his own weapon. He just . . . smiles.

And my steel stops just short of his neck.

What? It froze, without my order. I lurch forward, arms straining, hands gripping the hilt, trying to move, groaning with the effort—

But my blade doesn't give an inch.

Lord Rodin's laugh echoes through the forge. His voice is dripping in superiority. "You took an oath on your sword, stupid human. You can't kill me." He turns to motion toward his knights. "You can't hurt any of my men. Not while you're a *guest*."

It doesn't seem like that safety measure extends in the opposite direction.

Those knights inch forward, blades drawn. Lord Rodin's own freshly sharpened sword glimmers beside him.

My arms tremble, trying to break free from the oath's iron hold. But they can't.

And that's when I realize how fucked I am. I'm deep below an ancient Great House on Starside. I'm standing in front of an heir, surrounded by a dozen immortal warriors, each outfitted with massive swords that I can't even attempt to deflect. The God of Death is on his way here, to collect my head himself.

There's nowhere to run. No escape. No getting out of this.

The immortal warriors have me cornered. I'm surrounded.

And I might as well be weaponless.

"Your sword is useless here," the immortal lord confirms, eyes lit with nothing short of smug delight as a dozen blades close in around me. Then—

"Mine isn't."

That voice, dark and unyielding as this castle's obsidian walls, comes from right behind me. The immortal's eyes widen. His army turns with their immortal speed toward a new target.

They're too late.

As if time has slowed to a crawl, I watch as Raker hurls his glorious sword into the air.

And that blade spins, starting at the first guard that has me surrounded, then cutting off immortal head after immortal head, body after body dropping at my feet. One after the other, in rapid succession, they fall. *They all fall.*

He kills every single one of them.

I turn in a circle, eyes wide, watching as a dozen immortal warriors are cut down in seconds, until I face Raker himself.

His eyes are sharpened steel. His body is taut with rage. Gaze locked on mine, his arm juts out—and his sword slams back into his palm with a force I feel in my bones.

I swallow.

"Nice trick," I say, breathless.

He gives me a look that says, *Idiot*.

I give him one that says, *I fucking know it*.

Then, eyes still on mine, he throws his sword right at my neck.

No. Not my neck. His blade misses the side of my throat by less than a quarter of an inch, striking right behind me, where Lord Rodin is standing, his blade nearly to my pulse.

Raker takes a step forward. Another. I feel the whisper of his sword as he retrieves it, quick as lightning. I hear the body collapse behind me.

Raker has just killed an heir. He's just killed *everyone in this room except for me*, with half a thought. I look around at the bodies surrounding us in a circle, their heads lying next to them.

Then I fall to my knees and retch.

Raker watches me. He waits. When I'm done, he offers his hand. I spit at his feet, still angry. He frowns.

But the next time he offers his hand, I take it.

39

Raker killed all of them. In rapid succession. *Easily.* His blade flew, spinning, cutting down, besting even immortals. I've always known it would take little effort for him to kill me, but now . . . seeing it . . .

I'm grateful he saved me. Again. But it doesn't erase the time he didn't. The time he decided his duty, or whatever else, was more important than helping someone.

It was years ago. It was before . . . before all of this. Still, those days have marked me in more ways than the carvings on the base of my spine. I have pinned my hatred on him for so long. He represented everything I hated about the wretched king's guard I was taught to fear since I got my markings. He was their *leader*. He was the *warrior without marks on his armor*.

There's only one person I can think of that would be able to defeat him, and he's on his way here.

"The God of Death is coming," I say as we race past rows and rows of statues dedicated to him.

"Let him come," Raker says, not looking as worried as he should as he cuts through the wild parts of the untamed garden with his blade.

"Even you should fear the gods, Raker," I say through wild breaths.

In a burst of unchecked anger, Raker's arm juts out, his sword glimmering, and he slices the air in a flash. The nearest statue is reduced to rubble.

I swallow. Part of me expects the silver-haired god to emerge from the fiery depths of the underworld right now and strike us down. But he doesn't. By some small mercy, he doesn't.

And at the edge of Lord Rodin's lands, we slip into the quiet of a forest without incident.

The rest of the day we walk in silence before camping in a final stretch of woods, protected by the starlight necklace Raker kept with him.

I barely sleep, expecting the God of Death to appear at any moment, surrounded by his demons. But the sun rises, just like I must.

You rise, I tell myself, even though I'm tired. Even though I don't really want to. My knees crack as I get to my feet.

"Why do you say that?"

I blink. I didn't realize I said it aloud.

Raker looks at me expectantly.

"It's something—it's something someone used to say to me. He said *you rise, always*. Sometimes I have to remind myself why. Because sometimes rising is hard."

He looks deep in thought.

I start to make my way out of the clearing, but his voice stops me.

"Aris," he says. And for once—for once, he says my name like a plea.

Slowly, I turn to face him.

He's right there. And he says the last thing I would ever expect: "I remember you."

I tense. My pulse stutters. No. I wouldn't believe him if I couldn't see his face, if he hadn't lowered his hood, as if to show me. *To show me what he shows no one else.*

He's towering over me, just like he did that day as he keeps going. "I told them to throw you onto the streets. *Not* into the prisons." Anger flashes in his eyes, hard and blazing, before disappearing. "I didn't know they disobeyed. I didn't know . . . I didn't know they—"

"Carved their names into my back with rusted blades?" I say, my voice quivering. Tears sting my eyes, but I don't let them fall. I won't waste more of them on those worthless guards.

His eyes shudder, for a moment. And for that moment, I see a flash of true emotion. Hurt. Fury. Conviction.

"I should have known. I should have stopped it." His gaze sears into mine as he says, "I'm sorry."

All the words I was about to say die in my throat.

Because never in a thousand years would I think Harlan Raker would be apologizing to me.

I open my mouth. Close it. In the end, I just shake my head, and say, "It doesn't matter."

I make to keep walking, but his hand catches my wrist. That one touch. That *one touch* sends fire through my blood. I turn to look at him, and his eyes are blazing into mine. Shining, glorious gray, like clouds before a storm.

"It matters, Aris," he says. "You—*you* matter."

I don't know why those simple words go right into the center of me. I don't know why they make my eyes burn. I've blamed myself and hated myself for so long that anyone seeing past the worst I've done . . . anyone caring about me at all . . .

"I don't," I say, meaning it. "You said before that you are nothing beyond your rage and vengeance. I'm . . . I'm the same, Raker. Maybe I was someone, once. But that person is gone. I have one last thing I want to do. One last thing worth fighting for. And then . . . and then there's nothing left for me."

His eyes harden. He looks angry. "So what? You'll just let yourself die?"

I shake my head. "No. But I've known from the beginning what I signed up for. That . . . that most likely, the end of this journey is the end of *me*. And . . . I've made my peace with that. I'm willing to die for this."

He searches my gaze for something. Weakness? Anything short of pure conviction? What he finds has him scowling. "And how do you plan to kill these gods, Aris?"

I lift a shoulder. "With my sword. I've learned it's a good one."

"The one you don't know how to use?" he sneers, and I see right through him. He's trying to get me to doubt myself. He's trying to get me to change my mind.

"I do," I say. "You trained me."

His nostrils flare. I can almost feel the words between us, the ones he doesn't say. We stare each other down.

I turn away again, and his fingers fall from my wrist, as he lets me go.

We walk for miles without stopping, until the ground becomes so dry, there are cracks in the dirt.

"We're about to reach the desert," I say.

Raker nods like he knows.

We reach the last spring that's marked on the map. We drink from the running water and fill our pouches. It might be the last water we see for a while.

It's the forty-first day of the quest. Maybe if I use the oaths on my sword, I can portal to a Great House and gain passage back to the gates in time to make it through. Maybe this journey does really kill me. Either way . . . I'm almost to the gods. I'm almost to the end of this.

"Ready?" I ask Raker, as I stare at the endless sea of sand. Somewhere out in that desert sits the creature even Vander Evren couldn't face.

I'm not afraid of anything, Raker said. He looks hesitant now.

"Let's get this over with," he says.

THE DUNES SHIFT in sparkling shades of sunset. Flecks of silver are speckled throughout, catching the light, before being covered by another layer.

"I wonder how many things have been lost here," I say, thinking an entire city could be buried below, and we wouldn't even know it.

Raker's eyes are on the horizon. His sword is already in his hand. It's as if he can sense something I can't.

But it doesn't come. We walk the entire day, and through the night, without any movement at all. Though we're protected by the starlight necklace, the demons don't pierce these sands even beyond the light, just like they didn't pierce the mists. Which only makes me more afraid of what is slithering within them.

Every brush of wind makes me tense. I turn at even the slightest shift in the dunes. Nothing.

I start to wonder if the creature Vander mentioned has moved on. Maybe his own effort was centuries ago—I never asked. Or maybe this beast has better things to do than torment two humans.

We drain our pouches, washing our faces and soothing our throats. I wish for my high collar again, if only to hide my face from the dust. Then the thirst begins.

We don't speak. We just keep moving, feet dragging through the heavy sand.

Until my foot doesn't move.

I frown down at it. I try to pull it free, but it doesn't budge. "What?"

I jolt with pain as nails sink into my flesh—

And pull me under.

I don't gasp. I shut my eyes, shuddering as the sand scrapes my cheeks and slices against my clothes.

What feels like a lifetime later, I'm finally deposited in another part of the desert. I emerge clawing and gasping, shaking away the sand that has scorched every inch of exposed skin.

It's everywhere. I blink the grainy dryness away—and the dunes in front of me begin to shift. They rise, sand flinting, glittering, making shapes.

They make . . . people.

I tense, watching as the worst of my memories form around me.

My sister and I slipping out of the house in the rain to pick wildflowers. *It was my idea.*

Her eyes widening as the lightning strike came right toward her—and the rush of air from her lungs as I pushed her out of the way.

I shouldn't have pushed her away.

In that moment, I thought I was saving her. I acted on instinct, without question, putting myself in danger instead of her. *Always instead of her.*

Instead, I unknowingly sealed her fate.

As quickly as they are formed, the glittering sand falls away, and another gust of wind brings more figures.

My mother. Combing my hair in front of a mirror.

"Look at yourself, love. You're beautiful."

I shake my head. "I'm ugly. I'm strange."

The markings were a sign of my recklessness. My irresponsibility. *My sister could have died.*

She bends down to my level. "You are *you*, Aris. And that makes you perfect. Don't ever hide from yourself."

"You're the one who tells me to hide!" I yell, getting up from the chair. "*You* make me feel wrong! Maybe I should go outside like this," I say. "Maybe if the knights drag me off to the prisons, or to the king to cut me up and study me, I'll deserve it!"

I'll never forget the shock on her face. I never raised my voice at my mother. It wasn't fair of me to do so. All she ever did was for my protection. I know that now.

But it was easier to blame her for my problems. My mom never screamed back at me, and maybe that made her an easier target for my anger.

The thought roils my stomach now.

"I'm sorry," I whisper from the sidelines, feeling the twist of guilt as the sand falls away. "*You* were perfect, Mom."

In a flash, the sand rises in a column, right in front of me. My mother stands there, twisted and wrong. Her normally smiling mouth is curled into a smirk. "Perfect? I couldn't get the doors open. If I could . . . maybe we could have all gotten out. Maybe we wouldn't all be dead. Maybe you wouldn't be a ghost of your pain and worst memories, walking."

I swallow. "It's not your fault," I say, meaning it. "It's *hers*."

"And what have you done about it?" She takes a step forward. "I lied. You aren't perfect. You are *weak*. You are an *embarrassment*. *You* should have died that day. The world would be better for it."

It wouldn't hurt so much if I didn't agree with her.

Tears sting my already sand-crusted eyes, running down my torn-up cheeks.

She steps forward. "Your *sister*, she was perfect. She was always better than you. Prettier. Kinder. She could have made the world better. You? You just want to kill. Hatred lives in your heart. Love lived in hers."

The sand thickens, twisting around me, blocking the rest of the desert, trapping me with her. It circles like a cyclone, howling, her words echoing.

The air is being choked away. My senses are, one by one, being snuffed out. My knees buckle. Slowly, I sink to the ground.

"You are nothing. You are worse than nothing. You are the reason everyone is dead. You are a poison. You are a curse."

My breathing becomes panting as I try to suck in air that isn't there, my lungs filling with sand instead.

As I fall forward, the last words I hear are spoken right into my ear, as if my mother bent low to tell me, "Do the world a favor and die this time."

I STAY DOWN. For the world. For everyone that would be alive if I had just *stayed down*. If I had just died when the lightning struck me.

Sand brushes over me, covering me like a blanket. Soon I'll be buried, just like the rest of this desert's secrets.

And the world will be better for it.

For a while, only the sand whispers. Then there's nothing. A thick layer has overtaken me. I can't even feel the sun anymore.

The world is quiet below.

Until another voice ruins it.

Stellan. There he is, in the echo of a memory. "Why do you rise?"

"Leave me alone," I say, the words barely reaching my lips.

"Why do you rise, Aris?"

"Leave me. *Please*."

"Why are you doing this? Do you even have a reason?" The voice is above me now, as if he's trying to find me under the layers of sand.

A reason.

He sighs. "You don't, do you? Not a good one, anyway." He starts to walk away. I feel his steps receding, leaving me here.

Fury lances through me, my veins igniting. I couldn't feel my body before, but now I feel every limb, every bone, every muscle. They're all tensed in rage. I shake with it as I break through the crushing weight of the sand.

I can't even see the ghost of him—I can't see *anything*—but these emotions will not stay buried. My voice is unrecognizable, a primal growl. I don't need to just tell him. I will tell the *entire galaxy* if I need to. I will fill universes with my fury. I will shake the stars loose with my rage.

"I'm doing this because *she killed her!* She was my sister, she was innocent, she was *everything*, and that goddess *fucking killed her* because *she fucking could!* And now . . . I'm going to kill all of them. I'm going to burn those merciless gods to ashes, even if I burn with them. Even if I am skinned and broken and bleeding and all my bones are shattered, I will drag myself to those gods, and I will end them, and if it kills me, then I will die with a smile on my face, because it will have been worth it. They will be scourged from this world—and then, only then, *finally then*, will I know peace." My voice is a screaming rasp. "These ghosts . . . they're right. I am a blight. I am not honorable. What I want is revenge. That's *all* I want. *That* is the only reason why I'm doing this."

Blinking, panting, I finally see the shape of Stellan, in the sand. The shape of all of them, every single person I have loved and lost. All staring at me, on my knees, shaking with rage.

I remember what Vander said about the monster that makes you an enemy of yourself. I wonder if I'm looking right at it.

My lip curls. "Go ahead. Do your worst," I say to the invisible creature making these shapes, digging a blade into my ever-bleeding wound.

I unsheathe my sword and stab it into the sand below, using it to steady me. Slowly, on shaking legs, I rise. They continue to tremble as I take a step forward. The sand shifts beneath me, but I do not fall. I dig my feet into the ground and stand firm.

A wicked, twisted laugh leaves my lips. "I have lost my entire family. I have lost everyone I have ever loved. This world is not large enough to hold my fury. It wants to knock me down?" I scoff. "I would like to see it try." My hands tighten around my hilt, and my blade's energy runs through me, invigorating me. "My worst nightmare has already happened, and I'm still standing. I'm not afraid of *anything*," I bellow.

And the sand drops away to nothing. The dust vanishes with the wind. Everything settles.

Raker.

I race through the dunes, squinting through the grit—and that's when I see him.

The Warrior Without Marks on His Armor. The Battle-Ender. The Devil's Blade. So many names. And he's earned every single one.

His hood is partially up. He's battling an invisible source with the frenzied fury of a duel. His metal sings, it glimmers, it moves in arcs like water, he was made for this, he is *the best at this*. His face is almost expressionless, but I know him. By now . . . I know him. I see the coiled rage in the set of his shoulders. I watch as it bleeds into his movements. They become more hurried. More reckless.

The illusions . . . they're getting to him. I wonder what he's seeing.

I'm not afraid of anything, he said. I think he believed it too.

But it seems even devils have demons.

When I get closer, his eyes close, like he can't bear to even look at what's appeared. What's so bad that he can't face it?

He winces. *Winces.*

It's instinct to reach for him.

I take his arm, trying to pull him out of this dream, but instead of leaving with me, he lashes out, nearly slicing me through my middle. I barely jump away in time.

My chest is heaving. So close. He was *so close* to killing me.

I remember the circle of dead knights. I remember their heads, cracking against the stone floor, over and over and over.

A lick of fear slides down my spine. He can kill me so easily; I've known it this entire time. But I've never been afraid he might actually do it until now.

He's not himself. He thinks I'm someone else—

"Aris," he growls. I blink. He knows it's me. And he still swung his blade. *"Aris, leave me alone."* It's an order.

I should. It's the smart thing to do.

But aren't those the same words I said to Stellan? I begged him to leave me to die, but he never did. Even his *illusion* didn't leave until I was standing. Until I was free.

I will be a hand in the darkness. I will pull him out of this.

"I'm not leaving you," I say, yelling so he hears me over the roaring sand.

His face twists into a mask of cold, cruel amusement. It's as if the worst of himself has taken over. All the tenderness, all the understanding, has vanished. It's been replaced with the callous, heartless warrior I encountered in the rain. "You never did have great survival instincts," he spits. "But me—you won't survive me."

I have a feeling he's right. But still, *still*, I stay.

He can tell, even with his eyes closed. He shakes his head. "You are a fool, Aris. Searching for shreds of humanity in a broken world. Searching for care that has never existed. Looking for *beauty*"—he spits the word—"in *monsters.*"

His blade is still battling that invisible beast. His eyes are still firmly shut. I take a step forward and duck, barely missed by the metal again. "You're right," I say, my voice just a rasp in the whirl of sand. "I see beauty in dark places. If that makes me a fool, then so be it."

I reach for his hood, to pull it down completely, but he shoots back, then raises his sword right in front of him, a barrier between us.

"You ask why I hide? Why I wear the hood? The mask? The helmet?" he yells, face twisted. "I hide because I can't even *look* at myself, Aris," he says. "The things I've done . . . you have no idea."

"I can imagine," I say, inching closer. I just need him to open his eyes. Maybe if I touch him—

He senses me immediately and turns, raising his blade again. "You *can't*," he spits. "If you knew all the blood on my blade, you would run,

Aris. You would cower. You wouldn't look at me the way you do. You would never call me *beautiful*." He laughs cruelly. He's trying to scare me off.

"I'm not leaving," I say steadily.

"Then you will die." He says it like a promise.

I shake my head. My voice is unyielding. "I'm not afraid of you."

His is pitying. "You really should be."

He lashes out again—and this time, his blade meets mine.

The ringing of their joining echoes through the desert, muting the roaring winds for just a moment. The force of it spirals down my veins.

The one blade he can't break. He pushes, growling as if he's trying. He's *trying*.

I push back, teeth grinding together, feet sliding. I put every shred of energy and rage and feeling into that one motion. Slowly, in a high-pitched wail, our blades begin to slide together as I get closer. *Closer to him.*

"Open your eyes, Raker," I say. My arms are shaking with effort. We're too close now. One sudden move, and he'll skewer me on his metal. My voice is a whisper. "Please."

He shakes his head, then shoves against my sword, hard. I stumble back, and I should take this chance to escape. To survive him. But instead, I hurl myself forward, and my blade meets his again with bone-splintering force.

I press down, trying to get closer, but he blocks his face with his sword, using it like another mask to hide behind, just another sheet of metal to use as a wall between him and the rest of the world. Between us. But in these last few weeks, those walls have slipped. I've seen beneath the mask, beneath the warrior, beneath the deadly reputation, and that's why I won't let him succumb to this. I won't let the worst of him win. We break apart for a second, and then my weapon slams against his again.

"Raker," I say.

But it's like he's lost.

Whatever he's remembering, whatever he's fighting, I know he's trapped in his darkest moments, just as I was. The darkest parts of himself.

He was a stranger before this quest, but now . . . he knows me better than anyone else.

And I know him.

I know him.

I will be a map through the darkness. I will be a hand, pulling him out of it.

Our metals scrape together. He makes to move, but I move first. And instead of striking—I release my sword. It thuds against the sand.

What a stupid thing to do.

But sucking the poison from my blood was stupid. Summoning an ancient immortal to save him was stupid. What's one more stupid thing.

He lunges to attack me again. And instead of reaching down for my blade—

I reach for him.

My knuckles brush along his cheek, before pushing his hood back completely. It falls away, revealing his full face.

And his blade settles against my throat. I go still. One move and I'm dead. One breath and this entire journey will have been for nothing.

I fight to keep my voice calm. "Raker. You're not yourself."

His mouth twists into merciless amusement. "That's where you're wrong, Aris. This is me. Not whatever you pretend I am."

I shake my head, careful against the blade's edge. "No. No, it's not."

"You don't know me," he growls. "You don't know anything at all."

I swallow. My pulse beats along the metal. "I know your father was a fisherman. Your mother was a seamstress. You had siblings, once. You grew up near the ocean." He bares his teeth at me in rage, but I keep going. "You became a warrior to help your family. Your reputation is that you are a cruel, merciless knight. And you are."

My voice breaks.

"But that's not *all* you are. You use your skills to save too. You've saved me. You've trained me. You've . . . made the nightmares stop. I haven't had them in days, and I think it's because I finally feel safe. Even in a world of dangers, even when you're the exact person I was taught to fear, when I'm with you, I'm not afraid. Not anymore."

That makes him inhale sharply. His grip on his sword loosens—then tightens. It presses so hard against my throat, it becomes hard to talk. But I don't stop.

"You told me you are *nothing*, nothing beyond your rage and vengeance, but you are not nothing. You matter, beyond your blade. Beyond your skills. You matter to me. Because I see you," I say, breathless, as a tear slips down my face and lands on his metal. "I see beneath the mask. I see beneath the armor. I see past the fury, past the vengeance." One of my hands reaches up to his, the one that's gripping the sword against my throat.

His skin is burning hot. His fingers are trembling.

"*I see you, Raker.* I see past the blood on these hands. I see past your mistakes, and I hate that you can't look at your reflection, because . . . because I never want to stop looking at you, Raker." Careful not to move forward even an inch, my other hand reaches up to slide across his cheek. His body flinches, shaking with a chill. Still, his sword does not drop from my throat. One sudden movement and I'm done. I'll bleed out all over this sand.

"I see the good. I see the bad, and everything in between. I see you. *I see you*, and one day you will see a shred of what I see." I say it like an order. Like a promise.

"You see what you want to, Aris," he says, his voice just as cutting as his blade. He presses it deeper, and I feel a sharp flash of pain.

A drop of blood drips down his metal.

Shit. I should stop. I should give up.

But no. I'm not wrong. Even as I'm bleeding, even as he's moments from slitting my throat, I think back to our journey. I think back to his actions—not his words.

My voice is a choked whisper. "I have seen you be both merciless and kind. I have seen you kill and rescue. I have seen both the best and worst of you. I've seen it all. I have seen the evil in you, Raker, which is how I know the good exists. It's how I know . . . how I know you won't do this."

"You don't know me," he growls, his hand trembling. His blade scraping against the thin, fragile skin. More blood spilling onto his metal.

"I know enough," I breathe. Sword still against my throat, I do something foolish. Slowly, so he can feel my intention, I lean closer. I pause, waiting to feel the hot gushing of blood. I wait to feel the shock of death. But he's moved with me.

He hasn't cut me down—*not yet.*

Heart hammering, I press closer still, my face right in front of his. His eyes are still shut. I lean in until the metal stops me.

"*I see you,*" I whisper an inch from his lips. I feel him . . . feel his arm trembling. His fingers flexing beneath mine, as we both hold on to his sword. "I see the monster, and I'm still looking. I see the darkness, and I'm not flinching." My shaking voice sharpens. "Your blade is against my throat and *I'm. Not. Leaving.*"

He is the greatest warrior on Stormside. He is an infamous killer. But right now, with his sword against my pulse, he is hesitating. He is *shaking*.

Gently, so gently, I pull back an inch, the blade following, only to see his face still twisted, as if he's locked in an invisible battle.

"Open your eyes, Raker," I whisper.

He shakes his head. The pain clear on his face—I want to take it away. I want to heal it, the same way he has healed me.

"Open your eyes. Please." My voice breaks on the word.

The sand surges, circling, enclosing, caving in, as if to drown out my words. And that only means it's *working*.

"*Open your eyes*," I scream, because this sand . . . this sand will not silence me. It will not silence those moments where we have fought, and survived, and *lived*. Against all odds, we have endured, and even though I have hated him, and cursed him, every step of this has been side by side, and if he wouldn't leave me behind before . . . neither will I.

The sand rages. It's roaring. So. Am. I.

"I SEE YOU," I bellow. "I see you, Harlan Raker. I see you, and I like what I see. I want to see more. I want . . . please. I *want* . . ."

Tears spill, sliding down my neck, mixing with the blood.

Fuck it. If these are my last moments, then I won't let a single word go unsaid.

"I want *you*, Raker. I want to find you again when all of this is over. I want to see what life might look like beyond the misery. Beyond the vengeance. You make me want to see what's left for me. You make me want to build a life in a world of ashes. So please. *Please*. Open your eyes. *Open*—"

He does.

And his sword drops between us.

"I see you too," he says, eyes locked on mine, steel blazing through the desert.

I see you.

I know he does. Because at some point during this journey the moat I kept around myself lowered a bridge to him. He knows about my nightmares. He knows about my markings. He knows about my sister. He knows my fears and weaknesses and the things that make me smile.

Everyone else who knew me at all is dead. I almost just joined them, at his hand.

My knees buckle in relief, and he catches me around the waist. No one gets close to him. Everyone is too afraid. I should be too. He just almost killed me. But I throw my arms around him anyway. Together, we sink to the sand, knee to knee. I feel his arms curve around me tentatively as if he has no idea how this works, as if he hasn't embraced anyone in a long while.

"I thought—I thought you were going to kill me," I say, breathless, my cheek against his neck. Our hearts are both beating wildly, right against each other. I feel his hand against the back of my head, as he holds me to him.

He says nothing. He only holds me tighter.

40

There's a line of blood along my throat. We have matching marks, now. *A reminder of my weakness,* Raker called his, and I think that's right. It's a reminder that Raker—as much as I see him, as much as he sees me—is still my enemy.

An oasis awaits at the edge of the desert. It's an entire cliffside of waterfalls that glimmer like diamonds are threaded through its liquid. They spill into various lopsided, bright blue pools, one larger than the rest.

I rush to one of the falls, drinking directly from it, water soaking my body in a rush of welcomed cold. I groan. When I turn around, Raker is just standing there, lost in thought.

"I'm getting in," I tell him. He blinks, knocked out of his mind, then turns around. I turn too. Slowly, I begin to remove my clothing, sand spilling onto the rock beneath my feet. My skin has been rubbed raw. It's an effort to take each piece off.

Behind me, I hear Raker doing the same. I hear every piece of armor come off.

Without a look in his direction, I slowly sink into the biggest pool. I test for the bottom and feel that it's shallow. It takes a few steps to wade into where the water reaches my waist.

I hear the water part behind me. I can feel his presence. My markings glimmer beneath the sun. It's strange, being out in the open, with them on full display.

But I'm not hiding anymore. I see him. He sees me. We've made it close to the end, together. Only one more day stands between us and the Land of the Gods.

I duck into the water to wash my hair and face. When I emerge, I turn—
And there he is.

Without a hood. Without anything on. For a moment, I forget to breathe. The water is dark enough that I can't see anything beneath, but I can see his wide shoulders, and part of his broad chest. I can see parts of the thin, dark tattoos threading across his pale skin, down his muscular arms, to where they run down each of his fingers. I want to know what they mean. I want to look closer, so I can see the shapes they make. His hair is wet, small droplets falling from the dark strands onto his sharp cheeks, dripping toward his jaw, and I don't know why that simple fact makes me feel like I'm losing my mind.

He just stares at me. Only a few strands of hair keep me decent, but . . . he sees everything else. My bare shoulders, and collarbones, and the shapes of my breasts, and the silver markings. I remember how he traced his thumb down them, like I was his favorite constellation.

His eyes darken, like he's remembering too. Then his gaze shifts. He winces.

He's looking at my throat.

I reach up and tense. The skin is tender but not painful. That doesn't seem to matter. It doesn't seem to matter that he has a matching mark, fully healed, a thin line across his neck, from my own blade.

At my small grimace of discomfort, Raker's entire face melts back into that unfeeling mask. I open my mouth—

But he lifts himself out of the water.

I wash the blood away. Fill my pouch. As much as I want to spend hours in this pool, the desert leeched me of energy.

We collapse inside the closest cave, starlight sparkling through the darkness.

When I wake up the next morning the sky is still dark, and Raker is still sleeping. He's frowning, as if reliving a fraction of whatever he saw in that desert.

Whatever he saw . . . it's still haunting him.

Even devils have demons.

It's still early. I let him sleep. He'll need his rest. I carve the rest of the map into the rock. We're close, so close.

Today's the day.

We're lucky the cavalry wasn't waiting for us here, beyond the desert. But maybe the gods will be at the entrance of their lands.

Maybe they'll strike me down before I can even step foot into them. Maybe I'll actually kill them.

Either way, there's no going back now.

We need more water. I take our pouches, and head back to the oasis, drinking in the beauty of the waterfalls until the sky loses all hint of darkness, melting into flames. Time to go. I'm about to turn back to the cave, to wake Raker, when I see it. A dark smudge weaving through the clouds. I squint. It gets closer. Closer.

A dragon.

I know that dragon. It nearly burnt mine to a crisp.

It lands just beyond the hills of the oasis.

My sword is in my hand. Somehow, I know. I know what I'm going to find. I'm walking toward it anyway, led by pure and utter desire for vengeance.

I remember the words I spoke in the desert. *I am not afraid of anything.* I meant it.

I'm not afraid now. But I am filled with an anger that might burn me up from the inside out before I'm able to even reach the end of this journey.

The dirt is crusted orange and red. I don't walk far before something sparkling catches my eye.

A paladian dagger, its markings more familiar to me than the lines on my palm, sticking right out of the dirt, hilt-up. Waiting for me. Teasing me.

Beckoning me.

Pain and rage nearly blind me. I swallow. It's a trap. Of course it is. He wants my sword. Maybe he wants the bounty. But I'm not the same person I was at the beginning of this.

I take a step toward the blade. A boot sounds behind me.

"Still alive? I'm impressed," Cadoc says.

I turn very slowly, fury and satisfaction rushing through my veins, my hand gripped tightly around the hilt of my sword. He killed Stellan. *And now I'm going to fucking destroy him.* My metal hums, as if ready for the bloodshed. My mouth opens—

Then closes.

He grins as my eyes find his belt. And one of the many swords hanging there.

"No," I breathe.

Purple. The stone is *purple*. I know that carving, the flowers, the vines.

Kira's blade. Which only means one thing.

"*No.*" My voice breaks on a sob.

"I want you to know that she almost made it," Cadoc says, taking a step forward. "And with an injured leg, no less." He clicks his tongue. "Very impressive. She was just short of the gates when my friends caught her. She fought hard . . . kept mentioning, apparently . . . a *sister?*" Rage explodes behind my eyes. I bare my teeth, but that only seems to please him more. "They dragged her to me, keeping her just barely alive . . ." He smooths a finger down the metal. "So I could claim this." He shakes his belt, and the dozen swords clang together. "It was so fun . . . so fun to *break her.*"

"You're—you're lying," I say, trembling. The world is slipping away, but I use anger as a tether.

"Am I?"

Fury gathers in my bones as I step forward. My voice is pain and purpose woven together. "Then it looks like I'm about to have too many blades to carry."

At that, Cadoc smiles. "Or I'm about to add a new one to my collection."

He takes his stance. He holds up a weapon he must have claimed here, one of sparkling immortal metals.

I unleash everything this side has taught me, bellowing with bone-deep fury.

My arms might have trembled the first time I lifted this blade.

They do not shake now.

His sparkling metal meets mine and cracks. Sometime during this journey, through all the dangers, through the training, through the lessons, I got better. I see it now. Every inch of that skill, magnified by my rage. I grip my sword using both hands, slamming over and over and *over* until the blade completely shatters.

I lift my weapon one last time, to finally slay him, but he's fast. He pulls another blade from his belt, and his new metal clashes against mine. It seems I wasn't the only one who improved during this quest. Or changed. I see the jagged mark of a wound down the side of his throat. The skin is raised. Twisted.

He tries to go for my leg, but I pounce away, then swing for his sword-wielding arm. He barely deflects in time, but my blow is hard. The gold splinters. One more hit, and it's in pieces at his feet.

"Aris."

The word, the distant voice, distracts me.

The clash of metal must have awakened him. Raker is coming, any moment now.

Cadoc seems to know it too. He lunges for the dagger behind me. *Stellan's* dagger. I go after him, but he turns, blocking me with a new sword from his belt. He pockets the dagger, then fixes both hands on the hilt of his weapon.

"Aris." Raker's getting closer. I can hear the clanging of his armor. He's *running*.

Cadoc bellows a name I don't recognize, and then a sky-splitting roar rattles my bones. I turn, and my vision is wholly blocked by a monstrous shadow. His dragon is rushing right at us. It isn't stopping.

There's no time to move. Before I can take a single step, we're both knocked off our feet, and onto the dragon's back.

My head hits its jagged ridges, pain exploding behind my eyelids as my body skips down its spine. I barely manage to grip one of its many spikes, before it turns skyward, my feet kicking nothing as it spirals toward the clouds. I scream. My nails splinter as I fight to hold on.

Wind nearly rips me off its side, then the dragon steadies. My body slams down against its hard scales. My bones scream beneath my skin. Bile rushes up my throat. But there's no time to retch. I claw my way up to a more stable position. Cadoc is yards away, on his stomach. Staring at me with unflinching focus.

He stands. Slowly, I do too, on the other end of the creature's spine as it continues its flight through the fiery dawn. My head is pulsing, ears bursting with the rapid ascent. I swallow the pain and panic down, until only rage remains. I take a deep breath. Then, with a growl, I race forward, and not even the wind can smother the sound of our blades meeting.

Our duel continues on his dragon's back, in the air, and Cadoc's fighting might have improved—but his stamina did not. Of course. He had this dragon to take him across Starside. I made much of the trek on foot. I learned not to tire. *I trained for this*. As his movements get lazier, mine get more precise. One after another, his lesser blades shatter against my metal, and he replaces them with the others he's collected, slower each time. I advance, fury fueling me. I block each of his clumsy movements.

Stellan taught me everything he knew.

Now, I'm going to use every bit of that training to fulfill my promise to him. I'm going to kill the person responsible for his death.

For you, I think, tears stinging my eyes. *For everything you made me.*

Cadoc tries to kick my legs out from under me, but I jump, and slice through the air, in a move Raker helped me perfect. He turns his face away—

But he's not quick enough. When he turns back around, a deep gash slices across his face. Blood drips down into his mouth as he smiles. He takes a step forward, and it's as if the injury has invigorated him.

Suddenly, I'm hit with a wave of heat.

The City on Fire. It really does burn, and we're flying right above it. I can hear the flames, crackling, as if waiting to be fed.

Burning. Endless burning and—

I take a step back, burying the memories. The pain.

Cadoc tilts his head at me as though he can see my inner injury. Like that's what he's best at—finding someone's wound and twisting his inferior blade into it to win. Is that how he got so many other competitors to work with him?

That smug look grows. Eyes never leaving mine, he throws his sword over the side of his dragon, into the City on Fire, then reaches for another.

Kira's sword.

He smiles as I stumble backward, his teeth gleaming with blood. "What's wrong? Don't want to fight against your dead friend's blade?"

Memories flash. I see Kira, jumping into the water, desperate to keep that sword. I can hear her words like she's saying them right now, like she's still here.

I've—I've never been chosen by anyone. Or anything. This—this blade chose me. I can't leave it behind.

I didn't forget my promise. I'm going to reach the gods. I'm going to take a cup of their magic. I'm going to find a way to get it to Kira's sister.

Anise should have this sword. Not Cadoc. Anyone but him.

Silver overtakes my vision, and I stumble out of the way of his strike, not wanting to break Kira's blade. A few brushes with mine, and it will shatter. Fuck. The bastard's plan is working. I duck as he slices right at my throat, then lurch forward as his dragon jolts again. This time, the movement brings me to my knees. I nearly lose my balance and grip its spikes with one hand, my blade in the other, as the dragon rapidly descends. My teeth clench together.

It's in freefall. The heat of the burning city swells up like a wave. Sweat spills down my brow. It's like Cadoc knows the fire is bothering me. He's telling his creature to get closer.

All at once, the dragon goes still, and I almost lose my balance.

The fire is crackling right below us now. I peer over the side and see only a sea of flames. Memories rise up. So does panic. My ears are ringing. My mind is pounding.

I stand on shaking legs.

"How she screamed," Cadoc says, advancing, eyes glimmering with the thought. His face is bright red. "For anyone to help her. For her *friends*. But where were you?"

Where were you?

I let her down. Just like I let down my family. I'm blinded by the memory. That night. The fire, overtaking the room.

"Aris. Aris, it hurts."

But I was helpless. I couldn't make it stop. I couldn't save her—

The advance is so quick, I don't have time to move out of the way. I have to lift my sword. Kira's blade crashes into mine with so much force, it rings through my blood. A long crack spirals down its designs, splitting the flowers in half.

The memory—it cost me. It hollowed my grip.

At his strike, my sword slips from my sweaty hands, landing against the dragon's back.

Everything moves so slowly. I watch as Cadoc's eyes slide down to my sword. As the metal glimmers in warning, in pleading to pick it back up. I try.

But before I can bend to reach it, or call to it, Cadoc turns. He moves in a flash. He kicks me off the dragon's back—

Right into the City on Fire.

I think I hear a distant bellow, a sound scraped from the sky itself, of pure and utter agony. But it's too late.

I'm swallowed by the flames, and when I hit the ground, my body breaks.

41

Rise, phoenix, rise.

Stellan's voice is in my head again, the words familiar and from another time entirely.

A shaking girl in a pile of ashes.

A white-bearded man reaching out a hand.

Rise, phoenix, rise.

The world is boiling around me. My senses have been shredded. Slowly, they return. I hear the muffled crackling of the flames that have swallowed me whole. Even with my eyes closed, I see the relentless red and orange, like I'm trapped within a final sunset.

My body—I can barely feel it. My bones must be shattered.

Kira is dead. *Dead.* She died alone, begging for anyone to save her. I let her down. I let them all down. Every single person who has ever loved me has ended up dead.

This City on Fire should let me burn. My shame and guilt and fury are like these endless flames, forever roaring all around me.

Still, his voice is in my head again, insistent. *No one can heal you in here. You have to step out of the fire.*

Rise, phoenix, rise.

I can't, I think. *Not this time.*

Stellan's voice is angry now. His words are new. "*Every* time," he says, "You rise *every* time."

My eyes sting, remembering that hand that reached out from nowhere, toward a trembling girl covered in the ruin of everything she once loved, whose voice had given out from all the screaming.

He didn't leave. He didn't turn around. He reached his hand out for what seemed like hours, until finally, mine reached back. He gripped it with a strength I couldn't imagine ever having. With a firmness that I can still feel in my soul. But he didn't help me up. He said I had to do that myself.

No matter what, Stellan got up day after day. He was always there for me. Just like they were.

You rise every time.

For all of them, I will try.

The world is burning around me, my body is broken, but I grit my teeth against the pain and splintered bones and reach a hand forward. Another. I lift my head. Every aching muscle is pleading with me to stay down, to stay still, but I do not.

I rise until I'm on my feet.

My clothes are gone. My skin is coated in their ashes and the blood from my fall.

A single step. The first is always the hardest. My shattered knee nearly buckles. My arm is hanging at an unnatural angle. My skull is fractured. My ribs are snapped. It hurts to breathe. But even when I think I've reached my limit, my own strength surprises me.

Again. I step *again*. Once I've proven I can take one, the next comes, and then the next, until I'm walking through the raging flames, parting them like a blade that refuses to be melted down.

My flesh is hanging off my bones, I am gaping and bloody and broken, but I keep going, dragging my bare feet through this city, the one that burns with a thousand years of fury, the one that has burned for centuries before I was born and will for centuries after I am just dust in the wind.

I keep dragging myself forward until I reach the edge of the flames—

And then, I step through them.

Harlan Raker is rushing toward the City on Fire without signs of slowing down, as if he was going to *run through the flames for me*. That bellow. It was him.

When he sees me, he stills.

Our eyes meet. *His eyes*. His hood is down. It's down like it fell while he was running and he didn't care about putting it back up.

Those gray eyes are gleaming, they are wide, they are filled with a relief that I can almost taste. And something else . . . something like wonder.

A shriek peels through the sky, and slowly, I look up to where Cadoc is circling on his wicked dragon, close to the ground, as if he wanted to watch me burn. He's close enough that I see his shock.

He thought he killed me.

He is going to wish he killed me.

Gaze locked on his, I hurl my arm to the side, broken bones screaming, my shredded palm open wide.

"*Stellaris*," I bellow with every smelted piece of myself, the word a fractured roar.

And I feel it. My metal, singing a song only I can hear as it arcs through the sky like a shooting star, back into my hand, with a force that rattles my blood. Rattles the world.

Cadoc's eyes burn with wrath. My stare promises revenge as he takes off into the sky, until his dragon is nothing more than a mottled smudge in the burning horizon.

Then my bones finally give out.

Arms catch me just before I hit the ground.

I GASP.

"Shhhh," a voice says, so gently it can't possibly be from the source I think it is. "Just a little longer."

But I can't be quiet. Not when it feels like I'm swimming through a sea of blades.

I keep screaming, pain a blinding light. My body convulses, hurt lancing through me again and again.

"Make it stop," he says, his voice as threatening as I've ever heard it.

It is completely at odds with the gentle voice that responds. "The pool needs time. It will be over soon." I recognize that voice.

Este. She's here. How?

My body is on fire, burning from the inside out, the water so cold it cuts me down to the bone. I don't want to scream. I don't mean to scream. But my body has abandoned my mind, it moves of its own volition, and I hear my bellow and begging as if I'm listening to someone else.

I hear the slicing of a sword leaving its scabbard. "Make it stop."

I don't know what happens next. The pain is so great, it pulls me under.

WHEN I AWAKE, the pain is gone. All that's left is a distant numbness, the ghost of its memory.

My eyes open to find Raker sitting across a glimmering pool, staring. He looks lost in thought, brow furrowed.

He's by my side in an instant. His eyes are furious.

The necklace. Somehow, Raker used it to summon Este for help. The water in front of us is swirling with silver flecks, like the starlight was broken into it.

"You wasted the necklace on me," I say, my voice a croak.

If I thought that might tamper his fury, I'm wrong. The anger only grows. He makes an aggravated sound. "Your injuries were significant," he says tightly, as if that is a light way of putting it. His entire body is coiled tight.

I nod. I could feel them, of course. My body broken and shredded from the fall. I shouldn't be alive.

A heavy silence falls between us, and I remember those eyes. How those eyes *gleamed* across the desert. How they did not at all belong to the merciless warrior, to the fearless and fearsome head of the king's guard.

"None of them were burns, Aris."

There it is. An answer he deserves, but I'm not willing to give him. I don't meet his eyes. I stare very intently at the glowing pool in front of me, full of that starlight; then I feel long fingers curling around my jaw, forcing me to look at him.

My chin quivers with defiance. "What do you want me to say?" is what comes out.

"How you walked *through fucking flames* would be a start," he says through his teeth, voice shaking with barely leashed fury like he's working very hard to remain calm.

I try to move, but his grip is like iron.

"Now isn't the time for secrets. Have we not been through enough?" His voice. It's changed. He sounds . . . almost hurt.

My gaze locks on his. I look at him. *Really look at him.* He has saved me. I have saved him.

I've seen his face. He's seen my markings. My scars. He's seen me retch, and sob, and scream.

If moments can leave marks, claws on our minds and souls, then we have matching battle scars. No matter what happens after this journey, after these weeks together, if somehow I survive this, if one day, we are strangers, walking through a sea of people, we could share a look and *know*, know truths of this world that no one else could ever understand.

We have been through endless trials together. If ever I was to tell this secret to anyone, to speak the unspeakable . . . I would want it to be to someone who has seen me fight harder than I ever have in my life. Someone who has seen me broken and battered and still standing.

Someone who has seen me walk through flames.

"Ever since the day the sky touched me, I have been immune to heat. I could touch warm things. I was drawn to the hearth. I didn't test it. The markings worried my parents, so I hid them. I didn't tell anyone about the ability I discovered. I thought . . . I thought if I ignored it, it would go away, and I could be normal again, and maybe my parents would stop worrying. Then one night, my sister woke me up." I swallow.

My eyes close. My nightmare. The one I've had for years. I've never told anyone. Even Stellan. Not this part.

The worst moment of my life. A moment that has swallowed my entire existence. In a way, my soul remained there, in that night. In those flames. My body might be here, but my heart and mind and soul are still there in that pile of ashes.

Warmth against the endless chill. I open my eyes to see Raker's hand curled around mine. I look up to see his eyes fierce and steady. *I'm here*, his gaze seems to say. *You can tell me unspeakable things. You can tell me things that no one else will understand.*

He squeezes, firmly, almost painfully so, and that one movement has a thousand memories trapped within it, of all my toughest moments, as if to remind me of my strength.

My words are not steady, but they are out. "She said there was a fire. She could smell it. We tried to leave our room, but our doors were locked. Our parents were on the other side, trying to get in." I take a shaking breath and keep going. "They tried everything. We heard . . . we heard their screams, as the fire swallowed them. They could have lived, if they had left us. But . . . but they never left. They never stopped trying. It was the last thing they ever did.

"Then—" I choke on a sob. Raker is there, holding my hand, his other steady against my back. *I see you too*, he said. He sees me now. "The fire overtook the room. We knew it was done. So we held each other. She began to scream. Her hair caught fire first. Then her clothes. Her skin. Her eyes, they got so big. She was burning, burning away right in my arms, but I—"

Tears fall, endless tears, choking tears, forever tears, a bleeding vein that will never stop. An infernal agony.

His voice is rough with understanding. "You did not burn."

I did not burn. I wish I had. I wish it had been me instead of her, *instead of anyone* who had become ash.

I shake my head.

The world was fire around me, but I saw her. Through the flames, I saw her. A goddess, with silver-red, sparkling eyes, who then turned her back to us. She set the fire—I knew it like a truth buried in my soul.

Then she was gone.

I held my sister until she was just ash and bone, until there was nothing left to hold, and then I screamed until my voice gave out.

The next day, Stellan found me in the ashes of everything I once loved.

"I died that day, with my family. The only thing that has kept me going is the belief that I will see that goddess again." My eyes lock into his, and my sobbing calms. My voice does not waver now. "I'm going to kill her. I'm going to kill them all. I'm going to paint the sky with their blood. I'm going to unleash a wrath so great, even the stars will flinch."

I say it like a promise.

A muscle in Raker's jaw works. "You're going to die."

"I know. This will kill me."

He glares at me.

I shake my head. "Don't you see?" My voice is raw from the screaming. I form something like a smile. "I'm not afraid. She is waiting for me at the end of this, and then I won't be alone."

He studies me for a moment. Then he says something I would never guess. "Aris, you are not alone."

You are not alone.

We look at each other. More moments spill between us, yet the silence doesn't feel cold anymore.

"You don't understand. You never could."

"I understand," he says.

I swallow. "You don't have a heart. How could you?"

He scowls at my attempt at a joke. "I know you, Aris. You claim you don't care about anything but revenge, but I have watched you unfailingly, *stupidly* care about everyone else's life over your own. You are not the monster you think you are."

His words make all my hatred rise to the surface, because I don't hate *him*, I don't hate *anyone* more than I hate myself. "I am worse!" I say. "I am the reason they are all dead!"

He opens his mouth as if to say something else, but at that moment, someone steps behind us.

Este.

She's followed by a half dozen women that look almost like the faelings, draped in thin, white fabrics, flowers woven through their long hair, vines wrapped around their arms.

Relief melts through her expression. "You're awake."

"Because of you," I say, my voice heavy with emotion. "How—"

"You needed help," Este says simply. She looks over at Raker. "He reached for it." I remember now the final words she told me, before we left the Traveling City. Her gaze drops to my back. "Nothing we could do about older marks, unfortunately. It would have required more time in the pool of starlight. And pain."

I shake my head. "It's fine." I want them. They are a reminder, just like the mark I can still feel the ghost of against my throat.

I drop Raker's hand and don't miss how his fingers reach for mine again on reflex—before pausing.

"I hope you don't mind the clothes," Este continues, motioning to the dress I woke up in. It's thin, silky fabric, barely enough to cover me, just like the women behind her, staring at us curiously. I walked out of that City on Fire naked, broken, ash-covered but unburnt. I walked out the phoenix Stellan always told me to be. The clothes—they don't matter. Not when Este has given me a chance to finish this journey.

I lift to my feet and reach my hand to hers. "Thank you," I say, gripping her fingers, trying to convey in any way possible my endless gratitude.

She smiles, but I see a trace of sadness in her eyes.

Something is wrong.

I think about the Traveling City, and all its rules. The way the Eldress looked at her, when she reached out to give me her final parting words.

A pinch forms between my brows.

"You can't go back, can you?" I ask, hoping I'm wrong.

But she just lifts her head. "No. Once one of us chooses to leave through the gates . . . we're not welcomed in again."

My eyes widen. She sacrificed everything she loved . . . including her *sister* . . . for *me*.

Why?

"I—"

She silences me with a hand on my arm. "I made my choice, and I don't regret it." She looks up at the sky. "You are the ember that lights the torch, Aris. I know it. The world is about to change . . . and it's time we stopped hiding. It's time we actually do something."

Conviction rings through her words. She dips her chin.

"Now, come," she says, leading me toward the rest of the women. "Tomorrow, you finish your quest. You deserve at least one night of peace."

42

The faeling not only saved me—she brought us somewhere to sleep: a starless, black, secluded cave. The smooth stone is cold beneath my bare feet. My scabbard is heavy in my hand. Raker is a towering shadow behind me, following *me* for once. Maybe he's too tired to protest. He hasn't said a word in an hour. We walk down a tunnel until we reach a circular clearing with a waterfall trickling onto a slab of obsidian rock tilted slightly to the side, letting it drain somewhere below.

A few feet in front of it sits a bed.

Well, a makeshift one, anyway. The forest nymphs Este summoned managed to find dozens of thick, clean sheets, stacked together to make the most comfortable spot I've seen in a long while. All I want is to bury myself in it, and sleep forever, and ask Raker how comfortable the cold stone floor is in the morning. But first, I need to wash the remaining soot and ash away.

He says nothing as I head toward the waterfall in the dress they gave me. The nymphs' fabrics are barely there at all, translucent when wet—I've *seen* them—but I'm so grateful for the rush of clean, cold water that I don't care. It's not like Raker will be looking, anyway.

I take my time. I carefully undo my braid. I scrub the cinder from my hair and then my skin, until it's smooth again. I clean the blood off my sword. Then, after the evidence of the duel is gone, I sink to my knees. Sit on my heels. Tilt my head up to the water and let it soak my every inch, drops like cold fingers threading through the roots of my hair, smoothing my rough edges, letting me forget, for just a moment, how much of my own blood was shed today. How much more will be shed tomorrow. *Tomorrow.* The day I finally face the gods. I sigh and release a fraction of the tension in my stress-coiled bones.

When I'm done, I turn to see Raker standing very still. Watching. In the same place he was ten minutes ago.

His expression is the same as it's always been—closed off. Heartless. Cold. But we've survived weeks across Starside together. We've slayed creatures with claws like swords; we've made it out of castle rooms painted red with blood; we've survived demons that crawled into our minds. As much as I hate it, and him, I know him. I can see the slight tension in his shoulders. The way the vein down his sword-wielding arm is taut. How his frown doesn't reach his eyes.

Before, I would have thought he looked disgusted. Now I can see he almost looks pained.

Slowly, I rise. Water drips down the sheer fabric that might as well not even be there at all. He can see everything. Including the thin silver lines like roots down my neck, chest, and arms. Glowing faintly in the light.

And he's not looking away this time.

"I'm likely going to die tomorrow," I say, my voice coming out in a rough whisper.

He doesn't correct me.

"There's—there's one thing I haven't tried." I can't believe the words have left my mouth. The Aris from weeks before is screaming from the past, *What are you doing? Don't humiliate yourself.*

But even though I knew from the start that this would kill me, being so close to all too imminent death makes me fearless. It makes me ask for exactly what I want, for the very first time in my life.

I don't shrink under Raker's gaze, not the way I have before. I don't bend under his unrelenting scrutiny.

Because he seems to get my meaning immediately. His frown deepens. He's trying hard to look irritated—of course he is. His pride and position and a million other reasons make admitting to wanting to spend a moment with me that isn't for the good of the quest impossible.

"Are you truly so desperate?" he finally says, his voice harsh. But he's said worse. So have I.

"Yes," I reply.

His mouth was open, likely halfway to another barb, but my response shocks him into silence. It's always been a duel with us, hurling words like throwing stars back and forth, clashing swords, leveling glares across rooms that end in spilled blood.

Tonight, I've laid down my sword. It's still sitting beneath the falling water, its metal glimmering.

Still, he looks wary, like he's expecting this is a ruse, a way to kill him while I can. A way to finally lay claim to his own glorious blade.

I slowly uncurl my fingers, until he's staring at my palms. "Unarmed." I turn all the way around, for good measure. There's no concealing anything beneath these sheer, wet fabrics.

When I face him again, his hands are in fists, knuckles white, veins taut. He's standing so still, I'm not sure he's breathing.

Harlan Raker is a famed, merciless warrior—and right now, he looks every inch as deadly as his reputation. For even though I'm unarmed, he's armed to the teeth.

I should be afraid. I should be ashamed of myself. I take a slow step toward him.

He doesn't move a single inch.

I keep moving. When I reach him, I lift my chin, leaving any trace of emotion or anticipation out of my voice. "I hate you. This wouldn't change anything."

"Of course it wouldn't," he spits back at me.

Good.

He could leave, he could go to bed himself, he could do a thousand things, but here he is, looking at me, as if he's waiting. As if he doesn't think I'll have the nerve to do something next.

I stare him down the same way I have every other time he's challenged me. Instead of making for my sword, though, I move to unclasp my top, and his hand shoots out, grabbing my wrist. Stopping me.

At first, I think he's going to snarl and reject my advances. Or order me to remain mostly clothed while he has me against a wall.

But then his hand drags down the wet fabric, and it's the first time I've seen him truly lose control. Because he looks like he *hates himself* for touching me, but it also looks like he can't stop.

His rough fingers slide down my breast, and I'm not breathing. His callused thumb rubs across my hardened nipple, and I pinch my lips together to keep from making any sound at all.

He doesn't need to know how much I like this. He doesn't need to feel how long I've wanted this.

Our encounter underground could be blamed on the fire demon. We were in the dark, with our eyes closed. This . . . this is different.

He removes his hand, and my body shivers at the loss of heat.

"We shouldn't do this," he says, and I think he's going to leave me here, aching. Wanting. But then, in a flash, he reaches around and tears the buttons at my neck clean off. They bounce somewhere far away, clinking against stone. My dress slides down my body, onto the floor.

His eyes seem to go wholly black.

I shiver under his unrelenting gaze. It's cold in here, and I'm wet, small droplets of water running down my heated skin, across the markings he can now see clear as day. Since I got them, it's been instinct to hide, to shrink away from notice, but I don't move to cover myself. I don't do anything that would make him think of me as weak. Because even if we're really doing this, he's still my enemy.

The way he's looking at me, taking in every inch as if I exist for him alone to study, shouldn't send a jolt of need right to the core of me, but I am beyond shame. I am beyond reason.

His knuckles get even whiter as he stares and stares, gaze locked onto my chest, heavy with need and peaked from the cold. My thighs clench together, and that's where his eyes drop next.

This is purely physical. Raker hasn't ever let anyone kiss him, so I'm not expecting anything tender.

I'm not surprised when he says in a dark voice that seems ripped from the seams of his self-control, "Get on your hands and knees."

Fuck. We're really doing this.

I swallow. He traces the movement with his eyes. He's focusing far too closely on my neck. Carefully, very carefully, gaze never leaving his, I lower myself onto the sheets. I turn my back to him.

For a moment, I wait for the sound of his sword scraping out of his scabbard. I wait for him to betray me and slay me while I'm at my most vulnerable.

There is a sound of metal—

His armor. He's taking it off, piece by piece.

"I said your hands and knees," he says, his voice a dark and brutal command.

I bend over. Do as he says. I really am desperate, aren't I? Yes. Right now, yes. I'm desperate and aching. These weeks have been about survival, but right now, before my almost-guaranteed death, I want this.

My back arches and a shiver licks down my spine. I'm more exposed than I've ever been in my life.

I swear I hear a barely restrained growl behind me, but his voice is cold and cruel as ever as he says, "Look at you. Already gleaming and ready for me."

I clench my jaw, staring straight ahead. The sheets rustle with movement. My skin prickles at his approaching heat. "No one has touched me in weeks. Don't flatter yourself."

"Weeks?" he says, suddenly stilling behind me. If I didn't know better, I would say he sounds jealous.

"*Weeks*," I reply.

His fingers dig roughly into the sides of my hips as he drags me back toward him. His hands are burning hot.

Then, without any words or warning, the full heat of him is against me.

And I'm glad he can't see my face, because my eyes nearly roll into the back of my head at the contact. I can't see him, but I can feel him, and his sheer size against me—

I should have known. Should have suspected. I *felt* it, that night at the ball. Though now, with him right against my entrance, the clear difference in size has me sweating.

I brace myself, waiting for a flash of pain. Wondering if there is any way to do this that doesn't ruin me.

But it's almost gentle, the way he pushes in. And in.

My every nerve seems to flicker on, and this time I do gasp at the fullness, at the stretch, as it becomes immediately too tight. I don't expect him to stop, but he does. He does, until I can breathe through it.

Then he begins to pull my hips back, inching me farther and farther onto him. Slowly. It happens slowly, slowly, until every thought and feeling and sensation is narrowed to that searing point of contact as he pushes in and in, and, *somehow* he's still going.

He pushes in again. *Again.*

Until I'm so full of him, I can't think around it, can't feel beyond *him*, I can't get a full breath.

And then, just when I'm wondering how this is possibly going to work, he starts to move.

I curse into the sheets. "Did you have to be so big? I can feel you in my fucking *teeth*."

He makes what seems like a tortured sound behind me, but a moment later, his voice is smooth as velvet as he says, "And I can feel you trying not to scream."

He's right. Every part of me is clenched tight, because if I let go, if I give in wholly to this building pleasure, I'm going to scream, I'm going to whimper, I'm going to beg, and I'm not going to be able to stop.

He's going to know he has me all but ensnared, and I can't have that happen. He can't know that I've never felt anything like this, and that I hate—*hate*—that it's coming from him.

My voice is strained as I manage to say, "No. Not at all."

He laughs darkly behind me, and the sound makes my skin tighten across all the sensitive places I want to be touched. Everywhere is so raw, so needy. The pain has given way completely to a pleasure like melted-down gold, glimmering, sinking down to my core, curling into blinding, building, unrelenting need. He increases his pace, and I bite my lip to keep from crying out. "Really? I think you're lying, Aris. I think you're a fucking liar."

I'm surprised I can keep my composure as I say through gritted teeth, "Or maybe you're not as good at this as you think you are."

In a flash, he pulls me up, one hand palming my breast, the other firm against my hip, and the next thrust is so hard, so deep, my shoulders hike up. My lips part with a choked gasp.

He laughs against the top of my head. "Like that?"

I don't say a word. I seal my mouth shut. And his callused fingers just scrape against my sensitive skin, circling my hardened peak, in slow, languid movements, like he has all the time in the world to wait for my response. My pulse races as those rings get smaller. Closer. He's getting closer and closer to where I need him, and his pace is inching to a crawl, drawing it out—until his rough thumb finally brushes against my nipple, and I almost whimper. He does it again. He pinches it, and heat floods through me, but I keep my fucking mouth shut.

I don't want him to know that with just a few simple strokes, he's worked me into an aching, desperate frenzy. I don't want him to have that kind of power over me. But I'm fighting a losing battle with the moans crawling up my throat, and he fucking knows it. He knows exactly what he's doing, thanks to my body's own response to this pleasure, and he growls his approval as he feels just how much I like this. It's obvious. I can hear the proof of my enjoyment with every thrust, but that's not enough, he wants words, he wants the truth, and he's going to drag it from my lips with every punishing brush of his fingers. His callused knuckles scrape below the underside of my breast, testing, teasing, wanting me to cry out. Wanting me to break.

I don't. A moment later, his other hand splays out across my lower abdomen, pressing down hard as he continues to thrust into me—and I see stars. I fight to breathe. He has me pinned against his muscled body, palming my abdomen like he wants to feel himself inside of me, fucking me like he's trying to rob me of my sanity, and the pressure builds into a rising, blazing wave of need.

Just when I think I can't possibly feel any better, his fingers slip between my legs, to the aching core of me, and—

Fuck.

A burst of pleasure races through my veins, and my head is falling back against his chest, and I'm making a sound I've never made in my life.

"There it is," he says, deep voice right in my ear. And then, like a reward, his fingers stroke me into a mess of moans and throaty pleas.

It's official. He has me. Instead of pinned against a wall with a blade at my throat, he has his rough thumb pressed against my sensitive center, and he knows exactly how to make me cry out for him. I do. Again, and again. I can't help it. He makes a pleased sound. "You're going to be screaming my name in no time, Aris. And I'm never going to let you forget it."

The bastard.

But I'm not the only one enjoying this. I can feel the proof of it, the extent of that enjoyment dragging through me, hard as steel. I begin to grind my hips back, arching my spine, meeting him stroke for stroke. I sink down deeper, taking even more of him.

His movements falter. It's all the encouragement I need. I don't stop. I grind back onto him, riding him like this, clenching, writhing.

"*Fuck,*" he snarls right against the crown of my head.

A pleased smile spreads across my face as I realize, for the first time, Harlan Raker is completely at my mercy.

And I like it.

I don't know what I'm doing, but I wrench myself free, turn, and push him down onto the sheets, and he *lets* me, even though he's baring his teeth at me in warning.

I pin him down. I remember his promise. That soon enough, I'll be screaming his name. I press my hands against his chest and say, "You're going to be screaming mine, Harlan." I must be imagining it, but I swear he shivers.

Then I sink down onto him, taking every brutal inch, and we both curse at the same time.

Fuck. I feel so full it's hard to breathe. I'll never get used to the stretch, to the tight fit, but still . . . I want more. His eyes widen as he watches me begin to move on him, like he can't look away. I really don't know what I'm doing, but when I tilt forward, bracing my hands on his hard chest, and find a place that sends a jolt up my spine, I start to move faster, chasing it, wringing every ounce of pleasure I can from him.

His hand reaches toward me, as if on instinct, but he stops himself. Fists the sheets instead. He might as well be touching me, though. His gaze is casting flames. I can feel the heat of it on my chest as I ride him, on my stomach as I arch back, on my face as my lips part with pleasure.

I look at him too. His wide shoulders. Pale, tattooed skin over rippling muscle, unmarred by even a single scar, as if nothing has ever gotten close to hurting him.

At least, that used to be true.

There's a new mark, across his throat. One I gave him.

We're enemies. I've hated him for years. We both have wanted each other dead. He's right. We really shouldn't be doing this, but I also don't ever want to be doing anything else. Nothing has ever felt so good, so full, so all-encompassing. My every nerve is sensitive, prickling, fire-swept, embers dancing across my skin.

My nails rake down his abs, and he doesn't make a move to stop me. My head falls back as I chase my pleasure, as I grind against him, as I move with abandon.

It's not enough, though. I want more, want to feel him deeper, everywhere.

And I can't pretend any longer. There's an ache within me, growing and desperate. It's been building for a while, this fire between us, this inevitable battle. I don't care if this is wrong, or if I hate him—I want this. I want it so badly it scares me. "Raker, *please*," I say, willing to go on my knees, willing to beg for this. I don't even know what I want, but something tells me he knows exactly how to give it to me.

His hand moves to my throat. At first, I think he might squeeze it, but all he does is trace his thumb up and down my pulse and say in a voice forged from pure and utter need, "Say it again."

Fine. If he wants me to beg, I will.

"Please," I say, my voice raspy and out of breath.

But he shakes his head. His own voice is strained. "No. My name. Say it."

Satisfaction spreads through me. He's not the only one who holds power here. I see it in the desperate flicker in his eye. I see it in the way his muscles are flexing as if he's holding himself back, as if he too is afraid to let himself go completely.

He might be the greatest knight on Stormside. He might not have a single mark on his armor. But right now, he's looking at me like I can ruin him.

And he might beg for it.

I slow my movements. He watches, transfixed, as my tongue darts out to lick my lips. Taking my time, I drag my hands down his muscled chest.

Then I bend down low, and say slowly, right above his mouth, "Harlan Raker."

He flips me over in a flash, his hand curling beneath my knee, pulling one of my legs into an angle against his chest, and then he starts to fuck me at an unyielding, unforgiving pace that has me screaming.

I arch against his body, my nipples scraping against his hard chest every time he slams into me, my toes curling. This is Harlan Raker unleashed.

My spine is a bolt of lightning, gleaming with nerves, sparks spreading with every brutal stroke. His cock drags against a place so deep, so sensitive, I'm whimpering. I'm clawing at his chest.

My head falls back, but he tilts it forward again so that my eyes meet his. "Aris," he says, his voice a deep rumble I can feel in my bones. I nearly break, hearing my name on his lips like this.

"I," he says, slamming into me again, dragging me across the sheets. "*Hate*," he says, punctuating the word with another brutal thrust. "*You*." He slams again.

He's saying it as if he's trying to remind himself of that fact.

And the way he's looking at me . . . he means it.

He hates me the same way I hate him. He hates that this feels so good. He hates that we both know it. Because it's undeniable. This fire, flaming, raging between us is undeniable.

"I hate you too," I say, breathless, meaning it in all the same ways.

We glare at each other as he lifts my hips and takes me deeper, eyes widening, mouths tightening, neither wanting to break first. Neither wanting to admit anything other than hatred.

Then his gaze suddenly falters. He looks down and stops for just a moment. I see the surprise flicker over him and trace his line of sight. He's looking at my marks.

The sensitive silver markings along my skin are gleaming brighter than they ever have before.

His fingers dig into my hips. He rips his gaze from my markings and lifts my other leg. My ankles lock behind him.

And he fucks me like he hates me. Like he hates this. Like he hates that he's uttering a string of curses into the crown of *my* head. His movements are getting more desperate, rougher, hitting a place that makes me bite my lip, heating my blood until it's boiling.

Everything in this world has always seemed so limited, but this feeling, this pleasure, this fullness seems endless.

Until he slams into me one final time, and the pleasure crests and shatters. Together. We shatter together, our gazes locked, until he closes his eyes sharply and curses so loudly, it echoes through the cave.

The cave. I almost forgot where we were. How we got here. Who, exactly, I was doing this with.

His eyes open again. We're staring at each other, both panting, chests meeting. We're waiting for who is going to make the next move.

Embarrassment and shame sink through me. Maybe we shouldn't have done this. I feel so raw. So exposed. *And he's never going to let me forget it.* I open my mouth, and Harlan Raker does the last thing I would ever expect—

He kisses me. His lips crash against mine, and I gasp, then melt as his tongue traces my parted lips. It's not gentle. It's punishing, the way he kisses me, like he wants to swallow my breaths and words and protests. Like he didn't just tell me he hates me. Like he didn't say, days before, that this very act is more intimate than having sex and that he would never allow someone to get that close to him. He's doing it now. Very thoroughly. He's biting my bottom lip so hard he's drawing blood, and then he's licking that too, and he's stroking my teeth and the top of my mouth, like he's trying to taste and savor every single inch of me.

He's still hard inside me.

I start to move on him greedily, the ache building again, and he doesn't hesitate. He starts to take me with long, brutal strokes, matching the pace of his tongue in my mouth, and I'm on fire. I'm burning.

Heat floods my body, something in my blood calling to his, and *this*—this is different.

This is us giving up all pretense that we didn't both want this, *need* this.

I gasp for air when his lips slip down my neck, licking, sucking, teeth scraping against my pulse. His hand slides between us, and he bites down just as his fingers find my center again, then curses as I tighten around him, a scraping sound leaving my lips.

Then the world tilts. In one smooth movement, he's standing, and gripping my ass, and then he's hauling me up against the wall.

The stone is cool and smooth behind my back as he fucks me against it, his mouth still hot against my neck. He takes his time there, on the sensitive place between my neck and shoulder. There's another sting of teeth, and then my back arches off the wall at a blinding flash of pleasure. He snarls his approval, and then he's groaning, and I'm whimpering as he takes me deeper and rougher, like he's still trying to get more of me.

I'm beyond words right now. I'm only panting and insistent movements as my legs wrap around him, heels digging into his back, meeting him stroke for stroke, riding out this pleasure on his cock. He takes me again and again, shifting my hips and changing angles, each thrust tightening this coil of need within me, until it's wound almost painfully tight.

"Harlan," I say, my voice a ragged plea, and his hand moves between us. With a single brush of his callused thumb, my body bows off the wall as my world shatters into a thousand glimmering steel pieces. I gasp and then his mouth is on mine again, claiming it, swallowing every pant and cry, and I cling to him as he takes me through every shuddering wave, and then again, like he's trying to wring every bit of pleasure from my body.

It's still not enough. Not even close. "I need—"

"I know what you need," he says, and then my feet hit the ground, and he's spinning me and pressing me against the cold wall, and lifting me to my toes by my hips, and filling me and—

"Fucking *gods*, Raker," I cry out against the wall as he takes me hard and fast.

One of his massive hands curls around the back of my head, pressing my cheek to the stone.

"No. Fucking *me*, Aris. *Only* me."

And then he fucks me harder, like he's trying to mark me, trying to claim me, and I arch my hips back and meet his every stroke, doing the same.

This. This is what I've needed for weeks—the desires I couldn't even put into words. A pleasure I didn't even know was possible. This hatred between us has blurred and burned into something far more complicated, endless duels that have all led to this.

We've fought and battled and argued this entire journey and now every ounce of tension is being worked out, thoroughly, as if this is its own duel, its own language, and my entire body is going taut, then loose, and I'm tightening around him, and he's groaning. He's gripping my hips, and the world could be crumbling around me, and I wouldn't even notice, I'm too lost in this pulsing, insistent, desperate madness. He's giving me everything I need without me even having to ask for it.

One hand still firm on my hip, his knuckles slowly trail up the curve of my side, to my waist, his long fingers opening one by one, curling around the base of my ribs, then gently stroking the shape of me, like I'm a map he wants to memorize.

Chills erupt across my heated skin, and he touches all of them, feeling how my body responds to his, learning how to make me prickle even more, studying me not like an enemy he wants to conquer, but like an opponent he wants to surrender to. His thrusts are hard and fast, hammering into me like he wants me to see stars, but his fingers are featherlight. He's touching my body with the care and reverence he's only ever reserved for his sword, like I'm more precious than its metal, like I'm more dangerous than its edge, like he wants to claim me more than any other weapon.

Then his hand is in my hair, and he groans as he touches the long strands, rubbing them between his fingers. "I was right," he says, curving over me, mouth at my ear. "This is dangerous." It's what he said in the Traveling City, when he saw it down for the first time. He meant because it was a risk during dueling.

Now, he takes all of it in his fist—and pulls. My lips part. His grip is light, not enough to hurt at all, but the possessive move makes my mind spin. Because this isn't about either of us giving in. I see that now. No, this is just like when our blades meet. Two equal forces, coming together. A push and pull that merges into a perfect joining.

This pleasure is gleaming, ruinous, and I know in my blood it wouldn't be like this with anyone else. I don't just want this. I want *him*.

My arms reach back, wrapping around his neck, arching against him, nipples still pressed to the cold wall, pinned between him and the cave, and he molds to me, until his entire body is flush with mine. I'm on my toes, his legs against my thighs, keeping me upright. His hands are back on my hips, fucking me onto him, finding a place that makes a jolt of pleasure race up my spine with every thrust, and I choke out his name. He does it again. Faster. My eyes close tightly against the surging wave of pleasure.

"Like that?" he says.

This time, I nod against him.

That's not good enough. He reaches for my throat, thumb gently stroking where his teeth sank into my skin, and says, "I need your words, Aris," his deep voice echoing, vibrating through my blood. *"Please."*

Fuck. I never thought I would hear him beg.

So, I give him what he wants.

"*Yes*," I say, looking up at him. His forehead is leaned against the cave wall. He's staring down at me like he doesn't ever want to look anywhere else. His mouth is just inches away. "Just like that, *Harlan*."

His fingers dig into my hip and throat—and then he unleashes, dragging against that gleaming place in a ruinous, unyielding pace. I cry out, lightning spearing through my veins, and he growls his approval. He keeps going and going like it's his sole purpose in life to get me over the edge, like he wants to test just how much pleasure I can take.

I need to taste him. We're facing the same direction, and my head is tilted up, his is down, but my fingers fist his hair, and I pull his mouth to mine, and—

This angle shouldn't work. But my tongue brushes his lips and he groans when it meets his. The kiss is messy, and insistent, and he's holding me to his mouth by the throat, he's tasting me like he can't get enough, and I could die from this. From the perfect stretch of him desperately filling every aching part of me, from the sound of his moans in my mouth, from the all-consuming feel of him. He kisses me until I can't think, I can't breathe, and then I suck on his bottom lip, licking and stroking, biting him like he bit me, marking him, until another wave of pleasure rolls through me and I release him.

His eyes have darkened into ink. He looks half-crazed. Enraptured. He looks a moment from losing his fucking mind, like I control his sanity, and I'm about to snap its final string.

"*Aris*," he says, his voice a tortured rasp. "You will be the fucking end of me."

"Harlan," I breathe. "If *only*." Our gazes are locked. I throw my head back. His name is on my lips as my desire crests.

Then I'm falling back onto my heels again. Before I can miss his fullness, he's turning me back around, and lifting me to his height, and my legs are around him, and he's pushing into me again, and—

His mouth crashes against mine in a brutal kiss that's all teeth and smothered gasps, and this, *this* is how I want to finish, with me facing him. I'm close, and he seems to know it. His hand reaches down, thumb stroking me toward the edge of this cliff, until I'm on its brink, trembling with pleasure that's ready to pull me under. I try to fight it, give myself more time, bucking my hips, chasing this desire until its very end.

Now, it's his back against the wall. His forehead is pressed to mine. He's not even moving anymore, he's just watching me ride him, watching me take what I need, watching my thighs tremble as I stave off my release, as I curse because this feels *too fucking good*.

I try to take him deeper, but it's hard at this angle, and—

I don't even have to say a word. All it takes is a fold in my brow, and he's sliding to the floor, pulling me down with him, and I'm bracing my hands on his wide shoulders as I move on him. *Better. Much better.* He's curved, leaned close, watching me ride him needily, desperately. I'm panting right against his mouth.

"I still hate you," I gasp.

"Yeah?"

"*Yeah*." I say, breathing hard. "I hate you so much."

His hands tighten around my hips.

"Good. Hate me harder, Aris."

The same words he said as we dueled. *Hate. Me. Harder.*

I do. I ride him as hard as I can, and he groans, watching me take him, over and over, letting me use him. I lean forward and grind against his hard muscles, chasing my pleasure. My hands are in his hair, his face is just inches away.

Not close enough. I want him to flood my senses, I want to feel him, smell him, *taste him*. I duck my head—and slowly run my tongue along the thin line across his throat. The only scar he has.

A *reminder*.

He groans. I feel him twitch inside me.

"*Aris*," he says, my name like a prayer on his lips.

And I shatter. I pulse around him, crying out, and he seals his mouth to mine, swallowing the sound. He starts to take over then, fucking me faster than before, in hard, brutal strokes, like he can read me, like he knows this is exactly what I want from him. Then he stands in one smooth motion, holding me with what seems like no effort, presses me against the wall and fucks the sanity and attitude and anger out of me, never even breaking our kiss. He tastes me like he's starving, like he needs this, and when I suck on his tongue, then rake his bottom lip through my teeth, he groans and breaks too. I feel him, pulsing within me, our gazes locked, our mouths now just inches apart. We're panting, sharing breath, studying each other.

Fuck.

It wasn't supposed to be like this. He wasn't supposed to be the cure to everything I never knew I needed.

This was supposed to be quick, and meaningless. But—

His previously unmarred chest is now marked with long lines where I clawed at him. I can feel blood hot against my lip where he bit me. My neck is tender. There's an undeniable soreness between my legs and liquid dripping down my thigh.

We've ruined each other. And by the time we finally go to sleep in the pile of sheets, we've ruined each other even more.

When I wake up, my body is sore. Aching. Sensitive everywhere.

And Harlan is gone.

He took my sword.

He betrayed me, just like I always knew he would.

43

No.

My head is still spinning with confusion and regret, and *this can't be happening* and *why did I think it wouldn't*, when a step echoes through the cave.

Followed by several others.

Before I can get the sheet over me, three human men step into view. I recognize them. Questral challengers.

One of them has a long line below his jaw, as if someone almost killed him but didn't. It bleeds when he raises his head. "Well, look at this. She's already naked for us." He turns to the others and laughs. They all look hungrily, disgustingly, at me, as if they're going to have me and there's nothing I can do about it.

"What do you want?" I demand, my voice sharpened with pure anger. They've picked the wrong fucking time to find me.

The one with the line below his jaw just smiles. "We watched him. We watched him leave you, with your sword in hand. But that's not what we're here for . . . No, we're here for *you*." He looks at the others. "The god didn't specify in what state she was to be delivered . . . Perhaps he'll take you in pieces." He looks me over and smirks. "It's been a while since I've had a woman. You're going to see just how starved I've been."

I pull the sheet over myself, but it might as well be nothing.

Nothing.

My sword is gone.

He took it.

But that doesn't mean I'm defenseless. Because I have not gone on this great journey and survived both physical and emotional perils for three men to stop me.

I stand, letting the sheet drop, falling into my fighting stance. I ignore the heat of their stares.

"You don't have a sword," the man with the bloody mark says, laughing at me.

"You're wrong," I say, looking at the ones they're holding. "I have three."

Three glimmering blades. Won by these monsters. Or gifted by the God of Death.

Great swords can betray their wielders if they encounter someone stronger. By the end of this, these blades will answer to *me*.

This will not kill me.

Stellaris.

I hear her faint echo far away, and my pulse races. *Where are you?* Her song is muted, and that's when I realize my scabbard is gone. Stellaris must be inside of it, impossible for me to summon. Raker took that too.

He took . . . *everything*. And I let him.

I practically begged him to.

A deep, twisting sadness strikes me right through the chest, but I bury it. I won't think of him for another second. Not now that he's left me here to fight and die alone.

The men are still staring at me, reveling in my naked body in a way that makes fury pound through my blood. It's that distraction that costs one of them.

I lunge right at him and his sword, tackling him to the ground. I barely move out of the way of his blade.

I pin his wrist down with my knee, then grab his head with both of my hands and slam it down against the stone with all my might, over and over and over, my thumbs curling into his eyes, nails digging, popping.

This rage is blinding. It's unrelenting. Those eyes that looked upon me with the promise of violence are now in tatters.

His scream pierces the cave like a blade. I turn to see the other men standing very still, as if temporarily shocked by my brutality.

The one with the blood across his neck finally grins. "I like them with some fight."

The other races forward. "You crazed bitch!" he roars, and I spin off his friend's lifeless body just in time to miss his metal. It goes through his friend's chest instead, burying itself in his rib cage. He pulls and pulls at it, but of course he's too weak to get it back through the bone.

"You weak idiot," I say, kicking him from the side, watching him stumble back. He watches me as I force his own blade out of his friend's chest cavity.

Mine.

It glimmers in my palm, claiming me as I have claimed it. The connection is nothing like me and Stellaris, but for now, it's everything. The metal is recently sharpened, long and curved.

He races toward me with a dagger this time, roaring, and I duck, then turn, slicing hard and wide—cutting his legs clean off. He falls forward, screaming, blood shooting out of him.

The marked man watches me slowly rise from my crouch, gripping his friend's blade. He's still smiling. He's still looking at my blood-covered body with relish and the promise of cruelty.

He raises his sword—and I throw mine right at his arm, pinning him to the wall with the force. I aimed the blade high, so it didn't completely sever the limb. No, I want him trapped. Just like he thought he had cornered me. He screams, his blade now on the ground, his arm only attached by a few nerves and threads of skin.

He watches me stalk toward him.

"What was it you said you were going to do to me?" I say, turning the sword in my hand.

"No—nothing. I wasn't really going to do anything." He isn't smiling anymore. No . . . he's trembling.

"Right," I say.

He changes strategy. As if maybe he can say something that might pull at my heartstrings. "The god—he said he would take me straight to the Land of the Gods. He said I would get two immortal cups. I have, I have a family, and—"

"I don't give a shit," I say, grabbing the other blade from the ground and burying it in his chest. He bellows.

I drag both swords out of him, and he falls forward. He's able to gather enough strength to crawl. I let him. I let him make it a few feet. I let him hope.

Then I flip him over and pin him to the ground with my legs. His words run through my head, his promises. Then memories. Three men pinning me down. Carving their names into my skin. They spoke similar words. Made similar promises.

I'm blinded by rage as I stab him over and over, with both blades, wailing, screaming. I stab him so many times that I'm covered in blood when I'm done.

I thank the person that made it easy for me, who traced the line across his neck that I now run across with my blade until I hit bone.

Only then do I let both swords fall to the ground.

Dripping blood, I walk out of the cave.

44

He betrayed me.

I promised I wouldn't think about him again, but the reminder of the night, and the sinking feeling of discovering him gone, won't go away. Not as I chew the leaves from the sprig he left for me to find, a flower I recognize, a remedy for *afterward*. Not as I claw my way up the side of the mountain and sink to my knees when I reach the peak.

My blood-crusted eyes prickle, watching the world from this height, because it is *beautiful*, and that just makes everything so much worse.

I don't have my sword anymore.

I don't have a partner.

I don't even have *clothes*.

There are just days left of the Questral. At this point, I won't make it back to the gates, especially without my sword. I know that.

All that's left for me is this one purpose, and I don't know how to reach it. Not alone.

I look up at the sky, my chin trembling.

The only thing of mine I have left is this diamond necklace. It was waiting, on a rock next to that sprig. Raker must have held it for me and left it. It's almost like a message. *Go to him instead.* But he doesn't get to do that, he doesn't get to leave and then tell me what he thinks is best for me, he doesn't get to growl at me to take the necklace off then leave it for me to find.

Besides. I don't want it anyway.

With a shaking hand, I offer it to the skies, and say, "Please. Please, come back for me. I—I need you." Tears fall, blurring my vision. "I won't make it without you."

I cry, letting my agony spill out, my shame, my *everything*, every hope and want that shouldn't belong to me but did and is now in tatters. It all comes out in raking sobs, tears falling and falling and falling, until something sparkling blocks my vision.

But it isn't my dragon. No, it's a beam of light melting into the form of a woman. I lift my arm, blocking my eyes against the brightness.

When I drop it, the woman in silver is tilting her head at me. "You look lost," she says.

The diamonds tremble in my palm. "I am lost. I have been lost. I *have lost* everyone I have ever loved."

The star on her brow glimmers as she studies me. "You remind me of myself."

I laugh without humor. "We do look so much alike, don't we?" Me, covered in blood, my hair knotted with it. Her, glowing with ethereal beauty.

She doesn't laugh at all. "At one point in my life, I looked just like you," she says. "Covered in the blood of my enemies. Bellowing to the sky for someone to help me."

"Then help me," I say through my teeth. She says nothing, and I sink deeper into the ground, the fight leaving me. I will beg. I will plead. I have nothing else left. "Please, show me the way. Like you did before."

She shakes her head. "I don't need to. You already know the way."

"I *don't*."

"Ask me a different question," she says. She says it quickly, like we don't have much time, and I suppose I don't.

I have so many. *So many*. Very few will help me now.

But . . . but there is one.

"How did he take my sword while I'm still alive? Did it—did it choose him?"

Her eyes gleam. "Do you care for him?"

"No," I spit. But it's a lie.

She seems to know it too. "Let me tell you something about great swords, Aris. Swords forged by the elements themselves, by the gods, by the strongest emotions. Forged by love and fury."

"Godswords," I say.

She nods. "Great swords meld to your soul. To your heart. And when you let someone into it . . . they can take what's yours."

And let him in I did.

My hands shake with anger. My cheeks redden in shame. Did Raker know that? Is that why he's been working with me this whole time? To wait for me to fall for him, like a fool, so he could take my sword?

Why not just kill me, then? Why not claim my sword that way? It doesn't make any sense.

"Why mine? Why not any other godsword?" We came across a few. The one that was thrown in the mud. The one in the mists. He could have gone after either of them, but he didn't.

She nods again, like this was another good question. The star on her brow gleams as she says, "Your blade and his—they used to be one."

Even the pounding in my ears stops.

My word is a whisper. "What?"

"Your swords are two halves of the same blade. That's why they glow the same color. Long ago, they were split, for their power was too great as one. Your swords connect you." A shadow passes over her face. "If he seeks to merge them again, you must stop him. Those swords, joined, will lead to millennia of ruin."

I don't want that. I *do* want to stop it . . . but my only purpose is revenge. The Astral Queen seems to know it too.

"The connection to your swords binds you. He is a map. Follow *him*, and you will reach the gods you seek."

He is a map.

Even if that were true—even if I knew what that meant—how am I supposed to get there? Who knows when he left? He could already have reached the Land of the Gods. "But I . . . I have nothing."

She smiles. "That's where you're wrong. You are not alone, Aris."

You are not alone.

Raker said those words. He meant him, and he was a liar for saying so. But he was not wrong.

A distant shriek lances through the sky. I know that shriek. In the far distance, past the clouds, shines a creature brighter than all the stars combined.

My dragon. Her eyes glimmer when she sees me. As if she's been searching too.

Light blinds me for just a moment. And in that moment, my skin hums as all the blood is washed away by some curious magic. Soft fabrics and sparkling armor cover my naked body. When the light fades, the Astral Queen is floating there, shaping a beam of light into a sword of pure starlight. She hands it to me.

"Anyone can start a journey, Aris," the Astral Queen says. "Not everyone can end it." She shoots back up to the sky just as my dragon lands before me, shaking the mountain.

I fall back from the force, then lunge forward, throwing my arms around her. Our foreheads press together, and the star on her shines. *It shines.* And I feel something being seared into my skin too. I tremble with a sob.

Then she lightly pushes me back with her nose. Sniffs.

I laugh, knowing exactly what she smells. "Right," I say, tossing up the diamond necklace.

She catches it in her mouth. The diamonds crunch and shatter against her superior teeth. She swallows.

I tuck the starlight sword against my back, and it stays there, humming. Ready.

So am I.

I mount my dragon, and say, "Let's finish this."

45

Wind whips my hair back, but my eyes do not close against it. I am solely focused forward. The Astral Queen was right. I can *feel* him. Like a vise around my very soul, snaking through my marrow, tugging like a rope, I follow the glittering string across the world to him.

He's gotten far, quickly. Perhaps he was always capable of this speed. Maybe I just slowed him down. Maybe that's all I ever was to him—an obstacle to overcome.

Of course I was. Why would I ever think anything different?

I see you too.

Those words haunt me, my eyes stinging. "You saw me, and you *left me*," I say into the wind, my voice echoing through it.

After everything, foolish of me to think that something I cared about would ever be anything other than temporary.

Anger and agony and betrayal shape me, until I become more than just this body, just this armor and this glimmering sword of starlight. I become a sword myself, forged in fury.

The gods don't know what's coming for them. I don't fear death like they do.

This will kill me.

It's supposed to.

My dragon's wings push forward, conquering the skies, riding with the winds, fighting right beneath me, as if she has her own purpose. Flat on my stomach, I hear her strong pulse echo against mine.

"Your name," I whisper, and I know she hears me. "I never—I never got your name. Maybe that's why, when I called you, you couldn't hear me."

She hums below me, her scales trembling.

"I don't think I'm going to walk out of there alive," I say. "You saved me, for this. You helped me, for this. And for that, I thank you." I take a shaking breath. "I would like to thank you by name."

Don't thank me yet.

The voice isn't a voice at all, but a feeling strung into words. I can sense it, as if she's speaking directly into my mind. I can't hear her . . . but somehow, I know the words anyway. Just like my sword, telling me its name.

"How did you do that?" I breathe.

But there's no response.

The string in my chest tugs—*Raker*. He and our swords are close. "There," I say, seeing a shimmering arch even from the sky. It's blocked by a wall of clouds, thick as a storm.

I grip her scales as she dives forward.

Right through the tempest.

And we plunge into a sea of magic. It's everywhere, glimmering, poured into all my senses, drowning me from the inside out.

Everything pulls my focus. There are holes in the clouds, with rainbows spilling out of them, like paths, brushing against the sparkling ground. Every time I focus on one thing, the rest vanishes.

This place is its own test. Someone could make it all the way here, I think, and get lost in its maze of radiance.

Luckily, I have my dragon. She cuts through the beauty, landing in front of an arch formed from beams of silver light. This must be the entrance to the well of magic. I can't see what's beyond it. The place wears a cloak of enchantment.

I slide off my dragon's back. Just when I'm about to enter, a shadow casts around me. I tense. Snap around.

A beast is landing right next to my dragon.

Instead of reaching for my sword, I nearly fall to my knees.

Zane. He's on the back of a massive winged creature. My eyes burn. He did it. He claimed it.

A glorious Helmhawk.

His smile transforms his entire face. In a moment, he's on the ground, then pulling me into a crushing hug. "You're—you're alive," he says, staggering back from me, eyes wide with wonder.

"So are you." I frown. "Did you . . . go in already?"

He nods. "I got my cup." He pulls a silver chalice from his pack. It's filled with shimmering liquid that somehow doesn't spill. "I got here about a week ago. I've stayed to get anything else I can, but this place is like a labyrinth. I was just leaving, when I saw you."

I throw my arms around him again. Finally, some good news. Something positive from this deadly journey.

It reminds me of the bad. Slowly, I pull back. "Kira—Kira is dead."

The news melts the smile off his face. He curses. "I had hoped . . . I had . . . *hope*, I guess."

"Me too." His eyes meet mine, and my voice is poison. "It was Cadoc. He hunted her down, and—"

His eyes flare with something at the mention of that name.

"What is it?" I ask.

Zane's expression is serious. "He was just here, a few hours ago. He had a cup." Fuck. He actually made it. The bastard. Zane's gaze is hard. "I saw him drink it, Aris."

Silence.

"Did he—*did he* . . ."

"He was screaming. His dragon took him away. But . . . he was *alive*."

No. Cadoc—Cadoc cannot be immortal. I tense, knowing what that will mean for the other side. For any world with a person as terrible as him in it.

But that's not my problem. It shouldn't be.

Wrath still racing through my veins, my eyes dip to the chalice in his hands. The liquid inside swirls silver, like a cup full of stars.

"What are you going to do with it?" I ask.

He doesn't hesitate for a moment. "I'm going to take it home and pour it on our land. I'm going to save my mountain and everyone who lives there."

I believe him. He'll make it back to the gates on his Helmhawk, if he's quick. "Go, then. Go save them all."

Zane hugs me. One last embrace.

His hand grips the side of my arm, grasping the new, sparkling metal. "It was nice to meet you, Aris," he says. I know he means it.

"And it was nice meeting you, Zane," I say. I watch him mount his massive bird and disappear into the sparkling light.

My blood pounds with fury and grief and, most of all, purpose.

"Stay here," I tell my dragon. "And if I don't come out, know that knowing you was the greatest gift of all." I press my head to hers.

Then I turn toward the arch and the end of my journey.

46

"I'm going to kill her," I tell Stellan. "The goddess with the silver-red eyes."

He looks over at me. I'm twelve and can barely hold up even the smallest swords in his forge.

"And how are you going to do that?" he asks.

His doubt makes me sit up straighter, as if I could make myself seem more capable by adding a half inch to my stature. "I will cut off her head."

"And if she has many heads?" he asks. "She is a goddess. She is a being of many forms. Of many faces."

"Then I will cut off every head," I say through my teeth. "And every arm, and every leg, and every heart she has, I will cut them off and up and I will burn them." My voice changes, becomes something I don't recognize. "I will burn them all."

Stellan looks over at me. "And if you burn too?" he says.

I give him a rueful smile. "Then I'll rise from the ashes, just like you taught me."

THE GLIMMERING CAVE falls into focus the second I step through the arch. Goblets cover the ground, made of every metal. Some look like crystallized flame. Others look forged of ancient bone. Some are carved straight from priceless gems.

Most are piled high, in the corners.

The one blocking my path is made of pure, sparkling silver, just like my sword. I kneel. And the second I wrap my fingers around its stem, it begins to fill with silver liquid brighter than the sun, gleaming like a galaxy, swirling with shredded stars and melted down power.

Pure magic.

It doesn't stop until it reaches the goblet's rim.

I lift the cup from the ground. I test it, moving it to the side.

But the liquid does not spill. Even when I turn the goblet over completely.

One promise, finished. I got the magic. I will have my dragon take it to Kira's sister, if it's the last thing I do.

Now, it's time to finish this.

One hand holding the goblet of magic, I use the other to reach for my starblade. I slice my palm across its glimmering edge. My blood spills into the sparkling dirt.

Then, I dig my sword into it, my mind filled with a name that's haunted me this entire journey.

The gates are ruled by unbreakable magic. They cannot be opened by anyone—even the gods—outside of every fifty years.

Except, maybe, by the god who made them.

The god of journeys, and gates, and in-betweens. The god of the Questral itself.

"God of Travels."

Great Houses weren't the only thing I researched in Vander's library. I also looked up anything I could about summoning gods. They can ignore calls anywhere besides their own land. That's why they make it so hard to get here—why the archway is closed to anyone but them, outside of the fifty days of the Questral.

A moment later, a goddess steps in front of me, looking just like she does in my worst memories.

Her pale skin gleams like my sword. Her hair is the silver of the gods; she shines with ethereal and otherworldly beauty. Hundreds of gems decorate her skin as if growing out of it, in a multitude of brilliant colors. Emeralds, rubies, sapphires, diamonds, stones I can't begin to name.

All this emotion, all this rage, has narrowed into an arrow-like focus as I lift my weapon. I'm surprised my voice comes out steady, but it does. "Do you know who I am?" I ask.

She looks bored. Her perfect face is expressionless. "Of course I do. The one that didn't burn. You're here to kill me," she says simply, glancing at the starlit blade in my hands.

I don't care how she knows that. I don't care at all. None of it matters.

"I am." I take a step forward. "I have wanted to kill you every moment from the first time I saw you." Every word is edged in rage, the sharpest swords I have ever forged. This unmatched fury uncurls within me, my veins lighting with its fire. But my voice is steady. "You killed my entire family."

Not a single shred of regret passes across her glorious face. The gems that ornament her body simply keep shining.

I take a step forward. "My village. You burned it to the ground." Hundreds of lives reduced to ashes. I take her in. "You don't care, do you?"

"I'm a god," she says flatly. "I've lived millennia. I've watched millions be born and die. I've watched kingdoms and worlds rise and fall. I don't care about anyone, unless they threaten *us*."

Us. The gods.

"So *why?*" I demand, my voice shaking with the question. "Why me? Why my family? If you don't care . . . then why did you do that?" *Why did you have to do that?* Tears sting my eyes. I imagine a world where she didn't. Where she left us alone. Where I didn't have to trek across this beautiful and brutal world just to get revenge.

"Because of the prophecy," she says simply, without a morsel of emotion. "You posed a threat. I tried to eliminate it."

Prophecy. There's that word again.

She thinks it's about me. *The paladin who was promised.*

I step forward. It doesn't matter, I know that. This is all about to end, but I can't not know. I can't not know why everything I loved had to be ripped away from me. Because I was right. Now I know for certain. It *was* my fault.

"What *prophecy?*" I demand.

The goddess's lips just curl into a smile, like she finds my anger and ignorance amusing.

She still hasn't summoned a weapon to this duel.

"You should be more afraid," I tell her, voice echoing through this room that glimmers like we are sitting inside of one of the stones growing from her marble-smooth skin. "Because even if you are the God of Travels, I can imagine opening the gates was not a small task. That's a long way to go to eliminate a simple *threat*. You were *afraid of me*. Now I'm here . . . summoning you to a duel . . . and you don't look afraid at all."

"No," she says simply. "I'm not. Because I can smell your wants, human. I know everything you feel. Your emotions are like the strings of an instrument, and I have them all here, laid out nicely in front of me. Which is why I know there's something you want even more than your revenge."

My voice is full of rage. "I don't want anything—"

"You want them back."

The world stills. The rage in my blood freezes over. Everything goes very quiet. Because I would do *anything*. *Anything* . . .

"Of course I do. But that's impossible." My voice is a rasp.

"It's not," she says. "And, if you make an oath on your blood not to kill me, I will tell you how."

A blood oath. I imagine it's the same as swords, but if broken . . . *I will break.*

"You're lying," I say, the words trembling. I refuse to believe what must be a lie from this goddess I hate with every shred of my being.

"I do not lie," she says. She tears one of the gems off her skin, and blood races from the spot. It's silver, just like the swirling power in my goblet. She dips her fingers in it. "I swear on my blood that there is a way, and I know it. I will tell you . . . if you agree not to kill me."

Impossible.

The need for vengeance pounds through my skull. Burns through my blood. I have worked years for this. Fought countless dangers, survived endless challenges, just for this moment.

I lift the starblade, wanting to end her. *Needing to end her.* But instead of throwing it through her neck . . . I drop it at my feet.

The words feel wrong. I never believed, in a thousand years, that I would be speaking them. But I do. Clearly. Desperately. "I swear on my blood that I will not kill you, goddess."

It takes everything in me to step over my blade, to walk toward her as she smirks, placing her hand in mine.

Our blood mixes, and I feel the oath racing down my veins, straight to my heart. It's done.

I stumble back, slightly light-headed, almost tripping, wondering if I've made a grave mistake. When I finally face her again, my voice is steady. "Speak," I demand.

"Kill the God of Death, and you can bring back your family."

The God of Death. The silver-haired warrior who steals brides, who rules demons, who is famed for his ruthlessness, and who put a bounty on my head.

"Thank you," I say to the goddess. And *I never thought I would be thanking the woman who killed my entire family*. Her gems blink back at me as she nods her head. She turns toward the tunnel at the end of this cave, wide and tilted up, as if it leads straight to the stars. "But I'm not done with you yet."

I reach toward the connection between me and my dragon, the one it spoke to me through in the skies. *Are you there?* I ask.

The same resonance responds, the wordless language that translates in my mind. *Always*, she says.

I have something for you, I say.

Come and get it.

With knee-shattering force, my dragon breaks through the arch, shattering the silver beams, and lands right behind me, shaking the ground. I can feel the steam of her breath above my head.

The goddess's eyes widen. "You made a blood oath not to kill me."

"I never said anything about my dragon." I look up at my silver companion. "Eat."

The goddess can't even summon a flicker of power before my dragon swallows her and her thousand gems whole.

47

Kill the God of Death, and you can bring back your family.

I might have been afraid of him, I might have been running from him this entire time, but hope and love banish any fear from my chest. Because—I'll do anything. I'll climb up to the fucking stars if I need to. I will rip them from the sky. I will crush them in my hands. I will break every bone, shatter every tooth, skin myself alive if I have to, and none of it will matter if they can *come back*.

Without a second of hesitation, I dig my starlight blade into the ground, drip more of my blood into the dirt—

And whisper, "God of Death."

The cave falls away. My stomach lurches. *I'm* being portaled somewhere, instead of him coming to me.

Ice crawls through my veins, but I tighten my hold on the hilt of my sword, until a new room settles around me.

The ceilings are hundreds of feet high and intricately carved. The floors are solid silver. The door in front of me has been punched through, ripped apart. Metal is everywhere. Empty thrones surround me.

Slowly, I turn around.

There's a body on the floor, eyes open, with a blade buried straight through its chest. I know that blade. It's standing tall and proud right in front of a throne crowned with a stone black as the night sky. The throne of the God of Death.

When I meet the eyes of the person sitting in it, my heart finally breaks.

"No," I say.

Raker doesn't say anything at all.

My sword is across his lap, still in its scabbard.

"No," I say again, shaking my head, refusing to believe it.

A goblet just like the one I claimed is turned over by his throne. It's empty. He *drank it*.

"Aris," he finally says, standing.

"*No*," I say, with every smelted piece of my soul. "You don't get to say my name. You don't get to *look at me*."

His eyes flash with something like regret, but a moment later, it's gone. All emotion has vanished. Just like that goddess. He takes a step forward. "You shouldn't be here," he says.

"This is exactly where I should be," I say, my voice shaking. I tilt my head at him. "So did you just kill the God of Death?" I look at the man on the ground, but he doesn't look like any of the paintings from the Great House we visited. Not at all.

Not like Raker does.

"I killed the God of War," he says, his voice distant. Emotionless. "Who thought he killed me, the God of Death, five years ago." He steps over the dead god without sparing him a glance. "He's been trying to rule the underworld ever since. Badly, as you saw, with the demons and stolen brides."

"But you—you were human," I say, seeing every difference. Every lack of warmth. Every smooth place that was once rougher. Every glimmering place that was once matte. He was always beautiful, but now . . .

Now.

Because he drank the cup and became what he was meant to be, the magic illuminating everything that was already there, he is not just immortal.

He is a god. Again.

"I suspected the gods were plotting against me. So, during the last Questral, I traveled to Stormside and buried a shred of my soul there. When the God of War finally tried to kill me, he failed to kill *all* of me. I awoke on Stormside as a human," he says. He glances at the cup. "I needed the magic to access my powers again."

"So that's why you went on the quest," I say, voice trembling. "It was always your plan . . ." I shake my head. "Tell me. How did I fit into it?"

"Your blade—"

"Is the other half of yours," I say. He stills in surprise. I step forward. "But you could have killed me to get it. Easily. So many times." My head tilts. "So why didn't you?"

At that, he is silent.

I look down at the god between us. "Killing doesn't seem to be a problem for you. So why?"

"Aris—"

"*Why didn't you kill me?*" I demand, voice echoing through the room. My chest is heaving. Every broken piece of myself is showing, sticking out of my chest, like the blade of my heart has shattered after meeting a greater opponent. "Why did you pretend to care? Why did you pretend to see me?" I shake my head again, emotion welling up. "You should have just—you should have just killed me, Raker," I say, my voice breaking. "It would have hurt less."

His eyes finally flash with emotion. Pain. My pain affects him. He takes another step toward me.

And in an instant, that feeling is gone.

"Don't pretend you were honest with me, Aris," he says. "Do you think I don't know who you are?" He takes another step. "Aris Agron, heiress of House Agron? One of the Great Houses of Stormside?"

My teeth lock together. It's been years since I heard my full name spoken. I lost it that day, when my house burned to the ground. I don't know why that matters to him, but it looks like it does. It looks like my lineage could mean more than I'm aware of.

Hearing it, hearing my name, shifts my agony back to rage. "A house your kind *burned to ashes*," I scream. "You didn't just kill my family—you killed *hundreds*. The entire village, all dead because of you."

"I didn't set the fire," he says.

"You might as well have!" I take a step toward him. "You must know the prophecy. The one everyone else but me fucking knows." I motion toward myself. "So kill me, Raker. You couldn't do it before, but how about now? *Do it now!*"

He doesn't move an inch.

I laugh. "Don't pretend you care about me. I have lost everyone I have ever loved. *Everyone*. And—and I started to . . ." I don't dare finish that sentence. "And you . . ."

The words spill out of me as I look at him, eyes brimming with tears, and simmering with rage, and filled with every single moment we've had together on this dark and perilous journey, fighting side by side to the edge of the world. My words are like my pain—numbed at first, then searing.

"You left me," I say, my voice devoid of emotion.

"You *left* me," I say again, remembering the pain at waking up alone.

"You left *me*," I say, because I thought I mattered to him.

"*You* left me, weaponless, to die." He watches the emotions slide through me, his face, his eyes distant and cold. "After . . . *after*—" My voice breaks, and his expression finally shifts, but no. I won't get caught in this trap of caring.

Fury ignites me, and I close the gap between us. I rip the scabbard from his hand, and he lets me.

Scraping metal echoes through the hall as I peel my sword from its sheath.

Stellaris. She glimmers in my palm, awakening.

"Fine," I say, falling into a stance he helped me master. "If you can't strike me down . . . then duel me, Raker."

I've never been able to duel before.

We've done it countless times. Now he shakes his head. But he doesn't get to make that decision.

There is a way. Kill the God of Death.

With a bellow, I rush forward, going right for his neck—and in a flash, his sword crashes into his hand, wrenched from the god's chest, flying into his grip. It's up and meeting my metal before I can blink.

Memories from our quest echo. Me, in the cave, trying to get his attention. Cleaving my blade toward his to get him to listen. His meeting mine. Bending sound and space.

The same thing happens now.

The ringing our swords produce is poetry. It's the stars scaping across the galaxy. It's the sun melting into the sea.

But Raker is not the same human I dueled with before. He's not even just an immortal.

He is a god.

The force of his newfound strength sends me flying back, sliding across the stone, my head cracking against it.

For a moment, the world gutters out. But no. I cling to consciousness. I cling to the image that flashes in my head—my family and me, everything broken turning whole again.

Mind swimming with pain, I rise, only to find him right in front of me.

He could kill me in a second. I see that. I *feel* it. Part of me wants him to try, to show us both exactly who he is, the merciless God of Death.

But he doesn't.

I slam my blade down with all my strength, over and over, in a furious frenzy, using every move he taught me. I go for his neck, for his chest, for his legs, and every single time, his metal meets mine. He doesn't even attempt to hurt me. All he does is block my advances. And it's easy, the way he fights. Like he is lifetimes faster and stronger than I am, like all my years of training are absolutely nothing. Like I am the lowliest of metals against the highest grade of steel.

He's not even trying.

"Fight me," I say through gritted teeth as I fling my sword toward him again, with both hands and all my strength.

His sword echoes against mine. And the sound—it's a song. Life and death, sun and darkness, summer and winter—I feel them all, merging for that one resonant second, and I don't know if it's us or our swords, two halves meeting, glimmering, *wanting*.

"No," he says as our blades meet again.

A growl escapes from the back of my throat as I rush forward once more. He's not even looking at my sword.

He's looking at me.

"*Fight me*," I bellow, putting every piece of myself into my next hit. And this time, when our swords collide, they unleash a blinding light. I gasp—backing up a few steps, away from him and his weapon.

I expect him to strike, or say something else, or just leave and decide I'm not worth another moment of his immortal life, but all he does is throw his sword to the ground.

All he does is stalk toward me, until his hands are cupping my cheeks, like we could both forget everything that happened and start anew. I let him. *I want to let him.* My arms go slack by my sides.

"Aris, stop this," he breathes, right into my face, and I shiver, remembering how we panted words against each other's lips, how our eyes widened, how we both begged and gave, held tight and released. Over and over and over until we were boneless and spent.

He shivers too, as if he's doing the same thing. "I don't want to fight you. Not anymore."

He's staring at me so intently, looking into my eyes as if somehow he's seeing something new. His own eyes widen. He's so focused. *So entranced*. His lips part in surprise, then lower, as if he's going to kiss me.

"You left me," I whisper, chest heaving. Eyes prickling.

"I left," he says, gaze blazing into mine. "To save you."

To *save me?* I almost laugh. Save me by leaving me for dead? By stealing my sword? I spit the words. "From what?"

"From me."

My breath hitches. I swallow, looking over his perfect face, seeing the mixture of hurt and wrath, waiting to feel the cold whisper of fear down my spine. He's the God of Death. I should be terrified.

But I'm not.

His eyes narrow, as if sensing that. As if telling me I should be. Still, he doesn't move away from me.

Hands still threaded through my hair, he pulls me closer, and in his heated gaze, I see chaos. Conflict. An internal battle I don't understand. He finally shakes his head.

"I tried to do the right thing. I tried to leave you. But you summoned *me*." His pulls me even closer, like he can't stop himself. Like he can't survive with any distance between us. "And if you're still intent on killing the gods . . . I want you to join me."

I blink. "What?"

"Our swords. They're meant to be rejoined. They're meant to work side by side. Together . . . together, we could change this world. All the godswords combined are nothing compared to ours. Joined, this one sword . . . could shatter and claim them all."

Claim them all.

Because that's what great swords do. I read about it in Vander's library. They absorb the power they conquer.

I remember the Astral Queen's words. The destruction she said would be unleashed.

He seems to sense my hesitance and shakes his head. "I want the same thing you do, Aris. I want the gods to fall. I want power to be restored to the other side. I want everything to be as it once was."

That is what I want. It's what I believe.

"Join me," he says.

Then his lips brush mine, and that simple touch drags a brutal truth from the pit of my soul.

I want to join him. I don't want to be alone anymore.

Who was I kidding? Did I really think I could come here, see him again, and feel nothing? Did I really think all those emotions, all those moments, died in that cave?

They didn't.

So I kiss him. This time, it's me surging forward, and he groans like he's been waiting, like he's been missing my touch, like I am a drug, and he's already addicted. His lips are cold as my warm tongue parts them, but his taste—it's the same. His hands are hard as marble and just as freezing as he runs them through my hair, and I sigh as his mouth trails down my neck, as he pays extra attention to the place he bit last night, as he gently runs his sharp teeth against the same sensitive skin. "You left me alone," I repeat, because it's something I can't forgive.

"You'll never be alone again," he swears against my pulse, and then his lips capture mine. And this kiss—it's the ultimate blade; it cuts through everything. The pain. The rage. The purpose. His tongue meets mine, and the rest of the world just vanishes.

I kiss him back just as fiercely, sucking, biting, speaking in this wordless, desperate language, every part of me aching for every part of him. We kiss until we're both panting. Until I have to pull away to breathe.

"Raker?"

"Yes, Aris?" he asks, right against my mouth. And he says my name like it's the most important word in the universe.

My eyes prickle. Finally, I'm telling the truth. I'm being honest with myself about what this is.

"I think—I think I love you," I say.

And then I plunge my blade through his heart.

48

Raker's eyes widen. *Widen*. At my words or at the fact that I just plunged my sword through his heart, I'm not sure.

Slowly, his gaze drops to my blade, coated in his silver godly blood, before sliding back to mine.

And then he does something unexpected.

He *grins*.

He's supposed to be dying.

My hands tighten on the hilt. I push the blade in farther, releasing another torrent of silver, but he only steps *toward* me, skewering himself, his eyes never leaving mine.

His mouth nearly reaches my lips, as if he could kiss me like this, but I stumble back until my spine hits the wall. Until my wrist, still gripping the hilt, hits his chest.

My sword is entirely through his heart.

He only grins wider.

"Did you think that would kill me?" he says, tilting his head. He looks amused. He looks enraged. He looks enraptured. My hands are covered in his blood. "I am death." My breath catches in panic as he leans toward me. "You're going to need to try a little harder than that, Aris."

"I will," I spit, my words firm, conviction rooting in my very core.

If he is the only thing standing between me and seeing my family again, I will try for the rest of my life. I will make it my only waking purpose.

"I look forward to it," he drawls. Then his silver gaze hardens.

"Did you mean it? What you said?" he demands, leaning toward me. He says it like he needs to know. Like it's the most important thing in the world.

I don't answer him.

I don't do anything but slip out of his grip, taking advantage of his distraction. Then I reach for his sword, still on the ground where he threw it—

And I take it.

I don't miss the sharp inhale behind me, of Raker realizing what I've done. *I can move his sword.*

It all makes sense now. Why Raker was so miserable and cruel from the start. Why, just when we would make progress, he would burn it to ashes. Why he's always tried to keep a firm distance between us.

He knew the risk of falling in love.

And what it would cost him.

I look back, and our eyes lock. His are wide and full of surprise. Like he had been keeping some truths from himself too. My blade is still buried in his heart.

Stellaris.

My sword cuts completely through his body, and into my fist. It's covered in glimmering silver blood. He curses, reaching toward me, calling my name—before he collapses.

He might be a god, he might be death, but a hole through his chest has to fucking hurt.

I don't know how much time I have until he's up again. I don't hesitate. I put his sword into the scabbard.

And then I run like hell.

MY DRAGON IS waiting for me, surrounded by the broken pieces of the god's arch, standing next to my claimed cup of magic. I grab the goblet, mount my dragon, and then we're off. My heart is beating too quickly.

Did you mean it? What you said?

He seemed more concerned about my words than my sword sticking out of his chest.

I wish I didn't say them. I wish I didn't *mean* them. But the proof of what we feel for each other is in these very blades.

Great swords meld to your soul. To your heart. And when you let someone into it . . . they can take what's yours.

I slip Stellaris into the scabbard, right against his sword, to keep him from calling either of them.

Everything has gone both right and wrong at the same time. I wasn't supposed to survive this. I didn't *plan for this*.

The God of Travels' words have been etched into my very soul. I can bring my family back. There's hope.

But killing Raker is clearly not as easy as putting a blade through his heart.

I am death, he said. How does one kill death? I'm not sure. But I'll find out, even if it takes years. Decades. Lifetimes.

For now . . . I think about what the Astral Queen said. These swords cannot be united. Raker is the God of Death . . . and now the God of War too.

Who knows what immeasurable power he might have? Who knows what chaos he could unleash if he were to forge these blades back together?

I could see a glimpse of humanity in him—and I watched it harden as I left with his sword. Now he must truly hate me. He knows I meant to kill him. He could see the surprise in my face when he didn't die.

Once something like friends . . . back to enemies.

His words are in my head again.

I know you, Aris. You claim you don't care about anything but revenge, but I have watched you unfailingly, stupidly *care about everyone else's life over your own. You are not the monster you think you are.*

He's right. I do care. Even though this world has taken everything from me, I don't want to watch it burn.

This world doesn't need gods. It doesn't need a blade that *claims them all*. It needs peace.

I vowed to kill all of them . . . I killed one. Raker killed another. Two are now dead. The rest will follow. Somehow, some way, I will make sure they all fall. Even him.

But first I must make sure he never gets these weapons.

WE FLY THROUGH the day and night for nearly a week, only stopping to rest when absolutely needed. My dragon is fearless, unflinching, untiring. It's as if she knows how important it is for me to outrun him. As if she is invigorated by the goddess she ate.

Because I can feel that thread . . . Even with his sword in my possession, I *feel* him. I feel his fury. His determination.

He's getting closer. He's chasing after me.

No. Not me, I think. The swords. It's what he's wanted this entire time.

His rage washes over the world. The night flickers with it. The day bleeds with it. Of course. I told him I loved him, and then I stabbed him through the heart. The worst thing is, I don't regret it. If killing him will bring back my family, then I will try again and again until his death finally sticks.

We're not just racing against him—we're racing against time. At sunset on the fiftieth day, the gates will close, and I feel the hours counting down.

When that day arrives, my dragon's wings push harder. The sun begins to dip. She flies faster still.

Finally, the gates come into view, towering and glittering, and relief slithers down my spine. They're still open. So close. *So close.*

The sun is melting against the horizon. There are minutes to spare.

My dragon lands just short of the gates, and I turn, realizing only now that I can't bring her with me.

"You belong here, among the magic," I say, tears stinging my eyes. "I don't have anything to feed you over there." Gems don't exist. Even if I raided the king's entire castle, she would starve after a few years.

No. She deserves to be in a place just as glimmering as she is.

I throw my arms around her nose and make her a promise. "I will come back one day. And then . . . then you can finally tell me your name."

She nods, brushing against my cheek. We stay there, together, for a few stolen seconds.

Then, the world begins to tremble as those massive sheets of metal begin to close.

I can't be stuck on this side. I need to leave. She dips her head lower, telling me to go. With one last look at her, I turn and sprint toward the closing gates. I'm almost there.

"*Aris.*"

I hear his voice, feel it like a caress down my spine and a blade through my back.

He's right behind me.

I'm just a few feet away from the gates.

My heart thunders as I run faster than I ever have before. I run for all the people I have lost and all the ones who will fall if Raker gets his hands on these swords.

I run for the hope that I will figure out a way to kill him and bring my family back. I will be patient. I will be strong. *For them*. Always for them.

The gates are almost closed, and even the God of Death can't stop them. A growl sounds in the back of my throat as I throw myself through—

And a hand locks around my ankle, dragging me back.

Raker.

I turn, and he's right above me.

This is my last chance. I think about his words: *I am death*. Maybe the problem was I used my own blade. Maybe, to kill him, I need to use his.

I drag his sword out of the scabbard and bury it in his heart. *Again*.

His eyes blaze with fury.

It doesn't work.

The gates are almost closed. I thrash below him, but he won't let go. *He won't let me go.*

A shriek cleaves the sky in half.

My dragon lands behind him, rattling the ground. He loses his hold, for just one moment.

It's all I need.

In a flash, I'm on my feet—and then I'm soaring through the gates again, my body brushing the metal, just slipping through. I land roughly on the other side.

Raker crashes into the gates not a moment after, but he's too late.

He roars as he tries to wrench them open, to take them down. And under his godly power, those towering gates *shudder*. But they do not break.

His eyes slide down to me, still panting on the bridge. His own blade is still sticking through his chest. I rise to my feet and stand right in front of him. I grip the bars, just as he does.

We stare at each other through the silver, chests heaving, only metal between us. He looks down at the sword still in my scabbard. Then he looks back up at me.

"These gates won't keep me from you," he says. He says it like a curse.

I press as close to him as I can. He's just inches away—but he might as well be across the world. "See you in fifty years, Raker," I whisper.

Then I turn back toward my home of ashes.

Acknowledgments

Writing this book felt like its own quest, filled with surprises, many sleepless nights, and the magic of getting lost in a world that was once a blank page. It swallowed my entire life, and brought me back to why I started writing, so many years ago. This story is smelted from my soul. I woke up every single day excited to dive back in, and I'm so grateful to everyone who made it possible for you to read it now.

Thank you to my incredible agent, Jodi Reamer, for being my guiding star and driving force through all the deadlines these last few years. I've wanted to work with you since I queried you at twelve years old, and now that I do, I can say you're an even better agent than I ever could have imagined. *Thank you.*

Thank you to May Chen, my amazing editor, who took me on for my contemporary romance and then enthusiastically kept me for this romantasy series. Your exclamation points and notes in the margins of each draft are my sustenance. Every time you email me, I smile. You bring the best out of me and gave me all the time I needed to get this right—thank you.

Thank you to everyone around me who continues to make so much possible. Thank you to Berni Vann and Michelle Weiner at CAA for everything to come. Thank you to Amanda Della Ragione, Elise Mesa, and Emma Eales for all that you do. And thank you to Maja Nikolic, Alessandra Birch, Sofia Bolido, Peggy Boulos Smith, and Cecilia de la Campa for getting this series out to readers around the world.

I'm so grateful to everyone at HarperCollins for another magical publishing experience. Thank you to Liate Stehlik, for seeing the potential of this series from the beginning, and for your unmatched support. Thank you to Jennifer Hart, for your fierce championing of my books. Thank you also to Kaitlin Harri and Kelly Rudolph, for making so much possible.

Thank you to Kelsey Manning for never batting an eye at my marketing ideas, and always turning them into jaw-dropping reality, to Jes Lyons for two incredible tours, to Erin Merlo for your enthusiasm and support, and I look forward to working with Eliza Rosenberry. Thank you also to everyone involved with the production of this book, with special thanks to Hope Ellis, Brittani DiMare, and Andrew DiCecco.

Thank you to Vicky Leech Mateos for reading this early and giving me incredible notes, and to the rest of the team at my UK publisher, Bloomsbury.

Thank you to Elsie Lyons and François-Xavier Pavion for the silvery cover of my dreams, and to Diahann Sturge-Campbell for the beautiful interior design.

Thank you to my loved ones for understanding that writing has completely taken over my life, and for still being there when I surface from each deadline. I'm going to try to sleep more. I promise.

Lastly, and most of all, thank you to you, the reader. You are the reason I get to write these books, and I am endlessly grateful for your support. I wrote this for you. *Thank you.*

ALEX ASTER is a #1 *New York Times* and internationally bestselling author. She studied creative writing at the University of Pennsylvania, lives in New York, and is never too far from a coffee shop.